Loki

by

Mike Vasich

For Beth, Spenser, and Oscar

The Norse Pantheon

Loki (LOW-key)—The god of mischief and lies.

Odin (OH-din)—The leader of the Aesir (AY-seer), the main group of gods. He is also known as the Allfather and the High One. Odin wields the spear known as Gungnir (GUNG-neer).

Sigyn (SEG-in)—Loki's wife.

Tyr (TEER)—A god renowned for his battle skills.

Balder (BAL-dur)—The most handsome god.

Thor (THOR)—The god of thunder, lightning and storms. He wields the hammer, Mjolnir (MYAWL-neer).

Freyja (FRAY-uh)—A goddess of the Vanir (VAH-neer), a group of fertility gods.

Frey (FRAY)—Freyja's twin brother.

Heimdall (HAYM-dahl)—The guardian of the rainbow bridge known as Bifrost (BY-frost), the only way to reach the realm of the gods.

Others in the Norse World

Yggdrasil (IG-druh-sil)—An eternal ash tree that towers over all of creation.

Thiazi (Thee-OT-see)—One of the giants, a race of beings opposed to the gods.

Jormungand (YAWR-moon-gahnd)—Also known as the Midgard Serpent, he is a snake that lies at the bottom of the sea and encircles the entire world.

Fenrir (FEN-rear)—A massive wolf creature and the brother of Jormungand. Also called the Fenris Wolf.

Hel (HEL)—The half-living, half-dead sister of Fenrir and Jormungand. She rules over the dead in the underworld known as Niflheim.

Valkyries (VAL-kuh-reez)—Warrior maidens who serve the Aesir.

Einherjar (EIN-har-yar)—Dead warriors who have been brought to Asgard to fight for the gods.

Sleipnir (SLAYP-neer)—Odin's eight-legged steed, the fastest horse in the Nine Worlds.

Places and Events

Asgard (AHS-gard)—The realm of the Aesir.

Midgard (MID-gard)—The middle realm, the world of men.

Jotunheim (YAW-toon-heym)—The realm of the giants.

Niflheim (NIV-uhl-heym)—The realm of the dead.

Vanaheim—The realm of the Vanir.

Muspelheim (MUS-pel-heym)—The realm of fire, death to all living things, and the rumored home of Black Surt, the legendary fire giant.

Valhalla (Val-HAL-uh)—Odin's Hall of the Slain, where the Einherjar feast each night.

Valaskjalf (VAL-uh-skyalf)—Odin's hall.

Ragnarok (RAG-nuh-rock)—The legendary end time of the gods.

Prologue

As always, the venom dripped down slowly, like acidic syrup. The man below was fixed in position. He was strapped upright to a rocky outcropping, arms and legs bound, fetters around his neck limiting his movements so that he was nearly as frozen as the serpent that was embedded in the rock above him.

There was no way for him to avoid the flow of venom that splashed onto his face. His attempts to keep his eyes closed were useless as it burned through, dissolving the soft tissue below. He kept his mouth shut, but it did not prevent his lips and tongue from melting away. It wound its way down his throat laying waste to stomach and innards before exiting, leaving a bloody trail that drizzled down the rock.

For long seconds the venom would do its work, and his screams and thrashing would shake the earth above, his agony beyond comprehension. Relief would come, however, and his faithful wife would be there once more, bowl in hand, to catch the stream of poison above him.

But the relief was a cruel mockery. Where a mortal would have been dead, the misery over in minutes, it was his curse that he survive to suffer again. From inside, he could feel his guts knit together, healing the burnt hollows left by the trail of venom. His stomach made itself whole and his throat reformed and healed, turning pink what had been charred black. His lips and tongue grew back, dissolved flesh slowly reclaiming its hold onto his wasted frame. Even his eyesight hesitantly returned. His wife appeared above him once more, the anguish on her face an additional

9

torture.

Faithful Sigyn. During brief, lucid periods—those fleeting moments when his agony ceased—he pondered his worthiness of such a companion. He had failed to be faithful on numerous occasions, and had been more absent than attentive. He was a less than ideal husband, undeserving of her devotion.

These thoughts would be over soon enough. She could not hold the bowl over him forever. It was shallow and filled quickly, the venom trickling over the side and licking his flesh in a precursor to the scorching that he would soon endure. Weeping, Sigyn would slowly move the bowl from the stream and take it to the ever-growing pool nearby.

Again it would flow. Again his insides would be seared. And again she would return, empty bowl in hand. The process was eternal, and as miserable and wretched as he was, he feared even more the day when his wife would collapse and die in front of him, a wizened hag whose slavery he had engendered to her dying day.

He could not remember how long he had been in the cave. Time no longer had meaning for him, other than the ebb and flow of venom. But he remembered how he had gotten there, and his hatred for those who had done this to him was boundless. He could see them in his mind's eye, and every injury they had caused was still fresh. His desire for vengeance scorched his insides.

But he would not be free. His bonds had not slackened no matter how much he strained at them. He would be chained to this rock until the end of the Nine Worlds, his torment unending.

Sigyn returned with the bowl, stopping the flow, and as his body repaired itself again he suddenly heard something that he had not heard before. Sigyn held the bowl up high while he healed, and he strained his ears to hear the sound.

It was faint, and he wondered if he had imagined it.

His eyesight returning, he looked up to see Sigyn's grim visage, a clear sign that the bowl was nearing fullness. He forced it out of his mind and concentrated on the sound. It came from under the ground, far below even the cave where he was entombed.

He focused all his energies on listening. When the sound reached him again, louder this time, he thought he recognized a tearing, the sound of muscles being strained to their limit and then ripping. It was accompanied by other sounds as well, and he realized that something else was buried with him, far deeper, but equally tortured.

He heard steel scraping muscle and bone, and a low growl that sent reverberations through the rock. He heard the sounds of metal sliding out of flesh, of cold steel falling to the ground. His seared lips spread wide into a painful smile, the first that crossed his face since his imprisonment. He knew what the sounds meant. His own flesh and blood was breaking free deep below him, leagues under the surface.

He looked up to see Sigyn's arms quivering with the effort to keep the bowl from spilling. Soon she would have to dump it, and the venom would flow, causing him more pain than any being in the Nine Worlds had ever suffered.

It no longer mattered. There was an end in sight, and even if he faced a hundred more cycles, he could bear it. When his son finally broke free he would come for him. Together they would gather such armies as the Nine Worlds had never seen.

He had heard tales of the Twilight of the Gods many times, and he had wondered if they were real. He had feared it would come one day and destroy all that he knew. He had never before considered that he and his progeny would herald it.

As the venom streamed down once more, he heard the unmistakable sound of a wolf howling. It would not be long now. Ragnarok had come, and he would see Asgard crushed and burned till he trod on the ashes of all those who had wronged him.

The Rebuilding of Asgard's Wall

Not long after the wars between the Vanir and Aesir, Asgard's wall remained in ruins. The gods were loathe to rebuild it themselves, but were fearful that Asgard may be vulnerable should the giants attack. They were therefore quite happy to take up the offer of a lone mason who happened upon the council of the gods one day.

Standing amongst the gods, the builder must have felt very bold indeed to make them such a proposal. "I will rebuild your walls in eighteen months, higher and stronger than they were before, so that no giant or other enemy may breach them."

The gods could not believe that any mason, working by himself, could rebuild Asgard's walls in such a short time. Still, they would not dismiss his offer out of hand. They were enticed by the idea that the wall could be built without effort on their part. They were curious, however, to hear the price for such a task.

The Allfather, wise Odin, asked that very question of the mason. "And what would be your price? Surely such a task would require a high fee."

The mason was not shy as his looks lingered over one of the gods gathered in Gladsheim. Lovely Freyja, whose beauty froze men in their tracks with her hair of spun gold and flawless white skin, was the subject of his stares. "I want Freyja as my wife."

The gods grew angry hearing his price, and some needed to be restrained lest they slay the mason for daring to be so bold. Even wise Odin was angered, and he prepared to have the mortal removed from Gladsheim, the council hall of the gods. But Loki was there, whispering in his ear, working his schemes and plans.

"Wait, Allfather," the Sly One said. "Do not dismiss him so

quickly. Let us accept his offer, but allow him so little time to complete the task that he will not be able to do it. His lust for Freyja is obvious, and it will be his undoing."

Odin did not look as though he liked the idea, but Loki continued on. "Let him have till the first day of summer. He will not be able to finish—no one could complete such a task in so short a time—and we will at least have it partially done, and for nothing."

Odin nodded, weighing over Loki's plan.

"We will pay you your wages," he finally told the mason. "But you will have to complete the rebuilding of the wall by the first day of summer, and you must do it alone."

The mason was not happy with the offer, but his lust for Freyja was strong. "You make an impossible bargain," he said. "But to have Freyja as my own . . ." The look on his face made it clear what he intended. "I will accept your offer, but let me have the use of my horse to assist in the hauling of stone."

The gods chafed at this condition, but Loki was there once more, whispering advice into the High One's ear. "Let him have his horse, Allfather. What harm could be done? He will still fail to finish, and we will have most of the work completed. If we deny him this one thing we gain nothing."

Odin did not want to accede, but the Sly One's words eventually convinced him. "Very well. You may use your horse."

The mason made the gods swear an oath of safe conduct should Thor return from Midgard where he was smashing giant skulls. They agreed that none, not even the Thunderer, would harm him.

And so the mason and his horse began the rebuilding of Asgard's shattered wall on the first day of winter . . .

Chapter One

Loki was led up the spiraling staircases of Valaskjalf, Odin's hall, by a servant who glanced back at him furtively, fear evident on his face. Loki knew that rumors of his ways ran throughout Asgard, and even lowly servants such as this had heard them, but what did the fool think he would do? Stick a dagger in his ribs as he was led to audience with the Allfather? While such ignorance offended him, he would never wantonly slay a servant of the High One.

The servant did not know this, of course, and Loki flashed him a wolfish grin the next time he glanced back. The servant's pace increased up the stairs, and he hurriedly opened the door at the top, stepping out of the god's way and keeping his head bowed low. Loki walked into the room without another thought about him.

Odin stood with his back to Loki as he approached. He gazed out the window over the wide expanse of Asgard.

"You summoned me, Allfather?" Loki said.

There was no answer. Loki stepped closer. "High One?" he said.

"You have returned from Jotunheim, I see." Odin did not turn. "Were you successful?"

"Yes, Allfather. Mjolnir is back in the hands of its rightful owner." It was strange, Loki thought, to be telling Odin information that he already knew, but it was ever the way of the Allfather.

"Tell me how it went with the giant."

Loki stepped closer. The Allfather still stared out the tall window, failing to register Loki with even a casual glance.

He did not mind, however. Odin had the weight of the Nine Worlds on his shoulders, and he could not be expected to dismiss the fate of creation for a ritual greeting. Besides, he was the Allfather, the High One, and above notions that might apply to the rest of them.

"From Thor's discovery of his missing hammer?"

"No. Begin from the transformation."

Loki nodded. "I spoke the sacred runes and saw the Thunderer change before me. His beard thinned and disappeared, his skin grew softer, his hips grew wider, and his height grew by two-fold."

"Who provided the clothes?"

"Sif did, Allfather. It was a simple task to increase their size to fit Thor's new frame."

"What was Thor's reaction?"

Loki smiled to remember it. It was a sight he would not soon forget, and he would relish bringing it up from time to time so that Thor could be reminded of his humiliation.

"His eyes shown like lightning, Allfather. His rage was only kept in check by the reminder that he would soon have his hammer in hand. He had favored an attack on the giants from the start, but relented when I convinced him that they would never bring Mjolnir from its hiding spot, and that slaying the giants might cause it to remain hidden forever. But he was not happy to be wed to a broad-shouldered son of Jotunheim."

Odin nodded, still gazing out the window. If he found the story humorous he didn't show it. "And your own transformation?"

"Like Thor's, it was mere trickery, of course. But I grew as well, and donned one of Sigyn's gowns. Thor's anger would not allow me to disguise his voice, so I had to attend him as handmaiden to speak for him. But I would have attended anyway. I would not have wanted to miss the

16

wedding feast."

"When was the hammer brought out?"

"It took some time, Allfather. The giant was intent on satisfying his new bride, so he had his finest foods brought to her. He was surprised by her appetite, as Thor downed nine plates overflowing with meat, and washed it down with nine large horns of mead."

"But he did not see through the spell?"

"No, Allfather. Nor did any of the other giants present. They were too eager to see what they wanted to see, and maybe overconfident after the theft of Mjolnir."

"They thought to march on Asgard using Thor's own hammer against us."

"As you say, Allfather. But it was not to be. The giant showered Thor with presents. Thor tossed them all aside, as a fastidious bride might do. The giant saved the hammer for the final gift, undoubtedly thinking that the most fearsome weapon ever crafted would impress her. It was his last mistake."

"Thor was able to contain himself till then?"

"Yes, Allfather, although I could see the lightning in his eyes and the storm brewing on his brow. But any longer and I am not sure he would have been able to hold back his fury."

"And then all would have been lost."

"As you say, Allfather." Loki was not entirely certain that was true, but he would never openly question Odin's judgment.

"What happened when the hammer was brought out?"

"Once it was laid in front of Thor, a smile stretched across his features. I saw the giant smile wide, as well, content that he was finally able to please his bride. But his smile did not last for long. As soon as Thor grasped the handle of Mjolnir and hefted the hammer up, the disguise dissolved. If there would have been time for surprise, I am sure the gathered giants would have registered it, but Thor gave no opportunity for that. He swung Mjolnir wide and slaughtered every giant in the room. If I had not gotten out of the way, I might have fallen victim as well."

Odin nodded solemnly before slowly turning. He faced Loki and placed a hand on his shoulder. "You have done well, my son. Were it not for your craftiness, Asgard might have fallen to the sons of Jotunheim."

As Odin looked down at him, Loki marked the lines on his face and noted how much the Allfather had aged since the first time he had seen him. He still remembered it, although it was a distant memory, or even a memory of a memory, but it was there all the same. The face that now looked down upon him bore the same expression he had first seen all those eons ago. It was his earliest memory, and he could almost feel his swaddling cloth around him while he looked up at the one who had rescued him when his parents had been killed by the giants.

"Thank you, Allfather. Although it would be best if I avoided Thor for some time. I only pray that his satisfaction in reclaiming Mjolnir makes him forget that he had to become a giant's bride to regain it."

Odin smiled slightly, a rare sight. "The episode will fade in time. Be content that you have served Asgard. No other could have done what you have."

Loki bowed, and Odin turned back to the window, once more gazing out across Asgard. The audience over, he backed out of the room and swiftly made his way down through the winding stairwells and corridors of Valaskjalf.

The rest of the Aesir would not look upon his role in this as a boon to Asgard, but the Allfather recognized his contribution. For now, it was enough.

* * *

Deep in his storm home, Thiazi felt waves of chaos strike him, sending constricting pains deep into his body and forcing him to double over in agony. The pain subsided for an instant, but he was struck again, worse than the first time, and he fell to the ground curled up in a tight ball, waiting for the pain to pass.

The chaos washing over him was stronger than any he had ever encountered. His own chaos energy had risen instinctively when it had felt the first wave of power touch him, and it had set up a defense that was riven almost instantly, sending radiating spokes of pain through him. Grinding his teeth while he lay on the stone floor, he willed his energy to lessen its defense—slowly so as not to be subsumed by the assault—until he could interweave it with the chaos assaulting him.

Eventually the pain dwindled down to a dull thudding ache, and he was able to rise to his feet. He probed the invading chaos to see what kind of enemy he faced. He had never felt such raw power before, but as he sent tendrils out to probe the waves of invisible force, he was surprised to discover that there was no intent in the assault. He was not, as he initially assumed, attacked. Rather, the waves were the natural emanations of . . . something of greater power than he had ever encountered.

He made his way through the meandering halls of his keep and up spiraling stairs, finally stepping out onto a tall tower where he could see anything that might be approaching. The chaos force had been so strong that he expected he might find an army of fire giants at his door, or perhaps even Black Surt, the Lord of Fire, come to claim a facet of himself left over from before creation. At first he saw nothing, which was even more surprising, and somehow more disturbing.

After long moments of gazing out at the road that led up to Thrymheim, he saw a sole figure approaching, so far away as to be little but a speck. He could scarcely believe it, but it seemed that the waves of power that had laid him low emanated from this solitary creature. He continued to watch as the figure made his way steadily towards the gates of Thrymheim.

The figure was a giant, but aside from the chaos that radiated from him, did not look exceptional. He disappeared from Thiazi's view as he drew closer to the gates, and Thiazi stood looking out over the path, feeling the chaos stronger than ever. There was no longer any pain; he had made his own chaos to be a part of the far more powerful energy of the giant.

He suspected that his visitor was not fully aware of the potential he contained. Thiazi had thought that his own ability to wield chaos made him the strongest in Jotunheim. The power flowing from the giant at his gates made his own seem non-existent.

He looked towards the rainbow bridge that was only hinted at from this distance. The enemies of the giants were just beyond, but who knew when they might lead their legions of undead warriors and ghost-maidens across it to storm Jotunheim. The red-bearded wielder of the lightning hammer alone had slain hundreds of giants, slaughtering without regard. He showed up for no other reason than to wreak havoc, and did not leave until every giant he faced was dead. The others were little better, and every inhabitant of Jotunheim knew that the day would come when they would march on the land of the giants.

He heard the booming sound of fist on the wooden doors below. His servants would seek him out for instructions, and he would have them let this visitor in. He would listen to his reasons for coming to Thrymheim, and

20

then he would craft a way to use his power to help him destroy the gods.

Heimdall woke to the sound of footfalls on Bifrost. He rose from his bed to stare out the window, the rainbow bridge only a stone's throw from his keep. His ability to see vast distances and hear sounds from hundreds of leagues away were exaggerated by those who told tales of such things, but his senses were still far more keen than any other of the Aesir. Because of this, it was his duty to stand watch at the entry to Asgard.

He turned at the sound of servants entering, one carrying a tray of food and drink, the other armor and weapons. They could anticipate his needs almost before he was aware of them.

"An intruder on Bifrost, my lord?"

"So it seems." He grabbed bread and a cup of mead from the tray, tore off a chunk with his teeth and downed it with a swallow of the syrupy-sweet liquid. His breath sent out plumes in the cold castle air, but the weather did not bother him. He was used to the cold clime, and it was the beginning of winter, after all. The mortals down below on Midgard may imagine the High Realm being one of eternal summer, but Asgardian winters were no less cold.

He glanced out the window again, attempting to see if the intruder was in sight. He could hear the footfalls, but he could not see the intruder yet. His vigilance often saw threats where there were none, so he automatically thought of the unknown person as an intruder. Better to see a threat where none existed, he thought, than assume peaceful intentions and be caught unaware.

"My horn," he said, just as a third servant came in with Gjall, shining and golden, seated in its case. He put his armor on, not quickly, but with enough purpose so as not to waste time, and strapped on his sword. He hung Gjall on his belt as well. He rarely needed it, but would not leave without the horn, for who knew when the giants might march on Asgard?

It bothered him that he could not yet see the intruder. Something seemed amiss, but he could not understand what it might be. There were six individual footfalls, and he could tell by the gait that it was a lone traveler with a horse in tow. The sounds of their footfalls seemed heavy at times, and lighter at others. It was as though their weight shifted as they came closer. Perhaps they were shedding supplies, he thought, but he could hear no other sounds that might indicate a sloughing off of items. He put it out of his head for the moment as he left the keep and rode out to the edge of Asgard, where Bifrost arced down to Midgard.

Heimdall planted himself in the center of the path, directly in the way of the intruder and his horse. It wasn't long before he could see them both, but his sense of unease was not quelled. They appeared as he had expected based on the sounds of their approach. Although they were still leagues away, he could see that it was a lone mortal leading a single horse.

There was something unusual about the traveler, but he could no longer detect anything strange about his gait. He found himself relaxing his guard somewhat. If this mortal and his horse were a threat, then at least they appeared far less threatening than the thundering mass of giants he expected to come crashing down on Asgard one day, and he had no doubts that he could keep this solitary figure from holy ground if need be.

It was a long while until the traveler reached him, but when he did Heimdall saw nothing terribly remarkable about him. He looked strong, but not unnaturally so, and he could say the same for his horse. He considered that his original estimation was faulty, that too many years of guarding the path to Asgard might have caused him to see threats that were not really there.

Still, he eyed the two warily. The man had no apparent weapons, but did carry a bag over his shoulder. He could hear the clink of tools—hammers, chisels, wedges, and the like. The horse was likewise burdened. The traveler—a mason, clearly—was simply dressed, and his face bore the marks of one who had toiled under a hot sun or with an icy wind constantly barraging his face. His hands were rough as well; Heimdall could hear his fingers scraping together, the sound like grating sand on skin.

Heimdall felt a brief moment of alarm that was suddenly gone as the mason and his horse drew closer. It had felt as though the rays of the sun had been blocked, and an icy shadow had chilled his skin. He dismissed the inexplicable panic and focused his attention back on the man.

Heimdall nodded in greeting, and the mason and his horse halted a dozen strides away.

"What do you seek in Asgard?" he asked, eyeing the mason carefully. He could not see anything strange about the man—in fact, he looked almost painfully normal—but he could not relinquish the unsettling idea that there was more here than met his watchful eye. Still, it was inconceivable that any enemy could mask his true nature from Heimdall for long. Although his sword arm was strong, it was his keen eye that made him the most suitable guardian of Asgard. If this mason hid himself behind an innocent-seeming mask, Heimdall would eventually see through it.

"The wars are over?" the mason asked.

"What business is it of yours?"

The mason did not directly reply, but instead stared far beyond Heimdall, as if he could see the tall spires of Asgard from where he stood, a feat that none but Heimdall and perhaps Odin could accomplish.

"Does Asgard still stand?"

It seemed that he already knew the answer to the question. Heimdall's natural mistrust was proving valid.

"Asgard stands well enough." He paused briefly, as if the knowledge of the destruction that had been wrought on sacred ground caused him physical pain. "There is work that needs to be done, but it would take more than magic tricks," he nearly spat the words out with disgust, "to topple it."

The mason nodded, as if acknowledging the truth of Heimdall's words. "And the surrounding wall? Does it still stand?"

He was losing his patience. "Who are you to question these things? Make your purpose clear now or leave the way you came."

The mason did not look intimidated by his threat. This man was either uncommonly brave or a fool. Whatever the case, Heimdall had already decided that he would not pass. If he attempted to force his way through he would have no one to blame for his lost head but himself.

"I come to rebuild Asgard's wall," he said simply.

Heimdall laughed, softly at first, then louder as he considered the absurd proposal.

"You? Rebuild Asgard's wall?" He laughed harder. "Go back to Midgard and toil away your miserable life building hovels and carving tombstones."

The mason stood his ground, unmoved by Heimdall's mocking. His laughter was quickly ended by a flapping sound from above. He looked up to see Odin's ravens flying overhead. The birds circled high over Heimdall and then flew back towards Asgard. Odin's message was clear.

"It seems that the High One would like to have audience with you." There was a trace of confusion, but only a trace. If Odin decreed that this mortal be let onto Asgard to pursue his ridiculous goal, then who was he to question? Odin's wisdom was eternal, and he obviously saw purpose in allowing this mortal to pass.

As the mason led his horse to the end of Bifrost, Heimdall considered that the strangeness that he could not identify in the mason was the reason the Allfather wanted him to be let in. He contented himself with the thought of the Allfather's wisdom, keeping them safe from the evil that festered in Jotunheim, where the giants continually sought the death of the gods and the order they brought to the Nine Worlds.

The frozen crunch of grass under the mason's feet grew fainter and fainter with every step he took as Heimdall watched him dwindle in the distance, a lingering doubt mostly fading.

The Allfather's summons came while he fought a dozen retainers in the courtyard. Tyr was unarmed save his fists, and the warriors came at him with sword and axe, each intent on drawing blood.

Tyr was fast enough to avoid them, but it was not his speed which served him so much as his ability to anticipate. He read their motions and gestures, the eye movements that showed where they aimed. As one drew closer, he grabbed a sword arm in mid-swing and tossed the attacker into two others, sending all three roughly to the ground. He kicked the feet out from under one and bent under the clumsy lunge of another, sending him tumbling to the ground. A few more deft attacks and counters, and all of his attackers were disarmed, or on the ground, or both.

He picked up a fallen sword and approached the closest man. He held the point to his chest. "That did not go well," he said.

Orn wiped sweat from his forehead. "No, my lord. It did not."

Tyr stuck the sword in the ground and helped Orn to his feet. His other retainers rose and recovered weapons, some nursing bruises.

"You see our plans before we do, my lord. It is not a fair battle." Orn pulled his sword out of the ground. His tone did not ring of complaint, merely fact. The others nodded or grunted in agreement.

Tyr acknowledged the truth of Orn's words, if only to himself. It was true that even a dozen of them could never hope to beat him. His battle prowess was legendary, and none of the Aesir could match his skill with a sword. Only Thor was a match for him on the battlefield, and that was only due to raw power and strength. None could match the Thunderer for those, but in terms of pure craft with a blade, there was no contest.

"There is no fair in war," Tyr said. "You will not face one other of your exact skill on a battlefield."

"But you are Aesir, my lord," Geir said. "We won't face even one such as you."

"It's true, lord," Orn added. "Even unarmed we cannot touch you."

Tyr frowned. "What will be your excuse when the giants march on us? 'They're too big?'"

Another of his retainers, Kjallar, said, "But my lord, the giants will at least be easy to hit. We could just barely see you move. How could we hit you when your movements are faster than our eyes?"

Tyr sighed. "If I wanted complaining I'd have the women out here."

His retainers, embarrassed at the light chiding, forestalled further complaint.

"You are able fighters, but your skills of observation are

piss-poor. I did not beat you because I am faster or stronger. I beat you because I could see your clumsy attacks coming. You gave yourselves away with looks and gestures."

Geir looked abashed. "How, my lord? I barely thought before I launched myself at you."

"Your every movement gives you away. A step here, a glance there. And you attack me as individuals, not together. You will never lay a hand on me like that."

His men looked at each with some guilt. They all realized the truth of their lord's admonishments.

"Now come at me again. But this time, coordinate your attacks. Look around you quickly, and know what the one next to you and the one next to him is going to do before he does it. Don't wait till an action is undertaken before you commit to an attack. And once you do attack, read the movements of those around you, adjust your plan as you see the battle unfolding."

The warriors looked at each other, attempting to read the intentions of the others without giving their own intentions away to their lord. They knew it was unlikely that they would be able to strike him, much less best him, but they would at least show that they heeded his lessons.

A servant dashing towards him from the keep halted the attack. Tyr held up his hand and the warriors paused, some of them looking relieved to avoid another beating.

"My lord, the Allfather summons you." The servant was out of breath for running to deliver the message. "He has summoned a council at Gladsheim. A stranger has appeared."

He eyed the servant carefully. He looked agitated.

"What is known of this stranger?"

"Little, my lord, save that he is a mason. He has come alone except for his horse."

Tyr dismissed his men with a nod.

"Send word that I am on my way," he told the servant, who bowed low and quickly returned the way he had come. Tyr stroked his beard, wondering what this news boded, and why it was important enough to gather the gods at Gladsheim to hear it.

Odin's Sacrifice

Yggdrasil towered over all the Nine Worlds. It had always been, and it would always be. It was so large that its branches brushed the heavens high above, and its roots wound down into the underworld.

One root delved deep into Niflheim, coursing down into a blackened and foul spring. That land was filled with corpses and decay and the dragon Nidhogg, who spent his days devouring the dead and his nights chewing on Yggdrasil's root, constantly threatening the life of the eternal tree. From time to time he would cease his gnawing, but only to give insults to the squirrel that scurried up the trunk of the tree to deliver them to the majestic eagle that perched at the top of Yggdrasil.

Another root wound into Asgard underneath the Well of Urd, where the three Norns resided to decide the fates of gods and mortals alike. The Norns—Urd, Skuld, and Verdandi—would sprinkle the tree with life-sustaining water from the well, countering the evil of the dragon. As shapers of fate, they carved a thin channel into the wood for every being in creation. At the top of the channel, life began. At its end life would cease. Some channels were long, indicating a full life, and others were mercifully short. Such is the way with the fates of both gods and men.

Yet another root wound its way down into Jotunheim, where the giants dwelled, underneath the Spring of Mimir. Its water would grant insight to any who drank from it.

Standing at the spring in his gray cloak and with his mighty spear, Gungnir, disguised as a walking stick, Odin lusted for the knowledge he would gain from drinking from the spring. Reaching up he plucked an eye from its socket and tossed it into the waters in exchange for a single taste. Great wisdom and knowledge were now his, but this only caused him to thirst for more.

He approached Yggdrasil alone and impaled himself upon the tree with his own spear. There he hung for nine long nights, sacrificing his life so that he might rise again and gain the knowledge of what would be. When his ordeal was over, the High One was wiser, but also sadder and more brooding. For not only had he learned all, he had also seen his death and the death of all the gods at Ragnarok. It was with a heavy heart that he bore this burden, full with the realization that this fate could not be changed. And so Odin returned to Asgard to ponder the future he could see but not avoid . . .

Chapter Two

The present was hazy, sometimes more so than the past or even the future. Odin could see a wall of giants descending on Asgard, marching across Bifrost, the bridge shattering underneath their collective weight. It was a mass of chaos intent upon nothing more than the destruction of Asgard and any who resided there, and it was an irresistible tide that could not be halted.

And then the image was gone.

Instead, there was a lone traveler with a large draft horse in tow, steadily crossing Bifrost with a beltful of masonry tools. He would have an offer for them soon, an offer that they would accept. Or had they already accepted it? It was unclear. Odin could see, however, that the mason was not what he appeared to be, but the rest was vague and shadowy. For a brief second there was an image of destruction and horrific violence so intense that it sent a bludgeoning pain through his body But it was gone as quickly as it had come, leaving him to stare blankly at the empty council hall of Gladsheim.

Heimdall's messenger came meekly into Odin's presence. The Allfather had seen him enter through the front doors after telling his servants that he had an urgent message from Heimdall. They let him in quickly, and the old man, Edil, who Odin had known for decades as Heimdall's most trusted servant approached him with a message that he had known would come ever since he first plucked an eye out all those years ago.

"Allfather, I have an urgent message from my lord Heimdall." Edil lowered himself to one knee and bowed his head at Odin's foot. He could see visible shaking while the man knelt in terrified supplication.

"Speak it."

Edil would not raise his head to meet the gaze of Odin's one eye.

"Allfather, Heimdall sends word that . . ."

Odin's attention drifted. He was there in his hall, but at the same time elsewhere, too. He saw a snake plucked from its nest by one with a fair face and the air of sorcery about him. He saw the mystic runes carved into the air as the creature changed. The fair-faced one—Frey, he realized— disappeared with the snake into a cave.

The image shifted, and he saw the rustling waters of a narrow, cold stream. They hunted for a fish, one that was not a fish. It weaved its way into the depths of the stream. The fish was wily and small, able to be grasped in one hand. A net was thrown over one end, its weights dropping down to the bottom of the stream while two gods—Thor? Frey?—he could not see it clearly—waded in and stomped forward, pushing their prey closer and closer to the net while another perched over it. The fish, unable to see an escape through the legs of the Aesir, made a last, desperate leap, only to be grabbed in mid-air. It writhed and wriggled to be free, but to no avail.

". . . a lone mason has offered to . . ."

The scene shifted again. He stood in the hall of a one-handed god. A wolf as large as a horse was being wrestled to the ground. The image was dark, and the faces were not clear, but it looked as though Tyr was there. The wolf struggled, but he was already partially bound by a silver rope. The rope was being wrapped around paws and body, but the wolf's muzzle was yet free. The powerful jaws lashed out and clamped down tightly. There was a howl of pain and a final image of a bloody arm clutched tightly.

He returned to the present. An old servant—Edil, he thought—knelt before him, waiting for some sort of response.

"Allfather?" His voice shook with fear.

He looked down at the quivering servant. It was always thus when those who were not Aesir approached him. Few could stand in his presence without feeling his terrible aura.

He could well understand why they feared him. He was the Terrible One, the Hanged God, the Lord of the Gallows. He was the god of mystery, magic, and death, and the tales of his exploits were not sung by drunk warriors seeking to pluck up their own courage for an upcoming battle. Instead, they were tales to frighten small children, and grown men as well. They were grim tales of death and its certainty, the shade of One Eye appearing to send one to Niflheim with a thrust of his spear or a gaze from his eye. He was not a god to be loved; he was a god to be feared.

And it was well that it should be so. None could fathom his burden, the depth of his knowledge and wisdom. Even the greatest of the Aesir—Tyr, Thor, Heimdall—were but children to him, with their simple understanding of the ways of the Nine Worlds.

"Tell Heimdall I have received his message." He dismissed Edil with a nod, and the old servant backed away slowly, head down, before finally turning around and exiting the hall quickly.

Odin had already sent his ravens to signal Heimdall to let the traveler cross over onto Asgard; the messenger was a courtesy.

He called for his own servants to send word to the other Aesir to gather in Gladsheim for a council, and in an instant they were scrambling to the halls of each of the other gods. They would arrive soon enough, and Odin would then pretend that they had a say in the decision to come.

The mason would soon be there to present his proposal to the assembled Aesir, and he could not dispel his dread at the deal that would be struck. He would feign rejection, but knew that it would ultimately be accepted. While it was true that each day led inexorably towards Ragnarok, he could not question the outcome. The cycle of the Nine Worlds must play out as destiny intended, and even he—the High One, the Allfather—was not exempt from fate.

As she passed the threshold, all eyes turned to her, as usual. Freyja's beauty was nothing if not breathtaking, and no one—mortal or god—could see her pass without directing longing glances her way. The servants averted their eyes after the first initial glance, deference for being in the presence of one such as she. The seated Aesir turned back to their conversations while Odin sat mute and staring at the head of the table, his two wolves panting at his feet.

She was not surprised to see the High One sit thusly, separate from the others in spirit, and also seated apart from them at the head of the table. He was distant and often seemed to be pondering great mysteries with a furrowed brow, seeing things that no other could comprehend.

During the wars between the Aesir and the Vanir, Odin had been the most feared enemy. His gaze alone had slain many of her kind, and his sorcery was the rival of any of the Vanir, adept though they were in such arts. He was unique among the Aesir in this respect; while all were powerful warriors, he alone wielded death as a weapon. It was good that the wars had ended. While there had been many losses on both sides, the Vanir had suffered far more.

Freyja took her seat while servants scrambled to pull out her chair, fill her cup, and otherwise see that her needs were met. She noticed that all the main gods were present save two. She knew that Thor would not be joining them, but

Loki was expected. If it had been up to her they would have proceeded without him.

Loki was no friend to the Aesir, much as he pretended to be one of them. Like Odin, there was an air about Loki that set him apart from the others, but it was different than with the High One. Odin, for all his distance, was the tree from which the branches that were the Aesir spread. He was father to many of them, but his spirit infused them, as well, as it did the entire realm of Asgard. Without Odin, there would be no Aesir, no Asgard.

The same could not be said of Loki. Freyja sensed a strangeness about him, one that perhaps even he was not aware of. He acted like them in many respects, but he shunned their straightforward ways, their warrior ethos. He was skilled with a blade, of course, and powerful as well, as befitting an Asgardian. However, his true skill was in deception and cunning. In many ways he was the very opposite of Thor, the embodiment of direct, unrelenting, and uncompromising strength.

It was surprising to her that Thor and Loki did not appear to hate each other, despite their differences. She wondered if the Thunderer did not perceive the Sly One as a threat, and so was beneath his notice in that way. Certainly, Thor did not pay attention to small details, instead opting to assault enemies directly and head on. In fact, his current absence was due to his travels in Jotunheim, where he undoubtedly sought out giants to slaughter.

It was not surprising, however, to see the enmity between Loki and Heimdall. The guardian of Bifrost felt nothing but contempt for the ways of the Sly One, and it was no wonder. As the protector of Asgard, he drew a clear line between friend and enemy; the giants were deception and chaos. Those who used such means might as well be allied with the giants themselves. It was no matter to Heimdall that

Loki's ways were in service to Asgard, or so the Sly One proclaimed. In Heimdall's scheme, those who fought for the side of the gods did not use the weapons of the enemy. If not for the domineering presence of the Allfather, Heimdall might take it upon himself to slay Loki before he could cause the downfall of Asgard.

Freyja did not relish death, but she would find it hard to shed tears for Loki. It was strange that even her divining was unable to uncover the strange air that surrounded him. She only hoped that Odin was correct in his wisdom to keep the Sly One around.

Balder sat at the long table, impatiently drumming his fingers against the hard oak. Occasionally he would lift his cup of mead and take a long drink, servants immediately refilling it each time it touched the table, although he did not give any thought as to why his cup never emptied. His mood continued to sully as the waiting went on. Why must they all wait for Loki to rear his deceitful head?

Odin could never hold council without guidance from Loki, and it was an insult to the rest of them, especially him. To be held in thrall to that trickster galled him. What wisdom did Loki bring to bear that could not be gleaned from other sources? Why was it necessary to wait around for one who was so reviled by all?

He drained his cup in frustration before letting it hit the table, the last few drops of mead spraying out. In an instant, another servant rushed over with a pitcher and refilled the cup. His dislike of Loki had grown since his most recent dreams, and he could not dismiss the foreboding that ran through him every time he was in his presence.

For some time now Balder would wake in a cold sweat, sometimes still swiping at phantom images. Much of the dreams faded as he woke, but certain images stubbornly persisted. In all the dreams there was a gathering of the gods that would begin as a feast. As he ate, one of them would suddenly begin clawing at his or her throat and vomiting blood, only to fall face first on the table in a paroxysm of agony. Another would follow, and then another, until the entire hall was filled with violent eruptions. As the spasms died down, all those he knew and loved would be horribly dead except for himself and his brother, Hod.

It was not, however, the blind, handsome face he knew and loved, but rather a sinister face, smiling with derision and vileness. It was the pure face of an enemy, one who was opposed to him in every way. In the way of dreams, however, Hod was not Hod, but rather someone wearing his face as a guise.

He had told no one of these dreams. It seemed womanly to worry about phantoms that haunted one's sleep, and it was not hard to imagine that he would be made sport of for admitting the fear they left him with. But he carried them with him, and even though the dread lessened as the day went on, it returned as he lay down for the night, knowing that sleep would bring the images and feelings back, and that he would wake again with his bed drenched in sweat, vainly chasing away ghosts that could not be seen.

Tyr did not think he would ever be relieved to see Loki stride into a room, but he felt just that as the Sly One took his seat near Odin. Loki nodded at each of the assembled gods in turn, with no trace of anything other than respect. At least they would now learn why Odin had assembled them.

Tyr noted how quickly the hush fell over those assembled as all eyes turned to Odin to explain why they gathered. The Allfather raised his gray head and sat up straighter in his chair. He looked like an ancient warrior returned from the dead, but still housed within the thin body of a corpse. He stared out at them, saying nothing for long moments. He appeared to look beyond them, and Tyr wondered if he were going to speak at all just before his voice rang out.

"We have a visitor," he said simply. He motioned to the great doors of Gladsheim which were being pulled open wide by servants on either side.

Tyr expected someone of consequence. Perhaps a high ranking Vanir or Underlord of Svartalfheim, with their inky black skin and ugly features. He was even prepared for it to be an emissary from Jotunheim with a declaration of war, or possibly even some inclination towards peace, however unlikely that might be. He would not, however, have guessed that a council of the gods would be called for this visitor.

The doors were fully open, and the bright sunlight streamed into the dark hall, causing eyes to squint. A silhouette appeared in the light of the door, walking in slowly with a beast of burden in tow. The visitor strode to the center of the hall.

He stood impassively before the gods, awaiting permission to address them. Tyr could see nothing special about him. He was some sort of a craftsman, or so his tools indicated, and he looked strong, as if he were used to building things.

Tyr stared at the man for a moment, and then quickly glanced at the other assembled gods. His gaze finally settled on Odin, who indicated nothing whatsoever. The Allfather leaned forward in his seat and put his arms on his knees before speaking.

"You have an offer for us," he said. It was not a question.

The mortal did not look intimidated or uneasy, which made Tyr suspicious. He glanced over at Loki and saw him

38

with his chin in hand, obviously pondering the situation. The others simply stared, curiosity plain on their faces.

"Yes," the mortal replied.

Odin did not seem bothered by the familiarity and lack of respect, even if Tyr was. He wondered about the sanity of a mortal who would dare to address gods as if he were their peer, but for now he was content to abide by Odin's unsaid wishes to hear his words.

"Speak your proposal."

The visitor looked at them all, pausing briefly on Freyja. And short though his glance was, there was no mistaking the desire it held. If she noticed it, Freyja did not seem bothered. As far as Tyr knew, Freyja received such looks from all she met, so perhaps she no longer even noticed them.

"On Midgard we have heard of the war between the Vanir and the Aesir. We have heard of the destruction of Asgard's mighty wall, the enclosure that keeps Asgard safe from invaders.

"You see my tools." A hand indicated his belt. "I am a mason. I create strength with stone and mortar. There is much to rebuild in Asgard—I have seen ruined towers and halls, once proud structures now scraping the sky like broken teeth."

It was a good thing, Tyr thought, that Thor was not here. Odin's wishes or not, he would have split this mortal's head wide open to hear him speak such insults about Asgard. As it was, Tyr could feel his own ire rising. He wondered how long Odin would let this continue.

"With all that you must do, I only propose that you allow me to rebuild Asgard's wall."

Tyr could hear snickers and low murmurs from around the room. He silently echoed their sentiment. To say the least, it was presumptuous for this lone mortal to come to Gladsheim and claim to rebuild a wall that had taken the gods months to assemble. Why did Odin tolerate this? The Allfather's expression was blank, but that did not mean that he dismissed the idea outright. What madness was this?

"And what price would you ask?" Odin was nothing if not succinct.

The mason glanced around the chamber, pausing briefly on Freyja. She noticed his attention this time. Her brows lowered, and she looked over to Odin questioningly. Tyr thought he knew the price the mason was about to name, and anger welled up inside him. He glanced over at Freyja's twin brother, Frey. Either the Vanir prince did not understand what the mason was about to request, or Tyr could not read his expression. Either way, he could not predict what his response might be, although his own was clear.

"I would not ask for a fee that could not be paid."

"State your price."

"I do not wish to anger the gods with my price. Will you swear that I am safe here?"

Odin was nonplussed. "None will attack you." His gaze alone carried the weight of his authority.

"Very well." The mason once again looked around the room quickly before straightening up to his full height. He was a large, powerful man, but still an insect compared to the might of any one of the gods, much less their assembled personage. "For rebuilding your wall, I want Freyja."

Tyr had predicted the price correctly, but the mason's gall in saying it out loud incensed him. He noted that Freyja, however, did not seem angry or repulsed. There was even a hint of mild amusement on her face. She probably thought the bargain laughable, as if the High One would ever use her as payment for a service. While she was almost certainly correct, Tyr's anger rose from the presumptions this mortal made. Perhaps this insult would pull Odin from his complacency.

Instead, Odin simply stared. Tyr wondered if he was pondering the offer, or if he was simply lost in some other place, as he often seemed to be.

"How long would you require to rebuild the wall?" Odin asked.

Freyja's previous amusement turned to revulsion, or so Tyr guessed from the look spreading across her face. It was odd to see so lovely a face contort in such an unappealing way. As Tyr glanced around the room he could see anger rising on the faces of the gods, while others plainly registered shock. They all attempted to mask their reactions, however. Odin was the Allfather, the High One, and it was not the way of the Aesir to openly question his judgment.

"I would need six seasons."

Tyr narrowed his eyes. It was a short period of time for one mason to repair a wall that encircled the entirety of Asgard, and a likely impossible feat. What game was this fool playing at?

Until this point, Tyr had noticed that Loki sat silently near Odin, undoubtedly observing and taking in details that the rest of them might miss. Loki leaned over and whispered something to Odin, his hands subtly emphasizing his points. Tyr wondered what mischief he might be up to. Finally, he settled back into his chair, and Odin returned his attention to the mason.

"You have two seasons to complete the wall."

Tyr heard a thud, the clear sound of a fist slamming down onto wood, and he saw Balder shoot to his feet, his chair scooting backwards across the stone floor.

"Father, you cannot bargain with Freyja as if she were a piece of livestock!"

Odin fixed him with his one eye and said nothing, but the message was lucid and unequivocal. Balder took his seat quietly, although not without a sullen look of displeasure.

Nor did the mason look pleased.

"I cannot rebuild the wall in so short a time. It is impossible."

"The wall must be completed before the first day of summer. That is the offer."

The mason knit his brow as he considered first Odin, then Freyja. He turned back to the Allfather. Tyr could not imagine that he would accept the offer. Six seasons was far too short a time to complete such a monumental task, but to have the wall complete by the first day of summer was impossible, and the mason knew it as well. Could his lust for Freyja be great enough to cloud his judgment so severely? He would spend two seasons reconstructing a wall for nothing. Would this mortal be so foolish?

"I will accept the offer if I can use my horse to help me haul stone."

Odin looked as if he were about to say no, but Loki once again leaned over and whispered to him. After a moment, he returned his gaze to the mason. Tyr could not help but notice the smug smile crossing the Sly One's features.

"It will be as you say. You will rebuild the wall with no assistance save for your horse. You will have it completed by the first day of summer else you will forfeit your wages." Odin paused for a second to note acknowledgment from the mason. "If you do this," he paused briefly. "Freyja will be yours."

The mason smiled wide, and Odin rose from his chair, dismissing all the assembled gods with a nod of his gray head. He turned and strode from the hall, ancient and venerable, the high authority of his person evident with every step. There was no sound in the hall to drown out the faint report of Freyja's golden tears striking the table.

* * *

Loki had been asleep when he first received the Allfather's message. One of Odin's servants was at his door summoning him for an audience with the Allfather.

Sigyn's side of the bed was empty, and he was alone in his bed chambers. He dressed, although not hurriedly, and girded his waist with his sword belt. He did not care for the feel of it clanking on his leg, nor did he need it, but it was part of the normal dress of an Asgardian. Appearances were important, and it was always easier to give in to expectations than fight them.

He knew that he was viewed suspiciously. He heard the furious whisperings, often enough not even concealed, and even the complaints to Odin's own ear. He could feel their looks of contempt, their disgust for him. And why? Because he dared to contemplate a solution rather than instantly loose his blade from sheath? Because he did not live up to their vision of what an Asgardian should be?

He shook the thought from his head. It would not do to enter a chamber of surly Asgardians with anger on his face. As always, it was his role to quietly examine the problem from all sides and offer advice to the Allfather, he who had been a father to him—in deed if not in name—for as long as he could remember. He knew that his value to Asgard lie in his wits rather than in his blade, and he fulfilled that role well, even if the other gods did not value it. Above all, despite the derision of the others, he owed a duty to Odin.

Not that he couldn't fight if need be. He was not fool enough to think himself the equal of Thor or Tyr, but he knew how to use a blade. He had dispatched many of the Vanir himself, long before there was even talk of peace between the two. He had even faced Frey himself once, although circumstances intervened and the battle was ended before it could begin.

Now there was peace, and it pleased him to a degree. The Vanir dog Frey, and his bitch sister Freyja, could not be trusted, of course. But it was good that they were here in Asgard, nestled amongst them rather than far away in Vanaheim plotting. Their treachery was inevitable, and he would be the first to see that they paid with their lives.

He could see the duplicity in every action they took, in every word that eased itself from their silver tongues. They had been sent as a war bond to end the fighting, but he knew it was a ruse, that they merely lay in wait for the most opportune time to strike. And the Aesir were easy prey for this type of strategy. Both Frey and Freyja held qualities that the Aesir respected, and none but he could see beyond the surface of their actions to the guile beneath.

He would bide his time. This was his greatest skill, to choose the perfect moment to act. He would wait till the moment was right to expose them. The Aesir could no longer speak his name with derision once he proved the two Vanir twins false for all to see. Their skill and beauty would be meaningless. Betrayal was ever the Aesir's most hated crime, and the penalty—the blood eagle—was horrid indeed.

Loki was last to arrive at Gladsheim, and he took the looks of contempt he received with grace and nods to the assembled Aesir who loathed him. A large man, powerfully built and plainly dressed, was led in. Loki could see the man was not as he appeared to be, but he could see no more than that. His mind began to concoct possibilities and motives, reasons for why this strange, weather-beaten visitor stood amongst the gods.

As the visitor addressed them Loki gauged his actions, his speech, his manner of delivery. He was rough and plain, but this was no ordinary mason. There was a shifting as he spoke, like a second skin that clung to him that was visible only for brief moments, and only to one with the skill of seeing. He glanced over at Frey and Freyja, and was amused that neither had detected it.

The mason faced their anger when he named his price, yet stood his ground. Loki detected a slight smile on his face, the sense of satisfaction from infuriating a foe, from using words to drive an opponent to physical anguish. Loki had done this on many occasions, and he felt a sudden, odd kinship with this bold mortal who requested so much of those with so little sense of humor. He leaned in and whispered to the Allfather.

It was not necessary to tell him all of his suspicions. Odin was the only Aesir that Loki held to be his equal in powers of the mind. Surely he saw all—or nearly all—that Loki had observed. It was Loki's role only to point out the advantages to be gained in the situation, to explain how the mason's lust for Freyja could be turned to their advantage. Let her be thrown into the bargain—there was little chance that the mason could succeed. While there was something unseen about him, Loki could foresee no way that this could assist him in the monumental task he had accepted. He would fail, and yet Asgard's wall would be partially rebuilt for nothing but the mason's sweat and tears.

And if by some obscene chance he should complete his task, all the better. The Aesir would have a fully rebuilt wall and would get rid of Freyja in one stroke. The Aesir would never go back on their bargain, of course, but maybe they could be rid of Frey as well, for he would not concede to his sister's bondage so easily. Perhaps he would raise arms against the mason, and the Aesir would be forced to slay Frey, lest he violate the bargain, a principle they would die or kill for.

The mason did not care for the conditions imposed on him, but his lust for Freyja was like a foul stench poisoning the air around him. Loki knew this would be his undoing.

His counter—to be able to use his horse—was laughable. *Certainly,* Loki thought, *use your horse. We would not want you to drop dead from your efforts before the task was halfway done.* Odin was reluctant, but Loki's words assured him. He struck the bargain, and the Aesir fell silent, recognizing his authority if still not agreeing with his decision.

As the mason left to begin the impossible task he had accepted, Odin turned to Loki. "If the mason succeeds—"

"He will not, Allfather. It is an impossible task."

"That was true till you allowed him use of his horse."

"It will end better for us, my lord. He will get further in the rebuilding. But horse or no, he will not finish. Freyja is safe."

Odin leaned in close and fixed him with his stare. "If the wall is completed, you will learn why I am called the Terrible One."

Loki felt his insides tighten as he stared into Odin's eye, but he knew that he would be proven correct. And didn't Odin know the outcome as well? If he truly feared losing the bargain he would never have made it in the first place. He was reassured by Odin's knowledge of the future. The High One would not allow him to enter into a bargain where he would truly be at risk. The threat was for show, to remind all assembled that he was also the Terrible One.

The mason would fail, the wall would be nearly completed, and he would have served the Allfather once more. Odin's false threat to him would even work to his advantage. If the High One would admit to a council of the gods that Loki's advice had proven correct, no others would be able to spurn him openly. Even his naysayers would not be able to claim that he caused only mischief in Asgard.

Chapter Three

Balder and Tyr pulled their horses up short in the tall grass of the fields outside Asgard. They were higher up than the city, and could see the expanse of high towers and vast halls stretching out to the horizon on either side. Once unblemished and shining, the war had damaged many of the structures. Most were repaired, but the work continued. Even for the gods, rebuilding the destruction took time.

The wall surrounding Asgard had been the most heavily damaged structure. It was nearly decimated during the fighting, and had been reduced to rubble in many places. In others, lonely sections were left to stand at a fraction of the wall's previous height. From their vantage point the wall had once looked like a gaping maw of missing and broken teeth.

But now it was nearly summer, and they looked down upon a wall that was, astonishingly, almost completed. Where holes and rubble had once been, there was block upon block of stone towering up to a dizzying height. The gap in the enclosure, once so vast as to leave the entirety of Asgard unprotected, was now reduced to mere leagues. This distance seemed paltry when compared to what the mason had accomplished so far. Neither Balder nor Tyr doubted that he would finish by the first day of summer.

They could see him working from where they sat. He was barely a speck at this distance, but the wake of his progress was unmistakable. A cloud of dust rose up from where he chiseled and placed stone blocks, fitting them in perfect balance with those he had already placed. While any chipping and cutting of stone would cause dust to fly out, the mason worked so quickly and with such furious intensity that he created a whirlwind of dust, making it appear as if smoke was billowing out from an intense fire that could not be seen.

When he hauled stone from the quarry and unloaded it at the base of the wall, his movements were so rapid that he looked like an army of ants constructing their nest. Balder and Tyr marveled and wondered at his strength and endurance. He lifted stone blocks that would have given some of the gods a struggle. And he did not stop working. When they laid their heads down for the night, the mason continued to work. When they rose the next morning, he was still hauling or chiseling stone. None of the gods had seen him rest or even pause to eat.

But even at his unbelievable pace, he would not have come this far without the assistance of his horse. Each time they returned from the quarry, the animal—no bigger than any draft horse—hauled scores of enormous blocks in a wide net that trailed behind him for hundreds of feet. The load was so heavy that its rumbling could be heard for leagues, and it left a channel in the wake of its passing.

"The first day of summer draws near," Tyr said.

"And we draw closer to losing Freyja," Balder replied, clenching his fists. He turned to face Tyr. "No mortal could accomplish what this one has. There is sorcery here." He did not mention that his nightmares had increased in intensity since the mason's arrival.

"Undoubtedly. His strength rivals Thor's."

"Then we should renounce the bargain. It was struck in bad faith. That ought to justify breaking it."

Tyr shook his head. "You know that cannot be done. We cannot simply change the terms of an agreement because we do not like the result. You know well enough what it means to be Aesir," Tyr added, "And we cannot forget that even if we lose Freyja, we gain something from this bargain."

Balder was not mollified. "I do not care about the wall. How can a thing made of stacked bricks compare to one of the gods? What we lose is far greater than what we gain."

"You say that now, but what if the giants marched on us? I do not take the unhappy loss of Freyja lightly, but that wall may be the thing that prevents the destruction of Asgard. It may be callous to say so, but Freyja's sacrifice here may prevent the death of all."

Balder looked at him sourly. "Is that the cost of our security? Trade one of us so the rest can feel safe? That is a cowardly bargain."

Tyr was not surprised to hear Balder speak like this. His temper often got the better of him. Still, he would not allow Balder to speak of the High One in such a way without redress. "You do a disservice to your father. You know little of his sacrifices or his burdens. He bears the fate of the Nine Worlds on his shoulders, while you think only of one solitary goddess. While we value and honor her, would we sacrifice the whole of creation for her?"

Balder looked away, frustrated. "You seek to make it more complicated than it is. Do you really think the fate of all rests on this one ill-conceived bargain?"

"How can we know? It is not our lot to question the judgment of the High One. He knows things we can only guess at."

Balder was not satisfied. "Bah, that is an explanation meant to keep us quiet. If my father truly knows all, then why does he not share his knowledge with us? Does he think us children who cannot bear to hear sour news?"

Tyr shifted on his horse, uncomfortable with the direction of the conversation. "We do not yet know what the outcome of this bargain will be. It is possible that the wall will not be finished, and that Freyja will not be lost."

"He will finish. Look at him. He is a whirlwind. How can he work so furiously without rest? There is sorcery here."

Tyr nodded slowly. "You may be right. But the bargain was made; that is all that matters."

"And what of the sorcery? Does it not matter that this creature deceived us?"

"Not if it cannot be proven."

Tyr sighed and glanced over to the wall. He did not like the bargain, either, but it was made and none could change that. He doubted that the mason would be satisfied with some other reward. What could compare to Freyja?

Balder scowled. "Loki is to blame for this. He convinced my father to enter this bargain. You saw him, Tyr. Odin was prepared to reject the deal before Loki whispered honeyed words into his ear. Nothing good ever comes from his schemes. My father ought to know that by now."

"You know that is not true. There have been times when the Sly One's schemes have helped Asgard."

Balder looked disgusted. "He spoils all he touches."

"Was it not Loki who found Mjolnir when it had been stolen by the giant, Thrym? If not for him, Thor would not have regained the hammer."

"Mjolnir would have been discovered soon enough even without Loki's help. That giant was a fool. He could not even tell that his bride was a thundering, red-bearded brute."

Tyr did not argue the point. He knew that Balder's anger at the bargain prevented him from seeing clearly.

Balder said, "I will not just sit here and allow Freyja to be lost."

"There is nothing to do but sit and wait, and hope that the mason does not complete the rebuilding. You know that we cannot interfere with him." Tyr wondered if Balder planned to attack the mason or stop him somehow. Such an act would only bring dishonor to the Aesir, and Balder could find himself facing the blood eagle, his lungs sprouting from his back like wings. Tyr doubted, however, that Balder could survive an attack on the mason, and he wondered what might happen as a result.

"I can read your thoughts, Tyr. I will not do anything foolish. I will merely seek out the counsel of he who is never without a plan. Maybe his conniving will be able to undo what he has done."

"Do not do anything rash, Balder. I would not want to see you punished for interfering with your father's plans. His wrath can be terrible."

"I only wish to find a solution to this problem. I am sure the Sly One will be able to discover a way to save Freyja."

Balder spurred his horse and rode back towards Asgard.

Tyr watched him go, his brows creased with worry. Balder would never approach Loki. He could not even stand to be in the same room with him. Would he swallow his distaste and appeal to Loki for this one thing? Would he threaten him? And even if he did, could Loki's counsel be trusted? It was true that his schemes sometimes saved the day, but it was just as true that his mischief rankled many of the Aesir.

He watched the mason continue to rebuild till he ran out of blocks. He and his horse headed back to the quarry, traveling faster than could be believed. They would return soon enough with more stone to add to the wall. He did not think its completion could be halted. He hoped that Balder would find a way, despite his own misgivings.

There was little use in denying that the mason would probably complete the rebuilding of the wall, but it galled Loki nonetheless. He cursed himself for ignoring the sheen of sorcery he had seen on the mason at the council at Gladsheim. It was certainly more palatable to blame sorcery than to accept that he may have been fooled.

But why had Odin allowed the bargain to be struck if he knew that the mason would complete the rebuilding? The High One's threat was foremost on his mind, and he considered the punishment he might receive if the wall was completed. Death? Exile? But why would Odin allow him to endanger himself if he knew the outcome? Perhaps that meant that something would prevent the mason from completing the task.

He could think of little that could be done, however. Anything that blatantly interfered with the mason would be viewed as breaking the bargain. He was stuck with merely hoping that the mason would not finish, as unlikely as that might be.

He had observed the mason at work, convinced that the sorcery that hid his true nature was at fault. He did not work as one, but as many. His speed, his strength—they were not those of mortals, or even gods. None of the Aesir could have accomplished what the mason had so far, and that was disturbing. He could not conceive of a being who wielded such abilities. Even the giants, though they were strong beyond belief, did not have the powers of this mortal.

He had wandered out onto the paths of Asgard to observe the mason's handiwork. He was leery of getting too close, unsure of the creature's true nature. He saw him working from afar, hauling with ease stone blocks that would have given Thor difficulty. No one could have predicted that the mason would be able to do these things. This would surely be taken into account if the wall was finished.

For now, he would observe him and consider ways to stop the construction. If he continued at his current speed there were still several weeks left before the wall was finished. That was time enough, Loki thought, to devise a way to stop him.

As he moved around a corner, coming closer to where the mason toiled, there was a sharp blow to the back of his head. He stumbled to the ground, still conscious, but only barely. He was grabbed and roughly dragged before being dumped to the ground.

He lay with his face in the dirt, struggling to overcome waves of nausea. He got to his hands and knees and was rewarded with a kick to the stomach. He vomited, but managed to keep his position. His head and vision clearing, he anticipated another blow but it did not fall. He looked up to see his attacker.

There was a semi-circle of men surrounding him, a score or so of them, and a high wall to his back. The men wore battle-scarred armor and held pitted weapons that still looked solid enough to cleave flesh. The men themselves were just as damaged. Some were missing hands or even arms, one stood on one leg, propping himself up with a rough wooden crutch. Several lacked eyes or ears, or both. All had numerous visible scars, and more that were not visible. Their armor had plates missing, gouges and cuts where countless blades had stabbed, thrust, and slashed.

All in Asgard knew these men. These were Odin's army of dead warriors, the Einherjar. They fought on the fields of Asgard each day, feasted and drank themselves to a stupor each night, only to rise—both the dead and the living—to repeat the cycle the next day.

But though they rose to fight again, they did not emerge unscathed. Those that lost limbs did not have them magically regrown. Those with eyes stabbed out did not find their vision returning. In fact, some of the most badly injured Einherjar were barely human, but they dragged themselves onto the field of battle to fight in whatever way they could. Those that survived intact time and time again were fearsome fighters, but their numbers were few. All of these warriors would be needed at Ragnarok, or so the legend went.

Loki was less concerned with a legendary future than he was with the immediate threat they posed. Thor or Tyr might relish this situation—a score of fighters against one lone adversary—but he did not fool himself that he was their equal. While he was skilled with a blade, he was no match for all at once, at least not after being waylaid.

He rose slowly, wary of another kick. As he glanced over their gruesome faces he saw nothing that made him think that these warriors had once been living men. Their stares were dull and lifeless, their motions mechanical. There was no spark of life within any of them, and Loki could feel the dull bloodlust they exuded, like a foul stench. These were not men; they were ghouls.

"You strike a prince of Asgard," he said. There was no change in their expressionless faces. "The Allfather will not like this. You risk his wrath."

A large, bald one stepped forward. He was missing an eye, and there were scars above and below where the eye had been, as if a large blade had stabbed him there. His ear and part of his head were missing on the right side as well. The rest of him, though severely scarred, was intact, and he gripped an axe in one hand.

"He cannot finish the wall," the warrior said. His speech was halting and rough, as if he had not spoken in years. Loki considered that it was possibly true. This warrior could have been in Asgard for many mortal lifetimes, and there would be scant need for him to say anything. The other ghouls simply stared, and looked as if they were eager to hack and slash at any target.

The Einherjar had never attacked any of the Aesir before, nor did they look as though they had concocted this—or any idea—on their own. Someone had told them to do this. He suspected it was Frey, likely angry that his twin sister was the payment for the wall.

"I agree," he said. He would befuddle these warriors while he regained his bearing, discover who had sent them, and then kill them all. "We must stop the mason from finishing the wall. But we cannot do it here, fighting amongst ourselves. I must find your master so that we can craft a plan. Where is he now?"

The bald warrior did not respond, but had an air of confusion, as if he was not sure what he should say. "He told us . . ." He paused, searching for a response. "He cannot finish the wall. We will kill you if he finishes the wall."

Loki felt increased threat. He was not entirely sure they would not kill him now, before he could figure out who sent them. "The mason is the threat. We must help each other. Nothing can be done while we stand here trading words. Your master, is he in his hall? I must find him quickly. There is little time to waste. Where is he?"

The bald warrior looked at the other Einherjar. He signaled to some nearer to Loki and they grabbed his arms, one on either side. He stepped forward, bringing his face close. His breath was hot and fetid.

Loki opened his mouth to further persuade the warrior, but was hit in the stomach with the haft of the axe. He doubled over, but was kept on his feet by the two holding him up.

"You will stop the wall or we will kill you."

He could see that words were not going to work. "Yes," he sputtered. "I will go to stop him now."

He felt the two holding him relax the slightest bit, and then sent his foot into the groin of the bald one in front of him, who doubled over at his feet. He took advantage of the surprise and wrenched one arm free. His hand found his sword hilt and he pulled it loose quickly. Before anyone else could act he continued the motion and swept it in a wide arc, beheading the one who had been holding him.

The other instinctively pulled on Loki's still trapped arm, but that was his last mistake. Loki brought the sword back and ran him through. Even with a sword sticking out his other side he clutched Loki tighter, and the momentum of the blow carried them both to the ground. Loki wrenched his arm free, but the sword was stuck in the body of the warrior.

The other Einherjar advanced on him, but they did so haltingly, as if their bodies were worn out. He scrambled to his feet and pulled out a knife. As they drew closer, he slashed one across the throat and stabbed another in the chest. Both fell, but the rest were upon him, unrelenting. He was pulled to the ground and pummeled, finally disappearing under a mass of twisted and scarred bodies.

The Valkyries and the Einherjar

Odin looked into the mists of time and saw that the giants would come at Ragnarok. He despaired of the end, but would not sit idly by and wait for doom. He counted all the hosts of the Aesir, and while they were many, he was not satisfied they would be enough to stave off the giants. He called his ghostly Valkyries, and the beautiful warrior-maidens flocked around him in response, mounted on their steeds and eager to do the High One's bidding. Among their legions he called forth his favorites: Mist and Might, Screaming and Shrieking, Raging, Axe Time, Warrior, and also Spear Bearer, Host Fetter, and Kin of the Gods. He charged them with the task of increasing the armies of Asgard.

"You will fly down to the land of mortal men whenever there is battle or bloodshed," he told them. From among those that have fallen, you shall choose the bravest and strongest. You will bring these warriors to Valhalla, my Hall of the Slain. Once there, you will serve them wine and mead.

"They will fight on the fields of Asgard each day, and feast in the halls of Valhalla each night. Those that die will be reborn to fight again the next day. These men will be known as the Einherjar, and they will fight and die and be reborn each day until the time of Ragnarok.

"When the giants march on Asgard, the Einherjar will stand with the Aesir and their allies. These brave warriors will serve the gods in death as they did in life."

The Valkyries flew out from Odin's hall on spectral steeds and sought out those who would become Einherjar. They were known as the Choosers of the Slain, and all mortal men desired to see them, for what greater honor could there be than to be brought to Valhalla to serve the High One?

Chapter Four

The thud of fist on oak reverberated throughout the hall, startling Sigyn with its insistence and urgency. She dispatched servants to answer it, and then decided to see for herself as well.

As the doors opened wide, two figures were silhouetted by the sunlight streaming into the dark hall. They were tall and thin, but the light reflecting off the metal armor and weapons dispelled any impression of weakness. She recognized them as two of the Valkyries, Axe Time and Spear Bearer, although she did not know them other than by name.

Her attention was quickly drawn to the burden that one of them carried. What initially looked like a large sack in the darkness of the corridor took shape more clearly as the doors were shut and her eyes readjusted to the dimness of the hall.

A body was thrown over the shoulder of one of the warrior maidens. A sliver of alarm became full horror as she realized who they carried. She rushed forward.

"Does he live?" she asked, panic causing her breath to come in ragged gasps. Without waiting for an answer, she ushered them to a bedchamber. "Here! Put him here!"

Axe Time laid Loki's still body onto the bed somewhat roughly. "He lives," she said. "But he has been beaten severely."

Sigyn issued orders to the nearby servants, and they rushed off into the bowels of the hall to fetch what she needed. She bent over Loki's unconscious form. Using the sleeve of her gown she carefully wiped blood from his face. "How did this happen?" she asked, emotion threatening to overwhelm her voice.

Both Valkyries looked down on the pair impassively, no emotion registering on their faces. "We found him thus," Axe Time said. "He was near the wall, lying on the ground. His attackers were gone when we arrived."

Spear Bearer added, "There were many of them. The signs of the fight were clear."

Sigyn looked up at them, a range of emotions across her face. "What do you mean? What signs?"

"The signs of the fight," Spear Bearer replied, as if it were common sense. "They first struck him from behind. He fell, and they dragged him to where they would not be seen assaulting him. They surrounded him and then fell upon him, all attacking as one."

"How could this happen in Asgard? Are there enemies among us that we are unaware of?"

Axe Time shook her head. "No, mistress."

"Then who has done this?"

"They did not mean to kill him," Spear Bearer said.

Sigyn paused in her ministrations. Loki did not stir. "What do you mean? Look at him! How could this not be an attempt to kill him?" She felt anger rising up, but she forced it down. She did not want to take out her grief on the ones who had picked her husband up out of the dust.

"They used no weapons. He was beat with bare fists. And he spilled blood on them. He may have killed some, but they took their wounded or dead with them." Spear Bearer produced Loki's sword and knife, still covered in the blood of his attackers, and set them down for Sigyn to examine.

Servants rushed into the room and began cleaning Loki's wounds, applying healing ointments and bandages. As they wiped the blood away, they dipped their cloths into bowls of warm water which quickly turned pink.

Sigyn stood up but stayed near, one hand on Loki. She picked up his knife and examined it. "Whose blood is this?"

"Einherjar," Spear Bearer said.

"What? That cannot be."

The two Valkyries simply stared at her.

"How do you know?"

Axe Time said, "We have pulled them from their battlefield deaths for countless ages. We know these warriors like we know no other. We are tied to them."

Spear Bearer added, "There are no others who could have done this. You know as well as we that it could not be Aesir. None of the gods would attack another on Asgard's holy ground. And there are no other in Asgard who could do this to a god except Aesir, Einherjar, and Valkyrie."

"How do you know it wasn't one of your own then?"

If the two Valkyries were offended, they showed no sign of it.

"We live to serve the High One," they said simply, as if that quelled all question.

Sigyn looked back down at her husband. Under the servants' care he began to look better. She could see his bruises slowly fading, his immortal's healing ability already knitting his body together. It would not be long till he was fully recovered.

"Why would the Einherjar attack my husband? They have never done such a thing before."

Spear Bearer looked down at Loki. There was neither love nor hate in her eyes. "It is strange, but we cannot say why they would do such a thing. You should seek answers from the High One." Axe Time nodded in agreement.

"It does not make sense," Sigyn said. "My lord serves the High One as well. What reason would Odin's warriors have for attacking him?" She did not say it aloud, but she also wondered why they would leave him alive. There was a warning here, but from who?

"Seek the High One, mistress," Axe Time said, and neither Valkyrie offered more.

Sigyn thanked them for bringing Loki, and then had servants lead them out. She bade another to bar the main doors and let no one enter, then sat down next to Loki, grasping his hand lightly. His wounds, though serious, would heal. She was thankful that it was not easy to kill a god, although mindful that it was also not impossible.

She knew this was due to the bargain struck with the mason. Loki was never popular in Asgard, but the swift and unexpected near-completion of the wall had turned all of the Aesir sour towards him, even more so than usual. It hurt her that they did not value him as they should, but she knew that she was powerless to do anything to change their opinions of him. His ways were different, and he would probably never be fully accepted by the Aesir.

But she could not summon venom against them. She was Aesir, as well, and though she supported him and felt hurt at the rejections and ridicule he faced, she could not turn her back on her own kind. Feeling pulled in two different directions, she laid her head down on his arm.

She felt a stirring several hours later, and realized that she had fallen asleep. She sat upright and saw her husband staring back at her with open, dazed eyes.

"I was attacked," he said, almost as a question.

"Yes, my lord. You were attacked by—"

"Einherjar," he said, finishing the thought. "How did I get here?"

"You were brought by two Valkyries. They found you lying near the wall."

He nodded slowly, as if he could remember being carried by them. "How long have I been in bed?" He sat up, pushing her hand away gently and setting his feet on the floor.

"You should not be up yet. You were beaten severely and must rest and heal."

"There is little time for that," he snapped. "How long was I out?" His eyes bored into her, insistent and impatient.

"Hours only, I think. I fell asleep watching over you, but I do not think a day has passed."

He nodded and got to his feet. "Good. There is much to do, and time quickly grows short."

"Let me get the servants to do your bidding. You can direct them as you like while you heal. There is no need for you to even leave your bed."

His eyes flashed angrily, but he was able to mostly hold his tongue in check. "If I do not discover the secret of the mason, and soon, these injuries will be nothing compared to what I will receive at the hands of the Allfather."

Her face expressed alarm. "The High One would never harm you."

"Don't be a fool," he hissed. "If this bargain causes Freyja to be lost, the Allfather and the rest of the Aesir will blame it on me for urging the deal. Death will be the least of what they do to me."

"No, they would not do such things. They only threaten. Odin would not allow harm to fall on you, even if Freyja is lost."

He shook his head at her. "You know little of Odin." There was a dark edge to his words that made her pause.

"What do you mean?"

He hesitated, his eyes cast down as if searching his memories. "I am ever blamed for backhanded dealings, but the High One's schemes make mine seem pale. If you only knew the things he has done."

Sigyn clutched her hands, shaking her head slowly. "I

don't believe you. The Allfather is good and kind."

Loki stared hard at his wife, his lips drawn into a thin line. "Would you know his black deeds?"

She paled, but did not respond.

"Long ago on a journey in Midgard," he said, "we approached nine thralls working in a field. He revealed enough of himself for them to know that he was no mere traveler. He pulled a whetstone from his pouch and held it for them to see. 'This stone,' he said, 'will make your blades as sharp as those of the gods.' They did not believe him, so he sharpened one of their scythes and returned it. When the thrall swept his blade at the grass, it cut through the tall reeds with no effort. Their eyes went wide, and Allfather sharpened all their blades. The thralls were able to cut the entire field down in moments only, where it would have taken them hours."

"So he helped them. You see that he is kind and giving."

Loki eyed her before continuing. "Once the field was cut, Allfather told them he would give the stone to one of them. All the thralls were eager to have the whetstone, and they argued with each other over who should have it. I looked over at Odin, and there was a terrible gleam in his eye. He threw the stone in their midst. In the end, nine thralls lay slaughtered at his feet, each desiring the stone for himself. The High One smiled and pocketed the stone, and then we went on our way."

There was horror on her face, but Sigyn still could not believe that the Allfather would do such a thing. "There was a misunderstanding. The High One could not have intended it to happen."

He did not respond.

"It was their own greed that killed them. It is not Allfather's fault that they were controlled by their emotions."

"You fool yourself. He enjoyed seeing them destroy themselves. I will not be spared a consequence from the Terrible One."

"My lord, I am sure that—"

"Enough," he said. He put a hand to his head and paced the floor. "I need to discover what sorcery is behind this mason. I am a fool for urging this bargain, even while I could see that he hid something from us. But why can't I detect it?"

She folded her arms in front of her and looked down. No matter what her husband thought, she could not believe that Odin had done such a thing. Nor could she believe that Loki was in danger even if Freyja was lost. None would be happy with him, and they would certainly shun him even more so than they did now, but the Allfather would not turn on his own kind. There must have been some reason for the death of those thralls, something only Odin knew, and Loki misunderstood a look or gesture. She knew her husband well enough to know that he often saw things more starkly than they truly were.

She put it out of her mind for the moment. She had seen him cast the runes several times, and each time he had been ultimately frustrated, unable to find anything out about the mason. She approached him, lightly putting a hand on his shoulder. "You have found nothing from the runes?"

"Nothing." He spoke the word as if it were a curse. "Whatever sorcery he hides behind is beyond my ability to pierce. If I could see it, then perhaps we could justify breaking the bargain. But without that knowledge, it must stand. And the wall is nearly finished. It will be only weeks or days till it is done."

She leaned in, wrapping an arm around him. "If it is sorcery, you could consult with those who are adept at such things."

He turned his head to stare at her, breaking the embrace. He knew who she meant. "I will not go to them."

"But the Vanir have access to sorcery that may help you find an answer. It is Freyja who stands to be lost. Surely she would be willing to use her sorcery to discover the mason's secret."

"If they had an answer, would they not have already gone to the Allfather? And what if they are the cause of this trouble somehow?"

A look of unease crossed her face. "You do not think that they could be in league with the mason? They would not betray Asgard."

"And why do you think so, wife? They have not been in our midst long enough to forget that we were once enemies, that they once used their magic to kill Aesir."

"But they are Aesir now, as well. They have been accepted by the Allfather."

"Or so he allows them to think. Why are you so ready to trust those who killed your kin?"

She looked down. "The war is over, my lord."

"For now. But can you be so sure that it will not begin anew? And what poison might they spread while they are in our midst? What plans are they perhaps spinning even now, plans that might mean the death of all the Aesir? Why do we suffer the enemy to live among us?"

She held her head down and did not respond.

He turned away from her. There were a few brief moments of silence where all she could hear was the slow rhythm of her own breathing.

He did not turn back to her when he spoke. "There are none here that I can consult with. The Allfather does not reveal what he knows of the present or future, and there are no others that have the necessary skill to help me discover the sorcery behind this mason."

"Is there another who could help? Someone not in Asgard?"

He turned to look at her, thoughts already brewing in his mind. "Yes," he said. "Of course." He trailed off, staring into space. "They would know. Why did it not occur to me before?"

"Who is it, my lord?"

He walked to the door and pulled it open before pausing to look back. "Have the servants prepare my horse. I leave tonight."

"But my lord, where do you—" But he was out of the door before she could finish the question. As she moved to summon the servants the answer came to her, and her eyes went wide. They would know, of course. They would have the answer to the problem. But only the High One saw them, and he revealed little of what he knew.

It was said that they lived at the Well of Urd, but that place was far from Asgard. Even if Loki could find his way to them, Sigyn could not see why they would help him. She thought again about what he had said about Odin. What if she was wrong? What if the High One had a side to him that she had never seen before? What might that mean for her husband if Freyja were to be lost? Suddenly feeling despair wash over her, she sat down on the bed, put her head in her hands, and quietly sobbed.

The Wisdom of Mimir

Freyja's first journey to Asgard was unknown to all. Using her magic, she disguised herself as a witch and traveled to the land of the Aesir. In Odin's hall for the first time, she incensed the Aesir by talking again and again about her lust for gold, her need for gold. They could not stand to hear such greed, and so they raised their sharp spears and assaulted her.

She was riddled with spears and swords and arrows, and then she was hacked to pieces and thrown into the fire. Sitting by the hearth, the Aesir were satisfied that they had rid the Nine Worlds of her foulness. They were therefore quite surprised when she stepped out of the fire, whole and unharmed.

Angrily, they attacked her again and threw her back into the fire. Yet again, she strode out unharmed. Finally, she left the hall and made her way back to Vanaheim, a smile on her face at the trouble she had caused.

When the Vanir heard how she had been treated by the Aesir, they gathered their weapons and spoke their most powerful spells, eager to have revenge for the insults and injuries they had heaped upon Freyja. Sitting in his high seat, Odin could see all that the Vanir did. He sent his two ravens to bid the other Aesir to prepare for war.

And so began the first war in the world.

After much conflict, the gods tired of fighting and agreed to a truce. They exchanged leaders as a sign of good faith. Frey and Freyja went to live with the Aesir in Asgard, and became two of their most trusted and loved advisers. The Aesir never discovered Freyja's role in causing the war. For their part, the Aesir sent long-legged Honir and wise Mimir.

Honir and Mimir quickly became well-loved by the Vanir, for when they were together, their counsel was wise beyond measure. When they were apart, however, Honir could not be counted on to give such wise advice. He stammered and said nothing more wise than, "We shall think on it."

The Vanir felt deceived by the Aesir, and meant to show those gods what they thought of their exchange. They came upon wise Mimir when he was alone, held him down, and cut his head off.

Odin gathered Mimir's head and spoke the sacred runes to give it life once again. It sits in his divining chamber, there to consult whenever the High One has a pressing need. Mimir was wise in life, but has become even more so in death . . .

Chapter Five

The severed head of his friend sat on Odin's knee, the High One's hand resting on top of it. Its eyes were open, but it appeared lifeless. There was no spark of consciousness, no flaring of nostrils, no twitch of the mouth. It had a waxy appearance which made it look almost unreal, although a closer inspection would reveal the tell-tale signs that it had once been attached to a body.

Odin had fetched the head himself after the Vanir had hacked it off of Mimir's body. They had left it at the Well of Urd, knowing that he would find it there. He had seen them behead his friend countless times in visions, had seen them deposit it at the well, thinking they would shock or anger him with this act of violence against his wisest friend. But they did not know that he had sent Mimir to them even after he had seen the visions. He had known exactly what would happen, and he had come to the well that day knowing exactly what he would find.

It was not difficult for him to chant the runes while smearing the head with sacred herbs, bringing it back to life and returning to it the ability to speak. He remembered well the look on his friend's face when he opened his eyes and said his first words. They were faint and raspy, but they were clear enough for Odin to understand. Odin had simply nodded once, then tucked his friend's head into a sack and returned with it to Asgard. Even now, Mimir's first words echoed back at him, a symbol of his curse and his responsibility. *"You knew,"* he had said.

"Where is Loki now?" Odin asked.

The eyes moved slightly, but they did not appear to be seeing anything. They were like the eyes of a blind man. The mouth opened and closed, like a fish gasping for breath. Odin leaned in closer.

"He plans . . ." the head of Mimir said, his voice the sound of wind whispering.

"What does he plan?"

Again the mouth gaped, but the eyes became more focused, looking around and taking in their limited perspective.

"A journey . . ."

Odin sighed with impatience. Mimir's head was ever like this. His detachment from the Nine Worlds allowed him to see things that even Odin could not see, but he was never direct and straightforward. He spoke in hints and riddles, and it was tedious at times to get anything from him. Odin wondered if it was his way to get back at him in whatever slight way he could. But he could not refuse to answer altogether; the runes compelled him.

"To the Norns?"

"Yes . . ."

Odin nodded. He had seen that as well, but it was satisfying to have his vision confirmed. He stood and cradled the head, walking over to a pedestal in his chamber. He placed the head on the pedestal and stared up at the night sky. It was daytime outside, but here it was always night, and he could always see the star-filled sky when he looked up.

He looked back down at Mimir. "What will they tell him?"

"Nothing . . . and everything . . ."

"He will ask about the mason. What will they tell him?"

"They share . . . the same . . . spark . . ."

"They will tell him that?"

"No . . . but he will . . . learn it . . ."

"Will they tell him what the mason is?"

"They are . . . one and . . . the same . . ."

Odin narrowed his eyes. "They will not tell him that."

"Yes . . . and no . . .

Odin looked up at the night sky above. The stars were said to be sparks from the flames of Muspelheim, that fiery realm on the outskirts of the Nine Worlds. He had placed them there himself, part of his creation of the Nine Worlds, or so the story went. He did not remember doing such a thing, but it was difficult to recall events that happened so long ago, especially when he was ever drifting forward and backward in time.

The events he had set in place when he accepted the mason's deal troubled him, even while he realized the necessity. He was the Allfather, had been thus for so long that he could only barely remember a time when he was not. The Aesir looked to him for guidance, and he was always there to provide it. And yet he was their enemy, although they did not know it. Indeed, they might never know it, although they might have an inkling when he ordered the armies of the Aesir outside the wall to confront the two massive armies bearing down on them.

But perhaps not. They were so accustomed to the unerring wisdom of the Allfather that most would be loathe to dispute even so questionable a decision. There must be a reason, they would say. There is a strategy that only the High One knows. There would be a reason, of course, but he would never explain it. Nor would any of them understand it if he did.

He did not need understanding from them, but his actions felt like a betrayal. No, he thought, they *are* a betrayal, but a necessary one. It was ironic that they found deceit and treachery in Loki's every word and deed, that

71

they would condemn him for his actions, when he was merely a tool for the High One. In truth, Odin was their greatest enemy. Only a few would ever realize it, however. All others would be dead.

The World Tree Yggdrasil towered over all of creation. Its roots led down into the furthest regions of Niflheim, deep into the bowels of the underworld. It rose through Midgard, unseen by mortals who could not perceive its scale, and through the heavenly plane on which Asgard sat. Its branches spread out over all the Nine Worlds. It was the lifeblood of creation. Yggdrasil was there before the frost giant Ymir was killed and carved up, his body becoming the earth, trees, and sky. It was there even before Ymir's body was formed from a frozen block of ice. Yggdrasil always was, and always would be.

Loki had seen it once, and it had overwhelmed him with its majesty and size. It had been long ago, before the wars, and he had been searching the horizon for something long forgotten. As the sun set he squinted his eyes against its rays, and for a short moment he glimpsed the enormity of the World Tree. Its branches stretched further and higher than his sight could travel, and its trunk plunged down to Midgard and beyond. In the briefest of instants, Loki had felt its towering presence as a living thing, as a fundamental part of creation. While the sight of it had faded with the years, the feeling that had washed over him had remained as powerful as when he had first experienced it.

That feeling guided him toward Yggdrasil even now, where he would hopefully find the Norns. They would know of the mason. He was not at all certain they would tell him anything, but his own chanting of the runes had been fruitless, and he did not trust either Frey or Freyja to tell him anything of worth.

72

As he was immersed in thought, the tree seemed to come upon him at once.

It was dark everywhere, but not the dark of nighttime. It was not cold enough to be night, and as he looked up at the sky he could see sunlight desperately trying to pierce the tangled and intertwining branches of the tree. He was in the shadow of Yggdrasil, although it was strange that he had not seen it in the distance before suddenly coming upon it.

Yggdrasil, despite its mass, did not appear completely solid. He could see through it at times, and it pulsed from corporeal to transient, fading in and out as though it could not decide if it wanted to exist or not. He felt the way he imagined a gnat might feel when standing at the foot of a mountain. He could not even comprehend its immensity, but he felt waves of power and life emanating from it.

The grain of its wood where exposed by torn bark was wider than the front gates of Asgard. There was depth there as well. He could walk into the channeled grain of the tree and follow a path into Yggdrasil itself. Despite its appearance it felt solid, and his fingers tingled when he touched it, as if energy was being released. He stepped into the tree, plunging into the depths of the oldest and largest thing to ever exist.

He was engulfed in blackness and lost all sense of direction and time. The only thing he was aware of—other than himself—was an oppressive presence that pervaded his body, like a deep, thrumming heartbeat, the consciousness of a being that had existed since the dawn of time. It grew and threatened to overwhelm him, saturating each of his senses to the point where he could not tell where he ended and the entity began.

And then it was gone.

He had no idea how much time had passed while he

hovered in nothingness, but it had seemed as if time had been suspended. An instant had lasted an eternity. With difficulty, he put it out of his mind, forcing himself to contemplate the task and forget the pervasiveness of Yggdrasil's consciousness. It was not as difficult as he would have thought to do, for as he got to his feet he found that the memories and feelings were fading as quickly as if they were dreams.

The last remnants of the experience slipping away, he took in his surroundings. He stood on the edge of an enormous cavern. He looked up and saw bright stars dot the skyscape above him. He wondered if he were still inside the tree at all, or if he had been taken someplace else. The ground was covered by a fine mist which swirled slowly around a central point in the distance.

The mist was thick at his feet and barely moved as he walked through it. As he got closer to the center he could see that the mist emanated from a large hole that stretched a stone's throw from one side to the other. Whispered voices surrounded him as he stepped closer to what he realized must be the Well of Urd. He peered over the edge, but his eyes could not pierce its depths.

The voices were disembodied and faint, a jumbled mess of barely recognized words and phrases, although he would occasionally catch bits that sounded familiar. There were different tones and emotions in the voices; he could hear sorrow and confusion, joy and ecstasy, anger and fury. He looked around him, but saw no one. He walked carefully around the well.

He paused when the mist stirred. Tendrils rose up slowly, forming a vaguely human shape in front of him. It was a ghostly woman, insubstantial and incomplete, the connections between body parts only vague or suggested. Two other similar shapes formed on either side.

"Child of chaos . . ."

"Harbinger of twilight . . ."

"Thief of time . . ."

They opened their mouths to speak, but the voices came from everywhere at once, resonating throughout the cavern. Their forms shifted as they addressed him, folding in upon themselves and reforming.

He narrowed his eyes. It was clear that they addressed him, but he didn't understand their allusions. He was intrigued, however, wondering what their import might be. He pushed it from his mind; he was here to find an answer to the problem of the mason, not to decipher riddles.

"You are the Norns?" he asked.

The shapes swirled and blended into one, then collapsed, folding into the mist at his feet. There was a cool breeze on the back of his neck, and he whirled, seeing another mist figure just behind him with hand outstretched. It was not fear that he felt exactly, but there was something about this place and these beings that stirred awe in him.

"We are that which has become. . ."

"that which is happening . . ."

"that which needs to occur . . ."

"Fate . . ."

"Being . . ."

"Necessity . . ."

The mist women collapsed again. He looked around the cavern and saw tendrils reforming in three different places.

"I am Loki of—"

"We know . . ."

"who you are . . ."

"Loki of Asgard . . ."

He was unsettled, but at least satisfied that he had found them, and that they spoke to him. He had wondered more than once if beings such as this would address him, but his need to find an answer to the riddle of the mason drove him forward, despite the uncertainty.

"You must know why I am here, then."

"The . . ."

"stone . . ."

"builder . . ."

"Will you tell me what sorcery shields him? Can the bargain be broken?"

There was a pause as the mists reformed elsewhere in the chamber.

"The stone builder . . ."

"will not . . ."

"complete the wall . . ."

He was taken aback. The Norns knew all, or so it was said. He needed to know more, however. "How will he be stopped without breaking the bargain?"

"He will . . ."

"be cheated . . ."

"of his prize . . ."

"but you . . ."

"will be cheated. . ."

"of far more . . ."

He narrowed his eyes. "What do you mean?"

"Stare . . ."

"into . . ."

"the well . . ."

Loki turned from them slowly, suspicious, but still curious. He looked down into the swirling mists of the well, seeing nothing at first. Out of the darkness he began to see shapes and colors, a scene forming.

The mist began to form into creatures with multiple legs and arms and others who were half alive and half dead, beasts who were half man, a creature with a face of black fire, a bodiless head with one eye, and long-fanged serpents who dripped venom.

"What is this that you show me?"

"Monsters will. . ."

"issue forth . . ."

"from you . . ."

Impatience rose in his breast. "What does that mean?" he asked.

"You straddle two. . ."

"worlds and it will . . ."

"be your undoing . . ."

"but your . . ."

"strength . . ."

"as well . . ."

A mist figure formed next to him and pointed down into the well. He looked down again to see that the monsters had vanished. In their place, the mists roiled, forming something new.

He saw a tree form, and then another and another, until there was an entire orchard of trees in the mists of the well. They were bountiful and loaded with heavy fruit. Slowly they began to change, to wither. Their long branches formed into wizened arms with long, brittle fingers. Their bark became the rough and wrinkled skin of old age. They shrunk and stooped over, the weight of long life bending them close to the ground. Their holes became blank, gaping eye sockets that had seen everything, but now knew nothing. Instead of a vast orchard, he now looked on a forest of walking corpses, dead in all but name.

"You will steal . . ."

"and restore . . ."

"life, only to . . ."

"steal it . . ."

"again . . ."

"once more . . ."

The scene shifted. An eyeless face stared back at him. As the rest of the body began to form, it held a bowl up to him with white hands. The bowl was empty, but it slowly began to fill with a dark red liquid. The hands dropped it, and the liquid inside splattered over other shadowy figures, dozens of them who stood nearby. The stains spread over the figures until it had encompassed all of them, and they began to melt into the ground till all he could see was a pool of red.

The pool cleared and he could see a small fish swimming rapidly through the water. It looked as though it was trying to evade something. Dozens of grasping hands suddenly thrust down into the water, and the fish darted away from them. But wherever it swam, more hands darted down until finally it was grabbed. The hands converged on the fish, and it disappeared amidst the amorphous pile of flesh that consumed it.

"Father of the dead . . ."

"Bearer of flame . . ."

"Wearer of masks . . ."

The Norns chanted while their forms wavered before him.

"You will kill . . ."

"that which cannot . . ."

"be killed . . ."

"You will . . ."

"herald destruction . . ."

"and rebirth . . ."

He clenched his fists. "Why do you show me these scenes?" he asked. "How will this help me stop the rebuilding of the wall?" *Why do they waste my time with riddles and prophecy?* he thought. *The wall nears completion while I dally here.*

They did not reply, but the scene in the well continued to shift. He saw himself, but misty and insubstantial. At his feet were tiny figures. As the mist-Loki bent down to look more closely at the tiny men at his feet, his arms began to change. They grew longer and more sinuous, and scales became visible. His fingers melded together, and his hands became heads with slitted eyes, while forked tongues continuously flicked from their fanged mouths.

The mist-Loki recoiled in horror at what his arms had become, but as his mouth opened wide his teeth began to grow longer and sharper, and his mouth and nose elongated. His ears became pointed, and black hair sprouted across his lupine face. His legs withered underneath him. He could see the flesh shrivel and blacken, the bones nearly poking through as the flesh rotted and drew flies.

The image began to smolder, tendrils of smoke rising until he finally burst into flames. He waved arms wildly, and it looked as though he was in pain, but as Loki looked more closely at the face in the mist-image, he noticed that the expression seemed almost . . . satisfied.

The flames spread out and consumed all the figures at his feet. He noticed that one grasped a hammer and another a spear, but he saw little else as the tiny men turned to ash. The fire continued to growuntil the entire scene was nothing but fire, burning so bright that he had to look away. When he looked back the scene was gone, returned back to swirling mist and nothingness.

"The answer . . ."

"is . . ."

"within you . . ."

He looked over at them, curious and annoyed simultaneously. They had shown him something of the future, he was sure, but he did not know what to make of it. Were any of these scenes of use to him?

"What answer? I saw nothing but images of horror. You have shown me nothing of the sorcery that masks the mason."

"*You will . . .*"
"*be . . .*"
"*mother and . . .*"
"*father to . . .*"
"*your . . .*"
"*answer . . .*"
"*You are . . .*"
"*both one . . .*"
"*and many . . .*"

"You speak in riddles." He had lost his patience. What use was traveling here when all they gave him were vague images and suggestions about what might come to be? "If you will tell me nothing useful, then I am finished with you." He turned away from the well and began walking back towards where he had found himself on the ground. He gave only an instant of thought about how he might leave this place.

"*Sly One . . .*"
"*Trickster . . .*"
"*Sky Traveler . . .*"

He stopped and turned. Only one mist shape remained, vaguely female but with three heads. They spoke in unison.

"*Seek the stone builder. You are one and the same.*"

The mist shape collapsed upon itself and did not rise. He waited for the shapes to return or the voices to tell him more, but nothing stirred except the continuous flow of mist from the Well of Urd. Frustration eating at the edges of his mind, he turned to find himself thrust back into the black nothingness of Yggdrasil.

Chapter Six

Their words danced on the edge of his thoughts as he made the journey back to Asgard. He had found himself outside of the tree, his horse still where he had left it, almost as if it had been mere minutes since he had seen the animal. He swiftly rode it back towards the spires of Asgard, all the while pondering what the Norns had revealed — not much — and even more what they had hinted at.

They had called him child of chaos, harbinger of twilight, thief of time. He did not know what those things meant, and yet was certain they meant something. He could concoct a thousand explanations for those epithets and still not truly know what they meant. *Monsters will issue forth from you . . . You straddle two worlds . . . The answer is within you.*

He was not foolhardy enough to dismiss their riddles, but decided that he could not pursue them while the threat of the mason still hung over his head. Some of what they had said seemed more relevant to the problem at hand, while others touched on distant things. *You will be father and mother to your answer,* they had said. There was a sliver of truth there, if only he could pull it forth. He hoped a revelation would come once he returned to Asgard. He would seek the mason, as they had told him. *You are one and the same.* Perhaps he would understand what they meant once he found the mason.

His return was speedy. His mount was completely replenished while it grazed on the grasses at the foot of Yggdrasil, and it ran without complaint and without rest for nearly a day, at the end of which he could see Asgard in the distance. Time was short. The wall would be completed within days, at most, and he still had no idea what he would do.

Loki dismounted and let his horse rest for a while. The beast did not seem to need it, but it gave him a chance to wander about and consider his choices—or fret about his lack of them—before he returned. The Norns had not given him any solution to stopping the mason. Maybe his fate was to complete the rebuilding and claim Freyja, and thus to launch the Aesir on another path than the one they might be traveling. If so, his own life-line carved into Yggdrasil may very well be short indeed. It was quite possible that he could be slain in response to Freyja's bondage to the mason. All it would require was for Odin to allow it, or fail to disallow it. He could easily imagine Frey intent on settling the offense against him, and he doubted that he could best him in combat.

A rumbling in the distance stirred him from his thoughts. The familiar dust cloud in the wake of the mason's progress was headed out of Asgard and towards a quarry. Loki was closer, and he thought he could arrive in time to observe the mason at work. It was possible that he could find a weakness out here, away from the city, before it was too late. He mounted his horse and rode off at speed.

The quarry, a deep bowl on the edge of a thick, crescent-shaped copse of ancient trees, was littered with scraps of once irregular boulders that had been hewn down to enormous blocks by the mason's chisel. Some large boulders remained, and the mason would no doubt use these for his reconstruction of the wall.

Loki led his horse to the copse and wandered in, finding a spot where he could observe the quarry without being observed in turn. He dismounted and let his horse graze while he crept closer.

He could see the trail of dust in the wake of the mason's horse before he could see the horse itself. Its speed was incredible, and it came fully into view shortly after he spotted it. It was a powerfully built draft, mottled gray with a long, silver mane, and its body was covered with a fine sheen of sweat. As it drew closer, Loki could see the mason riding on the net that trailed behind the horse.

He looked little different than before. A large man with powerful arms and broad shoulders, he was ideally suited for heavy work such as this. As before, Loki sensed the sorcery surrounding him, a shifting that was out of place. It was as if each movement he made was an instant off, like he was a shadow of himself.

As Loki watched, the mason and walked down into the quarry. He approached a boulder twice his height and began hitting it with swift and precise strokes with his hammer, his hands moving faster than Loki could follow. In mere minutes he had finished crafting a near-perfect square building block. He moved on to another boulder and repeated the process, each blow sending chipped stone flying and dust wafting into the air.

After seeing him make quick work of boulder after boulder, Loki barely questioned how the mason would haul the blocks up the side of the quarry. He was certain that he would simply pick them up—ton upon ton of stone block— and cart them up the side, plopping them down onto the net for his horse to pull.

Loki abandoned any idea that he may have entertained of attacking the mason after seeing him at work. Aside from breaking the bargain, what truly stayed his hand was his perfect certainty that he would never survive to land a second blow should he be foolish enough to attack him.

As he continued to observe, he noticed the mason's

outline shifting subtly. He seemed at one point no taller than Loki, and then at another to rival Thor's height. His arms, as they struck stone with hammer, seemed to extend longer, and seemed to also be numerous, as if he could spy multiples while they quickly hammered away. It must have been a trick of his motion, the speed of his hammer striking making it appear as if he had more than two arms, but it was disconcerting.

Loki strangely felt a kinship as he watched. Secrets were being revealed as he observed the mason, and he felt different, as if he was beginning to tap into something that existed within himself. He was not sure he could put a name to it, but there was a sense that he knew more, that he was seeing secret things that others could not perceive.

The answer is within you, the Norns had told him. Something about his own nature was being revealed as he watched the mason, something fluid. He felt his skin as a restrictive container, something that attempted to prevent him from . . . what? He was not sure. He only knew that some secret contained within him was on the verge of release. The mason was not what he appeared to be, and Loki suddenly felt that it was true for him as well. *You are one and the same,* they had said.

The mason would be done with the blocks soon enough. After loading them, he would head back to Asgard and finish the rebuilding. He would need another trip back to the quarry, but all would be lost if Loki did not act soon. Glancing once more at the mason's horse, he silently cursed the condition in the bargain that allowed him the use of this beast. If only that condition had not been granted, the mason would surely have failed to get this far.

As he stared at the horse, he began to see as it saw. He could feel how it gauged its footing subtly, each step being instantly measured even while it set hooves down. He could

84

see the way the animal saw its surroundings, the hidden dangers in a stand of trees, the open plains filled with tall shoots that sustained life. He could feel its power and strength, the feel of the wind whipping its mane as it galloped.

Something stirred within him, and he slowly began to grasp the Norns' message. He looked over at the mason and was shocked to see his true form. Jaw agape, Loki now understood how he could complete so much of the wall in such a short time. Yet even while he felt disgust and revulsion at the mason's true nature, he also finally understood why he had noticed the sorcery when no others had.

He would not have believed it if he had simply been told by the Norns, and they must have known that. Instead, all they could do was hint at his own true nature, a nature that could be revealed by a monster who masqueraded as a simple stone builder. The realization stunned him, even as he recognized it as the truth. His ancestry was elsewhere, and he could not deny it now that he felt it asserting itself within him. *You are one and the same.*

He was staggered with the consequences of what this meant. His entire life—millennia of time spent on Asgard— was false. He was no more one of the Aesir than the mason was, and the thought sickened him, even while he accepted it as the truth.

He forced his revulsion down, at once concocting a way that he might use his newfound knowledge. He may not truly be Aesir, but that was something that could still be hidden. They would not need to know—they would likely kill him if they did. The mere fact of his true nature would not change who he was and who he served. It would be a lie to continue as he had, but he did not care. A lie that would never be revealed did not truly exist. The truth was that he served the High One above all, even now, and the bare fact of his true ancestry was meaningless.

As he looked back at the horse the answer came to him. The animal had allowed the mason to get further in the rebuilding than he would have been able to do alone. He would not be able to complete the wall without the beast.

The stone builder will not complete the wall, he recalled.

His idea would not have been possible without the Norns' hints and the revelation of his true self. It would not be something he relished, but it would cease the rebuilding and save Freyja, and he would not have to contend with the ghoulish Einherjar or angry Asgardians with more might than wit. He would sacrifice once more for the bond he held with the Allfather.

As he felt his form begin to change, he wondered if it was not more honorable for him to do this thing knowing who he really was. It gave him further satisfaction to know that no other of the Aesir would sacrifice himself in this way. They would rattle their swords and shout their fury to the heavens, but none would ever do what he planned. Nor would they be grateful for his sacrifice if they knew of it. All they need know is that he prevented the wall from being rebuilt. They may be suspicious, but they could not fail to honor him for his service.

The mason's horse noticed him for the first time, and Loki walked deeper into the copse. His form continued to change as he was enveloped by the trees. It would be complete soon, and the horse would follow.

The mason finished the final strokes on the last boulder and tucked his tools into his belt. He reached his arms as far around the block as he could, and hefted the huge stone with no more effort than a child lifting a toy block.

He walked up the side of the quarry and dropped the

stone onto the net before he noticed. His horse was gone, the loose harness lying on the ground where the beast had been only minutes before.

Disbelief quickly changed to anger. He clenched his fists at his sides. He felt himself shifting, allowing the chaos to reshape him, but he quickly contained it. He forced his temper down and thought about what could have happened.

He examined the harness. It had been cut, but roughly, not with a blade. The edges were ragged and looked as if they had been chewed through. He brought them up to his face. The cuts were uneven, and the leather had been pulled thin around them. He threw the harness down, his anger rising once more. The beast had chewed the harness and then pulled till it snapped. It had betrayed him. But for what?

He attempted to follow its tracks, but the trail was too dry and hard. There were scant hoof prints, but he was no tracker. He thought they might lead to the woods. He looked towards them and realized that if his horse had gone that way, there was little chance that he would be able to find it. And time was being wasted.

Biting back his rage at this unplanned for event, he realized that he could not waste time searching for a horse that he was unlikely to find. If the beast wanted to return, it would. If not, it could very well be miles away by now. The mason angrily returned to loading stones onto the net.

As before, it did not take him long before the net was filled. He grabbed the harnesses left behind and held them over his shoulder. Digging his heels in, he began to pull the net loaded with dozens of square blocks toward the last section of uncompleted wall.

The weight was not troublesome, but he could not manage the speed of his horse. At best he could only make the speed of a normal horse, which was nowhere near the pace of his own beast. He forced his body to move faster, but even at a breakneck pace he knew he would not finish the rebuilding before the deadline.

For the next three days the mason ignored the impossibility of the task. He did not pause to draw breath, while he carved boulders, pulled his burden, and stacked them onto the mostly completed wall. His speed was astonishing and his endurance was impossible, but they were not enough to finish the rebuilding. He watched the sun set on the final day as he pulled the last load through the gates of Asgard, but it was for naught. The bargain had been lost.

He continued to pull the last load of blocks up to the wall. He was not certain if it was an act of defiance, or if he simply refused to leave this final load undelivered. He pulled them to the last unbuilt section of wall and released the harness. He looked back at the dozens of blocks that lay unused. He would have finished the wall with these and one or two more loads. It was another day's work, at most, but it did not matter. The sun had set, and the time to complete the task had expired.

The streets were lined with watchers as he made his way to Gladsheim, insolent smirks covering each face. All knew the bargain, and all knew that he had failed to fulfill it. He could hear their laughs and boasts, their taunts, as he passed. He let loose the rage that he had contained since finding his horse gone, and it continued to rise with every step he took. The knowledge that he would have finished if his beast had not abandoned him burned his insides.

He became more and more certain that there was some treachery in the act. Why else would the animal leave when the task was so close to being finished? It had pulled free of its own will, but what had made it flee? His horse had never failed its master before. The mason knew it had been something the Aesir had done. They had cheated him of his prize.

He spat in the dust at the thought of it. They prided themselves on their "honor," but what honor was there in the cowardly stealing away of his beast of burden, simply because they could not bear to lose a bargain? They claimed they were as good as their word, but it was all lies and tricks. They would fulfill a bargain where it suited them, and play underhanded tricks when it did not.

He felt a roiling inside of him, a shifting of energy. He had held something back since before he set out for Asgard. He had not even known it was inside of him before he visited Thiazi, but the sorcerer had let it loose. And then Thiazi had shown him how to hide it, so that even the guardian of Bifrost would not see the truth. But they would all see the truth now. He would give his rage free reign and bring their city down upon them. If he could not have Freyja, then he would crush all of the Aesir under his heels.

He reached Gladsheim and paused for breath. The willpower he had used to keep his chaos energy from spilling out was fading as his anger built. He was already seeing things differently. Gladsheim looked smaller, more vulnerable. His mind felt murkier, as if it were harder to express the thoughts and ideas he had before. He did not feel duller, however, but wilder, as if something had been unstoppered and was now flowing freely.

Gladsheim stood before him. The last time he had been there he had come with a proposal. He had not felt fear then, but there had been a sense of awe for these powerful enemies. These were the gods of Asgard, and he had not taken his entry into their midst lightly. He knew they would attack him if they knew what he really was, but if he had fooled Heimdall, no others would discover him. And even though he was a sworn enemy, he would have honored the bargain. He would have finished rebuilding their wall, better and stronger than it had been built before.

He would not enter with a proposal this time.

He pushed open the massive wooden doors of Gladsheim. Where its entryway had been several heads above him before, the top of his head now scraped it.

The Aesir were assembled, as he knew they would be. They laughed as they saw him, and he felt his blood boil. His sides itched and felt as if something were trying to burrow its way out of his torso. His legs foundered, each step harder to make than the one before. He released the chaos, feeling the tendrils of sorcery peel away from him like a second skin. The Aesir became more and more ugly with every step he took. He did not see powerful figures in shining mail, but misshapen dwarfs with small heads and tiny hands that were too small for their bodies.

One stood at the front of the hall. The mason could no longer recall his name—his memories were fast dimming to be replaced by bitter rage—but he recognized him from his one eye and long beard. He was tall and held a spear, but thin, as if a strong breeze might knock him down. He spoke, but the mason had difficulty understanding the words. One Eye threw a bag at his feet and its contents spilled out. He looked down at the shiny yellow circles and wondered what he was supposed to do with these useless things.

He heard his clothes tearing as he outgrew them, could feel his skull expanding. New arms emerged bloodily from his torso, and he felt the ground under new legs that stood beside the old ones. The feel of cold stone on his newly sprouted bare feet stimulated him, and a smile crossed his misshapen face. He felt satisfaction in seeing the smug looks wiped from their faces as his head was pressed down by the wood and slate ceiling above him. The sound of rending timber and breaking slate was accompanied by the night air rushing in, and the moonlight illuminated the dust falling in around him. The little creatures continued to shrink and shrink, their features full with alarm and their hands grasping their tiny weapons.

He felt the chaos finish shaping him into the essence of what he was, and he had two overpowering thoughts. He saw the one he had come for, the one he had desired, and he felt a hot flush pass through him. He would still have her. His second thought was to crush the bones of the foul little creatures around him, to pound their flesh until they were no more than red stains on the ground. In the distance he registered a horn blow, but his blood-haze of anger quickly emptied the sound of all meaning, and he advanced upon the tiny things surrounding him.

Chapter Seven

Heimdall could hear that something was amiss. It was not the rebuilding of the wall; construction had ceased. The cacophony of the mason's furious efforts had drowned out virtually all else in the Nine Worlds since his arrival nearly six months ago. But now it was finished. He had noticed the lack of thunderous hoofbeats reverberating throughout Asgard for the past three days, and wondered what had happened to the mason's horse. The mason himself toiled on. Heimdall could hear each plodding step, laden with the weight of scores of building stones being pulled behind in an immense net.

He had missed the silence of the time before the mason had come, and was glad that it had returned. For a too brief time—hours, only—the pounding and lifting and slamming of block on block had ceased, and he was able to once more hear the rub of crickets' legs, the soft footfall of deer in the surrounding woods, the low throbbing of ants marching back to their hills. His senses felt reawakened, as if he was once more hearing all these things for the first time. But it did not last long.

At first there was the strange noise of something being broken, bit by bit. It was not anything he could identify, nor was it anything he had heard before. If he had been forced to describe it, he might have called it the sound of a thin shell slowly shattering, but even this did not evoke the quality of the sound he heard. It felt like sadness and anger leaking from a slowly cracking glass bowl.

He dismissed such poetic descriptions with a shake of

his head, focusing more on what he heard rather than any attempt to describe it, even to himself. It felt wrong, whatever it was, as if there was something unnatural encroaching upon Asgard. His hand went down to Gjall and he brought it to his lips. He hesitated briefly—he wasn't sure if this were worthy of sounding the alarm across the Nine Worlds. He lowered the horn slightly and continued to listen.

There was the sound of flesh growing quickly, the sound of blood splattering on stone, small drips that indicated birth rather than slaughter. He heard multiple footfalls, but they were too large and there were too many of them. It was as if several large beings occupied one single space. There was also a deep breathing sound, indicating lungs deep enough for a man to drown in. In an instant he was aware of the danger, and Gjall sent out a warning that shook Yggdrasil itself. He only hoped that it was heard in time.

Tyr had been in thousands of battles, and had seen even more in his lifetime. That was what it meant to be Aesir: the glory of battle, of vanquishing foes and letting your sword sing a blood-song as it carved its way through your enemies. Any type of creature that could be named had met his steel at one time or another: elves, dwarfs, Vanir, humans, and of course, giants. He had suffered countless injuries, and had dealt out countless more. He had faced insurmountable odds with a grim smile, and he had walked away from a battlefield strewn with the bodies of those who had dared to challenge him. His battle prowess was second to none, not even Thor, although even Tyr would admit that no one could match the raw power and strength of the Thunderer. After all the pain and death he had delivered, after all the countless hordes he had faced, he would not have believed that he could still be shaken. And yet, staring up at the monstrosity that towered above them, there was a gnawing in his gut that he had not felt in ages.

It had started innocently enough. The mason strode into the hall, seemingly prepared to accept defeat. He had labored hard and had come close, but had failed to complete the rebuilding of the wall as he had bargained. They had gained nearly all and had lost nothing. And yet they were prepared to reward the mason for his efforts. The Aesir were nothing if not fair.

It had quickly become apparent that something was amiss. The mason looked dazed as he slowly approached the Allfather. He stared beyond the confines of the hall, seeing something that was not there. His gait was staggered and halting. It did not seem to be due to weariness or exhaustion, but something else entirely.

The Aesir exchanged uneasy looks as Odin addressed the mason. He did not respond, but simply took step upon plodding step towards the Allfather. Hands were placed on sword hilts as he drew closer.

It was unnecessary, of course. If the mason intended any harm to Odin, he would quickly find the High One's thin frame belied his strength and battle prowess. Tyr had stood shoulder to shoulder with Odin in too many battles to recount, and had been awestruck at the Allfather's ferocity. He may look like a decrepit old man, but to face him in battle was to face death itself, and there were none alive that could claim otherwise.

Trepidation turned to alarm when the mason began to change. Tyr noticed that he looked taller than before, and broader as well. As he continued to grow, Tyr realized that they faced one of their mortal enemies: the giants. But he was unprepared for what happened next.

Swords were loosed from their scabbards, but the Aesir

hesitated, caught up in the grotesquery they were witnessing. The mason sprouted new legs from his old ones, each new foot hitting the ground amidst blood and torn flesh. New arms sprouted from his torso, punching through his skin and quickly growing to full size. His torso doubled upon itself again and again, each increase spawning more arms, while leg after leg emerged. His head shifted, elongated, and his face became distorted with multiple eyes and mouths set in a random pattern across his face. Some of the mouths groaned, while others screamed in outrage and anger, the effect being not unlike a chorus of misshapen dwarfs. Except the noise came from one vast and deformed head of the creature that had masqueraded as a mason.

It stood over them, and Tyr could see many of the mouths smiling in what looked to him like satisfaction. The creature was impossible—Tyr could not fathom how so many limbs could fit onto its frame in such a haphazard fashion. The creature looked like chaos itself, which was perhaps what it was. None of them had ever seen a giant that looked like this, yet they all instinctively knew that this was what they faced.

Its size alone was greater than anything they had ever seen. Its head had broken through the roof of Gladsheim, raining rubble down on those inside. Every motion of its body destroyed more of the hall. Tyr thought that his own height might just barely rival that of the mason's ankle, but he was not entirely sure of that. For the first time in centuries, he wondered if this were the day that he—that all of them—might die.

Odin summoned the Einherjar even as Gungnir flew from his hands. The spear sank all the way into the mason's stomach, and there was a deafening cry of what sounded more like anger than pain as it lumbered towards Odin and brought dozens of massive fists down upon him, quicker than any of them could react. The ground shook with the force of the blows, and the stone floor of Gladsheim caved in, leaving Odin buried and still in the rubble.

The Einherjar quickly streamed into the hall as the rest of the Aesir attacked the mason. Tyr slashed his sword into one of the creature's tendons, severing it with one expert blow, while the others attacked different areas. Frey loosed arrow after arrow into its back, even while his sword hacked and slashed on its own, Frey's will being served by his steel as if it were a thing alive. Aegir hurled loose stones and sent them crashing into its head with the fury of a tempest. Sif leaped up and sank her sword into one of its innumerable knees, and the rest of the Aesir attacked other areas, which was not hard because of the sheer size of the giant.

The Einherjar also swarmed, swords and axes sending bits of flesh and blood flying throughout the hall. The mason swept down upon them and picked up dozens in each hand, crushing some, their blood and entrails spilling from his wet paws, and sending others flying to shatter against walls. Some were launched out of the newly opened roof, their cries heard for leagues. Massive deformed feet stomped down upon others, leaving nothing but broken bodies in wet cracks on the stone floor.

The Einherjar fought on, oblivious to the insurmountable nature of this opponent. Tyr saw hands coming at him and slashed out viciously. Fingers the size of tree trunks fell around him, and he was covered with a torrent of gore. The giant was littered with thousands of wounds, yet none seemed to do him any real damage. Tyr would not have even characterized this as a battle. It was more like angry ants attacking a bear.

More of the Aesir were down. Balder lay crumpled against a wall, no match for this chaotic thing. Thor's son, Magni, who possibly rivaled even Thor's legendary strength, had been kicked by a monstrous foot and sent crashing through one of Gladsheim's walls, the bricks tumbling down in response.

The hall around them was crumbling, and there was additional danger from falling blocks and timbers caused by the giant's flailing. Hundreds of Einherjar had poured in to battle the creature, and hundreds had been ripped to pieces or crushed by massive fists or feet. He wondered if these Einherjar would truly rise again, or if any of the gods might see the next day.

Tyr and the remaining Aesir, combined with Einherjar still pouring into Gladsheim, fought on, though weariness and dread replaced the battle lust that usually possessed them. Tyr received a glancing blow that sent him sprawling. He only barely regained his senses before the stone floor where he lay was pummeled with a giant foot. He rolled away at the instant before it struck, but he had no illusions about what would have happened to him had the giant caught him underfoot. He scrambled back and slashed with his sword, cutting through skin and muscle as easily as if he were carving greasy meat. Though the blood flowed freely from this and thousands of other wounds, the giant showed no sign of slowing his assault.

Tyr could not remember the last time he had felt as if a battle was hopeless, as if there was nothing that could be done to defeat an overpowering enemy. He had faced more powerful or numerous enemies many times, but always he had risen to the challenge. This seemingly unbeatable enemy made him wonder if the battle was futile. He fought on still, for he was Aesir, but as he saw the scattered bits of his friends and fellow warriors around the ruined shell of Gladsheim, he realized that this might very well be the end.

Heimdall was more torn than he had ever been in his long life. He could hear the battle being raged in Gladsheim. He gripped his sword like a vise—it had been loosed from its sheath after the mason had revealed himself—and he paced steadily to and fro at the foot of Bifrost. More than anything he wanted to be there, to add his steel to the battle, but he could not leave his post. It was his duty to safeguard Asgard from any who would attempt to invade from the only possible entry.

What galled him even more was his failure in protecting their homeland. It was he who had let the mason cross. How had he not seen what it really was? How could he be so blind? He could hear grass growing from a league away, but had somehow failed to detect a giant who had walked right past him. And he had done nothing more than banter with him. He cursed himself for a fool and longed to rush to the battle to fight—and perhaps die—with the other gods.

And yet he knew he would not leave. He must trust that they would triumph over this giant, despite his strength and power. This could very well be a ploy to lead him away from Bifrost so that another assault could be undertaken while the bridge was left unguarded. Though it pained him to stand there and observe the battle unfolding from afar, he could do no more than that for now.

He was shaken from his thoughts by a blinding flash of light, followed by the crashing of a thunder clap. As he looked up, dark clouds formed, swirling through the sky. The rain followed. It did not start slowly, but was an instant torrent, soaking Heimdall to the skin and sending rivulets of water coursing across the fields at his feet. He could feel the anger and fury present in every drop that fell, the power surging through the clouds as the lightning flashed again and the thunder shook the earth. He smiled grimly, certain that his mistake was about to be rectified.

Thor had returned.

The rain fell in through the gaping maw that was, until recently, the roof of Gladsheim. The giant was not even aware of the rain, as his slaughter of the Einherjar and his destruction of the hall continued. Broken and mangled bodies lay everywhere in the ruins, yet still the Asgardians attacked, although they might as well have been gnats attacking an ox.

Tyr could nonetheless see some effect of their attack. Frey had put out several eyes with arrows that still stuck out from the giant's face, although it was difficult to tell if the giant had one continuous face across the whole of his head or if they were multiple faces. Still, too many eyes remained to count, and he could still see well enough to fight. Frey's sword continued to dance on its own, stabbing here, slashing there, drawing blood wherever it bit into giant flesh. It would occasionally be slapped away, but always returned to do more damage. Sif and Aegir lay amongst the rubble, however, and Tyr was not able to stop his own assault—and defense—long enough to see if they yet lived.

Nearly all his ribs on one side felt broken. His weariness had caused him to react too slowly to a flailing fist the size of a boulder, and the giant had caught him in the side. He had been flung across the room, but his fall had been broken by the mangled bodies of a dozen Einherjar piled haphazardly in a corner. He had gotten up quickly to rejoin the fray, and had felt stabbing pain in his right side. He doubled over and spit blood onto the floor, gathering his strength before charging back to the battle, ignoring the agony of shattered and protruding rib bones digging into his side.

Tyr renewed his attacks, feeling his will slip away as he became more and more enraged. He no longer fought with precision and strategy, but instead with animal ferocity and savagery as his steel slashed and cut, sending blood splattering throughout the ruins of the devastated hall. Somewhere in the back of his mind he realized that this was a last, desperate attempt; that abandoning his normal tactics was the refuge of a warrior fighting his last battle. Only the sudden flash of bright light and the crack of thunder overhead halted his change into pure berserker.

He looked up into the stinging rain, past the giant, to see a figure fall from the sky and land on its head. Even through the pouring rain Tyr could see the spark of lightning in Thor's eyes. He felt hope renewed and retreated from his berserker rage, once more falling back into his old tactics, his every thought focused on how he could give Thor the advantage he needed to kill this giant.

Tyr leaped up and grabbed hold of the giant's torn pants where they dangled in ragged strips near the floor. He pulled himself up while avoiding flailing arms and grasping hands. The giant's body shook, and Tyr was nearly thrown in the process, but he managed to climb up to the giant's waist.

Around him the scene was chaos. Einherjar still attacked, mostly with no effect, and the giant still rained blows down on them, killing them by the dozens. The rain pouring in made the footing treacherous, although only for the Asgardians, as the giant had too many legs to lose his balance. Arrows flew all around him, and some nearly scored hits on Tyr while they sped on their way to burying themselves in the giant's thick hide.

Tyr steadied himself as best he could and looked up to see Thor struggling to stay on the giant's head. One hand gripped a fistful of the giant's hair and his knees were dug in, the constant whipping threatening to send him flying at any instant. Tyr drew his sword back and mustered all the strength his body would give before driving it up to the hilt into the giant's abdomen. There was an unholy scream of pain, and Tyr felt something grab him and rip him off the giant's body. In one violent motion he was thrown into a remaining section of ceiling, breaking through timber and slate, and he landed onto the wet roof amidst the debris falling all around him.

He rolled over onto his stomach and pushed himself up to his knees, the rain threatening to send him skidding to the distant stone floor. He looked down at the battle and spied where he had stabbed the giant, his sword hilt gleaming through the rain. But his attention was more focused on what was happening on the giant's head.

Tyr's action had given Thor an opportunity. Thor was on his feet, one arm wound tightly in the giant's hair, and positioning himself for attack. Dozens of hands rose up to swat or grab Thor away. Some were avoided as the Thunderer yanked the giant head around to serve him, much like he might yank the reins of an unruly steed. Others met Mjolnir, Thor's massive strength channeling through the hammer and crushing giant bones with ease, breaking fingers and snapping wrists and arms.

Each blow from Mjolnir sent a thunder clap reverberating through the ruined hall, sending shudders through the bodies of the Asgardians. Tyr dug his hands into the roof and held on tightly, lest the force of Thor's blows send him sprawling across the roof and onto the ground below.

Lightning flashed again and again above their heads, and the storm increased its fury. The giant's flailing became more and more desperate. Tyr recognized that the tenor of the battle had shifted. The giant's actions became more frantic, his inability to dislodge this demon from his head fueling the fear that was now driving him. Yet it seemed there was nothing he could do against Thor.

Mjolnir rose up high and came crashing down directly onto the giant's forehead, the cracking bone louder than even the thunder that accompanied it. Again Mjolnir rose, and again it fell. The giant screamed in rage and pain as the blood ran down his misshapen face from the massive dent in his head where hammer met skull. A flailing hand reached up and grabbed hold of Thor, attempting to pull him off, but Thor's grip held. His feet came out from under him, but he held onto the twirled locks of twisted and bloody hair with a death grip.

The giant, caught up more and more in a blood rage that ignored everything but the need to get this impossible attacker off, latched onto Thor with several more arms and pulled. Thor's grip would not loosen, however, and as the giant pulled, a chunk of hair and scalp ripped free from his head, dangling from Thor's vise-like grip. Blood poured down the giant's face, and a scream of rage ripped from his multiple mouths. Still, Thor was now dislodged and caught in the grasp of the giant.

Without hesitation, Thor flung Mjolnir from his hands. The hammer smashed into the giant's face and he reeled with the force. Lightning crashed down, striking the hammer, and Tyr saw Thor's features lit up, his red beard giving the brief impression that his face was on fire. Mjolnir, glowing red-hot, returned to Thor's outstretched hand, and he sent it out again, once more smashing into the giant's head. Smoke rose up from where it hit flesh, and there was a hissing as the rain cooled down the boiling skin.

With Mjolnir back in his hands, Thor struck the wrist of the hand that held him with a blow that shattered bone, and he was dropped to the floor below. Through the pain and blood-haze the giant lunged down at Thor, rage and desperation fueling his desire to kill this creature who continued to cause him pain.

The rest of the Asgardians, inspired by Thor's onslaught, pressed their attacks. The giant contorted his body to rain blows down on Thor, and he was beset upon by Einherjar swarming over him like ants, stabbing and cutting every available surface. The remaining Aesir struck the giant in the most vulnerable areas they could reach.

Thor twisted out of the way of many of the fists and arms that sought to crush him, but Tyr could see through the rain and flurry of blows that one had struck him, even as Odin had been struck down. The hand came up again and again, smashing down upon Thor's position, and others followed, the giant ignoring all enemies save this one massive, red-bearded Asgardian who thwarted him.

As the giant turned to his other attackers, Tyr's eyes went wide. Through the haze a sole figure stood, a glowing hammer in hand and his eyes shining like lightning. The Thunderer had been struck dozens of times by this thing that had felled Odin with one blow, yet he stood, rage evident on his bloodied features even from Tyr's position on the roof.

Thunder cracked even louder than before as Thor raised Mjolnir high above his head. There was a moment where Tyr could feel the hair on his arms standing on end, the crackling energy in the air nearly visible. Thor's cry of fury drowned out even the thunder shaking the room, and a massive bolt of lightning streaked down from the sky, catching the giant full force with its power.

Tyr shielded his eyes from the blinding flash, but not before he saw the giant's dozens of limbs raised to the sky, caught in the destructive power coursing through his body. Einherjar were flung from him, instantly killed from the force of the bolt. Even the Aesir who still stood were caught in the backlash from the giant, either frozen in mid-stride or on their knees in agony, while tendrils of Thor's lightning reached out from the bolt that held the giant frozen in place with its surging energy.

The bolt retreated, and the giant crashed to his knees. Again the Thunderer's cry of fury issued forth. Mjolnir held high, once more lightning crashed down upon the giant, sizzling flesh and exploding eyes from their sockets. The remaining wall nearest the giant exploded with the force of the lightning stabbing down from the sky. Tyr was far enough away that he was not caught in the bolt's thrall as much as those who were nearer, but he still felt the tendrils of power reaching for him, sending pinpricks throughout his body. While he wished he was closer to be able to rejoin the fray, there was a small part of him that was grateful that he did not feel the full unleashing of the Thunderer's power.

Thor seemed to grow larger as he held Mjolnir high over his head, the energy crackling around him like a living thing. His face was plastered with the fierce and unmistakable look of conquest.

The lightning died out, but the giant remained on his knees; still alive, although his breath came in ragged gasps. His flesh sizzled and was charred black over most of his body, and blood ran like rivers from his wounds. Still, he was not down, and his size and ferocity had proven a match for the Aesir so far. Tyr wondered how the battle might have gone had Thor not shown up when he did.

The giant stared at Thor with his multiple remaining eyes. His face contorted into a grimace that appeared to be a mix of rage and pain, and his mouths opened wide as a scream of anger issued forth. Impossibly, he began to rise to his feet. Thor gritted his teeth and threw Mjolnir with every iota of strength he could muster.

Tyr had heard many legends of Thor's strength. It was said that Thor had reeled in the Midgard Serpent while fishing one day, and only the treachery of a giant had set the beast loose. Thor was even supposed to have survived a battle with Old Age herself, a foe that defeats all.

These were mere stories, but Tyr had witnessed the Thunderer's strength in real battle, and he had never seen its equal. Thor was virtually a giant himself, and Tyr had seen him lay waste to entire armies. He had felt the earth shake with a stomp of his foot. The unleashed fury of Thor was a thing more frightening than all the armies of Niflheim.

He witnessed this unleashed fury as Mjolnir was hurled from Thor's hand with a force that was unequaled throughout the Nine Worlds. As the giant staggered to his feet, the hammer hit him in the forehead with a resounding wave of force and continued through his head, only to emerge in an explosion of bone, blood, and brain on the opposite side. The giant's head was jerked backwards as if someone pulled it with invisible strings, before snapping forward and sending his entire body sprawling after it. The crash of the giant's body on the broken floor of Gladsheim shook Asgard.

Mjolnir flew back to Thor's outstretched hand as he approached the downed giant. He had a look of grim satisfaction on his face as he strode around the massive body, Mjolnir gripped tightly at his side. Even in death the giant's size was impressive. Its head was at least twice Thor's height, and it almost seemed absurd to Tyr that the giant had been felled by something that was so much smaller.

The injured Aesir scattered throughout the hall slowly rose to their feet. Hundreds of Einherjar lay dead around them, some so badly mangled that Tyr could not imagine that they would rise again with the morn, or at least he hoped they would not. He could not imagine how such mangled and damaged beings could continue to exist, and they would certainly be useless in battle.

Tyr climbed down from the roof. His strength was returning and his wounds were healing quickly. He headed past the massive corpse to see Odin.

The Allfather was standing in the exact spot where the giant had pummeled him, looking only slightly weary. Dried blood encrusted his face, but all signs of injury were gone. One of the remaining Einherjar brought him his spear, Gungnir, torn from the stomach of the giant and still dripping with gore. He held it like a staff and surveyed the scene of the devastation around him, a look on his face that Tyr thought might even be grim amusement. But he could never fathom Odin's thoughts, and he knew enough of his self-sacrifice to realize that Odin did not always exist completely in the present with the rest of them. He was often elsewhere, other times and places, while still physically anchored to the present. He probably knew that he would be struck down by the giant, but made no move to prevent it from happening. It was his way, Tyr thought, to know what would happen and to make no move to change events.

He ceased pondering the thought. No one could fathom the mind of the Allfather, and it was folly to try. It was enough to relish this hard-won victory, the defeat of an impossible enemy, although thoughts must eventually turn to how the mason had accomplished this feat, this trickery.

He had fooled all of the Aesir, where his true nature should have long ago been detected. It was unfathomable that the mason had fooled Heimdall, he who could hear the wool growing on sheep, who could feel the reverberations of crunching grass underneath the feet of a distant traveler. Once in Asgard, both Frey and Freyja had likewise been unable to pierce the veil of his disguise. The Vanir were well-known for their sorcerous abilities, and yet neither had seen the mason's true nature. It did not bode well that two of the Vanir could be so thoroughly fooled.

Tyr was also surprised that Loki could be tricked by the mason. And not only had he been fooled along with the rest of them, he had made the bargain possible by whispering advice to the High One. Tyr suddenly realized that he had seen no sign of Loki during the battle. As the wounded gods healed from their injuries, and the bodies of the dead Einherjar were taken from the hall, he confirmed that Loki had not been in Gladsheim while the mason attacked.

Balder would surely make much of his absence, and Tyr was not at all sure that he would argue the point. It was suspicious at best that the Sly One was not there at such a time. He wondered where he might be, and what words he might use to lessen the blame upon himself when he returned.

Chapter Eight

Thiazi looked away from the pool. The mason was dead, his brains scattered across Gladsheim. Even though Thiazi knew it would end in such a way, he was still surprised that they had bested the mason. After he flattened Odin, Thiazi had held out a small hope that the mason would not be killed, that he would destroy all the Aesir in Gladsheim, and then continue on a path of destruction across Asgard. He could easily envision the mason, with the hall crumbling around him as he grew even larger, absorbing the energy from the gods he had killed. He would go from there to crush Valaskjalf, Valhalla, and all the other halls of the gods, stomping the Einherjar and Valkyries into the dust on the way, while the Aesir could do nothing but rail against his assault. It was amusing to imagine, even if such an outcome was unlikely.

He had relished the looks on the faces of the Aesir. Even though he watched from Thrymheim, their expressions were no less satisfying than if he had been there to see them in person. Their fear was palpable, their hesitation in those last moments of his transformation speaking volumes.

But it was over, and the end result was as he knew it would be, despite the power of the giant. When Thiazi had seen the lightning that heralded Thor's return, he knew short work would be made of the mason. The hated Thunderer was the strongest being in the Nine Worlds, and nothing could stand against him.

But that would change soon enough.

The mason had fulfilled his role. He had caused the

gods to feel fear, to worry about what may soon follow. If the giants could send one like the mason, could they send dozens? Hundreds? Such a threat could not be ignored, and Thiazi knew that it would not be. They would not send armies to Jotunheim—not yet, anyway. Some would argue for that course; Thor would be one of them, certainly. But Odin would not be persuaded to take rash action by his hot-headed son. He would want to know the threat first before committing to action. He would send one who he could be certain would not attack, one who would discover what needed to be discovered and then return.

And he would send him alone. That would be the key to their downfall, for once Thiazi had ensnared Loki, the eventual death of the gods would not be long in coming. The one-eyed one would think himself clever and cautious, but he would discover that even he could be outmaneuvered. As wise as he may be, he still failed to realize his most dangerous enemy had been in Asgard for ages.

At the foot of Bifrost, Heimdall could hear the steady sound of horse's hooves striking dirt. He had first heard the sound hours ago, as the animal made its way towards Asgard, led by a lone male traveler by the sound of his gait. At first he thought the man led two horses, but the hoof beats sounded odd. They were spaced too close together, as if one horse were nearly on top of the other. As the beast came closer, almost within sight, he realized that it was one horse, not two. But how to account for the multiple hoof beats? He wasn't certain, and didn't like to hazard guesses too soon.

He could first see two small specks coming toward him on Bifrost, one larger than the other. Soon enough he recognized them as man and horse, although he could not make out the particulars of either. The horse was large, but the awkward, unpracticed gait marked it as a foal. He smiled to himself when he realized why it had sounded like two horses, but his face quickly turned sour when he recognized who led the horse.

Half a stone's throw away, Loki stopped short, weighing his welcome back onto Asgard. Heimdall folded his arms and stood at the edge of Bifrost, cutting an imposing figure. He was almost as large as Thor, well-built and powerful, and he was very nearly the perfect guardian for Bifrost, the only way to reach Asgard.

Loki took several more steps forward. "Am I still welcome here?"

Heimdall's expression did not change. "That is not for me to decide." It was clear to Loki that Heimdall did indeed wish it was for him to decide, and it was just as clear what the answer would be.

"You think me at fault for the mason," Loki said.

Heimdall did not answer.

"Maybe you are right to blame me. It was on my advice that the Allfather accepted the bargain, and the mason's price as well."

Heimdall's lip curled up. His hatred of Loki was legendary. "Do you seek to give me further reason to scorn you? There is no need. You can sink no lower in my estimation. A worm can only burrow so deep into the muck."

"You do me wrong. Look on Asgard and see the wall that now stands. When the giants march at Ragnarok, remember that the wall is there once more because I proposed the bargain. And the cost was nothing more than a few thunderbolts from Mjolnir."

Heimdall sneered. "You risk much when it is not your own hide at stake. Where were you when the mason attacked?"

Loki ignored Heimdall's accusing tone. Much as he desired to explain what he had sacrificed, he knew that his role in defeating the mason could never be revealed. Savior of Freyja or not, they would kill him if they knew giant blood ran through his veins.

"I am not here to argue. I seek only to bring this foal to Odin, as a gift."

"So that we can forget how you bargained with one of our hated enemies?" Heimdall narrowed his eyes at the horse. "Where did you get it?"

I birthed it myself after coupling with the mason's horse, he thought. He would have relished the look on Heimdall's face, but that moment would be cut short when the guardian withdrew his sword.

"It is the spawn of the mason's horse. It will be a fitting steed for the Allfather." It was a partial truth, at least.

"That explains little. Why does it have eight legs?" Heimdall's tone was laced with suspicion.

"I didn't ask."

Heimdall sneered. "Your mocking words will be your undoing one day."

Exasperated, Loki abandoned any attempt at conciliation. He adopted Heimdall's tone instead, striking him where he knew it would hurt most. "You seem to have healed well from the battle. Perhaps you could tell me your role in slaying the mason?"

Heimdall's teeth gritted and he let his arms drop down to his sides, hands curling into fists. "You know well enough that I could not leave Bifrost."

"Oh yes, there may have been some other danger." Loki nodded in mock understanding. "And what threat did you repel while your comrades were being pounded into the floor of Gladsheim?"

Heimdall's quiet seething gave Loki some satisfaction,

but not much. Mocking him only partially assuaged his irritation, but he took some solace in the fact that he had at least shut him up.

Heimdall took a step closer, hands still gripped tightly into fists. "I would not be surprised to discover that this was all your doing. Your schemes know no bounds. I honored my duty at Bifrost to keep Asgard safe from the likes of you."

Loki shook his head. "Heimdall, you are ever the brilliant tactician. This lone foal and I did indeed plan to take over Asgard by force. Unfortunately, we could not realize our plan because of your unwavering duty."

Heimdall glared at him.

"Since my evil scheme to destroy all that is good has been thwarted, I suppose I will make my way to Gladsheim, unless you feel the need to draw your sword and end my terrible threat." He paused, palms up in a gesture of supplication. "No? Then I suppose I'll abandon my evil plans for now. Maybe next time we meet I'll be leading an army of giants across Bifrost."

Loki led the foal around Heimdall, who merely stood there. After a few dozen steps, he turned and looked back. "Are you certain that I am not a giant in disguise, Heimdall? I would hate for you to be fooled by the same trick twice."

The guardian did not turn, but Loki could see the corded muscle on the back of his neck stand out with the strain of containing himself.

After Heimdall's reaction, he knew he could expect no better from any of the others. They would see only what they wanted to see, and would fail to listen to any words to the contrary. Still, there was little choice but to face them. He would explain what he could, present his gift to the Allfather, and hope for the best.

He made his way to Gladsheim. The hall had been rebuilt since the attack, and from afar it looked as well-constructed and intact as it had ever been. Einherjar stared at him as he passed, but did not interfere. He was surprised to recognize the bald one who had threatened him months ago. The warrior stared at him blankly, but Loki ignored him as he led his gleaming white foal through the meandering streets of Asgard.

The massive wooden doors of Gladsheim slowly opened, and he entered the hall with the foal in tow. He walked confidently towards the Aesir seated around a large table near the front of the hall.

Odin was at the head of the table, and also seated were Tyr, Balder, Frey, and Thor. The other seats were empty. The remains of a large meal was scattered across the table and on the floor around them, and servants scurried to and fro cleaning up the mess.

Odin's ravens squawked and flapped at Loki's approach. Odin looked up and brought the attention of the others who sent sour looks his way. They remained calm and seated, but Loki could see the anger and resentment. It was plain that they blamed him for the mason's attack, and it was just as plain that they ignored the rebuilding of the wall and the saving of Freyja.

Balder spoke up as Loki drew closer. "The Sly One returns after nearly causing the destruction of Asgard. What clever bargains will you propose today? Will you invite the rest of the giants as our guests and give them our women?"

Loki ignored Balder and addressed Odin directly. "Allfather, it is true that I erred in judgment." There were grunts and snorts of derision from the other gods. "I, along with others, failed to see the mason's true nature," he made brief eye contact with Balder, "and there was a price to be paid for this failure. As a gesture to show my regret, I humbly ask that I be allowed to present you with this gift." He indicated the foal.

"You have caused much mischief," the Allfather said.

"My lord, I only wished to have the wall rebuilt for our continued defense."

"You let the enemy onto our sacred ground."

Loki bit his tongue. Why was Heimdall not to blame for this mistake? Why was he not here to face Odin's wrath?

"Perhaps you are right, Allfather. I should have seen through the mason's guise. I realize this one small gift will not make up for the damage caused, but it is a worthy gift."

Balder said, "So you bring an unnatural creature here to Asgard to curry favor with the High One? Where did you get this beast?"

Loki did not immediately answer. He considered how they would react to his change into a mare, his birthing of the foal, and knew that that fact alone would be enough to cause disgust.

"The foal is a gift for the Allfather. It is the—"

Balder cut him off. "You still do not tell us how you came about this horse."

Loki bit back an angry retort. "The Norns gave me the foal," he said. "In a sense." The gods quieted down and eyed him carefully.

"You have been to the Norns?" Tyr asked.

"Yes. They told me of a mare with . . . certain qualities that could lure the mason's horse from its work. I used the mare for this purpose. Without his horse, he was not able to complete the wall."

"And this foal is . . .?" Tyr asked.

"The product of the two."

Frey spoke aloud to the others. "It is likely true that failing to have the use of his horse prevented the mason from completing the wall. We all saw the power and speed of his horse, and how much slower he was without it those last few days."

Balder could not contain his disgust. "This story casting Loki as the hero is ridiculous." He turned to Loki. "Nothing could be more absurd than any vision of you as the savior of Asgard."

Loki's irritation rose, as it had with Heimdall. "And what was your role in defending Asgard, Balder? Did you slow the giant down by getting in the way of his fists?"

Balder stood up, his fists clenched. Before he could draw his sword, he was halted by one word from Odin.

"Hold."

Balder stared hard at Loki, but reluctantly retook his seat. He turned to Odin, nearly spewing venom. "He should not escape punishment for his role in this, father."

Thor spoke up for the first time. "I tire of this. A giant arrived in Asgard and we killed it. What else is there to say?"

"There is much to say," Frey said, "if Loki is responsible for this."

Thor pushed his chair back from the table. "Bah. Even if he is, what can mere words do? Jotunheim sent the strongest giant any has ever seen to destroy us, and now his brains are scattered across Gladsheim. I hope they send more. I would like to face a dozen like him."

The others ignored Thor's boast. Frey said to Loki, "You hide something, that much is true."

Loki successfully prevented himself from sneering at him. He glanced at Odin. The High One stared at him without expression, but he knew the truth. As ever, though, he would not reveal his secrets to the other Aesir. Loki was glad for once that Odin did not tell all. If he were to reveal Loki's secret, death would be the least of his punishments. He was confident, however, that the gift of the foal would

115

allow Odin to smooth the way for him with the others.

"I cannot reveal all the Norns told me. They were clear on that. I regret hiding things from the Aesir, but I was made to swear an oath before they would agree to help me."

Balder was not satisfied with the answer. "Half truths are nothing but lies by another name."

Loki ignored him and spoke directly to Odin. "Allfather, I offer you Sleipnir. He will one day be the fastest horse in the Nine Worlds, and he will be able to carry you farther than any other. I have cast the runes and seen that he is destined for greatness. He will be a fitting steed for the High One."

Sleipnir stepped forward without any nudging and presented himself to Odin. The other gods, except for Balder, could not help but admire the animal, and there was some quality about it that echoed Loki's words. Its presence was imbued with an ephemeral power that was clear to nearly all assembled.

Odin seemed to truly see the horse for the first time. If he found the eight legs unusual, he did not indicate it. After appraising the animal silently for long moments, he spoke. "I have seen that he will serve me well. The normal boundaries of the Nine Worlds will not contain him, even while his destiny is intertwined with their ultimate fate." He stood. "I will ponder on your own fate, Loki. Go now. I will summon you when I have reached a decision."

Loki stood for long minutes, feeling that more needed to be said. Finally, realizing that his audience and plea was done, he turned and left. Cold stares followed him as he walked out the doors of Gladsheim, uncertainty about his fate growing within him.

It was not been long before Loki received Odin's summons. A wizened old servant led him beyond the main hall of Valaskjalf and to one of Odin's private chambers. They stood before a black door with carved runes. The servant opened the door and Loki stepped inside, the thunk of the door's closing breaking the silence inside.

He was in a round chamber with runes carved on the floor and walls. He looked up to see the darkness of a cloudy night sky. When he had first stepped into Valaskjalf only moments ago, it had been midday.

Mimir's head was on a pedestal in the middle of the chamber, but there was no one else in the room. Loki approached the head. The eyes were closed and it looked lifeless, but this was not the first time he had been here. He knew that Odin counseled with the head. Mimir had been wise in life, and Odin relied on that wisdom in death—or whatever this was—as well.

The eyes popped open and stared at him, the mouth moving soundlessly.

"Do you have any words of wisdom for me?" he asked it.

The mouth continued to work while the eyes stared at him. Loki heard faint whispering and leaned in closer.

" . . . chaos rages within you . . ."

Loki narrowed his eyes.

"Mimir sees you clearly."

Loki turned, surprised by Odin's voice. The Allfather stood just behind him, although he had heard no one enter the chamber. He wondered how long he had been there. Recovering quickly, he bowed his head.

"You sent for me, High One?"

Odin moved past him and lifted Mimir's head from the pedestal, cradling it gently in the crook of his arm. He walked to a chair that Loki did not remember being there and sat down, placing the head on his knee. He made a gesture with his free hand, and Loki turned to see another

117

chair next to him. As he sat down, he wondered if the seat had been summoned, or if it had been there the whole time and he had missed it.

"You have changed since you visited the Norns," Odin said.

Loki paused, pondering what Odin meant before answering. "An audience with such beings would change any, my lord. Except you, of course."

Odin was looking down at Mimir's head, the mouth now closed. "They see what no others see. They are unlike any other beings in the Nine Worlds." He lifted his head to stare at Loki. "But I see even what they do not."

Loki looked down.

"I sacrificed myself on Yggdrasil for nine nights, and much was revealed to me." He turned back to the head on his knee. "Mimir, what does the future hold for Loki?"

Mimir's mouth moved again, the whispering louder than before. " . . . *the treasure of Jotunheim . . . the youth of Asgard . . . the golden flesh of the goddess . . . will be taken . . . he will consume fire . . . twilight will come . . .*"

"What do you make of these words?" Odin asked.

"Nothing, Allfather. I am sure his wisdom speaks to one such as you, but I cannot make sense of it." Mimir's words echoed the Norns' in some ways, and he thought he understood some of it. Twilight referred to Ragnarok, and he wondered if the youth of Asgard meant Balder, the youngest of the Aesir. Was the goddess of the golden flesh Freyja? As with the Norns, however, Mimir spoke in riddles that could have many meanings.

"All is laid out for you in his words. You have only to pierce their meaning." Odin had a faraway stare in his eyes, a sure sign that he was seeing more than what was presently there.

"I am not wise enough to understand, my lord." He

118

was always careful to subjugate himself when in the presence of Odin, cautious not to overstep boundaries.

"... *you are one and many* ..." Mimir mumbled. "... *legions will follow ... you will ever be alone* ..."

Loki did not like hearing Mimir. Like the Norns, he spouted riddles and half-truths that could be interpreted in many ways. "Is Mimir always correct, Allfather?"

"What do you know of your parents?" Odin asked, ignoring Loki's question.

"My lord, you know well—"

"Answer."

"I know nothing of them. Yours was the first face I remember seeing. I was raised under your auspices."

"And who have you served for as long as you remember?"

"You, my lord."

"And do you still?"

Loki swallowed. "Yes, Allfather. I serve no other, and never will. Everything I am I owe to you."

"... *he will serve the flame ... the flame will serve him* ..."

"I can make no sense of his wisdom, my lord." He was beginning to be annoyed by the talking head. Every word that issued forth was designed to incriminate him for some imagined misdeed.

"You will look down on my person one day. I will be Mimir to your Allfather." Odin had a hazy look in his eye again.

"My lord?"

Odin's eye cleared. "The mason is not the final threat that we face. We must meet the further threat."

"How can I serve you in this?"

Odin paused and looked at him oddly. "It is strange to hear you ask such a question."

Loki cocked his head, perplexed. "How so, my lord? It

119

is ever my wont to serve you."

"We shall see," Odin said, so low that Loki almost did not hear him. He stood up and placed Mimir's head back on the pedestal, keeping his back to Loki. "You will fly to Jotunheim. You will seek the giant Thiazi, in the storm-home known as Thrymheim."

"How will I fly, Allfather?"

Odin turned, and Loki could feel his probing stare go deep into him. If the chaos inside him were a physical thing, he was sure that Odin could see it. Odin, of course, knew his secret, just as he knew all, yet it would remain unsaid. Both knew the roles that must be played. Neither could ever acknowledge Loki's true bloodline.

". . . you will wear the falcon skin . . ."

"Thiazi sent the mason. He will further attempt to bring about the downfall of Asgard. You will seek him out."

"What do I do once I find him?"

Odin eyed him carefully. "He will find you. And then you will serve him, as you have served me."

He did not like Odin's tone, but knew there was no other choice than to do the High One's bidding. He would trust to Odin's wisdom, although he could not help feeling a foreboding at the task he was given.

The Theft of Idun's Apples

While the Nine Worlds were still new, Odin and Loki decided to explore those parts of Midgard that were unknown to them. While journeying through an unfamiliar forest, they came upon a herd of oxen. Being hungry from their travels, they took one of the oxen, built a great fire, and began roasting its great joints and flesh.

After a time they became eager to eat the meat roasting on the fire. Loki tested it and found it to be still undone. They waited longer for the meat to cook, and Loki tested it a second time, once again discovering that it was not yet cooked. They remarked how strange it was that the meat was still raw, and wondered what could cause such a thing to happen.

They heard a voice from a tree above them. "I am the reason your meat does not cook," it said. Looking up, they saw a giant eagle perched in a large oak. It was the eagle who had spoken. "If you let me take however much I want from your ox, I will allow it to cook."

The gods grudgingly agreed to the terms, thinking that they had no real choice in the matter. The large bird swooped down into the fire and grabbed the bulk of the ox, whereupon it devoured both shoulders and two of the legs in an instant.

Loki grew angry when he saw the eagle take so much of their dinner when it had not done any of the work of catching it and slaughtering it. He rushed forward with a large stick and struck the eagle, forcing it back from its prize. The eagle took to the air with the stick imbedded in its body. Loki, unable to release the stick, found the ground swiftly retreating as the bird carried him high into the air.

121

The eagle dived down towards the ground and dragged Loki onto stones and scree and bushes, causing him great pain, till he begged it for mercy.

"You must swear to do a service for me," it said.

"Yes, I will swear it. I will do whatever bidding you like."

"You must bring me Idun and her apples. Swear to this and I will set you free."

Loki realized what would happen if Idun was brought to this creature, and was reluctant to swear to his terms. "Ask me anything but that. I cannot bring Idun to you."

The eagle dipped lower once more and scraped Loki's body across the ground, ripping his skin from his body. He could no longer bear the agony. "I swear it! I will bring you Idun!"

The eagle dropped him to the ground and landed nearby. The eagle landed before him, and both gods knew they had been tricked when it changed its shape and became the giant Thiazi, whose hatred for the Aesir was well-known to all . . .

Chapter Nine

It felt right to be back in the copse near the quarry after so many months had passed. It was not hard to relive those moments, especially feeling his form shift, his consciousness change. The memory of what it had been like to be another creature was dim, but lingered. Somehow the horse that he had become had managed to retain a singularity of purpose, despite the fact that his normal self was almost completely gone. He was certain it would be the same this time; that he would be able to put one thought into his head and pursue it even while he became another creature entirely.

He closed his eyes and felt the energy flow through him as it had before. His thoughts changed first, becoming quick and fleeting. He could not hold on to a single idea or image for more than a few seconds. Muscles tightened and quickened. His eyes opened, and his neck and head began to turn back and forth instinctively, as if he were searching for something, although he did not know what it might be. A fear began to spread through him, but it did not feel out of place. It seemed that it was a fear that always lay below the surface, a fear that danger was nearby and imminent while he was on the ground.

Small protrusions began to grow from his skin, sprouting all over his body. His nose elongated and his fingers stretched to an obscene degree, while at the same time the skin between them began to spread out. He felt himself shrinking, a very different feeling from the vast and powerful expansion into a horse. Instead, he felt delicate and fragile. And yet there was power as well. He stretched his arms wide and reveled in their near-weightlessness. He felt lighter and airier than he had ever felt in his life, and the touch of the ground under his curling toenails began to repulse him.

He did not belong on the forest floor, a target for any larger creature with an appetite and some speed. He stretched his arms out to their greatest width—his bones felt so light! His newly-formed wings easily caught the wind and sent him skyward.

His vision was astoundingly clear. As he soared over the treetops he could see movements that he would never have noticed before, even if he had been only inches away. The fields below teemed with life of all kinds, and he was attuned to the smallest movements. He noted with some amazement that rodents were everywhere in the tall, swaying grasses below him—mice, rats, rabbits—and each one sent involuntary impulses to dive through his body. His talons flexed, anticipating a death grip on one of the creatures below.

It was not long before he gave in to his instincts and adjusted his flight suddenly, streaking towards a quickly moving rabbit that sensed death swooping down upon it. In a matter of seconds, he could feel his talons sink into its back, all fight leaving its body as it was hoisted off the ground. He landed on a dead tree, its leafless top offering a platform for his meal. Still alive, the rabbit was nonetheless paralyzed, either by fright or instinct. Loki's beak dug into its belly and voraciously fed while the creature's life slowly drained out into the dead wood underneath.

Soon after, he was soaring over Bifrost. Heimdall stood still as a stone at the entrance to Asgard. His bird-consciousness felt nothing in particular for this being—it only knew that the creature was too big to eat, and too slow and far away to be a threat. It was thus of no consequence.

Buried deep within him there was a feeling that he could not identify, a small, unpleasant burning in his tiny brain, something that his bird-self could not understand. It was akin to hunger, but it would not be sated with meat. For a brief second he understood the contempt and anger that dwelt within him, but then it was gone, to be replaced by newly-formed instincts. The only remaining thought of his prior self was the desperate need to travel to the land of the giants.

Midgard passed below him quickly and his submerged consciousness occasionally rose up. He could see his destination far in the distance, although it would not take more than a day to get there. The land below was much like Asgard, but some crucial element was missing. It was as if the life had been drained from this place, as if it were only a shadow of his homeland. Humans were scarce, but animal and plant life were plentiful. The forests were vast, and they blanketed much of what he saw. He could see part of the expansive ocean encircling the land, and beyond that even. It seemed that the smoke from Muspelheim was just barely within his sight, although he could detect nothing more of that fiery realm that stood on the outskirts of creation. Even his bird-self acknowledged relief that nothing could be seen of that place.

Jotunheim loomed behind a massive enclosure of mountains far to the north. The land seemed to arrange itself into a protective citadel, and even from a great distance he could sense the chaos that infused the place. He could not see it exactly, not even with his hawk's vision, but he sensed it, like a thick fog that lay over the entire land. It was concentrated around the massive citadel, Utgard, which he could just faintly make out, but there was another point as well. Odin had told him of this place. It was Thrymheim, the storm fortress of the giant Thiazi.

Thrymheim was carved from the tallest peaks of the mountain that made up the protective enclosure around Jotunheim, and it would have been difficult to spot from far away for any who did not possess a hawk's keen eyesight. He circled the tallest tower several times, looking down upon the massive fortress with little of his true cognizance, but being driven by a deep need to be there.

As he banked off towards the forest that lay at the base of the mountain, his eyes were drawn back to the tallest tower. Without his gift of vision he would not have noticed the solitary figure that stood on the tower at the top of the peak. He could see that the figure watched him, and he veered back.

His true consciousness rose slightly, and a single thought formed in his brain, one that would be impossible to conceive if he were merely a bird. The thought echoed in his head, and he felt an inexplicable link to this figure. With this thought gaining intensity, he circled down closer, eyes always on the figure in order to satisfy the distinctly unbirdlike curiosity.

The figure stared at him, clearly aware of this lone bird who circled above, with a gaze that was inviting and strangely . . . expected. The caution that would normally have pervaded his bird-self began to evaporate, and he drew closer.

The tower was wide, and he landed on the edge a safe distance from the figure. As more of his true nature asserted itself, he became aware that the man was a giant, although his size was nowhere near that of the mason's monstrous form. He was twice Thor's height, but lacked the Thunderer's commanding physical presence. Still, there was an undeniable aura around him; Loki could see a sheen of what he would have thought of as sorcery before, but what he now instantly recognized as chaos. It was the same shifting aura he had first seen surrounding the mason. It was also the same energy that he felt roiling inside himself.

As he stared at the giant, the single thought that had drawn him there—Thiazi—grew more prominently in his brain. This was who he sought. This was who had sent the mason to Asgard. This was the enemy of the Aesir.

Thiazi spoke, but Loki did not know the words. Comprehension came slowly as his bird-self gave way. Still in hawk form, he nonetheless began to perceive his surroundings with his own faculties.

"You have flown far," the giant said.

Loki was unable to form words to respond. He perched on the edge of the tower, intrigued but ready to take flight should Thiazi show threat.

As if reading his mind, Thiazi said, "I offer you no threat, Loki of Asgard. I would no more harm you than I would harm any other of my own kind."

Loki watched him carefully, but Thiazi made no move or threatening gesture of any kind. He merely stood on the opposite side of the tower and stared.

"The one-eyed one sent you here to find me, but he did not know that you had first found yourself. You have discovered much about your own nature, and more importantly, you have discovered that you have never been one of them."

Spoken aloud, the words caused him some pain. Though he had begun to accept it, the truth became more real when issued from the mouth of another. He was not Aesir, and although he had thought it settled in his own mind, there was a sliver of denial.

"You were sent here to discover how the mason was able to wield such destructive power. It was I who allowed him to attain that power, and it was I who sent him to Asgard. In time, I will send more like him. I will continue to

127

be a threat to the gods until Asgard has been reduced to rubble.

"So now that you have discovered what you sought, you may fly back and tell all you know to One Eye."

Loki tensed, waiting for some movement or threatening gesture after the revelation. Thiazi simply stood there.

"Or you may step inside Thrymheim as a son of Jotunheim—for that is what you truly are—and I will teach you how to wield the power that you feel emerging within you. You will discover that there are far better uses of your power than merely changing your form. The threat posed by the mason was nothing compared to what you will be able to do. And those who have shunned and derided you will be forced to treat you with the honor you deserve, or else they will all lie dead at your feet."

Thiazi took a step towards the stairs leading down and into the tower. "I will be within. None will attempt to harm you if you choose to fly back to Asgard, and our paths may never cross again. Or you may choose to enter as my disciple, and I will teach you how to wield the power within you. It is your choice; remain who you are and be a servant to those who despise you for the rest of your days, or join me and learn how you can rise above even the gods." He disappeared down the spiral steps of the tower, leaving Loki alone, still perched on the edge.

He turned his head and stared back towards Asgard. Even with his hawk's vision, it was too far away to see, but he could just barely make out what he thought was Bifrost. Heimdall was there still, and Loki remembered the sneer on his face as he had walked across with Sleipnir. He remembered as well the sting of Balder's insults and the derision of the other gods at Gladsheim.

He spread his wings wide. The chaos swirled within him, and he felt his body slowly revert back to his normal form. He stood up to his full height and looked back once more towards Asgard. He could no longer make out the rainbow bridge, but he imagined its presence, a shining beacon that announced the entrance to the realm of the gods, the only home he had ever known.

He turned towards the tower and began walking down the steps to the heart of Thrymheim.

Chapter Ten

Loki sat atop the same tower he had perched on many months ago, his feet dangling out into open space, looking down across the sprawling expanse of mountain ranges that encircled Jotunheim. He did not turn when he sensed someone approaching from behind.

"They serve as an impressive barrier between Jotunheim and the rest of Midgard," he said.

Thiazi stood next to him. "They are Ymir's gift to Jotunheim."

Loki looked up at his mentor, who towered over him. "The Aesir believe that Odin carved up Ymir's body to create the Nine Worlds. These mountains were his bones and teeth."

"And do you believe that?"

"I once believed all that Odin said. But that was before I learned what I am."

Thiazi nodded and looked out over the mountains. "Now that you know the truth, do you long for the ignorance of your past?"

"No, but it would be a lie if I claimed I had no regret. It is strange to wake up one day and realize that you are not who you thought you were."

"But you now know, and you can make up for those long years of service to your enemies. It will be a simple task now that you have been shown how to use the chaos that resides inside you. You can have revenge on those who wronged you, and we can turn our enemies into doddering fools."

"You have still not told me how we will do that."

Thiazi did not answer, but instead closed his eyes. The space in front of him moved and shifted, as if the air were slowly melting to reveal another reality behind it. Loki could see an orchard of trees, evenly spaced, each hanging full with golden apples. Weaving through them was a young girl with golden, curling locks, dressed simply in white. She moved from tree to tree with a small basket in her arms, picking apple after apple. It was half full, but no matter how many apples she picked, it never filled up.

Loki recognized her, although it had been years since he had seen her. She looked as young and unblemished as the first time he had seen her. And it was rumored that she was as old as Odin himself, perhaps older.

"Idun."

Thiazi nodded. "She is the lifeblood of Asgard. Without her, the Aesir will wither and die."

"But she does not exist in the Nine Worlds. Her orchards are unreachable."

"Yes, but she is tied to Asgard. And I will show you where. You will only have to travel there and find your way into her orchard."

"And then what? Would you have me kill her?"

"No, she must be taken from her place and brought here."

"What will you do with her?"

"Nothing. Merely keep her from returning. That is all that need be done."

"And once the Aesir feel the effects of her absence . . . ?"

The vision closed. Thiazi smiled and turned. "Then we will walk into Asgard and end the threat they pose to Jotunheim."

Loki nodded. "It will be satisfying to see them weak and feeble. Must they all perish?"

"Do you have doubts?"

"No, but it will be difficult to see ones who I considered kin destroyed. It will not be easy to walk among them and see their faces as they are cut down."

"Any who live will never rest until they have killed you. They will see you as a betrayer of his own kind, and will spare no mercy for you."

"You are right, of course."

"You need do nothing after Idun is captured, however. There is no reason for you to go to Asgard, if you wish to stay behind. Once they have been ravaged by time, it will be a simple matter for me to end their threat myself."

"No, I will go with you. If anything, they should see the face of he who has brought them down. And I would not refuse myself the satisfaction of seeing their faces when they realize that it was their own actions that made me their enemy."

"All of Jotunheim will owe a debt to you after this. The Aesir have ever been a sword hanging over the heads of all giants. It would only be a matter of time till they marched on us, and for no other reason than we bear the spark of Ymir."

"They do not suffer any who are different from them. I have been an outcast in Asgard for as long as I remember, and only because I am unlike them. My service to them has ever been nothing compared to my nature."

"Now, at least, you understand why you are different from them. They will regret spurning you."

Loki stood up. His head reached only to Thiazi's waist. "How will I get past Heimdall?"

"He will not see you just as he did not see the mason. While his senses are keener than any other, he can only see what is there. You already know that when you shift, you do not simply change appearances. You in essence become the thing itself."

"Yes, it was that way when I enticed the mason's horse."

"He will see a bird flying overhead, nothing more. But now that you have learned how to retain your own true self while shifting, you will look down on him with your full senses."

"I hope that he survives Idun's absence long enough for me to reveal how I deceived him."

"He may, but he will not survive much longer than that. None of them will."

The space in front of Loki looked vast and unoccupied, but he knew there was more there than was readily visible. Months ago he would have passed over these fields without a second glance. But now he could feel his chaos energy tugging him to this place, allowing him to pierce the veil that tied Idun's orchards to Asgard.

His eyes closed as he tapped the chaos inside him. It flowed throughout his body, changing him. His perception altered, and he could see the air in front of him shift and roil, its vaporous nature dissipating before him to reveal a window into another place, as if the reality he thought existed was nothing more than a cover for what lay underneath, a cover that he had just ripped through.

He stepped into the hidden space and found himself in the midst of a sprawling apple orchard, the gentle wind jostling fully ripe, golden apples on the branches and sending yellow leaves fluttering to the ground. It was warm here, although not uncomfortably so, the sun's rays sending shadows across the ground with the movement of leaves and branches. The sound of birds near by filtered to him.

He reached up and plucked an apple from the closest tree. He examined it closely before sinking his teeth into it, the juice running down his chin. It was sweet and ripe, a perfect apple, and he could feel the lifeline to the Aesir within it. It was one small slice of their immortality, one facet of Idun's gift of never-ending life to the gods. He could feel Idun's presence in the fruit itself, her power flowing through the apple, through the trees, through the ground beneath his feet. She was a living part of this orchard, an integral component that made its existence possible. Without Idun, this orchard would wither and die, and with its death, the gods would also wither and die.

He spat out the half-chewed apple flesh and reached up to grab another. He did not pull it from its branch, but instead closed his eyes and concentrated. As he held it firmly, he imagined it ripening fully, quickly becoming overripe. In his vision, its flesh softened and shrank, becoming too full of sickening sweetness. The skin dimpled and withdrew as the apple slowly shriveled, becoming smaller and smaller with each passing second. Finally, it was a wizened and grotesque orb hanging on a branch.

He felt the energy flow out of him, through the apple and onto the branch, where each apple that it encountered shrank while the leaves detached and fell to the ground below. The whole tree was soon completely engulfed, and then Loki felt the energy spread out to the surrounding trees, each one succumbing to the same fate—shrunken and rotten apples, weak and lifeless branches. The entire orchard visibly shrank under his assault, until all he could see were bleak and decaying trees, lifeless and gray, hollow caricatures of what they had been only moments before.

He opened his eyes. The wind had ceased. Even the sun's rays failed to shine down on the once vibrant orchard. Instead, he was amidst a tangle of dead and dying wood, shriveled fruit hanging from branches that looked as though they might break at any moment.

Even the singing of the birds had stopped. In its place, there was sobbing, the forlorn tears of a young girl. Loki weaved among the dying trees, listening carefully for the source.

She was on her knees, sobbing gently into her hands, the tears flowing through her fingers and falling onto the lap of her simple white dress. Her golden curls shook with every sobbing motion of her head. He approached her slowly and knelt down.

"Idun, it is Loki." He spoke softly, his voice filled with soothing empathy for a suffering sibling.

Her crying slowed and her hands fell from her face. She looked up in mild surprise, the oddness of seeing him there barely registering alongside the shock of what had happened to her orchards.

"Loki?" She looked at him imploringly, desperate for some answer or explanation for what had happened. "My orchards. My sweet orchards. What could have done this?"

He put his arm around her shoulders and gently embraced her, warmth and caring emanating from every iota of his being. She leaned her small body into him, but lifted her eyes to meet his, imploring some answer to the devastation she witnessed.

"I cannot tell you what has happened here," he said, the air of one who truly did not have an answer infusing his voice. "But we will discover what has happened, I promise you." His words were followed with comforting looks of reassurance, designed to give her a measure of peace.

"But now we must leave this place. It is no longer safe for you here."

Her eyes showed alarm. "I-I cannot leave my orchards." There was rising panic in her voice. "My trees, what will happen to them without me? I cannot leave them."

He grasped her upper arms in his hands and turned her to face him, a figure of strength and fatherly sensibility. Both still kneeling, he towered over her.

"Idun," he said, as if speaking to a child. "You must come with me. Whatever has poisoned your trees may be a danger to you. This is no longer a safe place."

Although it felt natural to speak to her this way, a sliver of unease remained. Despite her child-like appearance, she was vastly older than Loki or any of the Aesir, with the exception of Odin. Still, it was difficult not to speak to her so in her current state.

"What will become of my trees? You must save them. We cannot simply leave them here like this. There must be something that can be done. Odin could—"

"There is no time. Odin could not reach us before this disease spreads and claims both you and I, in addition to your trees."

He reached down and grabbed an apple that had fallen to the ground. It was slightly overripe, but not to the point of rottenness. It had fallen before its tree had been infected with his blight. He held it up to her. "We will begin anew. We will take the seeds from this fruit and plant them in a new place, a place where you can tend them, where no one can find you. I know of such a place, but you must come with me now."

There was a glimmer of hope in her eyes, borne from the inherent need to protect and nurture her charges. It was barely there, but some distant part of her recognized that her survival was crucial, that many depended on her, that the forces of chaos could destroy everything if not for her. She nodded to him, tears streaming down her face, and he smiled gently, pulling her to her feet. He guided her back to the window where he had entered, and the two stepped out onto Asgard. She buried her face into his chest as the window slowly shrank, leaving the vision of blackened and dead trees behind.

He glanced back only once, just before the window had

closed entirely. The smile on his face was not consoling, but deeply self-satisfied. The illusion faded even as the window closed, leaving only Loki with the last true imageof Idun's orchards—full, bountiful, and healthy.

Freyja disrobed and stepped slowly into the bath her servants had drawn. Her flawless, snow-white skin slipped under the water as she slid down into the warm bath, and her silver hair splayed out, creating a halo around her head. Her remaining two servants—those that always stood near to wait on her for whatever she needed—left after a dismissive nod of her head. She wanted to be completely alone for now, a state that she was not always able to achieve.

She was glad that Loki had been sent from Asgard. Of all the Aesir, she understood him least. He alone among them was immune to her enchantments, her beauty, and she did not know why. She had not sought him out—in fact, she had never sought out any—but they came for her still. More often than not, she was willing to accede to their desires.

In Vanaheim, there was no stigma to such acts; all gave of themselves freely, with no guilt, shame, or apprehensions. Nor was there any sense of unwanted attachment once those brief moments were gone. For a time she might stay with a lover, but it would be over eventually, and the two would find others. And even if Freyja were to stay with one for a time, that would not preclude the taking of others as well— on both sides. Such was the practice of the Vanir, and it was the very essence of their rituals that trickled down throughout the Nine Worlds, life begetting life in an act of physical and spiritual communion.

Here it was not the same. Asgardians she had mingled herself with often felt an entitlement, as if there was ownership implied by such acts. And even when there were no possessive inclinations, oft times a wife or other lover would send her angry or jealous glances. Freyja was more perplexed than angry at such responses, since she had never witnessed them before coming to Asgard. Yet she did not attempt to make amends for these acts or stifle them; she did not view it as her role, hostage though she may be in Asgard, to sublimate herself to the ways of these gods. She was a goddess of Vanaheim, and she would act as such, despite their discomfort and misgivings.

Still, Loki presented a puzzle to her. He did not act as the other Aesir did, letting their gazes linger after her, their countenances shining when near her, desiring her. She had had nearly all of them in turn, at one time or another, and she would do so again, whenever she felt the whim to do so. All save Loki. He alone had never lain with her; there was little desire for her in him.

When in her presence she could feel, almost like a physical sensation, the feelings of those around her. They would revel in her beauty, her scent, the allure she radiated. Her silver hair and tall, perfect form stirred longing in their souls, and these sensations gave her pleasure, happiness.

Loki emanated with darkness and confusion, and with venomous spite. He was not capable of feeling love for others, but merely jealously, envy, and arrogance. His emotions and thoughts caused her discomfort, and some small measure of pain. There were times when she could feel his glare burning into her with disdain. It was not that he did not find her beautiful, however; she could feel, buried under the other emotions, the bare stirring of lust in his breast, much like the others. But his was subdued, hindered by the darker resentments he felt.

Although he was one of the Aesir, she hoped he would not return from Odin's task. She had heard that the High One had sent him to Jotunheim, and it seemed possible that he might meet his end there. Freyja did not speculate further on what that end might be, nor did she even consciously acknowledge it since it was so contrary to her nature. But there was a part of her that found a measure of peace in the notion that she might not be plagued with his presence any longer.

She stood up and let the water drip from her bare form. Leaving the bath, she strode over to the tall windows that overlooked the green plains of Asgard, the rainbow bridge just barely visible far in the distance. The sunlight streaming in warmed her naked body, the water that remained on her quickly drying with the heat from the sun. As she gazed out the window toward Vanaheim, the home she had left so many years ago, she felt a longing to return, but realized that was an impossibility if peace were to remain between the Vanir and the Aesir. Still, Asgard was majestic and magnificent in ways Vanaheim was not, and the Aesir—even with their strange ways—intrigued her with their unusual sense of honor. They were to be admired in many ways, even if they were different from the Vanir.

She glanced down at her hands and frowned slightly. They were wrinkled, as if from being in the water too long. She held them up to her face to examine them closely.

As she studied her hand, thin, blue veins became slightly visible just under the skin, and small, brownish spots appeared. Mouth aghast, she could only stare in horror as she witnessed her nails grow thicker and turn to a sickly yellow. The blue veins became darker, more pronounced, and they began to travel from the back of her hand up her forearms, each second staining more of her unblemished skin. She brought one hand up to her head, and pulled it away clutching a clump of dull gray, coarse hair.

She held her arms away from her, one still clutching the clump of gray hair, as if they were things alien to her body,

139

as if she could somehow distance them from herself. She would have screamed, but she was so overtaken by a mixture of horror and disgust that she was unable to utter a sound even while her mouth was gaping.

She ran to the mirror in the corner of the room, noting that with even the few steps it took to cross the chamber she felt winded and weak. The first thing she noticed was her breasts. They were shriveled and sagging, like lifeless and dry prunes hanging from her chest. Her stomach was hollowed out, and her ribs were prominently displayed, as if she were a victim of famine. Her bones nearly protruded through at her hips, shoulders, and knees, but her skin hung on her in most places like ill-fitting and wrinkled leather, with the color of brittle, yellowed parchment. Spidery blue veins criss-crossed her legs and arms, although her mottled and splotchy skin made them harder to see than they otherwise would have been.

Her face was the most severely affected. Her once radiant, glowing eyes now glared dully at her from above folded bags of flesh and meandering wrinkles. Her mane of silver-gold hair, lustrous and shining even in darkness, was now a patchwork of bare skin and long, brittle wisps of gray thatch haphazardly attached to her scalp.

She stared at a folded-in version of herself, one consumed by the ravages of time. And she was also keenly aware that her eyesight was blurry and imprecise, and it was this one small favor that allowed her to keep some semblance of sanity, to tell herself that what she saw might not be real. It was not convincing, however, and as she stared at the old crone in her mirror, she finally managed to let loose a scream, but it was the breathless scream of an old woman, pathetic and weak.

Heimdall's sword belt fell to the ground with an

audible thud, his wizened body no longer retaining enough heft to keep it around his waist. Teetering, he put one hand out to steady himself against a small tree. His armor was weighing him down, and his helmet, suddenly and inexplicably too large for him, rode down over his eyes, obstructing his vision. He raised a weary hand and flipped it backwards, where it tumbled to the ground and lay there, inert and empty.

Weariness overcoming him, he lowered himself to the ground slowly and leaned up against the tree. His breath came in ragged gasps through his open mouth, and his head rocked back and forth with the effort of breathing. They were shallow breaths, borne of sickly weakness and frailty, not the cavernous gulps of a warrior exerting himself. Indeed, he had done nothing to even cause exertion. As always, he stood watch over Bifrost, when a soul-wearying tiredness had come upon him.

With effort, he reached around and undid the straps of his armor. He was unable to summon the strength to pull it over his head, and so had to slide his body down the trunk of the tree, like an ancient snake relieving itself of its old skin for the last time. His armor propped against the tree, he managed to crawl slowly out from underneath it, only to collapse with the effort.

After a time, he was able to get to his hands and knees, and then to sit up. His arms were like two thin sticks covered by the tent of his shirt, and his chest was hollowed out and shrunken in upon itself. The only reminder of his once broad and muscular chest was the rolls of skin that sagged lifelessly from it. And his physical frame was not the only thing affected.

His razor sharp senses were now dulled and useless. Where before he had been able to see for leagues upon leagues, his eyesight alone standing as a bulwark against any who might seek to cross into Asgard, the thin film of old age now covered both eyes, and he could barely see the outline of Bifrost from where he sat, not more than a stone's throw away. Nor had his hearing fared well. He had heard legends about his fabled hearing, caught snippets about his godly abilities from other Asgardians in low, awed tones. They said he could hear the grass growing on Midgard, and also the wool growing on sheep. He had done nothing to discourage these stories, even if they were greatly exaggerated. But his hearing was still greater than any other Aesir, and it stretched for long distances. This, however, was gone as well, to be replaced by a dull ringing that would not end.

None of these troubled him, however, as much as his one overriding thought. He became preoccupied with the idea that the end of his days was near, that soon he would shrivel and die. And worse, he would die weak and powerless, cringing in a bed, or right there on the fields of Asgard, a decrepit and useless old man. There would be no glorious end, with him beset upon by countless legions of giants and monsters, each tasting his steel in turn while the bodies of his enemies piled up, and he blasted Gjall that one final time to signal that Ragnarok had come. No, there would be no heroic end to one such as he, a pitiful shell of a god, the heart of a warrior beating only weakly in a decrepit bone-house.

He had only two other clear thoughts, occasionally rising to surface from the constant and all-encompassing fever of his woe. The first was of Idun. In these brief moments of lucidity, he knew that his state—the state of all the Aesir—was due to Idun's absence. She was gone from her orchards, and the link that kept them all eternally young was gone as well.

His second thought was one filled with venom and

anger, one that drove out, if only momentarily, all feelings of self-pity and desolation. It was an empowering thought, one that filled his feeble limbs with renewed vigor as he imagined having the one responsible for this state at his mercy. In these brief moments, he knew with perfect certainty that it was Loki who had caused this to happen, and he swore countless times that he would make the Trickster pay for this indignity, no matter the cost.

Chapter Eleven

The little goddess was safely locked away in the bowels of Thrymheim, and Thiazi's satisfaction grew with each passing day. The Aesir grew older by the minute, weaker, more feeble, and it was only a matter of time till they collapsed into nothing but bags of bones. He imagined Jotunheim's armies sweeping down onto Asgard like a force of nature, destroying everything in their path, desecrating the gods' lands, and annihilating any trace that they ever existed. He would see the stain of their existence purged from the Nine Worlds with fire and death, their bones trampled to dust underneath his heel.

He had used his power to erase the space between Jotunheim and Asgard to spy on one or another of the Aesir and revel in their wretched state. Idun's link to them had been severed quickly, and he had enjoyed seeing them wither before his eyes without the gift of her life-sustaining presence. He had not been able to see all images clearly and at length, but what he had seen had pleased him greatly.

Freyja had hobbled out of her keep as a withered old crone, constantly weeping and bemoaning her lost beauty. She had been attended to by her servants, as always, but never before had they been forced to support her weight as she slowly left her hall, step after plodding step. Her head bowed low, she mumbled to herself as she walked, her mind clearly addled. Who would have her now? Not that any of the others would have been capable of engaging with her in their pathetic states.

Tyr looked even worse, if such a thing was possible.

Once broad shouldered and lean, a warrior in his prime who knew no peer, he was reduced to a shrunken and doddering old fool who had to be carried from place to place by his retainers. They had hoisted him onto his chair laden with blankets so his thin blood would not freeze in the cold Asgardian air. His hands on top of his blankets, he held onto the sheathed sword that lay across his lap with knobby hands that trembled with rapid and uncontrolled motion. The flesh of his neck hung loose, and his eyes stared blankly at nothing.

Thiazi looked at them all in turn, basking in their infirmities. Balder the handsome, Balder the young, lay in his bed in a puddle of his own excrement. Frey could do naught but repeat the same complaints and worries incessantly while his overwrought servants wrung their hands in despair and hopelessness. Hod the Blind, faithful brother to Balder, had also become Hod the Deaf and Hod the Incontinent. Sif, the beautiful, flaxen-haired wife of Thor, merely sat and stared at an empty wall for hours at a time, lost in her own shriveling awareness, understanding less and less as each moment passed.

He could not see the one-eyed one, but no matter. Odin was nearly as old as creation itself; it was likely that he had already succumbed, and that was the reason Thiazi was unable to view him. Even if he still lived, how much more frail and impotent would he be than the others? Thiazi imagined Odin lying dead in his chambers, worms crawling through the empty socket of his missing eye, while maggots devoured what was left of the other.

While he derived much pleasure from the suffering of these gods, there was far more satisfaction in knowing that he had destroyed them from within using one of their own. Or at least they had once thought of him as their own. Loki was no more one of them than he himself was, and it would

145

be to their everlasting sorrow that they had sent him into Thiazi's hands.

How simple it had been to kidnap Idun and bring her to Thrymheim. Buried in the bowels of his keep he enjoyed seeing her, gloating over her in her dank cell, powerless to change the tides that flowed against her kind.

Thiazi made the long, winding trip downwards to the black caverns underneath Thrymheim. It was there that a rough dungeon had been carved long ago. Although it was never meant for one so small as her, it was an apt dwelling. It lacked light and life, and any who found themselves there drew desolation and despair from the very rock it was carved from. Idun, the giver of eternal life, would wither and die while imprisoned there, and it was fitting that she be forced to spend what little time she had alone and in the dark.

As he wound his way through the meandering tunnels underneath Thrymheim, he could feel her presence as he drew nearer. The force of her life was intensely strong, especially for one so small, but Thiazi knew better than most that appearances could be deceiving. For all that she looked like a young girl of no more than ten summers, she was likely as old as Odin, far older than Thiazi himself, in fact. Realizing this made him feel powerful, and even more confident that this was the end of Asgard. While he did not believe in their ridiculous prophecies, perhaps he would declare that Ragnarok had come when he trod onto the holy ground of their city just to see their spirits crumple along with their withered flesh. "Ragnarok has come for you, One Eye!" he imagined himself saying before stepping on the god's chest and crushing the last remnants of life from him.

He was drawn from his musings by another presence that he recognized, and he could feel his grip on the god as tightly as before. Loki was his to command, even if he did not truly recognize it, and he would have him at his side while he slaughtered the Aesir, a last insult to heap upon them, a final farewell from one of their own who had finally turned against them. It would be sweet indeed to bask in their bitterness and impotence.

As he stepped into the dungeon, he could see Loki standing near Idun's cell. He looked tiny standing next to the enormous door, like a small child unable to manipulate the basic objects of his fully grown parents.

"Keeping Idun company?"

"Watching her. Trying to understand her link to the Aesir and how she was able to provide them with eternal youth. It seems strange that her captivity here does not affect me. I had wondered if I might age along with them."

"But now you see yet again that you are not one of them. Idun holds no sway over you. It is the chaos within you that keeps you vital."

"I feel some regret bringing her here. She has never wronged me."

"Her very existence is an attack on our kind. Without her, the gods would have withered and died countless ages ago. Instead they remain a threat, and would continue to be so until one or the other of our races is extinguished."

"I know, but it is difficult still. She looks like nothing more than an innocent child."

"Do not be deceived by her looks. She is old beyond reckoning. And besides, we do nothing to her but prevent her from returning to her orchards. It is far better treatment than you or I would receive at the hands of the Aesir."

Loki nodded, recognizing the truth of his words.

Thiazi said, "Let us take a look at our guest and see how she is faring. That should salve your conscience."

He stepped over to the door and pulled it open. It had not been locked; there was no need here in Thrymheim.

147

Even if she could manage to open the massive door, she would not be able to find her way out. The keep was maze-like, and only Thiazi knew the ways in and out.

Although the room was quite large for Idun, it would not have been so for a giant. Her small frame, however, was completely swallowed by the massive room. As the weak light from the open door struck her, she seemed to be the lone point of whiteness in a pool of black.

The room had been carved from the solid rock of the mountain, deep in its bowels, and so of course had no windows or any source of light other than the flickering torches that were held in sconces on the walls. The door had no window in it, so the only light that would have reached her while she was in her cell would have come from the narrow space between door and rock floor.

She sat on her knees in the middle of the room, hands in lap, head and eyes downcast, golden hair limp. Her simple white dress was covered in dirt and her pale skin—once radiant and glowing—was now the white of a sickly worm that had never seen daylight.

Thiazi walked slowly into the room, his bulk taking up most of the doorway. If Idun noticed him she did not indicate it. She simply sat in the middle of the cell as if a statue, eyes staring down at the floor.

Thiazi could not deny that she projected a sympathetic image, but he would not allow himself to forget who this creature was in reality. Idun was no more a girl than he was, and it was her power to keep the gods eternally young and strong. More than any other of the Aesir, she was the most dangerous enemy of the giants. If not for the god's longevity, Jotunheim would not be under constant threat of destruction from the arrogance of those who lived on high.

Remembering that this one stroke against the gods could end forever the danger that he and all other giants

148

faced from the Aesir set his purpose firmly once again. This was no young girl, but in reality a god whose very existence was anathema to him and all his kind. She would rot in this cell until the gods themselves were dust under his heel, and then she would die as well, once he was certain that they were all dead.

"Can you feel them dying? Can you feel their anguish even here?"

Idun did not move from her position, but a soft voice rose from her, imploring and weak. "Please let me go. I have done you no wrong." If she noticed Loki behind him, she did not indicate it.

"Oh, but you have. You keep the gods strong. Without you, they are doddering old fools who can barely control their own bowels."

Again the weak voice, so like a child's, seemingly so innocent. "My orchards are gone; I have no more power. I can save no one. Please let me go so that I can die with my kind."

It was true that her orchards were gone. He had seen Loki infect them and cause them to wither and die. But he did not know for certain if her power remained without her orchards, and he certainly would not take such a foolhardy chance by releasing her, even if it was true that she was now powerless.

"No. You will be my guest till I have trodden on the fetid corpses of those you love." He noticed her head lower just the slightest bit, as if this was one further blow, one last hope that he had trampled. "However, I will not leave you alone." He motioned with his hand, and Loki was now more visible, standing to the side and just behind Thiazi.

Idun did not move, but instead muttered one word, as if it were the only thing in the Nine Worlds that could crush her spirit more completely than Thiazi had already done.

"Loki."

Thiazi smiled. This was the most satisfying feeling yet. Forcing the most powerful enemy of Jotunheim to share a room with he whose betrayal had caused the destruction of everything she knew and loved. It did not even matter if Loki said nothing; his presence alone was enough to quell any hope she might still have that she would ever be free from his possession.

"Loki will keep you company till we raze Asgard. I will bring you a souvenir—Mjolnir? Gungnir? Balder's skull?— so that you can remember the Aesir when they are all gone."

Thiazi turned to Loki. "Enjoy your time with her. She is yours to do with as you will. You may be able to discover her link to the Aesir."

He turned and left the room, the slamming of the door sending loud reverberations echoing throughout the stone chamber. As he mounted the stairs back to the upper parts of the keep, he felt Loki's own will coincide with his own. The Sly One was truly one of them.

Tyr slumped in a chair piled high with blankets, staring out the window of his hall. In his trembling hand he clutched a note with runes scrawled by someone he knew, although he could not remember who that person was. His eyesight was failing, but if he squinted just right and held the note close to his face he could read its message. He felt it was important, and had an overwhelming need to do as the note said, but was unable to comprehend the full import of the message. He read it again, for perhaps the ninth time, his lips mumbling the words as his eyes passed over them, his finger touching each word in turn.

He called one of his servants into the chamber. His wizened hand clutched his sword—he had been using it as a cane—and he struck it against the wooden floor sharply.

Moments later, a young man who he had seen before scrambled into the room and stood near his chair.

"What do you want?" Tyr did not understand why he was being disturbed. He noticed that he was clutching something in his hand, but he could not remember what it was.

"You called for me, my lord." The boy looked troubled about something.

"I called for you?" He did not remember doing that.

"Yes, my lord. With your sword."

Tyr looked down and was surprised to see his sword leaning against his leg, one hand resting on the hilt.

"The note, my lord? Was there something in the note?"

Tyr did not like the look on the boy's face, as if he were mocking him. If the weariness in his bones was not weighing him down, he would strike him for his insolence. What was it that he had said? The boy had said something and it sounded familiar.

"The note in your hand, my lord. I delivered it to you not an hour ago. Could that be the reason you called for me?"

"The note? What note?" Tyr looked down at his hand and was surprised to see that he clutched something in his withered claw. He held it up to his face, squinted, and read it slowly, his lips mouthing the words as his eyes passed over them.

"Who is this from?"

"The Allfather, my lord."

"It says to gather wood and pile it up against Asgard's wall?" He looked at the boy questioningly. He did not know what to do with this information.

"Yes, my lord."

Tyr stared at him. There was something he should do, but it was unclear. His thoughts were like fish—slippery and

151

difficult to grasp, there one moment, only to quickly dive beneath the surface the next.

"Perhaps your servants and retainers should be sent out to gather wood as the High One has instructed, my lord?"

"Gather wood?"

"Yes, my lord. As it says in the note."

Tyr was tired of this. The only comforting thought he had was to rest in his chair and stare out the window, as he had been doing before this whelp disturbed him. He would strike him if he were within reach.

"Do as you like," he muttered before turning back to the window. Without realizing it his hand released the note and it fell slowly to the floor, fluttering in the hot gusts from the fireplace nearest the window. He replaced his hand in his lap and stared out at the vast and sprawling towers outside his window, wondering only for a moment why there was such movement and activity on the roads that weaved in and around Asgard.

Thiazi would be coming soon.

Odin had sent instructions to prepare for his arrival to all the Aesir, as he had foreseen doing while he hung on Yggdrasil all those years ago. As ever, the past and future merged within his mind, constantly streaming images before him, feelings and impressions that he could not always differentiate from the present. It had seemed clear to him what he would do, however, and that his commands to the others would be followed, although hesitantly due to their enfeebled conditions.

"Is this the end?" he asked the only other occupant of the room. The bodiless head stared at him, mouth agape as always.

"*. . . it is not the end . . .*"

Odin could be certain that Mimir's head was always

152

correct. He could not say, however, that it was a blessing to know such things, for this wisdom perversely made him powerless.

"But Thiazi is coming?"

"*. . . he comes . . .*"

"Will the Aesir be restored? Will Idun be returned to her orchards? I see her there, but I cannot tell if it is past or yet to come."

Mimir was silent. He did not always respond to needs for reassurance, and Odin already knew the answers to the questions posed. Mimir was there to tell him only what he did not already know, or to help him sort the past and present from the future.

He stared up at the starlit sky above him. It was brightest day outside, but here in his chamber he could always see the stars lighting up the night sky, see the branches of Yggdrasil brushing up against the highest reaches of the heavens.

He attempted to push himself up out of his chair, but he was not immune to the weakness of old age that had recently stricken all of the Aesir. He let his hands fall back down onto his lap. If need be, he could summon servants to help him, but there was no pressing need. He was content for the moment to slump in his chair, infirm and frail.

Odin was nearly as old as creation itself, and it had been eons since he had looked young. All of the Aesir knew his visage as that of an old man, but his current state was far more wasted. While he had looked old before, this appearance had never extended to his strength. Without Idun, however, he felt the effects just as any of the others.

It was gratifying, at least, to have retained his wits while the old age had wasted his body. Tyr slouched in a chair in his hall, uncertain of what was said or done only moments before. Heimdall lay in a stupor in his bed, attended by servants who could only shake their heads while he mumbled incoherently over and over again. Bragi sat weeping on the floor in a puddle of his own waste, unwilling or unable to move, even with the help of his servants. Freyja was nothing but a hollow shell of her former self, so devastated by the loss of her beauty that she was incapable of thinking of aught else. It was far better, he realized, to retain his wits, even while they were cruelly trapped in a doddering frame.

"Where is Thor?"

Mimir's eyes rolled back in his head.

". . . in his hall . . ."

"Does he still wield Mjolnir?"

". . . Mjolnir hangs at his side . . . unsure of his ability to wield it . . ."

Odin narrowed his eyes and stroked his white beard.

"Is he a match for Thiazi?"

". . . no . . ."

"Are any of the Aesir a match for the giant?"

". . . no . . ."

Odin sighed. He considered his plan. If it did not work as he intended, then Thiazi would be free to roam Asgard unmolested, slaying anything in his path, and none could stop him. He was a far greater threat than the mason had been.

He could see Thiazi dying at some point in the future, but it was unclear when and where. There were flames, but they could be a funeral pyre. And did the flames consume Asgard as well? He could see the wall through the red haze, but he could not tell if the wall were part of the flames or merely beyond them.

"But this is not Ragnarok?"

". . . it is not the Doom of the Gods . . ."

"Then what is this event that looms over us and fills me

154

with such dread if it is not Ragnarok? I cannot see it clearly."

Mimir was silent for a moment, eyes closed as if pondering the question. His lids slowly opened, although he simply stared out into space, his eyes unfixed on anything in the chamber.

"Answer me!" Odin felt a hot rush of impotent anger. He would not have been so impatient before this wasting disease took him, he realized. Perhaps his acuity was not as untouched as he had hoped.

"It is not Ragnarok," Mimir said slowly. *"But it is the beginning of the end."*

There was woe on Odin's soul. He knew that this would come to pass, had known for an eternity, but its imminence weighed him down. Even more baneful than knowing that it would come, however, was the knowledge that he himself had set it into motion.

After what seemed like an interminable waiting period in the dark of the cell, Loki felt it was time to act. Idun had done nothing but sit on her knees with her head down the entire time. He had likewise been silent, and she had not acknowledged him. He knew that she was aware of his presence, but chose to remain silent and still, perhaps waiting to see what he would do. Or more likely, so devastated by the loss of her orchards that she was unable to do anything but wait for the end.

He approached her, feeling the chaos inside him shift and focus, begin to flow outward. He was beginning to master the shifting of his own form, but he had not yet tried it on others. He had little choice, and precious little time. It must be attempted, and he would have to simply hope that it would work as he planned.

Loki knelt down beside Idun. Invisible tendrils of chaos flowed from him. When they brushed against her, questing,

155

she started.

"Loki?" she said, as if waking from a deep sleep.

"Yes."

She looked over at him. He could barely make out her features in the blackness of the cell, but he could feel her gaze upon him. There was confusion there, but also anger and the agonizing stab of betrayal. He recognized the latter feeling well; he had felt it himself innumerable times. But Idun's feelings were weak and faint. She would not be able to sustain her own life for long if she remained in Thrymheim.

"I feel something strange. What are you doing to me?"

He closed his eyes and concentrated on sending the tendrils of chaos into her, pervading her person with his energy.

"I do what I must."

He could feel her resisting, but it was instinctual, reflexive. She did not know what she was fighting against, and so could not really withstand his assault. As he sent the strands deeper he found her essence, the shining beacon within her that summed up all she was. It was faint, which was good, because otherwise he might not be able to affect her. He surrounded that beacon with his own energy and willed her to transform.

The shifting came from inside her first. Her consciousness became slowly less coherent, less aware, as if her knowledge and intelligence were being drained. Unlike his own early transformations, where his consciousness shifted somewhat into the thing that he changed into, her own simply became fainter and fainter, more and more suited to the change he was forcing upon her.

As her awareness dwindled, he could feel her body diminish as well. Slowly she shrunk in upon herself, her arms and legs withdrawing into her body, her innards

156

drying up inside her. Dull, golden tresses shortened and were pulled inside her head, which grew smaller and smaller, her skin growing from pale white to brown. Her entire body seemed to collapse upon itself till little was left of her but an oval-shaped seed no bigger than a child's fist lying on the cold stone floor of the cell.

He opened his eyes and steadied himself. He felt much weaker, drained. It had taken more out of him to project his energy outward, to change something outside of himself. He stared down at the brown seed at his foot and wondered if he had been fully successful. Idun was transformed, certainly, but did some remnant of what she was remain, or was she gone completely? If so, then he had failed, and all would be lost.

He picked up the seed gingerly and held it, bringing it close to his face, examining it for some sign that the core of what Idun was remained in this small promise of potential life.

At first he could detect nothing, but after holding it close, feeling it up against his skin, he could detect stray thoughts borne on his own chaotic tendrils, energy seeping slowly from the nut and bearing feelings and impressions; things that a seed alone would never have, things that belonged only to a being with thoughts, ideas, feelings. Wafting from the seed was anger and confusion, love and hate, desire and hope. It was all the things he would have felt in the goddess herself if she were standing in front of him rather than lying transformed in his palm.

Loki stood up slowly, grasping the seed firmly in his hand. He turned and swiftly left the cell, making his way to a stone staircase and up through the bowels of the keep.

Thiazi was in his chambers or somewhere near there, which gave Loki enough space and time to find his way to the top of the keep. The giant had been keenly aware of

Loki's presence for months, ever since he had first reached Thrymheim. His shifting abilities must seem like a bright flame to the giant. But he had learned since then. While he could feel the giant's thoughts poking around inside him like an unspoken command, he had never felt compelled to listen, although it served his purpose to let Thiazi think that he was his to command.

He wound his way through Thrymheim, and his path led him to a tall tower jutting up from the mountain keep. Once there, he looked out over the mountain range surrounding Jotunheim. The cities and villages of the giants spread out across the land as far as he could see.

Grasping Idun in his palm, he closed his eyes and concentrated, willing himself to shift. It was easier and faster than it had been before he had come to Thrymheim. He felt as if he were simply shedding a layer of clothes and putting on new ones. Thiazi had taught him well.

Transformed once more into a hawk, he clutched the seed in his talon. Once he returned her to Asgard, the seed that Idun had become would restore what had been lost. Far in the distance he could barely see a multicolored arch. He flew from the top of the tower towards Bifrost once more.

Idun's Return to Asgard

The gods were upset at the disappearance of Idun, and at the same time increasingly dismayed at their quickly graying heads. They held a council in Gladsheim to discuss what had happened to Idun.

Heimdall said that the last time he had seen Idun was when she had crossed Bifrost with Loki. It was then that the gods realized that the Sly One had spirited her away. It was decided that he would be captured and brought forth to tell what had become of her.

He tried to hide from the Aesir by turning into various animals, but the far seeing eye of Odin watched him closely, and the others were able to drag him back to Gladsheim.

Once there, Loki first expressed outrage at his shabby treatment and swore oaths against those who had so roughly taken him against his will. Odin, however, threatened him with the blood eagle if he did not tell what he had done with Idun. The Sly One became frightened as he imagined the knife carving lines in his back, his lungs springing out like bloody wings. He told the assembled gods that he was forced to bring Idun to the giant Thiazi.

All the Aesir were furious with Loki and wanted to kill him right then for his offense. Odin, however, stayed their hands and charged him instead to recover Idun from Thiazi, and Loki left quickly for Thrymheim, happy to be away from angry gods and the threat of the blood eagle.

He changed into a falcon and flew quickly to Thiazi's home. He was relieved to discover that the giant was out rowing on the sea, and he would not have to contend with him before rescuing

Idun. He turned her into a nut, grabbed hold of her in his talons, and then flew back to Asgard.

Thiazi arrived at Thrymheim soon after, furious at discovering Loki's handiwork. He saw a falcon flying towards Asgard with his prize and recognized it as the Sly One. He changed himself into an eagle and pursued.

Sitting on his high seat, Odin could see the eagle chasing the falcon. The falcon would arrive at Asgard's walls before the eagle, but only just. He ordered the Aesir to gather up all the plane shavings from all the woodwork that had been done since Asgard was young, and to pile them up against Asgard's wall. They stood ready with torches in hand, waiting for Odin's command.

Loki swiftly flew over the wall with the giant just behind. As the eagle crossed the wall's threshold, Odin gave the order to fire the shavings. The Aesir used their torches to light all the plane shavings, and a great fire blazed up high into the sky, catching the eagle by surprise and setting his feathers on fire. The Aesir surrounded the eagle with their mighty spears and stabbed him to death while he lay flaming in the courtyard.

Loki released the nut that was Idun, and she formed back again into herself. She walked amongst the aged gods and fed them from her basket of apples. At once, they grew young again and thanked her for her gifts, and all was well again in Asgard . . .

Chapter Twelve

Thiazi realized the deception when Loki was at the summit of Thrymheim. He had thought him still in the bowels of the keep with Idun, and was confused. As he realized how he had been completely fooled, he cursed himself. The two-faced god had tricked him and was escaping with Idun.

He could scarcely comprehend it. He had trained Loki for months, each day subtly influencing him more and more with his own power until the god was his, even though he did not realize it. He had interweaved his own chaos with that of Loki's, gently nudging him in the direction he wanted, so that each time he spoke of one of the Aesir he planted ill will within him. He knew that he could not simply erase Loki's allegiance to the Aesir in a day, and so he had taken his time and done it slowly, all the while masking his true intentions by showing him how to wield his own chaos energy.

But now Thiazi was forced to the conclusion that Loki had never been in his will at all, and that meant that he had been utterly and completely deceived all the while. And now he was headed back to Asgard with Thiazi's prize.

His rage threatened to overwhelm him, and he let loose a roar of frustration that shook the foundations of the keep. He charged forth from the chamber, the transformation already begun as he mounted step after step, his massive bulk moving forward far faster than it would have seemed possible. He could feel Loki shifting, and his rage increased when he realized he would not be able to reach him in time.

161

The top of the tower was within sight as he rounded the final set of stairs, but he did not slow down. Instead, he propelled his bulk up the stairs and into the open air, changing into his eagle-form and taking to the air as he did. He glanced around for Loki but could not see him. His rapidly improving eyesight quickly caught sight of a large hawk flying from Thrymheim, a brown seed clutched tightly in its talon. He was headed to Asgard with Idun.

He flew after the two-faced god with anger and mounting ferocity. He had made a mistake, had under-estimated Loki and his burgeoning abilities. He was far more savvy than he had let on, far more than Thiazi had suspected. He would not be underestimated again.

The hawk flew swiftly, but Thiazi had used his eagle-form for centuries. He would catch Loki, and when he did, he would rend his body apart and watch the remains flutter to Midgard.

Odin's retainers and the Aesir who could still stand manned Asgard's walls with torches in hand. They were confused. Though they did not doubt the Allfather, they did not know why they were there. Odin saw looks of bewilderment on their faces as he looked out the window of his highest tower. He periodically glanced from the scene below to the open sky.

While he did not possess Heimdall's ability to see for leagues, Odin had other ways of sensing. When he sat on his high seat he could view nearly anything in the Nine Worlds, although it was not the same as sight, exactly. It was as if the scene unfolded in his mind, like a memory, but happening right then. He saw Loki's swift flight, Idun transformed and clutched tightly in one talon. His progress towards Asgard was rapid.

The eagle gained ground, however. He was an

enormous bird, brimming with chaos, and he cut the distance between he and Loki with every driving beat of his massive wings.

Odin had taken Mimir's head from its customary pedestal in his chamber and sat him on his knee.

"How long till Thiazi overtakes him?" he asked the head.

" . . . soon . . ."

"What will happen when he catches him?"

" . . . death . . ."

Odin grunted, mostly to himself. He was tired. The weight of Ragnarok was on him, as usual, but it was compounded by his infirm condition, as if the eons of his existence had suddenly caught up to him in one fell swoop. Mimir had said that this would be the beginning of the end. Odin did not see the point of telling him that he would not prevent Ragnarok even if he could.

He looked out his window, high above the plain of Asgard. Far in the distance, he could see a small speck rapidly approaching. Loki would arrive soon, and the giant would follow. The flames would be lit, and he would save all those who called him Allfather. Would they think of him so fondly if they knew that saving them now only cursed them with a worse death later?

As he looked at the other Aesir around him, Balder realized that he suffered from Idun's absence far less than the others. While his body was wracked with palsied trembling and his strength was no more than a distant fraction of what it had been before, he was still far more able-bodied than Tyr and many of the others. He could stand on his own two feet, at least, and his mind was still sound, or as sound as it could be for his advanced age. The clarity of thought that normally marked him was faded, but most of his wits were still about him. Others barely recognized the sound of their own name, their minds lost in the same way as their bodies.

The only other who had remained as able was Thor, but even he had suffered greatly. His muscular frame was mostly reduced to flab, and he stooped low with age, unable to even wield his own weapon. While he could not lift—or even carry—Mjolnir anymore, he still stood ready with weapon in hand; a hammer larger than his own, but a mere mortal weapon with none of the legendary power of the mystical hammer forged by the dwarfs so many ages ago.

Balder looked up to Valaskjalf's highest tower. In the window he could see the Allfather staring out beyond the wall at something that only he could see. There was a look in his eye that Balder could not identify. Odin looked troubled, as if a heavy burden were weighing him down. He had rarely seen him like this. Usually his countenance was elusive, and it was all but impossible to guess his mood or thoughts. Balder was unnerved to so plainly see the trouble etched across Odin's face.

As he watched, he saw Odin rise to his feet and lean partially out of the window, his hands bracing his weight on the sill. Something was approaching. The thralls and retainers held torches high in anticipation, waiting for a sign from the High One.

Balder pulled his sword free from its sheath, its weight now heavy in his hands. It would take effort to wield now that he was merely a shadow of what he had once been. But if this day was to be his death, then so be it. He gladly faced that fate with blade in hand, and felt pity for those too decrepit to stand here with him. It was not death the Aesir feared, but the slow creep and impotence of old age. He considered that dying in battle now might allow him to redeem his infirmity. A smile curled his lip as he imagined a song about "Old Balder's Stand at Asgard's Wall." It was easy to be heroic when young and strong; how much more glory would be gained from a final, desperate stand while trapped in an old man's body?

He focused his attention back on the wall in time to see a hawk soar just over it in a downward arc towards the ground. He did not hear Odin utter a word, but in his head there was an urgent command to fire the wood against the wall.

Everyone that held a torch acted nearly in unison, and the kindling that had been piled high roared loudly with a fire that crested the top of the wall in a blazing red inferno that burned skin, clothing, and hair of all those near it. Balder had not had a torch and was back from the wall in a strategic position, and so did not feel the kiss of the flames. He did, however, feel its heat like a wave, and considered for a brief moment that the servants who had just done the High One's bidding had paid a price for their loyalty. But that thought passed in an instant as the eagle met the roaring wall of flame.

The enormous bird seemed to realize the danger just as it soared into the flames, and it swiftly changed its flight path upward. Balder realized its fatal mistake. If it had instead continued through the flames, it could have perhaps survived, its feathers severely singed, but it may have otherwise remained intact. When it flew instinctively upwards, it caught itself in the wall of flame longer, and the heat was greater the higher up it rose. The eagle's feathers burst into flames at the crest of its upward path, and then it fell like a star shooting down to earth.

The Asgardian response was swift. Einherjar rushed upon the creature that was already in the midst of a transformation into his true, giant self. Screams of agony accompanied his change, and then swiftly turned to screams of rage when spears and swords pierced him. With a massive hand he batted away a dozen warriors, killing at least half of them outright and sending their crushed bodies into the flames. He stood to his full height, dwarfing the warriors around him, and beckoned them on with a sneer of defiance. It was obvious that he was hurt, but it was just as obvious that the damage he had sustained was not enough to bring him down.

As the Asgardians rushed forward to renew their attack on him, they paused when long, sinuous and ghost-like appendages erupted from him. They were reminded of the multiple limbs of the mason, and while they still charged forward to attack, the dread on their faces was apparent. It grew into fear when they saw the giant's size increase as well.

Loki had been in the midst of his transformation when he witnessed the assault on Thiazi. After exiting the flames severely burned, the giant had withstood a wave of Asgardians. But while they damaged him to some degree, he was still strong enough to cause much death and destruction.

He finished shifting back into his own form as he watched the giant swat away Einherjar by the dozens. Thiazi was calling forth his chaos energy to help him destroy the Aesir. Loki had seen him use it in many ways during the months he stayed with the giant while learning to control his own chaos. He had suspected that Thiazi did not show him all he knew, but what he had shown him would still be enough to deal with the Aesir in their feeble state.

His own power was nowhere as strong as Thiazi's, but he did not have to counter him strength for strength. He had fooled him for months, made him think that he was a son of Jotunheim, when in reality he had been learning all he could so that he could end the giant's threat to Asgard. Each time Thiazi had used his power, Loki had sent a small portion of his own to intertwine with the giant's, reinforcing the submission and cooperation he thought he received.

He called upon that chaos energy now, willing it to arise from its dormancy within the giant. Thiazi used his own to begin shifting his form into a creature like the mason. In their state the Aesir would not have been able to withstand another such creature, and Thiazi no doubt intended to crush them all as the mason very nearly had.

All Thiazi's energy was focused on increasing his size and threat, leaving none for any kind of defense. His arrogance left him vulnerable to an attack from within. As Loki's energy arose within the giant, the multiple arms that had sprouted withered and slumped to the ground, while his increasing size halted.

Loki enjoyed the look on his face when he realized how he had been tricked once more, but he knew he would not be able to prevent Thiazi's power from reasserting itself. He only hoped the Asgardians would seize upon the opportunity.

Balder cursed his frail body as he moved forward as fast as his weak legs could carry him. The giant weakened somehow, and he knew that it was time to press the attack.

The giant was already being weighed down by a score of warriors, and a few dozen others stabbed at him with spears and swords. Balder reached the giant and managed to just duck his head before a massive fist sailed above him, threatening to take his head from his shoulders. He slashed at the giant's leg, cutting through skin and muscle, and the giant's scream of pain fueled Balder on, sending his sword slashing again and again, as fast as his trembling old arm could manage.

The giant was too damaged from the fire and too overwhelmed by Asgardian attackers to focus on any one assailant, so Balder was able to continuously plunge his sword into the giant's hide without much fear of retaliation. Blood poured from his wounds, and Balder wondered how the creature could even continue to stand while covered in attackers.

A sound like cracking thunder shook the ground, and Balder could see Thor launching himself onto the giant. The giant was nowhere near the size of the mason, so the Thunderer was able to leap up and strike his head with his hammer. While Mjolnir would surely have shattered the skull in one blow, the diminished power of his current weapon seemed to cause an increase in the savage ferocity of Thor's attack. He relentlessly smashed the hammer into the giant's face and head, drawing blood and cracking bone with every blow. The giant grabbed him with one hand that was still weighed down by attackers, but could not pull the crazed old god from him.

Thiazi's limbs slowed, and he fell to his knees. The remainder of those Asgardians still standing redoubled their attacks. Balder hacked at the blackened and bloody body that still towered over him without any need to avoid an attack. The giant was swiftly dying, only its pure stamina keeping it from completely succumbing.

Thiazi finally collapsed under the weight of his attackers after Thor's hammer caved in part of his skull. He crashed to the ground and lay there unmoving, while Asgardian and Aesir ceased their attack and stood up from the corpse.

Balder gasped for breath and let his sword drop to the ground, strength failing quickly now that the battle rage had passed. He bent over and put his hands on his knees for support, desperately trying to regain his breath. Out of the corner of his eye, he could see that Thor had fared only slightly better; the Thunderer was leaning with one hand over the shoulder of a retainer, the other hand clutching his chest tightly.

Balder was slow to recover, but eventually was able to stand upright again. He turned to see someone standing there. As the face registered, the victory against the giant suddenly turned sour. Of all the faces he least wanted to see, the one before him was the most hateful in his sight.

The seed was cradled in Loki's hand. He had risked much to bring Idun back to Asgard. His life might have been forfeited, but what was one life compared to all those in Asgard? If Thiazi had been successful, Asgard would have fallen to the giants, destroying all he knew. The mere fact of his true heritage would not cause him to betray those he still thought of as his own kind.

But the cost had been high.

The Aesir were decrepit, barely clinging to life in some cases. Idun's absence had debilitated them far more than any battle injuries ever could. Worse than any bloody death was their pathetic lingering, a cruel insult to battle gods who expected to meet their end with steel in hand and fire in their eyes.

His reputation was also likely to be far more sullied than it already was. The Aesir would not care that he was forced to steal Idun. They would only see that his actions had put them at risk and caused them insult. Nor could Odin be counted on to explain his role. The High One was not given to explanations.

Idun's return, he hoped, would go some way towards showing them his loyalties. And he would take one further precaution to ensure that she could not be stolen again.

Loki approached the gathering of gods around the dead

giant, gripping the seed firmly in his hand.

Balder turned, and recognition spread across the once young, once handsome face. He sneered, the loathing that he felt not even partially hidden. Loki brought up his hand, the seed perched comfortably in the middle of his palm.

"I have brought Idun back to Asgard."

Balder's curiosity overpowered his disgust for the moment as he stared down at the seed in Loki's hand.

"This is Idun?"

Loki nodded.

"And you have done this to her?"

He nodded again. "Yes, it was the only way to bring her from Thrymheim."

Balder could not take his eyes from the seed. He took a step closer.

"And what is it that you have done to her?" The disgust was creeping back into his voice, spurred by the appearance of Idun changed by some power that was distinctly unlike anything the Aesir possessed.

Loki considered how to explain it. He did not want to reveal the chaos thriving inside of him, the energy that made him kin with their enemy.

"I have made her into the very essence of what she was."

Balder was dissatisfied with the explanation, but still curious.

"Does she live?"

"In a way. But she is not as she once was."

"Can you restore her?"

Loki paused. He did not know if it was possible for her to return to the form she held before. She lived, of a sort, but this transformation was different than his own. While he retained conscious thought in any form he took, Idun had become the seed. There was only the barest hint that she had

170

once been a goddess. He was certain, however, that her presence, in whatever form, would return the Aesir's youth and vitality to them.

"I will use the runes to restore her." He would chant them, but it would be the chaos that flowed from him to transform her, not Asgardian magic. But Balder, he knew, would look no deeper than the surface, as usual.

Before he turned from Balder, he noted the sour look that crossed his face. He ignored it. When the gods had regained what they had lost, they would view him differently.

He walked to an open patch of ground, untouched by the battle and marked only with scattered wildflowers. He knelt down and dug his hand into the moist dirt, feeling the life within it. He buried the seed and closed his eyes. He chanted the runes, but it was only a ruse. Instead, the chaos flowed from him, unseen tendrils enveloping the seed. He could feel the essence of what she had been trapped inside, the link to the immortality of the Aesir. She would live again, but not in quite the same way.

The chaos withdrew and he opened his eyes. Standing up, he turned back to see that Balder and Thor had drawn closer. Balder still bore an expression of disgust, but it was colored by an accompanying bewilderment, like that of an old man who did not fully comprehend what he was witnessing. Thor's expression was blank. He stood by, still gripping his hammer, hunched over and trembling with the effort of remaining on his feet.

After long moments, Balder spoke, his voice dripping with venom. "What have you done?"

Loki looked back at him. "I have returned Idun to Asgard. I have brought you back your lives."

"And why is it that you were not affected as we were? What bargain have you struck with the giant that has kept

171

you young?"

Loki ignored him and focused instead on the spot where he had buried the seed.

The small mound of dirt trembled slightly before one thin, green shoot fought its way out and continued its upward creep. As it grew, it thickened and turned brown, and offshoots eventually split and traversed their own path, upward and outward, creating a quickly spreading lattice of green and brown branches. Balder gaped open-mouthed, and even Thor registered awe as the young tree's bark grew thicker and the branches sprouted small leaves.

Loki craned his head upwards to watch the progression of the tree. The trunk expanded, moving earth around it, and smaller branches shot off from larger ones, the leaves creating a canopy that blocked the sun. White petals formed and swiftly grew into blossoms, and then just as quickly fell to the ground, creating a snowstorm around him. Where blossoms had been, small orbs grew, green at first, then tinting more and more yellow till they were a gold that rivaled Sif's hair.

He reached up and pulled one down. He handed it to Balder.

"Idun is here, even more a part of Asgard than before."

Balder hesitantly took the offered fruit and held it up to his face, inspecting it closely with his tired eyes. He looked back at Loki with suspicion.

"This does not erase your misdeeds," he said, before slowly bringing the apple to his mouth and sinking his remaining teeth into its flesh.

Chapter Thirteen

Loki walked through the doors of Gladsheim. He had been summoned by Odin, and he made his way there quickly. It had been only days since Thiazi had been defeated. After having eaten of Idun's fruit, the Aesir were regaining their vitality and vigor.

He had seen Tyr rise from his chair to stand on his own feet, the fog on his brain disappearing. For the first time in weeks, Tyr appeared to know where he was and what was going on around him. Thor stood up straight once more, regaining his stature, and the flab that encircled his arms and legs had returned to iron sinew. Balder, the youngest and once most handsome of them all, began regaining that clearness of complexion that marked him as eternally young and vital. Freyja, previously bald save the long, white wisps that pathetically clung to her wrinkled orb, saw her features smooth, her figure fill out, her silver hair return. No longer was she merely a bone case for her brittle and papery skin. And although she was not yet as radiant as she had been, it was undeniable that she would be so again.

Loki witnessed these transformations with anticipation. It was true that they blamed him for their decrepit state, but it was also true that such suffering had been necessary to end Thiazi's threat. Now that their youth was returned, would they not see that his actions formed part of a larger plan? And even if they did not, Odin would acknowledge his role. The others, spiteful as they may be, would have no choice but to accept him.

The Aesir were assembled in their customary seats.

Odin sat on his throne, his wife, Frigg, to his right. On either side the rest of the Aesir were gathered: Thor and his wife, Sif of the golden hair; Balder and Nana, his consort; Bragi the master of poesy; Njord of the Vanir; and Odin's sons, Vali, Vidar, and Hermod all sat on one side of the hall. Tyr, the twins Freyja and Frey, Ull the master archer, Forseti the just, Thor's son Magni, said to possibly rival his father in strength, Aegir of the oceans, Heimdall on a rare excursion from Bifrost, and Loki's faithful wife, Sigyn sat on the other. All faces were somber, all eyes on Loki as he approached.

"You summoned me to council, Allfather?"

Odin stared at him. Loki wondered if the Allfather were seeing him or something entirely different, even while they locked eyes.

"Tyr, speak the charge."

In response to Odin's command, Tyr stood from his chair slowly, his strength not fully returned.

"Loki, you stand accused of betraying Asgard, of consorting with our mortal enemies in Jotunheim. You stole Idun from her sacred orchards and brought a plague upon the Aesir. You brought the giant Thiazi to our very doorstep. If not for the all-knowing wisdom of the High One, all would have been lost. You failed to . . ."

Loki's attention trailed off as he looked around at the assembled faces. Only two did not appear overtly hostile; his wife, Sigyn, who looked sympathetic, and Thor, who looked bored. He could bear the anger of the others. It was Odin's proclamation that counted here.

When Tyr finished his litany, the others mumbled in angry tones. Balder was engaged in fierce complaint with Nana and angrily gesturing towards him. Heimdall glared silently. Sigyn held her head down, looking guilty and uncomfortable.

A gesture from Odin silenced them. "What say you in

your defense?"

Loki paused, taking one last look at the gods glaring at him. He felt strangely at ease despite the discomforting stares. The Allfather would soon forgive his trespasses, would explain how he himself had given Loki the task of luring Thiazi to Asgard, and he would derive great satisfaction in seeing the surprised looks on their faces.

"All here have judged me as lacking," he began. "Yet my efforts have preserved Asgard, have protected us against our enemies. I have suffered indignities that none here could know, and I have persevered, for the sake of Asgard." The angry glares continued.

"It is true that my ways are unusual. I do not have Tyr's skill with a blade, nor Thor's strength. But my gifts, though different, are used only to defend Asgard.

"We have opened our doors to two who are different, and accepted them as our own, despite the fact that at one time they were our sworn enemies. Now that Vanir and Aesir no longer fight, we welcome Frey and Freyja. If welcome is offered to strangers and their ways, why should it be refused to one who has been here since the Nine Worlds were young?"

Some of the gods looked at each other briefly, but Loki could not tell if he had persuaded any of them. Odin sat stone-faced and silent, no indication on his face of where his opinion would fall. But he had sent Loki to Thiazi, and of all of them, the Allfather would appreciate his service to Asgard.

"You call me 'Sly One' and worse, but it is my very ability to craft plans that has allowed me to contribute in the greatest manner to Asgard. Would the strength of my steel have lured away the mason's horse and won the bargain? And now our wall is rebuilt, better than before, so that when Ragnarok comes we will be better prepared to face it.

"It is true that I took Idun, but had I not done so the giant Thiazi may have found her and done it himself, and the cost would have been severe. I was able to convince her to go with me and still keep her orchards unharmed, and it was I who rescued her from Thrymheim, luring the giant here to his death, ending his threat and securing the safety of Asgard once more.

"Every sacrifice, every plan, every action I undertake is in service to Asgard. Before you pass judgment on me, consider what you have gained, and what you might have lost if not for my actions."

The hall was silent. As he looked from face to face, he saw some softening of expression, although not much. Still, any change in their view of him was unexpected.

Loki stood still, anticipating the response. He had no delusion that one plea could change their perception of him. It would be a slow process, and only a fool would think that all would accept him. Heimdall would never see him as anything but an enemy. Balder would probably always have enmity for him. Many, however, might be able to let go of past grievances and allow old wounds to heal. He could envision Tyr doing so, and even Thor, who he had aided many times. For his part, he would let old grudges fade. There was nothing to be gained by nursing them, and much to be lost.

Odin glanced over at one side of the assembled gods and then the other before addressing them. "Speak your thoughts."

"The end of Asgard was nearly upon us due to him," Balder said. "Time and again, Loki has shown that he has no regard for anything but his own skin. He claims to serve Asgard, yet his schemes bring trouble to our door."

"But it is true," Tyr said, "that Loki helped end the threat of Thiazi. If the giant had not been killed, he may have

176

continued to threaten Asgard. Could more like the mason have been sent?"

Balder spoke again, still fervent. "Allfather, he is a stain on the sanctity of Asgard. If he remains, he will surely cause the end of all. He must, at the very least, be exiled."

Freyja's soft voice arose. "He is not like the Aesir," she said. "There is a darkness inside of him, something shifting and black, and I fear that Balder is right. He does not belong here. To allow him to stay is to court the death and destruction that hangs over us."

"I am sorry, but I do not agree, sister." It was golden-haired Sif, wife of Thor. "While Loki's gifts run contrary to our ways, I do not believe that he is the harbinger of Ragnarok, as you imply. I do not think it is wise that we cast out one of our own when the purpose of his actions was pure, despite the stain of those actions themselves. Mistakes have been made, but who can say what might have happened without Loki?" Loki remembered Sif's fury when, long ago, he had shorn her hair in a moment of puerile abandon. He was happily surprised to see that she could put aside that old grudge.

"You are ever-forgiving, sister," Balder replied. "But what might his actions be next? What enemy might he bring to our doorstep? I would not like to wake one morning to find the dragon Nidhogg outside my window, and to later hear Loki explain how necessary it was to bring such a creature here so that he could save us from it."

Sif did not respond.

Loki looked at Sigyn. Her eyes welled with tears. He regretted the anguish he had caused her, and would have excluded her from this council if he could, despite the fact that she would plainly support him even against all the others. She was not strong-willed or bold, but she was faithful, and he wished that he had been a more attentive

177

husband. But the past could not be changed. After Odin lent his support and ended this council, he would pledge to be a better husband.

Odin spoke. "None of you have any further complaints." It was a statement, not a question. He had foreseen it, and had made a plain observation.

Loki directed all his attention to the Allfather. Fists clenched at his sides, he awaited the pronouncement.

Odin saw two rows of gods, one on either side, facing each other. One stood between the rows, anticipating some form of judgment. They were in Gladsheim, and all was well in Asgard. Or was it? Was this the present?

The scene shifted, and where the gods sat he now saw an army looming over the horizon and a shattered rainbow bridge in the distance. Broken bodies lay at their feet as they advanced forward, slaying all who stood between them and Asgard. While their sizes varied—some were only twice the size of Thor, others towered nearly as high as the mason— they were all sons of Jotunheim, and they had come to crush the gods.

Far in the distance, one figure stood overlooking the devastation. He was massive and enshrouded in a loose column of smoke and fire, emanating death and destruction. Most of what could be seen of him was outlined by flames. As he drew closer, Odin observed that he was carved from the very flame itself, an elemental being more than a flesh and blood creature. He wondered if such a being could feel the bite of steel.

He looked upwards. A ship sailed high overhead, floating on the clouds above them. The crew staggered about the ship, hobbling like lame rats. At the bow, one stood that he marked as different from the others. He could see the face clearly for a brief moment, and he knew the name, but his vision did not hold.

And then he was elsewhere. He looked around the hall, sensing its familiarity, trying to adjust himself to the circumstances. All the Aesir were gathered, one row on each side, and they looked to him for an answer. One stood in the middle.

In a rush, the roof above him was gone, and he stared out into the black night sky. Some others gathered around him, once more seeking advice, although circumstances seemed far different. He put hand to chin and was surprised when his fingers struck smooth skin. He must have expressed his confusion based on the quizzical looks on the faces around him, but he quickly regained his composure. He had learned to adapt quickly to the shifting circumstances he continuously found himself in.

The faces looked familiar. One of them was speaking.

"What do we do with the body?" The question was directed at him.

He knitted his brow, but could not recall what body the man—his brother Vili, he now realized—spoke of. "What body is this?"

Vili and his other brother Ve exchanged looks. "It is the body of Ymir, brother." The name sounded familiar—all names sounded familiar to him; it was maddening. But he could not place where he had heard it before.

"Who is Ymir?"

Again, there were looks between the two. Instead of words, Vili gestured to something behind Odin. "There," he said.

He turned to see the bottom of a giant, blue-white foot, towering high above him, lifeless and bloody. The foot was attached to a leg that stretched nearly as far as he could see. Beyond that, there was only the vaguest suggestion of a body that dwarfed the mountains themselves.

"Ymir," he said, and memories trickled back again. He had been a frost giant, the first of his kind, and his evil had been plain to the three brothers, Odin, Vili, and Ve. They had . . . slain him? Was that correct? But there was some sort of tie to the creature that he could almost name. It came to him suddenly, and he shuddered for a brief second. This dead monstrosity that he had helped slay, was it true that its blood ran through his own veins?

"He was our kin?"

The two were plainly finished with the conversation. "Enough of this. What do we do with Ymir's body?"

Why was he being posed this question? But he knew the answer as well. Bones, teeth, hair, all could be used for something. He opened his mouth to answer, but the image faded.

There was great pain in his side. He found that he could not move his body, and that even his arms were restrained above his head. He could just move his neck so that he could see his side. The head of a spear was stuck inside him, and blood flowed from the gaping wound. He was unclothed, and so far above the ground that he could only see vast landscapes and the features of the land below. He remembered this happening, was certain that it had happened in the past. It was Yggdrasil, his sacrifice to gain knowledge and wisdom.

He was weak. He did not know how long he had been on the tree. Before he could question further, the scene shifted again.

Balder was speaking. He was making a complaint against someone. They were in Gladsheim. He was in the present again. Loki stood before him, before them all, waiting for an answer.

The Sly One had done his bidding well. The giant Thiazi had been slain, and Asgard's safety had been assured.

180

But that was not why he had sent Loki to Thrymheim. In his mind's eye, he saw again the procession of giants pressing down upon Asgard, the smoke-obscured figure in the rear, the leader of all the armies of chaos floating on the ship above. Standing at the bow, peering over the edge, Loki looked down at his army with vengeance plainly etched across his face.

It was as Odin had intended. It was not for him to deny the fate that crawled ever closer. Did his sacrifice not show him clearly the preordained destiny that awaited them all?

He rose from his chair to address the assembled Aesir. "You have cause for recriminations against Loki, and I must see those charges answered, for you are all my children, and I am the Allfather. But as children, you see no further than the hand in front of your face and think you are wise. None of you can know the destiny that I have seen, have already experienced, and so none of you are fit to pass judgment here."

He could see Loki's eyes and chin raise slightly, anticipating an answer to the charges laid before him. Even he, the most crafty of all the gods, was but a fawn in a vast wood, thinking the copse of his birth to be the entirety of his world. In another time, Odin may have felt some measure of pity from his manipulations, but he was far beyond that emotion. All he felt was the burning necessity to answer fate's summons.

"Loki, you have served Asgard and the Aesir, and you have received poor treatment as reward. It would be fitting that you be given the respect that has been lacking."

A slow smile crept onto Loki's face.

Odin felt a momentary pity for what he must do, but it was quickly gone, to be replaced by the certainty that the actions he took were correct.

"I cannot, however, bestow that respect on one who is

181

not truly one of us." The smile on Loki's face disappeared. "You are not Aesir, nor have you ever been one. You are a son of Jotunheim, and so are an enemy to Asgard and all who dwell here. I banish you from this realm forevermore. You shall not set friendly foot on Asgard again."

Even the other assembled gods were speechless.

Loki stared, open-mouthed, but Odin offered nothing but a blank return stare. Slowly, the surprised expressions on the faces of the Aesir were replaced with dawning realization. They had not expected such a pronouncement, but now that the truth had been revealed—that Loki's veins ran with the blood of enemies who were prophesied to destroy Asgard—it allowed them to finally comprehend Loki's manner.

"Allfather, you cannot banish me from Asgard." Loki's reply felt weak, as if the full consequences of Odin's pronouncement had yet to be realized.

"You are no more one of us than the mason was."

Loki was visibly shocked by the comparison. He could barely find words. "But Allfather, I—"

"No. I am not Allfather to you. To you I am now the Terrible One, the One-Eyed God of Those That Live Above, the Gray Bringer of Death. I am eternally an enemy, and will slay you without hesitation if I chance upon you. Your name will forever be unclean. The skalds will sing songs of your treachery and deceit, and call you Trickster and Father of Lies. You will be known as the Bringer of Chaos, and all who harbor you will be our enemies. I will amass armies of Aesir and Einherjar and Valkyrie to destroy you and your kind, and I will fight you at Ragnarok. No longer are we kin or kind; I and all other Asgardians renounce you here and forevermore."

Loki no longer stared in surprise. Instead, his fists were clenched and his eyes were fire, burning into Odin with clear

182

and obvious rage. He spoke, his voice low and filled with threat. "You—all of you—" he turned his head both ways to lock eyes with each of them briefly before returning his attention to Odin. "Will regret this day. I swear that this will not be the last you see of me." He turned and angrily strode out the large wooden doors.

Odin knew that Loki was right. They would see him again. He had done this thing, had set events into motion that could not be changed. Loki's vengeance, crafted by Odin, would fall on Asgard, and they would all pay the price for the decision he had made. He would not speak of it, of course. It was his burden to carry. The cost of knowledge was heavy indeed, but it must be paid. Even Odin was not immune to the inevitable hand of fate.

He closed his eye and saw Loki walk across Bifrost. As the Sly One slowly disappeared from view, Odin felt a momentary pang of regret. It was gone soon enough. When Ragnarok came, there would be time enough for regret. He opened his eye, stood up from his chair, and addressed the stunned Aesir sitting in council with him.

Loki's Children

The Sly One, after having been banished from Asgard, took to spending long nights in Jotunheim with the giantess Angrboda in her hall. She was beautiful to look at, although her beauty did not compare to that of Freyja or golden-haired Sif. Loki had had enough of goddesses, and had even forsaken his own wife, Sigyn, in favor of the fair giantess.

Her hall had been carved from the solid rock of a mountainside in just two days, and was large enough to fit an army in its main hall, with room left over. But it was not in the main hall that the two spent most of their time.

After many a long night, Angrboda felt a quickening inside her, and months later she gave birth to three children. Loki and Angrboda's eyes were blinded by the love that parents feel when cradling their newborn children, else they would have realized that the creatures that had sprung forth from her loins were monstrous indeed.

The first to come out was covered in fur and had a long snout and tail. They named the pup Fenrir, which means 'wolf from below', and he eagerly suckled at his mother's teat. The second to come out was hairless and limbless and covered in scales. They named the hatchling Jormungand, meaning 'mighty wand', for they saw that he was destined to grow to an immense size and strength. The third was a beautiful daughter from the waist up. Below that, however, she was blackened and corpse-like. They named her Hel, which means 'covered up', for their first instinct was to cover her lower half so that no one could see it.

It was not long before word carried to Asgard about Loki's three children. The gods met with the Norns at the Well of Urd to *ask their counsel.*

"The wolf will eat the sun and the father," said Urd.

"The snake will swallow the lightning," said Skuld.

"The corpse will bring forth legions," said Verdandi.

All three Norns agreed that they were evil, and that they would mark the downfall of the gods.

"They will herald the end," said Urd.

"They will arise at Ragnarok," said Skuld.

"They will destroy the best among you," said Verdandi.

The gods were alarmed and decided to take action to prevent the prophecies of the Norns from coming true. They stole away during the night into Jotunheim. Unseen due to Odin's magic, they burst into Angrboda's hall while she was sleeping. Before she could open a single lid they had bound and trussed her. Loki was nowhere to be found, and the gods were happy they did not have to contend with him, for it is often said that a father is most furious in the defense of his own home.

Odin came upon the snake first. He pulled it from its cradle and hurled it with all of his strength. Jormungand flew out of the hall, across Midgard, and landed in the ocean at the edge of the world, where he sunk down to the bottom and fed on passing fish. Unmolested and more and more angry as time passed, he grew to an enormous size, eventually encircling the entirety of Midgard under the sea and, thinking his own tail was food, sank his teeth into it. He would rise at Ragnarok to take his vengeance on the Aesir.

Odin came upon Hel second. He gasped with disgust when he saw her decayed lower half, and hurled her with all of his strength downward. She burst through the floor of the hall and then the stone of Midgard, eventually landing in the underworld known as Niflheim. There she made the dead her servants, and they erected a hall for her on the edge of a sheer cliff. At Ragnarok she would send forth an army of the dead to take her vengeance on the Aesir.

Odin came upon the third child, the Fenris Wolf, and was

185

about to lay hands on him when Tyr spoke up.

"Have pity for this one, at least, Allfather. He is but a pup."

"You have heard the prophecy of the Norns. He cannot be allowed to grow."

But Tyr felt for the small creature. It did not look monstrous as had the other two. He said, "I will care for him in Asgard. I will feed him and ensure that he does not have reason to take vengeance on the Aesir."

Odin relented, and the gods went back to Asgard with Fenrir in tow . . .

Chapter Fourteen

Freyja stood gazing at her image in the mirror. She spent much of each day going over and over her face and body, taking in her replenished beauty, but always with a hidden fear that it might fade again. The memory of her crinkled flesh and sagging breasts was a physical pain to her, sending shudders through her body and nearly bringing her to tears. Letting her robe fall to the floor, she examined and re-examined herself in the mirror from all possible angles, looking for any blemish, any imperfection that may be a sign of the hideousness that she had endured. As ever, she found none. She was pure physical perfection, in face and body, and yet the pall that hung over her because of Loki's misdeeds could not be erased from her mind.

She drifted to the still pool at the edge of her room. Freyja knelt down and trailed her fingers in the silvery water in slow circles, attempting to bring an image up. She saw many things—her home in Vanaheim, Odin in his chambers with Mimir's head slowly issuing dire portents, Heimdall vigilant as ever at Bifrost. Jumbled images arose along with some clearer ones, images that spanned the expanse of the Nine Worlds. Some things she knew and could name—the light elves of Alfheim weaving among the trees, the dwarfs of Nidavellir holed up in their underworld home, busily crafting tools and weapons. But she saw more that she did not know—quick glimpses of a face of fire, an ice white corpse, eons old, stretching for miles. She turned from the pool and stood to go.

She was drawn back by swirling images that danced

just inside the waters, hinting at secrets. She knelt back down and brought her face close to the water, peering deeply into its depths as the images unfolded.

She saw a girl with raven hair. She was beautiful, but it was not the beauty of a goddess. Rather, her beauty was that of a warrior, well-toned with darkened skin from much time in the sun. She lay on a bed, and her face alternated between violent spasms of intense pain and periods of utter exhaustion. Her brow was drenched with sweat, and her enormously swelled belly was the source of her pain.

The image remained, so unlike the fleeting nature of most images in the pool, and Freyja was transfixed. After a brief rest, the contractions began again, and the girl visibly contorted, bringing her hand into the scene shown in the pool. She clutched the hand of a child tightly, perhaps an older sibling standing by his or her mother, witnessing the entry into life of a new brother or sister. By the size of the belly, Freyja thought it likely that there might be twins.

The child, seen only by the firm grip on the mother's hand, was resilient despite his young age. Freyja marked it to be a boy by the lines and wear of the hand, and he showed no signs of letting go.

Freyja continued to watch the intimate scene. Lost in a moment that was sacred to her and all of the Vanir, the introduction of a new life, she did not question the pool's focus on this one particular event, even though it was rare to remain on one scene for long.

The woman—Freyja could not consider her a girl any longer—continued to suffer the throes of contractions, but the ferocity of her expression was striking. Freyja could see scars of battle across her, so she was accustomed to pain. Her reaction to the quickening children within her marked this pain as far more intense than any she had endured before. Freyja found herself admiring this mortal woman, and she drew closer to the pool.

There was no midwife at the bed save the faithful boy, who was still yet to be revealed as anything other than a disembodied hand in the fuzzy darkness of the chamber. Freyja found herself concocting notions of this woman's life. The father, no doubt a well-bred warrior himself, was likely out in battle, perhaps fighting an enemy just on the borders of their land. He could not be at his wife's side because that would mean death for all those he had sworn to protect.

Freyja smiled at the thought. While she was not a goddess of battle, she honored duty and sacrifice. She was torn by the hope that the pool would show an image of him, and the fear that she would miss the birth of this woman's children.

The woman's throes grew more intense and frequent. The children would burst forth soon enough. She felt privileged to be observing this birth, and felt certain that this was the reason the pool had shown her the scene. It had sought a significant birth, one which might have import for the race of men down below on Midgard.

Unexpectedly the scene in the pool dimmed and wavered, and Freyja willed it to show her more. She would not miss the birth of these children. The scene steadied, and she was able to see a slightly wider area than before. The woman's knees were up as she pushed, her face becoming crimson with the effort, and her hand tightened on her son's. Cords of muscle stood out on the woman's forearms, and her knuckles were white with the effort. The boy was still a small child by the size of his hand, yet he held tight and voiced no complaint that she could detect.

Freyja was momentarily distracted by the thought. A woman as strong as this would likely break the hand of a small child, even a hearty one, but she did not attempt to hold back. It was obvious that she squeezed his hand with all her might. And still there was no complaint.

She looked more closely at the boy's hand and the small part of his arm that was visible. She could not see much, but it seemed that the skin on his hands was not as pristine as it should have been for one so young. It was difficult to tell in the dim light of the chamber, but his arm might have had a thin layer of reddish-blond hair, which would surely be lighter or nonexistent for a child of his age, would it not?

The woman contorted again with a stab of pain in her abdomen, and the boy was yanked forward momentarily, becoming visible for the slightest of seconds before retreating back beyond view. Freyja fell violently backwards with shock, thrusting herself from the pool as if the dragon Nidhogg itself had suddenly burst from the water.

She sat there dazed and uncomprehending, eyes wide with disgust and horror. It cannot be true, she thought. She felt sullied and filthy, all her alluring fantasies disappearing in an instant. She wanted to flee the room, but she had to see if what she had witnessed was true.

He had been in her thoughts for months, so it would be understandable to see him in the pool's image. The pool had probably conjured him from her thoughts and mingled it with the scene she had been witnessing. The initial shock faded, she began to replace the horror with more reasonable explanation, and it was this that allowed her to crawl forward and view the scene again.

It was the same as it had been before, although the woman was coming closer and closer to the moment of birth. Freyja watched more cautiously, fearful to see him again, but desperate to see if it was true. She kept more of a distance at first, but found herself peering closer again, anticipation and fear wrapped up as one within her.

After long moments she finally convinced herself that she had been wrong. It was then that the boy leaned in closer to his mother to stroke her head and chant words of encouragement. The first thing Freyja noted was that the proportions were all wrong.

The boy had reddish-blond hair and a light beard of the same color. His arms were wiry and muscular, but not excessively so. His eye bore the clear glint of one who had lived and schemed for millennia, one whose maliciousness knew no bounds. As she watched in rapidly unfolding horror, she noticed how small he looked in comparison to the woman, as if he were a small boy. Realization finally struck her as Loki's tiny hand touched upon the woman's cheek in an undeniable gesture of attachment. Stuck to the scene by mounting horror, she watched the woman give one more massive push with all her might.

She reeled backwards again, falling less elegantly onto her backside. She scrambled to her feet and ran from the room, summoning her servants to attend her instantly. Odin must be told at once. And while she could have voiced her concern about Loki's coupling with one from Jotunheim, she was less sure of her ability to explain what she had seen emerging from between the giant's legs.

Balder was not happy to be here asking for advice from these witches. Precious time was being wasted, and his temper was barely being held in check. "Will you tell me what I need to know?"

"We will . . ."

"provide . . ."

"answers . . ."

The voices came from nowhere and everywhere at the same time, hollow and icy. None knew what the Norns even were, but they had knowledge that no others possessed, not even Odin. It was even said that they were the tree, although Balder did not wonder overly on such things.

191

It was enough for him that Odin had sent him here to speak with them. He would perform this task and then leave, hopefully to raise an army to march on Jotunheim. The Allfather had said that it was not yet time for war, but who knew when the time may come? And if the Norns were to advise him to attack the giants, then he thought it likely Odin would acquiesce.

He gazed around the chamber, brow furrowed. "I come to seek your—"

"We know why . . ."

"you are . . ."

"here . . ."

Balder clenched his jaw. "Then show yourself. I am no threat to you."

A thin and hollow laughter trickled down to him.

"You . . ."

"are no . . ."

"threat . . ."

Balder continued to look around the chamber. As far as he could see, there was no one here but him. He stepped away from the well and felt a light touch on his back, almost a caress, but there was something unnatural about it. He turned his head, but once again there was no one there.

"What do I . . . what is to be done with Loki's children?"

He counted the seconds in silence, awaiting an answer. Something slithered between his legs and he started, but it was gone.

"Come closer . . ."

"to the . . ."

"well . . .

"gaze into . . ."

"its . . ."

"depths . . ."

Hesitantly, he took slow steps to the well. He knelt

down and looked into the black depths. He began to lose patience until he saw the darkness moving and shifting. Where there had been nothing, he could now make out three figures, vague and insubstantial. As he watched, they slowly began to change into a new image.

"*Your name . . .*"

"*will be . . .*"

"*legendary . . .*"

He saw himself, only a strange version. He looked thin and weak and very beautiful. He stood laughing while the other Aesir threw all manner of weapons at him, each striking, and each falling to the ground with no affect. Thor's hammer struck him directly, and there was no damage. In fact, the strange version of him laughed out loud. The entire scene had the strange air of falseness to it, as if this were a twisted story of something that had actually happened.

"What is this? What do you show me?"

His brother, Hod, approached holding something in his hand. It looked like a small plant with white berries, but as he raised his hand, the entire image collapsed in upon itself.

"Wait! What did he have in his hand? What is the meaning of this image?" Balder felt that he had been shown something important, but it had been withdrawn before he could make sense of it. Without realizing it, he leaned in closer, his head nearer the well.

"*Your . . .*

"*fate is . . .*"

"*at hand . . .*"

The image reformed, and he saw a newborn babe being cradled by the darkness. As the image expanded slowly, he saw a mother where the darkness had been, holding the baby, a sad expression on her face. It was his own mother, Frigg, and he realized that the babe in her arms was himself, freshly breached. As she held him tears tore down her face.

Like the first image, it seemed false and manufactured, again the distortion of a real event rather than the event itself.

Before he could delve further into it, the scene shifted yet again. His mother, barely recognizable due to her haggard and frail appearance, approached a dark woman on a throne. She knelt and the woman nodded. Frigg rose, gratitude spreading across her features, but worry as well.

Frigg disappeared down an unseen corridor, and Balder saw a shadowy figure—a man—watching from beside the throne. The man took a step forward, and the woman held a hand out to one side, halting him suddenly and refusing him any further steps forward. Balder gasped when he recognized his own face, insubstantial and rotting, staring after his mother with obvious anguish.

He felt his blood boil. "I am dead? Is that the meaning of this? If this is my fate then show it to me!" His ire continued to rise. They stood on the possible cusp of Ragnarok, and they wasted time on useless augury. It would have been better by far to take action against Loki and his spawn rather than listen to the useless prattle of these witches.

The swirling mists reformed, and he saw Frigg enter a cave. She was older still and tired, but there was a pleasant air about her, as if she were at the end of a long journey. The darkness of the cave was pierced by burning torches, and a gaunt old woman came into view. She was wrapped in a worn cloak, and time had not been kind to her. She mumbled to herself and rocked back and forth, and continued doing so as Frigg approached her. Balder could not hear any of the words, but the old woman ceased her ramblings as Frigg spoke.

The old woman's mouth opened wide in a vile and toothless smile, and she laughed, but not with glee or happiness. She shook her head from side to side, her answer to Frigg's request clear, even through the silence of the image. The effect on his mother was plain; she withered and her head hung low, tears streaming down her cheeks as she turned and left the cave, the crone's cackle following her out.

The old woman's face poked out of the cave, a dark and knowing smile spreading across her features. If Balder did not know better, he would have sworn that this was not even the same woman, so changed in demeanor did she seem. What was more shocking was the shifting of the face itself as it withdrew back into the cave, revealing the face behind the mask.

Balder felt rage creeping up inside him. "Loki," he spat. "Always Loki."

The blackness swirled and the scene shifted.

He saw Yggdrasil take shape and rise higher and higher, spreading its branches wide. Flames formed at its trunk, burning and smoldering, threatening Yggdrasil. The tree shrunk as the scene grew wider, and Balder could see that it was not just the base of the tree that burned. Flames engulfed everything that he could see, and they burned hotter and hotter, turning everything to ash.

From a breach in the tree a figure emerged, and as he did so the flames waned and eventually died down. The figure stood unmolested, surveying the scene of carnage and devastation. Balder could not tell who the figure was, but he did see a faint smile form on the face before the image faded completely, leaving nothing but darkness.

"Who is that figure?" Balder pulled back from the well. "Is it Loki, gloating over the destruction he intends to cause?" He paused, but there was no answer. "What must be done to prevent this from happening?"

Three shapes materialized from the mist, assuming vaguely feminine forms, although they remained faceless and intangible. Their voices came from all around him.

"What must . . ."

"be . . ."

"will be . . ."

Balder's anger flared. "Why do you show me visions if there is no way to change them?"

"You will . . ."

"not survive . . ."

"his wrath . . ."

"Loki's wrath? He will try to kill me?"

"You will . . ."

"survive . . ."

"his wrath . . ."

"Which is it? This riddle makes no sense."

"It . . ."

"is . . ."

"both . . ."

He silently cursed his father for sending him here. What was the point of this?

"You will seek. . ."

"the accursed . . ."

"spawn . . ."

"Loki's children?"

"Bring he . . ."

"of the single . . ."

"wolf-joint . . ."

Balder's mind spun, trying to grasp the meaning of the Norns' message. Balder had not heard that expression before.

"Who is he of the wolf-joint?"

"You . . ."

"will . . ."

"know . . ."

He clenched his jaw. *Damn these witches,* he thought. Who were they to thwart the will of Asgard? And yet what

196

could he do but unravel their riddles? Odin had sent him here for advice on what should be done about Loki's children, but they revealed next to nothing. Besides, what did he need advice for? He knew what should be done, but his father did not want the Aesir to go to war with the giants yet. *It is not yet time*, he had said, but he had revealed nothing further.

"You must tell me more." He tried to keep the irritation from his voice. The mist shapes swayed, but remained in place. He took a hesitant step forward, and they collapsed upon themselves, losing all coherence and drifting to the ground.

"Your fame will . . ."
"wane in life and . . "
"wax in death, only . . ."
"to wane and wax . . ."
"once more upon . . ."
"the Ash . . ."

He waited for further communication, but the Norns were silent. After a time, he turned and headed back out the way he had come. He did not know the exact meaning of the Norns' words, but he would not wait till all the riddles were unraveled before he struck out for Jotunheim and sought out Loki's children.

Chapter Fifteen

Sleipnir's back looked only wide enough for one rider, but Balder, Frey and Tyr discovered that there was ample room as they mounted the strange horse. He would take them, Odin had said, in between the Nine Worlds, but they were unprepared for the bizarre journey.

Sleipnir had taken off much as any other horse, although the gods were impressed with his speed and obvious strength. Odin's steed galloped with little effort, and the three gods felt no slackening of pace as he continued. Before they left the Nine Worlds completely, they marveled at the unearthly rate of speed the horse had attained.

Then Asgard faded. In its place was only a blankness. It was as if they had been struck blind, but they could still clearly see Sleipnir beneath them, the muscles on his back and neck rippling as he continued pounding his eight powerful legs on no surface whatsoever.

Shadows slowly became visible, and they thought they could detect a mountain range looming over them while grass and dirt materialized under Sleipnir's hooves. They passed by shadows of enormous structures with large figures scattered about.

They knew this place. They had been here many times, although it was always with swords flashing. This was Jotunheim, the land of their ancient enemies, the giants.

Sleipnir did not slow down, and they moved far too fast for any of the giants to even notice them. A few heads turned, but it was only to marvel at the unknown thing that raced past. With astounding speed, they crossed through

Jotunheim's villages and towns, their ultimate goal somewhere ahead.

The sheer face of a mountain lie ahead, directly in their path, but Sleipnir did not stop or even slow. They had little time to fear the collision before they hit the wall and went through it as if there was nothing there.

Sleipnir slowed drastically, and the world jerked back into view.

They were in a tall chamber that had been carved from the rock of the mountain. It was lit by torchlight, and several corridors led deeper into the keep. They dismounted, and Sleipnir faded, leaving the three alone in the large room.

"He will return when we have the children," Balder said.

Tyr nodded, looking around at the oversized dimensions of the room, the tables that were above their heads, the bowls large enough for them to bathe in.

Frey said, "I have never seen giants as existing anywhere other than the battlefield. It is strange to be in one of their halls and see such . . . normalcy."

Balder said, "Yes, I had not considered them sitting at a table and eating a meal. But we are not likely to be invited to dine if we are caught. We had best be swift. Can we be seen?"

Instead of answering, Frey closed his eyes and chanted while his fingers drew runes in the air. Blue-white letters glowed briefly, hovering before them, and then faded.

"We are mostly unseen."

"What does that mean?" Tyr asked.

"If we stay to the walls and are quiet, we will not be noticed. Anyone who looks at us directly will likely see us, so we should take care to avoid that. Any confrontations or loud noises will allow us to be seen."

"What if we encounter giants?" Tyr asked.

Balder replied, "My father said to avoid any fighting unless there was no other way. We are to find Loki's children and return with them—unharmed—to Asgard."

He remembered the oddness of the conversation. Odin had spoken, and then suddenly had seen something else beyond view.

When you exit the Ash, you will live again, he had chanted. Balder was unnerved, but Odin would not respond to his questions or explain what he meant.

"And if we encounter Loki?" Tyr asked.

Balder brought himself back to the present. "We will not see him."

The three made their way through the winding corridors of the mountain keep. Occasionally they saw giants, but they were not detected. Still, they were awed at the size of these creatures as they walked past. They had met giants many times on the battlefield, but to be so close, to be able to observe them nearby, was unusual.

Frey led them to a large door, the handle just slightly above his head.

"They are here with one other."

"Who?" Tyr asked.

"Their mother."

Balder nodded, realizing that this would be difficult. He did not relish attacking a female, even if she was a giant, but was not sure of how they were going to take the children without harming her. For a brief instant he wished that Loki was there; he would be able to craft a scheme that would get the children without any fighting. He half-smiled to himself when he realized again whose children they were.

Tyr asked, "If we open the door, will she see us?"

Frey said, "It is difficult to tell. If she is looking in that direction, then it is likely she will. If her attention is diverted, then perhaps not."

"Is there any way to tell before we enter?"

"Not now. We are too far from Vanaheim for me to work any other spells."

Balder said, "Then we go in slowly, and hope that we do not draw her attention."

He reached up and grasped the handle, pulling it down slowly and as silently as possible. The door swung inward and Balder looked in before entering. He stuck his head out and nodded to the other two. The three slipped into the room.

The room was Angrboda's bedchambers. Much like any of their own, it was filled with all the requisite items: fireplace, bed, chests, and other items. Near the large bed there were three cradles, and sitting on a chair nearby was a female giant with a swaddled baby in her arms, suckling.

The giant was in her bedclothes, and they could see her lean musculature. This was no nursemaid, but a warrior. Angrboda paid no attention to the three gods, and it was clear that she was not aware that they had crept into her chambers. She rocked the baby at her breast slowly, lost in the timeless ritual.

Balder looked back at Tyr and Frey, but was met by blank stares. None of the three were certain about what to do, although their directive to gather the children was unequivocal. After long minutes of waiting, Balder made a decision. He gestured to Tyr and Frey to stay by the door, and then strode slowly and quietly toward Angrboda.

He stopped at the three cradles and peered into the first one. The infant was asleep, but it looked like no baby Balder had ever seen before. Its skin was scaly and tinted brown, and the child was hairless and reptilian. He considered drawing his sword and slaying it right then, but remembered his father's admonition that the children be brought back unharmed. Still, it took some effort to choke down the grotesque sight of this vile child. What kind of god could produce offspring like this?

He glanced first at Angrboda, still feeding one of the infants, and then back over to Tyr and Frey who stood ready by the door. They had curious looks on their faces, and he realized they had no idea what he planned. He was not sure of it himself, but he thought it preferable to simply slaying the giant mother.

At first he had considered letting himself be seen and then issuing her an ultimatum: give over the children or die. He realized quickly that neither she nor any mother would willingly give up her children, and that such a command would only begin a fight in which she and possibly one or more of the children would die.

Instead, he would use her protective instincts against her by threatening to kill one of the children if she did not hand them over to Tyr and Frey. She would be furious, and would seek to find a way to avoid giving up her children. But she might give them over temporarily, thinking that she could get them back once her hands were free and Balder's sword was away from the infant. By then, Sleipnir would reappear, and Balder could hold her off or kill her—in battle instead of in a cowardly way—while Tyr and Frey made off with two of the infants. After he dealt with her, Sleipnir would return for him and the last child.

He was not sure it was the best plan, but he felt an urgency to do something before they were revealed. In time, Angrboda would notice them—she might leave the room or simply turn her head in their exact direction, or they might make some noise that would give them away. Something needed to be attempted soon, or the entire scheme was at risk. He wondered what Loki would have come up with if he were in their party.

He stepped over to the second child asleep in the next

cradle. Unlike her sibling, this infant did not look unnatural, aside from the fact that it was about as large as he was. Though he did not relish doing it, he drew his sword slowly and held the point over the infant's throat. When Angrboda saw the perilous position of her child, she would surely not be so foolish as to attack. He looked over to her, still unaware that they were there. Just as he was about to speak, he heard a quiet cooing from the child.

He turned back and saw that the infant was stirring, although the eyes were still closed. He nearly turned away before he saw something strange. The face began to change color, to grow pale and gray while the skin shriveled and withdrew, and black lines of decay shot across the face. The lips withdrew from toothless gums. The eyes opened, and they were empty sockets with flies crawling out of them.

In shock and horror he struck out, driving the sword into the grotesque infant. It stilled all movement, and he stepped back, barely grasping what he had done and forcing down a wave of nausea.

Tyr yelled, "Balder! Behind you!" but he did not turn in time. He was struck across the side of his head with something very hard, and he flew across the room, crashing into the stone wall of the chamber.

There was an unholy scream of rage and anguish that shook the room as Angrboda looked down upon her dead infant. She turned to Tyr and Frey with her fists clenched around a wooden cudgel, and the most horrible rage on her face that either of the gods had ever seen. The cudgel dripped with Balder's blood, and he lay unconscious against the wall.

She stared at Tyr and Frey with hatred and fury, and then charged, cudgel high and jaw clenched tight.

Both drew their swords, although they were unsure of this battle. Tyr could not get over seeing Balder stab the

203

infant in its cradle, and it had caused his hesitation in warning him of Angrboda's attack. Still, they could not change the fact, nor could they ignore that they were being attacked by an enemy who wanted them dead, one who was at least twice their size.

Tyr turned to Frey before she reached them. "See to Balder." Frey nodded and dashed off quickly while Tyr took several paces forward to meet the giant's attack.

Angrboda swung the cudgel hard and low, but Tyr deflected the blow with his sword. She recovered quickly—she had obviously been in battles before—and swung it again on a downward angle. Tyr side-stepped the blow and sliced his sword through her weapon, cutting it in two.

She surprised him by dropping it instantly and grabbing for him. He stepped backward, but not far enough to completely avoid her grasping fingers, and he was suddenly hoisted off his feet and then thrown. He struck the wall with his back and fell to one knee before she was on him again.

Frey had roused Balder and used the runes to speed up his healing. Recovering from the blow and from the shock of the infant's change, he pointed toward the first cradle and the bed where they saw that Angrboda had set the other child down. Glancing to see how Tyr fared, they could see that he kept her occupied and allowed them the time necessary to secure the children.

Balder went to the first cradle and hoisted the large infant over his shoulder, while Frey did the same with the infant Angrboda had left on the bed. Sleipnir appeared suddenly between them as the two infants began wailing.

Angrboda turned with a look of horror, realization of how she had been tricked painfully etched across her face. "No!" she screamed, and turned towards them. She was held back by Tyr, who grabbed her wrist. She turned back to him

204

quickly and grabbed him by the throat, lifting him up off his feet and crushing his neck in her large hand.

He was amazed at her strength, but had been in too many battles to be caught by surprise for very long. Staring her in the eye as she attempted to choke the life from him, he knew there would be no reasoning. Her fury was ignited as he had rarely seen before, and she would kill them all with her bare hands if she could.

His sword still in hand as he dangled at her eye level, he brought it up swiftly and sliced through her neck. Her head fell and her body followed, Tyr dropping to his feet even before Angrboda's fresh corpse hit the stone floor. He sheathed his sword and walked over to where Frey and Balder were mounted on Sleipnir.

"Why did you kill the child?" he asked.

"It was a vile thing. You did not see it."

Tyr looked over at the cradle of the dead infant. "There is nothing to do about it now. We can only hope the Allfather will not be too displeased."

"I will take the responsibility for the action, and the consequences."

Tyr nodded.

Frey said, "We must leave."

Tyr mounted Sleipnir. As before, though the horse did not look large enough to carry three gods and two giant infants, there was enough room for all. As it ran toward the wall, it faded into the spaces in between the Nine Worlds on its way back to Asgard with its cargo.

Chapter Sixteen

Odin could remember well the day that Loki's two children were brought to him. Laid out before him, wailing in his presence, he could see them clearly. One was the snake, and the other was the wolf. He almost found it amusing that these two helpless infants—large though they might be—would cause such destruction when the time came.

As he gazed upon them, Balder had spoken of the third infant.

"Father, the third child—"

"Is dead. I know."

"It was unintentional."

"Do not think on it more. She has been in Niflheim for countless ages already. Her death was fated."

Balder had been confused, but Odin did not elaborate.

"Take this one," he had said, nodding to the reptilian infant, "to the edge of Asgard and toss him into the seas surrounding Midgard."

Balder had blanched. "Father? Do you jest?"

"Have you ever known me to jest, Balder?"

"But it is only an infant, no matter how hideous. At least let me end its life quickly before sending it to a watery grave."

Odin had stared down at him from his high seat. "It will be no grave. Now do as I command."

Head bowed, Balder had said, "Yes, my lord," and left with the infant.

Odin had turned to Tyr. "You think my

pronouncements cruel?"

"It is not my place to question the Allfather."

"This one will have a different fate. What do you think of this infant?"

"It looks half beast, but it is not as ugly as the other."

"Take it to the woods surrounding Asgard and leave it there for the wolves."

Tyr had not flinched. "Yes, High One."

As he turned to leave, Odin called after him one last time. "See that the child survives. No harm may come to it."

Tyr looked at him oddly for a moment, but said, "Yes, High One. It will be as you say." He left with the infant in his arms.

From his high seat he had looked down on both infants, although they were infants no longer. They had grown quickly, and the chaos at their cores had redefined them according to their surroundings. The snake had attained an enormous size at the bottom of the ocean, where it had fed on whatever creatures swam or crawled near it. It would grow larger still, but he would not need to think on the creature till the time they met again.

The wolf was a different matter.

He was not as large, but he was more dangerous because of his size. He had needed to be fast in those early days in the forest in order to survive, snatching food when available, avoiding those that would feast on him. Tyr had fed him for a time, which was how he had survived. The wolf now reigned supreme in those woods, and all other creatures either fled from him or fed his insatiable hunger.

Odin had watched the wolf roam the fields and forests of Asgard for some time now, considering his upcoming confrontation with the beast. He did not relish where he would send him, but of course there was little choice. He felt a small regret for what must be done and who must be harmed, but such feelings were useless. The High One could not afford emotions interfering with the fate of the Nine Worlds.

Tyr's servants led the cart to the edge of the clearing. With a nod, they began unloading the contents and tossing them towards the tree line. They made several trips, nervously scanning the trees for any sign of Fenrir. The wolf did not show, but even back near the cart, well behind Tyr, they were still fearful. Some of them had seen him devour the meat that Tyr left for him, and those that had not had at least heard about the size and ferocity of the beast from the others.

Unn, a younger servant, meekly approached him. "My lord?"

Tyr did not turn to face him, but kept his eyes on the trees. "What is it?"

"What if the wolf—"

"Call him by his name."

"Yes, lord. What if Fenrir is not satisfied with the meat you have left for him?"

Tyr glanced at the servant, noting the clear terror in his eye. "Have you come with me to feed Fenrir before?"

"No, my lord."

"But you have heard tales of him from the others?"

"Yes, my lord."

"What have they told you?"

Unn swallowed. "That the wo—that Fenrir is very large and terrifying. That he chokes down all the offered meat and glares hungrily at anyone standing nearby."

Tyr grunted. "There is some truth there. Are you afraid?"

"Yes, my lord."

"He is large enough, that is certain, about the size of a

small horse. But he does not always take the meat that is offered. Or at least not while we stand nearby. Sometimes he simply stares. Other times he approaches and offers a word or two."

"The beast can speak?"

"Yes, although his voice is not pleasant to hear."

Unn looked even less comfortable. "Are we in danger, my lord?"

"There is always danger, even in the realm of the gods. But Fenrir has made no move towards me. I cannot say for certain that he will never attack, but it does not seem likely that it will be today. And even if he did attack, he would face my sword."

Tyr turned to see the telltale signs of fear on Unn's face. He placed a hand on the young man's shoulder and leaned in. "No Asgardian of my house will come to harm while I draw breath." Unn nodded and stood up the slightest bit taller.

There was hushed whispering from the servants behind him as a dark shape slowly walked out of the woods and headed towards them. Fenrir stopped at the meat that had been thrown for him, sniffed it once, and then looked up at Tyr. He came closer, ignoring the offering.

Tyr could see Unn blanch as Fenrir walked towards them, but the young servant was frozen in place, incapable of stepping back to join the others. Tyr gently nudged him backwards.

Fenrir stopped a sword's length from Tyr and sat back on his haunches. His head was level with Tyr's, making him the largest wolf the servants had ever seen. His fur was dark, and there was an intelligence about his eyes that made it clear that despite his size, he was no plain beast.

"Tyr," he growled.

"You do not eat."

"I hunger for more than meat, Tyr." Again, the name was uttered like a growl.

"I cannot answer your questions, as I have told you before."

Fenrir bared his fangs. He stood up on all fours, and Tyr heard the collective gasp of the servants behind him. Fenrir turned and trotted back to the meat. He reached down with his head and grabbed the largest piece, swallowing it down quickly. As Tyr and his servants looked on, Fenrir devoured the rest and then loped slowly back to the trees.

Before disappearing into the forest, he turned and looked back at Tyr one last time. There was menace in that glance, but he had seen the same each time he fed the wolf. He was not entirely certain why he continued to bring these offerings to the beast, but he could not erase the vision of Angrboda's head being sliced off and falling to the ground.

Freyja stepped carefully over a fallen tree, worry knitting her features. All living things—save for the gods—died, and those deaths were not upsetting to her. It was part of the cycle of the Nine Worlds, and as a Vanir she was not only a goddess of life, but of death as well. The delicate nature of life made it all the more valuable, even though mortals rarely understood that.

Witnessing the destruction wrought by the wolf, however, she did not feel any sense of beauty or closure in the death he had brought to the forest. Trees were savagely shredded, plants were trampled in his wake, and a slew of animals lay butchered, a bloody path that none could fail to follow. And all these things were destroyed for nothing. He had not even killed the animals for food, but merely rent them apart for the sheer pleasure of slaughter.

Sadness creeping over her like a funeral pall, she

followed the trail, not really knowing why she did so. There was a need to see this creature, to try to understand why any being would so senselessly butcher the living things around him. She could feel the malice lingering in the air around her, the wolf's aura permeating this holy place. The thought that he could continue to wreak destruction unchecked sent a chill through her body.

She continued on, her connection to the things around her bringing more misery with every step. She reached a clearing and paused. An unusual feeling crept over her, something she could not remember feeling before. There was an unpleasant tingling sensation low in her stomach, and she felt an overwhelming need to stay still and silent.

At the other end of the clearing Fenrir squatted, noisily chewing on a large, dead animal. Its legs were splayed out, forming a sort of half circle around the wolf. His head and shoulders bobbed and jerked while he fed.

Fenrir was not as large as she had imagined him to be, although he was certainly not small. She watched him before taking a step forward, a difficult task to accomplish. She realized that this feeling was fear, and while she had felt it before during the war with the Aesir, it was only a fear for the survival of Vanaheim and the Vanir. She had not felt fear for herself, no matter how many Asgardians threatened with bloody swords and axes.

This fear was different, and she realized that it was fear for her person. Something about this beast instilled a more primal fear in her, something that she would not have thought possible. What was this thing to cow a Vanir goddess by its mere presence? It was more than the sight of the wolf. It radiated something, some kind of aura that caused an offense to her senses. She wondered if the Aesir were so affected.

As she took another step forward, the beast froze. She

211

paused, and he craned his neck around to see his visitor.

His face was very much like a wolf's, with a long snout and pointed teeth, visible with his lips raised in a snarl. But he did not sit on his haunches like a wolf. He was more man-like, although he was covered from head to toe in coarse black fur. There was something unquestionably intelligent lurking behind his eyes as he stared at her.

She wanted to avert her gaze, but feared that he might pounce. There was a good distance between them, enough that it would have taken him several bounds to reach her, but she had every confidence he could cross that span quickly.

"You watch me," he growled. She was not surprised that he could speak, but the low menace in the primitive voice was unmistakable.

She did not know how to respond, but felt compelled to address him. "Why do you do this?" She indicated the destruction with a gesture.

He stared at her for long moments, his expression as unchanging as it was unreadable. "Who are you?"

A subtle shift occurred as she looked at him. At first she thought it might have been a trick of the light, but she realized that his form was changing in front of her. His snout grew less pronounced, and his body shifted, making him look more human. She wondered if this were a conscious shifting or an instinctual response.

"I am Freyja," she said simply.

He regarded her carefully before speaking. "You are not one of them. You are different."

"No, I am not Aesir. I am Vanir. We are not the same."

He looked around at the chaos he had caused and then back at her. "This is yours?"

"Yes. Why have you destroyed it? What could be gained by doing this?"

He did not answer, but after a brief moment, a smile crossed his lips. He turned back to his kill and stuck his head back into its flesh, ignoring her completely.

She felt bile rise in her throat. She considered addressing him again, but was certain that he would not respond. She slowly backed away before turning around and quickly making her way to her hall.

Odin could see the frightened look in Freyja's eyes.

"He destroys all he touches. He should not be here. I saw the look in his eyes. It is only a matter of time till he attacks one of the gods."

Odin did not reply. He knew what she told him was the truth, but he also knew that it was not yet time for Fenrir to leave Asgard.

"You saw him in the forest?"

"Yes. I was drawn by the death and destruction I felt, and I followed the path. I did not know it would lead to Fenrir. But when I saw him," she grew pale as she remembered the look on Fenrir's face as he turned back to his kill, "I sensed the lust for destruction. Allfather, he will not be content to roam the forests and kill woodland creatures for long."

In fact, Fenrir had already killed and eaten several of the Einherjar, although none knew but him. Those warriors had not risen the following day.

"Would you have him slain?"

"No. You know I would not want life taken wantonly."

"Then what? Would you have me send him somewhere on Midgard where he would spend his time feasting on mortals?"

"No, of course not. I would not send him where he could harm another." She looked down, considering the possibilities. "Could he be bound?"

"He would not be held by normal means. He is a creature of chaos, and even he has not realized his full potential yet."

"They would have a way to craft such a thing in Nidavellir."

Odin smiled. He wondered when she would think of the dwarfs. He pretended to ponder the solution. "Yes, they could craft a bond that would hold him. Go to the dwarfs, then. Tell them we must have a fetter that will not break."

"Yes, Allfather. I will go to Nidavellir right away."

Freyja left, and Odin felt himself shifting in time and place. He saw a wolf, a silver ribbon, and a grievous wound.

Chapter Seventeen

The smell in the large cave was repulsive. Freyja had heard Odin's tales of how he had crafted the dwarfs from the maggots of Ymir's flesh, but she had never really considered it to be true until this moment. Overwhelmed by their odor and appearance, she had no problem imagining them as maggots.

"Do you have what I seek?" she asked.

The leader of this clan, a thin creature called Radsvid, spoke. "It is likely we have what you want, but if we do not, it can always be created. We are very eager to serve the gods, beautiful Freyja." He flashed a smile with brown and crooked teeth, his eyes crawling over her body.

"If you have it, then bring it forth," she said.

The other dwarfs in the room, a dozen or so, also ogled her, although less brazenly. He had introduced them all, but she could not tell them apart.

Radsvid was all sycophantic reassurance. "Oh yes, we will bring it indeed, good Freyja. We are honored to serve the whims of the gods." Freyja noted the intentional hesitation. Despite his pleas to the contrary, the dwarfs were eager to serve none but themselves, and she knew this. She signaled to her servants. They produced a small chest and set it down at her feet.

"I have brought payment." The chest was opened. The gleam of gold brought more light into the dark cave, and she smiled at the satisfied sound the dwarfs made as they gazed at the treasure.

"There is more for you if you can deliver this fetter to

me and it serves its purpose."

"Certainly this is fine payment, lovely Freyja." He looked up at her. His eyes were pale gray, giving an impression of blindness. She could not tell if he were old or young, but the movements of his body conveyed the sense of a worm wriggling, and she thought once again of the maggots of Ymir's flesh.

"But surely there is more you can offer us?" Radsvid's hand came up and traced her dress, touching the skin of her thigh.

She reached down and grabbed his throat, pulling him off his feet in one swift motion. She squeezed, and an audible snap reverberated from the walls of the cave. She dropped the lifeless body to the floor. The other dwarfs stared at her, fear evident on their faces.

"You would do well not to test me again." She let her eyes touch each of theirs, searing her threat into their brains. "Who speaks for you now?"

A smaller and slightly less repellent dwarf stepped forward. "I do, goddess." She detected no ulterior purpose in his voice. "I am called Aurvang."

"Will you bring me my fetter?"

Aurvang looked down at the body of his former leader and grunted at some of the others. He issued quiet orders in a guttural language that Freyja did not know, and they hoisted up Radsvid's body and took him deeper into the cave, to disappear in the darkness.

"We do not have it, but can craft such a thing. It will take time." He looked up at her with a glimpse of defiance but kept his distance. "And more gold."

Freyja nodded at her servants and they brought forth two more chests, setting them down at Aurvang's feet.

"Give the fetter to my servants when you are finished."

Aurvang nodded and bowed, keeping one eye on the

216

goddess while she quickly swept out of the cave.

Odin never ceased to be amazed at the ingenuity of the dwarfs. They were not gods, nor did they have access to any sorcery, and yet they were able to craft things that rivaled anything the Aesir could have created.

The thin, silver ribbon in his hand was certainly one of their finest achievements. It did not look like much, but Odin could sense its power and craftsmanship. This fetter would hold any creature in the Nine Worlds who was bound with it, and it would hold till Ragnarok, when all bonds would be broken and chaos would reign.

There was a knock on his door, and he summoned Balder inside his chambers.

"You summoned me, father?"

"Do you fear the Fenris Wolf, Balder?"

The question caught him off guard, although the answer was simple enough. "It is a dangerous creature with an evil sire, but no, I do not fear it."

"You think to be a match for its power?"

"Yes, father. It is a beast, and could not stand against any of the Aesir."

Odin nodded. "So if it were to attack me, you would not worry for my safety?"

Balder narrowed his eyes. "Why these questions? Does the wolf plan an attack?"

Odin considered the question. There was no plan, at least not yet, and Fenrir would not be a true danger for some time. He wondered if his son would remember this conversation when he emerged from Yggdrasil to begin anew.

"Answer my question," Odin said.

"It is a ridiculous thought, father. There are none who could stand against you, and you know this well. What is the meaning of these questions?"

Odin sighed. It was a heavy burden to know events to come but be unable to share them. He held out the silver ribbon to his son.

"What is this?"

"It is called Gleipnir, and it is a fetter created by the dwarfs. Take it."

Balder gently took it from his father. He held it in his hands and looked down at it with curiosity.

"It feels strong despite its weight. Why do you give it to me?"

"The time will come when you will have need of it. Keep it on your person, and be prepared to use it."

"Yes, father." He tucked it into his belt and wondered why his father would ask him questions that seemed to have such clear answers.

Fenrir turned when he heard a sound behind him, surprised that anything would be able to get so close without him knowing. He looked around and saw no one, although there was a faint scent in the air, one that smelled vaguely familiar. It was the scent of something he had smelled long ago, but he could not place it.

"Who is there?" he growled. There was no answer.

His time in Asgard—as he had eventually learned this place to be called—was filled with survival at first. There were creatures that lurked in the woods that were more powerful than he. But he was fast and smart, and ferocious when the need arose. Eventually he had become the one to be feared, and all other creatures either gave him a wide berth or became his victims.

But he had quickly become dissatisfied with being merely master of these woods. Once he was no longer concerned with his own safety, his rapidly developing intelligence drove him to seek answers to the mystery of his existence. He had seen the packs of wolves many times, and knew that he did not belong with them. They were basic creatures who were driven only by instinct, while he was aware.

He prowled closer to the cities and towns, listening at windows and doors, gathering what information he could. He had learned much that had been hidden from him.

These creatures called themselves Aesir, and they had much in common. Their stories told of battle and war, of fighting against enemies that threatened to destroy them. These enemies were giants, but it was strange that the Aesir hated them so much for something that had not yet happened.

Talk always led up to a thing called Ragnarok, but he was unclear about what it meant. They dreaded it, although Fenrir would not have said that they feared it exactly. It was more a thing to rail against, to present as if it were an enemy that could not defeat their spirits, even while they spoke of the Nine Worlds burning. It did not make sense to him, but there were particulars of the story that drew his attention.

Before the giants arrived, a massive wolf would swallow the sun, leaving the Nine Worlds in darkness. Talk of this wolf always sent waves of satisfaction through him. He did not know where it came from or how it could swallow the sun, but he liked the story nonetheless.

He also learned of a banished one, an Aesir who had been exiled. This being was spoken of with loathing and hatred, and he was rarely named. He was called Sly One or Trickster. He eventually learned his true name and recognized it, even though he had never heard it before. The name stirred something in him.

He had tried to pry answers from Tyr, but the one who had fed him, had helped him survive, would not tell him anything. Fenrir was certain that he knew, however, and loathed him for failing to reveal it.

He looked carefully amongst the trees in the darkness, searching for any sign of an intruder in his woods. The scent was still in the air, and he knew that this being was close, even if he could not see him.

"I will find you," he said to himself, his voice low.

He heard a faint voice then, like a whisper on the wind. He froze and pricked his ears up, carefully listening. Someone spoke in a voice so low that he could just barely make out the words.

"You are the rootless one," the voice said.

"Who are you?" He turned slowly, attempting to find the source of the whispering. In the edge of his vision, he saw something flapping in the slight breeze. He turned, but there was nothing there.

"You will be buried deep in Midgard."

"You speak boldly for one who hides in the trees."

"You have been betrayed."

His ears lowered at this. "Betrayed by whom?"

"He who offers you life even while he has taken it from you."

"You speak in riddles. Show yourself."

"You know nothing of she who birthed you."

The voice taunted him with the knowledge he sought. He remained silent.

"She was taken from you when you were new. And more were taken as well."

"What do you mean?"

"You are alone and not alone. There are none like you and there are two others like you. They were taken from you along with she who birthed you."

"Bah. You speak in riddles again." Despite his curiosity, he turned to walk deeper into the forest. He did not trust this disembodied voice.

He halted when a vague shape materialized in front of him. It was a man, lean with a fair face and reddish-blond hair. He appeared insubstantial; Fenrir could see the trees through him.

"Who are you?"

"I am the Sly One, the Trickster, the Sky Traveler. I am he who bore Sleipnir, he who takes many guises. I am Loki. Your father." The voice remained the same whispering on the wind.

"You are my father? What are you?"

"I was once of the gods, but have been exiled wrongly. And now you bear the brunt of their evil. But they have wronged you far more than me."

"What do you mean?"

"Your mother was murdered while you suckled. Your brother and sister were murdered, as well, innocent babes who had done no harm to any."

Fenrir felt the truth of what the apparition told him. Rage boiled up inside him. He had sought answers, and they had been bleaker than he imagined. While he did not feel for those he had never known, he felt for how he had been cheated.

"They will come for you as well. You were only let loose here for a time. They will bind you and torture you as they will do to me."

"Who killed them?"

"You know who. It is he who has a debt to repay, he who has attempted to make redress for those murders, he who has provided you with life to balance out those he took."

"Tyr," he growled, baring his teeth and tensing his muscles.

"Now you see why he could not provide you with the answers you sought."

"I will kill him." He pictured the god tossing him great

221

joints of meat and felt the hot stab of betrayal.

"He sees your threat and plans to move against you even now. It may be too late. He is powerful."

"I've grown strong here. I will come for him. I will feast on his insides."

"Then you must be swift. Any delay and you will be lost as well."

"You will not join me?"

"I cannot now. I lack the power. But we will meet soon enough, and I will relish the tale of how you killed Tyr."

Fenrir grunted in response and then sprinted away. As he ran into the darkness of the trees, Loki's form shifted.

He grew taller and thinner, and a gray cloak covered him. His skin wrinkled and his beard grew gray and long. In his hand was a tall spear. He watched Fenrir's form disappear into the darkness with his one good eye.

The Binding of Fenrir

Fenrir grew quickly on the golden fields of Asgard, and in time attained an enormous size. All the Aesir feared him, but would not stain Asgard's holy ground with his blood. Instead, he was allowed to continue roaming unfettered and unmolested.

As he grew in size the anger in his heart grew, and his grumblings worried the gods; so much so that none would agree to feed him for fear that they might be made into the wolf's meal.

All, that is, save Tyr. He alone of the gods did not fear the wolf, and would regularly throw him great joints of meat that would be greedily devoured. Fenrir, however, felt no gratitude towards Tyr. In fact, he felt nothing but hate and anger towards all of the Aesir.

Odin called a council one day to discuss the threat posed by the wolf.

"He is a danger to all," said Balder.

"He only bides his time before swooping in for the kill," said Hod.

"He must be bound before he does any harm," said Freyja. "I will travel to the dwarfs and have them craft a fetter to bind him."

Freyja traveled to Nidavellir to meet with the dwarfs. Deep in their underground world the dwarfs worked on all manner of objects, continually crafting items. Despite their ugly and base appearance, they were master craftsmen and could make anything if given enough time.

The dwarfs were not eager to do anything for the gods without payment, but once they had seen the size of Freyja's purse, the dwarfs set to work on a fetter so strong that nothing in the Nine Worlds could sunder it.

After nine nights, they produced the fetter and brought it forth for Freyja to examine. She opened the box they had placed it in and was surprised to see a slender ribbon, barely heavy enough to register in the hand of the goddess.

"What is this?" she asked.

"This is the ribbon Gleipnir, and it is the strongest bond ever crafted. Even the mighty Fenris Wolf will not be able to break it."

Freyja was doubtful. "How can so slender a ribbon hold the wolf? He would snap it in an instant."

The old dwarfs' eyes gleamed with mischief. "It is made from things that are rarely seen or felt. That is the secret to its strength."

Freyja was still not convinced, although she was loathe to voice the doubt she felt in front of such master craftsmen, old and ugly though they be. "What is it made of?" she asked.

The old dwarfs smiled wickedly. "It is made of six things: the silence of a cat fleeing, the beard of a woman, the roots of a mountain, the strength of a bear, the breath of a fish, and the spittle of a bird. These things may not seem to exist, but many such things are in our safekeeping."

Freyja was satisfied with the answer and took Gleipnir back to Asgard.

The Aesir knew that Fenrir would not agree to be bound, so they decided to use trickery on him. Fenrir was roaming the fields of Asgard when a group of Aesir approached him. "Certainly you have grown strong feasting on lamb and cattle raised on Asgardian soil," Balder said.

Fenrir regarded the bunch of gods with contempt. "Yes," he said. "I have grown large, and I can see that you are afraid of me."

The Aesir could see the evil smile on his snout, and were more certain than ever that Fenrir needed to be bound. Balder said, "You are indeed strong, but I am sure there are some things that are beyond even your abilities."

Fenrir's smile faded, to be replaced with a sneer. "It is said

224

that I will swallow the sun one day. How could there be any limit to my strength?"

Balder smiled inwardly. The wolf's vanity had ensnared him. "I am sure your strength exceeds all normal bounds, but the dwarfs in Nidavellir have crafted items that would deny even your ability."

Fenrir growled low and took a menacing step forward. The gods felt cold fear at his advance. "No item—dwarf or otherwise—can withstand my might."

Balder brought out the slender ribbon.

Fenrir eyed Gleipnir cautiously. He was not unwise, despite what the gods may have thought, and he suspected trickery in their actions. Still, he could not back down from a display of strength for fear of looking cowardly. "What is that thing?" he asked.

Balder took a step forward and held the slim ribbon out at arm's length. "It is but a ribbon—called Gleipnir—crafted by the dwarfs in Nidavellir. They claim it is unbreakable, but they are obviously too boastful. How could this light ribbon compare with your strength?" He made as if he were putting Gleipnir away.

"Hold, little god," Fenrir said. "I will allow you to wrap the ribbon around me if," he paused, eyeing the group of hated gods carefully, "one of you places his hand in my jaws as a sign of good faith."

Balder and the others had not expected this condition, and none were willing to put a hand in the wolf's mouth for the knowledge of what would happen should Gleipnir hold. Finally, Tyr strode forward and stuck a hand out bravely. The wolf's jaws closed lightly over the god's hand, and he said, "Wind the ribbon round me."

Balder lost no time in binding the wolf with Gleipnir. When he was finished, there was barely enough slack for Fenrir to breathe. The gods watched with anxiety as the wolf arched his back and strained his muscles, but there was no effect; Gleipnir held. Aghast, Fenrir pushed his muscles to their utmost. The ground

225

shook with the effort, and some of the gods were thrown from their feet, but in the end he was unable to even tear the mighty ribbon.

The deception now fully clear, he closed his jaws and sank his teeth into Tyr's arm. The god howled in pain as the wolf ripped his hand off and choked it down. From that day forward the wrist was known as the wolf-joint. The other gods laughed to see him bound.

Balder approached him, fear dissolved now that the beast was fully bound. "I suppose there are things that rival even your strength, like the wit of the gods."

Fenrir would have bitten Balder's head off, but he could not even move, and it felt as though Gleipnir was constricting him further with every breath.

The gods fastened Gleipnir to a large boulder and drove it down into the earth, into a hollow cave far below the surface where his struggle to be free would not even be felt on the surface. Fenrir snapped his jaws and attempted to do further damage, so one of the gods drew his sword and rammed it into the wolf's snout, a gag to keep his jaws closed.

And as Fenrir lies there, bound under the earth, his slaver continuously runs, a flowing river of spittle. He will lie there bound till Ragnarok, when his fetters will split and he will burst forth to have his vengeance on those who wronged him . . .

Chapter Eighteen

Unn dropped another load of logs near the fireplace. He was tired from hauling them, but was grateful that he was not in the kitchen. Restocking the supply of logs for the fireplaces throughout the hall was hard work, but at least it was not the sweaty drudgery of kitchen work where the fires never ceased. He would likely be chopping down wood in the next few days, and while that work was strenuous, he would relish being out in the open air.

He walked through to the main hall with his cart in tow. There were still large piles of logs stacked outside the front doors, and he had much work to do before Lord Tyr returned from Lord Balder's hall.

He had been both flattered and terrified to be asked to accompany Lord Tyr to deliver meat to the wolf. Those who went with him on such an errand were usually servants who had been there for much longer than Unn, and he wondered if it boded well for him. He was eager to impress the god so that perhaps he could rise in the ranks and become a personal servant, one who interacted with Lord Tyr on a regular basis, instead of one who simply attended to the day-to-day duties of the hall, as most servants did.

And had there not been a gesture? Lord Tyr had laid a hand on his shoulder, had told him that he would protect him if the wolf attacked. None of the Aesir were given to reassuring servants, but all Asgardians knew that they would protect this holy realm and its inhabitants—both gods and mortals—against the forces of chaos. To be personally reassured by a lord of the Aesir was surely a prophetic sign.

This thought in mind, he stepped up his pace. He did

not fool himself that one job well done would bring the attention of a lord of the Aesir. It was possible, however, that if he continued to serve with distinction he could become more than a castle hand.

The look of determination on his face faltered when he heard something slam into the front doors just ahead of him. He stopped, fear spreading through his body. The large wooden doors, strong enough to withstand pounding by giants, had buckled. Small wisps of dust from around the frame were caught by the few rays of light that streamed in from windows high overhead.

As he stood there, uncertain of what to do, the doors shook again. More dust fell from the frame, and Unn could hear the wood planks splinter. He backed away slowly, forgetting to let go of his cart.

Once more something slammed into the doors, and one was ripped from its upper hinge. The door twisted to the floor, and a dark shape climbed through the newly created hole. It saw him, and jaws filled with teeth opened as it prowled closer.

Unn was frozen in place, the handles of the cart firmly gripped in his hand. His eyes grew wider and he began shaking as Fenrir drew slowly closer to him, a low growl wafting through the space between them.

"Where is Tyr?" he growled. Fenrir brought his muzzle close enough that Unn could feel the hot and heavy breath on his face. It stank of rotten meat. Unn could not find the ability to answer. He simply stared up at the wolf in abject terror, unable even to look away.

"Where is Tyr?" he repeated.

Unn somehow managed to force his mouth to move, and squeaked out one word: "Gone."

Fenrir snarled, and Unn thought that he would now be eaten. Instead, the wolf drew back. As he looked on, he saw the flesh and fur on Fenrir's face rippling. His snout withdrew, and the face took on the slightest human quality. He sat back on his haunches, and Unn could see the arms change as well. The paws spread out and became hands with clawed fingers. He stood up, and his legs were that much more human.

He still towered over Unn, but he was no longer simply a wolf. He was somehow more terrible as a blend of wolf and man than he had been as merely beast.

He reached out a heavy, clawed hand and placed it on Unn's shoulder. "We will wait," he said. "But you will do something for me."

Unn nodded, grateful that he would not be ripped to shreds. Fenrir brought his head closer and stared Unn in the eye. Apart from the fear, he felt something quite different. He could hear the wolf's thoughts, and he knew what he wanted him to do. Reluctantly, Unn moved away to complete his task, compelled by the will of the creature.

"Have you ever seen its like before?" Balder asked, holding Gleipnir up for Tyr to observe.

Tyr reached out a hand and took it carefully. He was surprised by its weight, and he examined it closer.

"The Allfather said little about it?"

"Only that I would need it and that I should keep it close."

Tyr continued examining its length. "The dwarfs are indeed masterful craftsmen. It is slight, but brimming with power. I would not want to be bound with that slender ribbon."

"Nor I, but I wish that my father would be more forthcoming. Why does he not tell us what he knows?"

Tyr handed Gleipnir back. "To him, we are like children. One does not reveal all he knows to children."

"It is not the same. I am not some mewling brat who pisses himself. Are we not Aesir?"

"Even gods are not all-powerful, Balder. None but the Allfather has seen what is yet to be. Neither of us even existed when he pierced his side with Gungnir and hung on Yggdrasil. And we cannot know what it is like to see what is yet to be."

Balder was not satisfied with the answer. "That explanation is—"

He was cut off by a breathless servant. "My lord! I beg your forgiveness!"

"What is it?" Balder asked.

"Something is amiss at Lord Tyr's hall! The doors have been broken down, and Einherjar collect outside but will not enter!"

Tyr started from the room. Balder caught his arm.

"I will go with you."

He nodded, and the two gods sped from the room and through the main hall of Balder's keep.

The gathered throng of Einherjar outside of Tyr's hall was uneasy. They made way for the two gods as Balder and Tyr strode quickly to the splintered doors. Tyr grabbed one of the warriors nearby.

"What has happened here?"

The warrior stared back at him, glassy-eyed, and said two words that explained the entire situation for Tyr: "The wolf."

Tyr turned to Balder. "It is Fenrir." He turned back to the warrior. "Why have you not engaged him? Why do you stand out here milling about when one of the halls of the Aesir has been attacked?"

The warrior's face had a perplexed look on it, as though he did not understand the question. After an interminable amount of time in which Tyr felt tempted to throttle him, he said, "He will kill them."

Tyr let the warrior's arm loose. He and Balder drew their swords and walked to the entrance to his hall.

The doors were broken and splintered, but still partially attached to the frame. They could see little as they peered in, save that there was a group gathered in the middle of the hall. They looked at each other once before walking through the shattered doorway.

Their eyes adjusted quickly to the low light of the hall. In the middle of the large room a tight semi-circle of servants knelt on the stone floor, some whimpering with heads in hands, others quietly sobbing, still more silent and frozen with fear. Balder and Tyr could see the tall man-wolf just behind the protective throng, within easy striking distance of any of the poor souls who knelt in front of him.

Standing directly in front of Fenrir was another servant, one whose face he remembered. It was the boy who had brought out the meat for Fenrir, the one who had needed comforting. Tyr felt bile rise. The wolf had his hand clasped over one of the boy's shoulders, the long nails trailing down. It was a mock-protective gesture that held menace for the boy, even while virtually daring the two gods to move forward.

They stood their ground. The smile on Fenrir's face told Tyr what would happen if they came too close.

Tyr addressed Unn. "Are you harmed?"

"Tyr," Fenrir growled. "I have not harmed the man-child. I would not harm such a defenseless creature."

"What is it that you want?"

Fenrir brought his mouth down to Unn's ear and whispered something. Unn spoke, his voice wavering. "My lord, he wishes me to tell you that all servants in the castle have been brought here."

Tyr could see that it was true. There were dozens of them around the wolf, some close enough to feel his hot breath on their necks. "What do you want?"

There was a low growl. Tyr could feel it pass through him.

Unn said, "He wishes to know where he came from, my lord. He wishes to know the answers to the questions he has posed you." His voice shook, but he maintained a steadiness that Tyr admired, especially in one who was no warrior.

Tyr and Balder exchanged brief glances. Both knew that this would not go well. Fenrir was far closer to the servants than they were. If either of them moved forward, Fenrir could kill a score of them before they even reached him. This was not a situation that could be solved with steel. Tyr found himself wishing that Loki was there. He thought how the Sly One would have a way to trick the wolf, but then he realized whose spawn it was that he faced.

Tyr saw nothing to do but give Fenrir what he wanted.

"You wish to know where you came from? How you came to be here?"

Fenrir growled, "Yes."

"And you will release them," he gestured to the servants with his sword, "once I reveal the answers?"

"Yes."

He paused to gather his thoughts before beginning.

"You were taken from your mother when you were an infant and brought here."

Fenrir whispered again to Unn. "My lord, he says he knows this. He desires to know the full tale."

"There is little more to tell."

Fenrir's hand shot out, and he dug his claws into the shoulder of the closest kneeling servant. The woman was pulled to him, but did not have time to register any complaint before Fenrir leaned his head down and tore out the side of her neck. Bloody and twitching, he dropped her body to the ground at his feet, the whimpers and sobs of the remaining hostages increasing to a frantic pace.

Tyr moved forward, rage on his face, but was held back by Balder's tight grip on his arm.

"He will only kill more," he whispered. "We cannot win this way. You must tell him what he wants to know."

Tyr could only barely contain the fury he felt while staring at Fenrir's bloody smirk. The thought that he could have prevented that senseless death was like a dagger in his gut.

"Tell me all, Tyr."

"You will pay for that, beast," he mumbled under his breath. His knuckles were white on his sword hilt as he fought down his anger.

He told all he knew: traveling to Jotunheim to take the three children, the death of the infant, killing Angrboda, the stealing away of Fenrir and his brother, the casting of the one into the sea and the other into the forest. He only changed one thing. He claimed responsibility for killing the infant himself. When he was finished, Fenrir stared at him with plain loathing on his face.

"The exiled one is my father?"

"Yes."

"Where is he?"

"It is not known."

Fenrir stared at him, but said nothing.

"You know all. Now set my servants free."

"Tyr, you took all from me."

Tyr did not answer.

Fenrir smiled a toothy grin made the more insidious by the blood coating his fangs. Tyr did not like the look, but realized an instant too late what it meant.

"Release my servants," Tyr said, taking one step

forward.

Fenrir nodded slowly. He turned his head toward Unn and leaned in closer, as if to whisper something in his ear, as he had done before. Instead, as his face drew closer, his jaws opened wide, and he sank his teeth into the side of Unn's head.

Unn's hands flew up to his face in a reflexive gesture, but even if it had not been too late, he would have still been unable to counter the wolf's power. There was an audible crunch as Unn's skull was cracked, followed by the rending of meat as his head was torn in half. The boy dropped to the ground at Fenrir's feet.

Tyr's eyes went wide and he screamed out, "No!"

He charged, his sword flashing in the dull light of the hall, his eyes fixed on Fenrir. Balder was just behind him. But both were too far to prevent Fenrir from lashing out, eviscerating those servants who were closest to him. A few got to their feet and ran, escaping with their lives, but most were frozen in stark terror while the wolf gutted and slew those nearest him.

In the few seconds it took Tyr to reach Fenrir, the body parts of nearly a dozen servants lay scattered in front of the wolf. Tyr did not bother to slow his assault or level an attack with his sword, but instead plowed headlong into Fenrir. The two crashed to the ground, their limbs a flurry of movement.

Tyr smashed his sword hilt again and again into Fenrir's face as the two struggled on the stone floor. What his attacks lacked in precision, they made up for in brute strength, and Fenrir roared in fury while he attempted to throw the god off.

Balder herded the servants out of the way as a stream of Einherjar came in through the front doors.

"Get them away!" he screamed at the Einherjar. "Leave

the wolf!" He held his sword out like a barrier, and the warriors scrambled to lead those servants who could still walk out of the hall. Those that lay bloodied at Balder's feet were carried out. Some might survive, but most that Fenrir had attacked were already beyond help.

Tyr and Fenrir rolled on the ground, and Balder could see that Fenrir had reverted to his wolf form, his slavering jaws snatching at Tyr's face while they struggled. Balder drew closer, ready to charge in with his blade. The two flailed so wildly that he feared he would skewer Tyr in an effort to stab the wolf.

Tyr had his arms around Fenrir's neck and was attempting to wrestle the wolf to the floor. Straining with the visible effort, he called out to Balder, "The fetter! Ready it!"

Balder cursed himself for not remembering it. His father had said to be ready, and even though he had it on his person, he had still forgotten about it. He sheathed his sword and pulled out Gleipnir just as Tyr lost his footing and was thrown to the stone floor.

Balder leaped at Fenrir, but the wolf was faster than he had anticipated. He ducked down underneath the attack and sunk his teeth into Balder's thigh. The god yelled in pain, but the cry was silenced as Fenrir whipped his neck and shoulder muscles and slammed Balder to the ground. He released his hold on Balder's leg and pounced onto his chest, bringing his jaws to Balder's throat.

He was able to grab the wolf's throat with one hand and stop the muzzle from getting any closer, but he could feel the hot breath and spittle on his face, could see the rows of teeth as the wolf snapped at him. The beast was strong, far stronger than he had thought, and he was not entirely sure that he could continue holding him off. Gleipnir was clutched in his other fist, all but useless as he felt the steady, crushing pressure of Fenrir's attack.

Tyr was suddenly there, grabbing the wolf's muzzle and wrenching him off Balder. He flipped Fenrir onto his back and pressed one knee down onto the beast's throat while the wolf scraped at him with four claw-tipped paws. He was gouged in multiple places, each claw drawing a long cut across his chest, but he leveraged his body onto the wolf and managed to avoid most of the worst attacks.

"Bind him! Now!" he yelled at Balder.

Balder tackled the lower half of the wolf, immobilizing his rear legs, and began wrapping Gleipnir around them. Fenrir's fury increased. He curled his body up and then flexed out with his rear paws, tossing Balder from him. Tyr shifted his body to keep the beast still, but his moved position gave Fenrir an opening. He twisted suddenly and Tyr lost his hold.

Fenrir turned back and lunged at Tyr. His jaws snapped in front of the god's face, but fell short as he was grabbed from behind. He turned back to see Balder holding onto his tail with both hands. He jerked it loose and sent Balder stumbling, before launching himself at the unprotected side of the young god.

Tyr saw that Balder was about to be gutted by the wolf. He charged in and grabbed for the snout once more. He clamped his hands around the muzzle and prepared to flip the wolf onto his back, as he had done before.

Fenrir pulled his head back quickly, and Tyr lost his grip for the briefest of seconds. It was long enough, however, for Fenrir to sink his teeth into the meaty flesh of Tyr's right arm. The jaws clamped down, Tyr's entire hand stuck inside the wolf's mouth.

Fenrir wrenched his head away from Tyr violently, the arm still clenched in his teeth. There was a tearing sound and then a snap, barely audible over Tyr's gasp of pain. And then the god was on the ground, his severed hand now in the wolf's mouth.

Fenrir turned back to Tyr and smiled before choking down the hand. But his momentary gloating gave Balder an opening. He brought his fists down on top of Fenrir's head with all the strength he could muster. Caught unprepared, Fenrir bore the entire brunt of the god's attack on his skull. He crashed down to the floor, dazed.

Balder did not hesitate. He began wrapping Gleipnir around the wolf quickly, binding neck and then front legs first. Fenrir was quick to recover, and he shrugged Balder off, although Gleipnir remained loosely coiled around him.

Nearby Einherjar joined the fray. Fenrir attacked them wildly, but was less effective now that Balder had him partially tied. His jaws closed onto some of the Einherjar, but others continued to grab and hold him. They slowed him down enough for Balder to wrap Gleipnir around him several more times, bringing him gasping to his forepaws. Balder continued to bind him with Gleipnir, the fetter almost taking on a life of its own as each loop confined Fenrir's movements more and more.

Tyr slowed the flow of blood from his severed wrist with torn cloth, looking more angry than hurt. Once Fenrir was almost completely bound, he approached. He snarled menacingly, but the dwarfs' fetter had served its purpose, and he was now helpless.

"Tyr, your hand . . ."

"It will heal," Tyr said simply, a trace of bitterness in his voice. "We have stopped him. That is all that matters."

Fenrir growled at him. "I will take more than your hand! When I am free—"

Tyr cut him off. "You will never be free. You could have roamed these fields in peace, but you instead attacked those who sheltered you."

Fenrir spat his disgust. "Peace? What do you know of

peace, you who murder infants?"

Balder pressed Fenrir's face into the stone floor roughly. "Enough. You will not speak to your betters like that."

"Let him speak. He can do no harm now."

Balder reluctantly removed his hand, Fenrir's furious eyes on him as he withdrew.

"I will be free, and I will feast on your entrails. You will have to slay me."

Tyr grimaced as he tightened the bloody cloth around his stump, the flow of blood lessening with each passing moment. "No, we will not slay you. The Allfather has forbidden it. But you will never run free again." He turned to one of the nearby Einherjar. "Go and tell the High One what has happened here. Tell him we require his advice about what to do with the Fenris Wolf." The mutilated warrior nodded, but as they turned the Allfather was there, clad in his gray traveler's cloak with Gungnir in hand, disguised as a walking stick.

"He is bound," Odin said.

"Yes, Allfather," Tyr said.

"For now." His back to Tyr and Balder, Odin approached the wolf who could do nothing but wheeze through the tightening coils of Gleipnir. Odin put his hood up and brought his face close.

Fenrir saw the old face shift and change, the wrinkles smooth out, the gray beard withdraw and lighten. The familiar face—the face of his father—smiled once before shifting back. Trussed up, Fenrir could do little but feel the rage roil inside him.

Odin dropped his hood and turned back to Balder and Tyr. "Have him brought to Gladsheim," he said, before walking back out the door, leaving the two gods alone with the bound wolf, wondering what Odin had said to him to increase his fury.

Balder's Dreams

The sleep of the most handsome god was most troubled. Balder tossed and turned in his bed, unable to shake off the creeping sleep demons that haunted him night after night. He would wake with a sheen of sweat covering his body, mistaking the shadows for the rapidly fleeing wraiths from his disturbed slumber. Moments later he could not remember them; there was only the persistent feeling of dread hanging over him like a funeral pall.

All the gods were dismayed when he told them about his visitors. Despite their concerns and hand-wringing, however, none could offer any solution to what could be done to banish these dreams. It was his own father who finally decided to visit Niflheim to find an answer.

The one-eyed god mounted Sleipnir and galloped off for the underworld, the home of Hel, the half-corpse creature who reigned over the dead. Sleipnir crossed nine backwards flowing rivers before he stood face to face with Garm, the huge hound that stood guard at the gates of Niflheim. With a sharp spurring of Sleipnir, Odin leapt past the jaws of the beast and rode past the cold fields of the dead, onward to Hel's hall.

At the door, Odin found pathways strewn with gold, a welcoming for someone important.

He found Hel on her throne. Odin addressed the creature he had banished to this place so long ago. "Who is it that you plan to welcome into your realm?"

Hel did not answer at once, but instead let a sly smile spread across her face. "The tribute is for the one who will soon be joining me here."

Odin felt a sharp pain at her words. "You do not mean

Balder?"

"The handsomest of the gods will be my guest ere long."

Odin's brow was knit with distress. "Who is it that kills him? At least you can tell me that."

"It will be a tragedy that will rend the hearts of all in Asgard, made the more tragic by the blind hand of he who slays his brother."

Odin knew she meant Balder's brother, Hod. "Why does brother slay brother?"

"It is Hod and not Hod who will lay his brother low."

Odin said, "What can be done to prevent this from happening?"

Hel's smile grew wider. "You of all should know that fate cannot be prevented. You set Balder on this path long ago." With a gleam in her eye, she added, "Your own crimes will ever be your undoing, One Eye." And with that she closed her mouth and refused to say another word.

Odin reluctantly turned and left. His ride back was somber and silent, although he imagined the faces of the dead laughing at him as he made his way back to Asgard . . .

Chapter Nineteen

It had been months since Fenrir was bound and his stain removed from Asgard. They had taken him, wrapped and immobilized in Gleipnir, to Nidavellir, and sought out the expertise of the dwarfs once more. Masters of underground spaces as well as masters of craftsmanship, the dwarfs led them deep underground, till the stinking rot of Niflheim seemed only a breath away. Tyr had come, as well as Frey, and their servants carried Fenrir on a litter that dragged behind them. It took ten servants to drag the beast over the rough and rocky ground of the cave.

The dwarfs led them down long, winding tunnels into the blackness of the underground till they came to an expansive cavern with a wide platform of rock in the center. They dragged Fenrir onto it, and Balder brought out a sword and chain he had brought with him. In the center of the platform was a metal ring embedded in the rock, and the dwarfs attached one end of Balder's chain to it. He slid the other end around the blade of the sword and approached the silent beast.

Kicking him over onto his back, he put one foot on Fenrir's throat to hold him in place. With two hands he rammed the sword into the bottom of Fenrir's jaw and out the top of his muzzle to fully gag him and bind him to the boulder. He snarled savagely, but was unable to struggle because of Gleipnir's tight coils.

It was thus that they had left him. Chained and muzzled, frozen in that place till he died of starvation, or perhaps stuck there for eternity. Balder had no idea if the beast was immortal or not, but if he was, all the better; his suffering would be never-ending, a fitting punishment for so foul a creature. Balder could feel Fenrir's burning gaze on him, the anger thick and palpable. He could not keep a grim smile from his face as they left the wolf in the cavern to begin his endless agony.

Tyr ran his hand over the stump for the thousandth time. Despite the long months since the wolf had taken his hand, it had still not healed. It would never be healed. He could still feel the jagged teeth sinking in, ripping muscle and sinew from bone, separating flesh from flesh, and the memory of it made him sick.

It was not as if he had never suffered an injury before.There had been many over the course of his battles, and each time he had healed—sometimes quickly, other times more gradually—but all wounds had eventually closed, and he had been made whole again in time. But he had never been wounded like this before.

Never had a piece of him been so savagely ripped away, so effectively separated from his person. The loss went far deeper than simply a loss of a limb. It felt as if part of his identity had been ripped out, and in its place was a stinking abscess that refused to heal.

He paced his bedchambers, anger and frustration building in equal amounts, as they had each day since the injury. His servants stayed away from him, aware that he did not want to be bothered, and also fearful of his silent anger. They had never seen their master in such a state, and it worried them. His manner had ever been measured, rarely showing anger even when warranted. Perhaps those loyal to Thor were used to mercurial passions, but Tyr's servants had come to expect balance in all things with their lord.

He was aware of their misgivings, but could not contain

his feelings. Instead of roaming through his hall angrily, he chose to stay in his bedchambers and pace the floor to exhaust the bile inside him.

Despite the punishment Fenrir had received, he was not satisfied. In the moment he had not questioned the Allfather's dictate that the wolf not be killed, but as the months went by, he grew to resent it more and more.

He knew that the only thing that could sate him would be to meet the wolf in combat. Fenrir would not escape Gleipnir, however. The only possibility was that he might be freed at Ragnarok, although who knew when or if that would happen.

He found it curious that all his life he had felt dread at the thought of the end, but now he strangely looked forward to it. He was not patient, but he could wait. And while he did, he would anticipate the feel of his sword slicing Fenrir open.

Heimdall had seen the old woman crossing over Bifrost for leagues now, slowly and laboriously making her way to Asgard. It was not unusual for mortals to cross over onto Asgard for various reasons. The mason, to Heimdall's shame, would never have been able to cross had it been irregular to request entry onto Asgard. Many village wise men and witches made their way there to request audience with one or another of the Aesir, and such audiences were granted often enough to make the long journey across Midgard worthwhile.

Occasionally, bereaved fathers and mothers would attempt to see sons who had been sped from a battlefield death by Valkyries. Some left satisfied that their sons were serving the High One, constantly preparing to defend Asgard at Ragnarok. They could see their son, now an immortal warrior, and feel a measure of peace upon learning that his death had meaning. Others left with different emotions, seeing instead a hollowed-out ghoul with missing limbs and scars from repeated injuries. They likely thought that their sons were restored, as if a blade had never even touched them when the Valkyries swept them up to Asgard. But Odin did not promise such things; he had no need for warriors that were fair of face and body, only those who could wield cold steel.

Heimdall scoffed at the notions of these mortals. How could they pay homage to the Aesir—gods of battle—and think that their sons would somehow become beautiful once taken to Valhalla? Those that valued such things would do better to worship the Vanir. Or better yet, they should stay where they belonged in the realm of mortals, where they would not have to see a dead son who still walked after having the top of his head shaved off by a blade, his ill-fitting helmet the only thing keeping his brains from spilling out onto the ground.

He did not know who this old crone was who so slowly made her way across Bifrost, but he knew that she was here either to beg audience with one of the gods, or to see a long-dead son. Whatever the reason, she was bound to leave disappointed, and Heimdall had little patience for the small concerns of those who dwelt below.

As she got closer, Heimdall marveled at how she had managed to make this entire journey, so slowly did she move. He had never seen such an old human before, and he wondered how she had survived the perils of her journey. Usually they came in groups. The dangers were too numerous to count: wolves, thieves, and murderers, not to mention giants and other evil creatures that preyed on humans. And yet here she was, alone and feeble, as old as Yggdrasil itself by her looks. And she was hideous. Her face was like an old, dirty sack that had been gnawed by goats.

Her body was bent over so far that Heimdall wondered if her jaw might scrape the ground when she spoke, and her back bore a mountainous hump that could have carried a small child had it been hollow. Even her smell was foul, the stench of death and piss.

"Hail, brave Heimdall," she said weakly, as she came close enough to hear his response. What little remained of her teeth were blackened stumps that hung precariously in her gums, ready to stick into the flesh of any apple she bit into.

He narrowed his eyes at her, this ugly old crone who so presumptively attempted to gain access to the realm of the gods, and felt an odd amusement creeping through him. This pathetic, wizened shell of a human, this shambling sack of bones and skin, had made a trip from her village to the foot of Asgard by herself. Despite her appalling nature, she was worth some small measure of respect for her sheer tenacity.

"What do you seek in Asgard?" he said, not unkindly.

The old crone took long minutes to catch her breath and answer, her hump heaving with each gasp. "My son was long ago taken by the Valkyries. I would like to see him before I pass into Niflheim."

It was as he thought, although he shook his head at the futility of the request. "When was he taken to Valhalla?"

"Many years ago, when I was much younger. He was defending our village against marauders, but there were too many. Our men managed to fight them off, yet the toll was heavy. My son stood against them and killed many before he was cut down."

Heimdall was not so hardened that he did not feel for a mother's pain, although he constantly wondered at the thoughts of these mortals. They longed to go to Valhalla and serve the gods, and they railed against an ignominious death that sent them to Niflheim. Yet they sorrowed for their sons when they achieved a glorious death and reward. He could not understand them.

For this woman he felt a bit more pity when he considered what she was likely to encounter in the person of her son. If he had been taken to Valhalla when this old crone was young, then it was likely he had been in Asgard for more than a mortal generation, fighting and preparing for Ragnarok. Few of the Einherjar escaped injury for long. Would there be much for her to even see? Would the boy even have a jaw left with which to speak? Would he have arms to embrace her?

"I will send you to the High One's servant. He will hear your request and pass it on to the Allfather, who will decide whether to grant it."

Her smile of gratitude made Heimdall wince. "Bless you, Lord Heimdall. My village will sing your praises."

He nodded. "I will send servants with you, to cart you to Valaskjalf." He turned his head and motioned for some of his servants. A small cart was brought, and he helped the crone into the seat.

"May the Allfather grant your request," Heimdall said as the cart began to pull away.

"Bless you, Lord Heimdall," she said once more before turning. Heimdall was glad to be rid of her. Tenacity or no, her appearance was so foul that it lingered like the stench of rotten leeks. He hoped that he would not have to see such decrepitude in a mortal again. He turned back to watch the cart pull further into the distance, and some movement around the old crone caught his attention. He looked closer and saw nothing, grateful not to have to gaze at her visage again.

He did not see her wide, wolfish smile as the cart pulled her away from Bifrost.

246

The servants could barely keep up with Thor's relentless demand for more food. Despite having his plates—there were many in front of him—repeatedly filled to capacity, the Thunderer continued to make the contents disappear almost as they were filled. His insatiable palate was legendary, and he was proving that once again at this feast.

For all his respect for Thor's immense power and strength, Balder detested sitting next to him at these gatherings of the gods. The red-haired, red-bearded giant inhaled nearly everything within reach, and there was scarcely a word emitted from him while food and drink were proffered. At most he would grunt, point, or simply say "more" to whatever servant happened to be unlucky enough to be near, and then they would scurry forth to grab another heaping platter.

Balder usually busied himself with trying to avoid the spray of food that came his way, while simultaneously keeping his own plate out of the Thunderer's reach. There was scant time for anything else; each time he diverted his attention from the boundless stomach to his left, he would feel wet droplets of mead or crumbs of whatever food was being stuffed into Thor's gaping maw striking him.

To his right Tyr was mostly spared the assault of food and drink. He sullenly stared out at nothing in particular while most of his food went untouched.

Balder slid his chair to the right and leaned over, ignoring Thor's assault. "You do not eat," he said. "What troubles you?"

Tyr turned to him, arms folded. He looked at him for long seconds before answering, some thought brewing behind his dark eyes. He looked away before answering. "It is nothing."

The servants continued their flurry of activity, most concentrating on keeping Thor's plate full, but a significant number were dedicated to refilling horns and cups with mead and bringing large plates laden with meat for the other gods who filled Gladsheim's vast main hall. At the head of the table, Odin sat eating slowly, lost in some other time or place. The other gods talked amongst themselves while they indulged in the bounty of Asgard. Gladsheim was filled with stories of battles won, trolls defeated, and bawdy tales that sent roaring laughter high up into the rafters.

Balder leaned closer to Tyr so the other gods seated nearby could not hear. "It is plain on your face that you are thinking of the wolf."

Tyr looked back at him and unconsciously stroked the stump from his missing hand. The wound had been covered over with a metal sheath of dwarf design, a thing that both eased the pain and provided a weapon or defensive foil. "How could I not think of Fenrir when every moment of every day I see the handiwork at the end of my arm?"

Balder felt uneasy. It had been his fault that Tyr had lost his hand to the beast. But his guilt was useless; it would not bring the hand back.

"If I could hack off and give you my own hand I would," he said, fully sincere. "Maybe the witch," he indicated Freyja with a nod of his head, "could use some of her sorcery to bind my severed hand to your arm."

Tyr eyed him squarely. There was a nervous moment before he suddenly burst out in laughter. "Ha! I believe you would, at that. Careful, lest I take you up on your offer!"

He seemed to lift out of his mood as he clapped Balder on the back. Balder felt some small measure of relief. He knew that the matter was not entirely resolved; in fact, he was not certain it would ever be. For now, here in Gladsheim at least, the two could nearly pretend that the incident had never happened.

He looked up to see his brother, Hod, walking over to him with two cups held carefully out in front of him, his blind eyes staring vacantly ahead. He set one down in front of Balder and held on to the other.

"What is this, brother?"

"It is a mead I have had brewed with a new spice. I wanted you to be the first to try it. I thought this feast a good time to bring it out."

Balder held the cup to his nose and sniffed. "What is the spice? I have not smelled it before."

"It grows on the trees near my hall. It has small white berries, or so I am told. It is said to increase strength in . . . certain pursuits."

Balder smiled. "Well, I suppose one can always benefit from increased strength." The two laughed. "Let us have a taste then." They both lifted cups to their lips and took a slow drink.

"What do you think of it?" Hod asked. "I cannot see your expression."

"No, I suppose you cannot. It is unique. I have not tasted anything like it before." He looked into the cup and saw the liquid swirling. "I do feel the beginnings of a strange sensation. Nana will have to attest to my increased strength later."

Hod smiled. "Then you should be careful, brother, that you not drink too much. You would not want your consort to be injured."

Balder chuckled. "We should get her a cup of it, as well. Perhaps we will shake the walls tonight!"

"I am afraid I only have this small amount for now. It was brewed especially for you."

"I suppose I will have to carry the weight, then. Thanks to you for bringing it. I must return the favor soon."

"There is no need for that, brother. Your drinking it is reward enough for me."

Balder tilted his head back and drained the remaining liquid. When he set the cup back down on the table Hod was no longer there. He looked around to see where he had gone, but there was no sign of him, although he could easily have been absorbed in the movement and activities of the servants.

The quick movement of a rat's tail scurrying across the stone floor distracted him for a moment. He wondered why his brother would leave so quickly, and also how he had managed to do so. A conversation for another time, he supposed, and he returned to his plate.

None could fathom his burden. To be simultaneously present, past, and future took a toll on Odin that none of the other gods could know. It had been thus since he had hung on Yggdrasil, learning the way to unlock the paths to the future and past. And it had proven to be his everlasting sorrow.

Even in so simple a place as Gladsheim, in the middle of a feast, he could not be fully present for long without drifting off to another time and place. He knew what the others thought—did he not know all?—that he stared out into empty space, present yet absent at the same time. They would never dare voice any derision, and not because they feared him, but because he was the Allfather: he who had carved up the giant Ymir's body and created the Nine Worlds, he who had drunk from the Mead of Poetry, he who had created the race of men, or so the stories went. The truth was far murkier than the legends, and even he could not remember the events themselves, but rather memories of memories of things that might have happened in such and such a way.

As he traveled through the past, seeing events unfold time and again, he was struck by how new and unfamiliar they were at times. They were always uncertain, though, and there were times when he witnessed a series of events that were the same and yet different. In one instance, he stood together with his brothers, Vili and Ve, and they had slain Ymir. In another, he was alone and had done it himself. In yet another version, Ymir had slain him instead. He could not tell which was the right version of events, if any, and it led him to further question any vision he might have.

More problematic was the doubt he felt even while he lingered in the present. He could never be completely certain that whatever he was experiencing was indeed the here and now. At times he was fairly sure, but there was often some small thing that cast his mind to doubting. By far the most troubling experiences he had, however, were when he saw the past, present, and future all at once and could not separate them. This did not happen often, but when it did, he was so disoriented as to be nearly useless. What might it look like to Balder, Thor, and the others to see him talking and gesturing to nothing but open air? He had been lucky not to have had that experience yet, but who knew what might happen in the future?

He laughed bitterly. *He* knew, and that was his curse.

For the time being he was in the present, and he sat back in his high seat witnessing the scurry of servants, sniffing the odors of the feast, savoring the sounds of laughter and talk. It was rare that he would be attached to the present for such a length of time, and he enjoyed the feeling, recognizing that it was likely fleeting.

As he let his eye wander through the main hall, he was struck by a feeling of familiarity that went deeper than normal. This was not a feeling of having been in a place before, since he had of course feasted and held council in

Gladsheim thousands of times across the eons. Instead, it was a feeling that he had seen this exact scene, this exact feast, somewhere before.

He was not surprised; he had this feeling often, one of the perils of perennially wandering about through time. There was a nagging feeling about it, however, and he suddenly remembered why. The look on his face becoming grimmer, he slowly scanned the hall. It did not take long before he found what he sought.

Hod turned his head on the way to Balder and met Odin's gaze for the merest of moments. In that brief time, an understanding passed between the two—both knew what was to happen next, and both also realized in that sharp moment that Odin would do nothing to prevent it from happening.

Before turning his head, Hod gave a brief and shallow smile, so slight it might not even have occurred, and then the moment was over. He brought a cup full of mead for Balder, and the two talked for a moment before draining their cups.

In the instant before Balder could set his empty cup down on the table, blind Hod looked once more over to Odin. Their eyes locked again, and then Hod melted away, the only evidence that he was ever there the small rat darting through the maze of servant's feet.

He turned his gaze back to Balder, who was animatedly talking to Tyr. He was glad to see that the wall between them was beginning to crumble, that Tyr would not forever hold his injury against Balder. It would not go away easily, for the reminder would be with him forever, but after a time he would remember that they were brothers and comrades-in-arms, with a common enemy and a common goal.

But of course, the time for such a reconciliation was too short. It would never occur.

He felt a tightness in his chest as if someone squeezed

his heart when he thought of the moment to come. He felt powerless, as he often did when faced with the unforgiving tide of time, but he wondered also if it were inevitable, as he had always thought. He could stop the events in motion with but a simple gesture. His son could live, could stand by his side at Ragnarok to face the tide of chaos that threatened Asgard.

And yet he did nothing.

He watched as the first convulsions changed Balder's expression from carefree frolic to panicked terror, as those around him stared wide-eyed for a moment before calling for help, imploring that something be done. Tyr's voice was loudest of all, even over the horrified screams of Balder's own mother, Frigg.

Odin sat stone-still as he watched his beloved son first froth at the mouth, and then vomit blood and bile while his body jerked painfully this way and that, sending plates and cups sprawling to the floor of the hall. He observed quietly while the hall erupted with outrage and horror, while Frey and Freyja rushed over and hurriedly cast whatever spells they could, all for naught, as Balder's insides betrayed him and turned to writhing liquid. He continued to sit in his chair as Balder's last throes slowly died down and he slumped onto his back on the table, his arms thrown out, while the gathered throng of gods screamed and howled curses to the heavens with red, tear-streaked faces.

And then it was done. His son lay dead on the table not twenty steps away, the paroxysms of his final moments now only existing in the memories of those who had watched him die.

Odin stood and walked slowly over to Balder's body. The knowledge that he could have prevented this from happening weighed heavily upon him, but he sloughed it off. None could fathom his burden, could understand the decisions that must be made by him alone.

He put his hand on Balder's chest and whispered, "Good journey, my son." And then he turned and quietly walked away, the image of Loki's Hod guise permanently etched into his mind's eye.

Chapter Twenty

The gods watched in silent stillness as the servants piled belongings and treasures onto the sturdy and finely-crafted long boat. They formed a long, slow-moving procession, laden with weapons and armor, silver utensils for eating, hollowed-out drinking horns gilt with gold, finely-wrought clothing and tapestries, chests filled with gold, silver, and gems, and other goods that had previously been in Balder's hall. Each in turn laid the items carefully onto the deck of the boat, mindful to leave a small space around the pyre in the center, the wooden platform upon which lay Balder's lifeless body.

The procession of servants, deprived of their burdens, filed away with heads hung low. The snake-like file crested a hill, and the row upon row of Asgardians standing shoulder to shoulder parted to allow them to pass. Once the last of the servants had disappeared behind them they closed ranks, creating seamless lines at least ten deep stretching out along the shoreline as far as could be seen. All wore somber looks upon their faces, with jaws clenched in anger.

The Aesir surrounded Balder's boat, awaiting a final push into the surf.

With a silent nod from Odin, Tyr strode forward into the shallow breakers with torch in hand and set fire to the kindling at the base of the pyre. As the flames rose and Tyr stepped back, Thor walked to the prow. Pausing for a moment while the pyre became slowly engulfed in flames, he grasped either side of the dragon figurehead with his massive hands and pushed the boat out onto the calm, dark sea.

The boat drifted slowly, the flames rising ever higher, climbing up the mast steadily and setting the square sail ablaze, spreading from the pyre to the crossbeams of the deck, and from there to the sides, all the while moving further and further from shore. The assembled gods looked on in silence, none taking their gaze from the fiery last rites.

The reflection on the calm waters created an aura of light as the flames consumed the boat, leaving no part untouched. The fire reached high into the night sky, sparks emanating like fireflies giving one final homage to the lost. The conflagration reached a peak, the warmth from the flames touching those who stood on the shore, before the rapidly disintegrating hull began to fail and the ship started its slow descent into the dark water.

Eyes followed it sink down, the water extinguishing the flames with an audible hiss. The mast remained intact in defiance of the fire that ravaged it—the sail had turned to cinders almost instantly—and it stubbornly remained vertical as the boat descended to the depths, finally disappearing with a brief and final snuffing out of the last of the flames.

And then it was done. What remained of Balder's body was food for the fishes, and the once-fine longboat that had carried him with speed and steadiness across turbulent seas was no more. He had taken all his prized possessions with him, although even the gods themselves did not really know if they would be of use in Niflheim.

Those on the hills turned first, almost as one, and slowly walked back towards the sanctuary of Asgard to resume their lives. A pall hung over them, and not one failed to consider how this tragic death might signal the beginning of the end. The Aesir lingered for some time before finally approaching Odin, each placing a hand on his shoulder in turn, and walking away with eyes cast down, a slow and staggered procession leading back to their great halls.

Finally he stood alone, still gazing at the empty sea where Balder's boat had gone down. The High One smiled a rueful, bitter smile. "You may approach," he said. His voice, despite the low, whispered pitch, projected clearly to the solitary figure on the low, rocky outcropping. "I am alone here, as you sought."

The bird perched on the rocks that hung over the sea grew larger and changed form till it was no longer a bird, but a man. Loki hesitated only briefly before jumping down to the sandy shore and making his way over to the Allfather.

"You knew I was here." Loki paused, waiting for a response before realizing that none was necessary. "Why did you let Balder die?" he asked.

"Who are you to question my motives? You are less than a flea to one such as I, one who has crafted worlds with his bare hands." Odin stared at him with menace in his eye. "You put your life at risk in coming here."

"If you wanted me dead, you would have acted on it by now," Loki replied, failing to be intimidated. "Why not point out my presence to Thor? Or Tyr? You did not reveal me to the gathered throng just as you did not reveal me in Gladsheim when I served Balder his final cup of mead. But why?"

Odin turned away and stared out at the empty sea. "You cannot hope to understand." The menace was absent. In its place was cold apathy.

"As ever, you misjudge me, Allfather. I know far more than you give me credit for. Perhaps the other Aesir would be interested to know how we locked eyes in Gladsheim, how I gained your approval for my dark deed."

"They would not believe you. You are the Father of Lies."

257

Loki was nonplussed. "So it is said. Still, there could be insinuated the tiniest doubt, which would be fed till it bore sour fruit. What would they think of the High One then, when it is finally revealed that you as much as murdered your own son, and in conjunction with he who is most hated in Asgard?"

Odin turned to look at him, the expression on his face impossible to read. "You will not tell. I have foreseen it, just as I have foreseen all that has led to this moment, and all that follows. Do not fool yourself that you rule your destiny."

Loki felt cold annoyance rising in him. He should have expected that Odin would attempt to diminish what he had done. He stabbed back at him with his words. "And what is my destiny? To sow discord and misery throughout Asgard? I have done at least some of that."

"You bring forth what must be brought forth. You begin what must be begun."

"You speak in riddles. You still have not answered my question."

"There will come a time—sooner than you dream—when you will lament what you have set in motion. Your suffering will be great, greater than any who have ever existed. And it will turn your heart even blacker than it already is." He paused, narrowing his eye at Loki, gauging the effect his words had on him. "None can comprehend my purpose, and you are only an ignorant pawn being moved by my unseen hand. You flatter yourself to think that you are of higher import than that."

Loki refused to be taunted. "You do not lessen my revenge for your petty manipulations. I have taken one from you, and you do not fool me that the wound does not go deep into Asgard's heart."

"It was a necessary death."

"If only the other Aesir realized your scheming. Who

258

will you sacrifice next for your grand purpose?"

Odin glared at him silently, and Loki was chilled by his cold stare. "I will see the Nine Worlds burned. And you and I will meet one last time. Then you will learn the truth of my manipulations, to your sorrow."

With difficulty, Loki forced down his awe of the High One. "I have no need to continue on this path. I have taken from you, and need do no more than let the wound fester. From here on, our paths diverge."

Turning his head to stare at the empty sea where Balder's boat went down into eternity, he felt again a satisfaction at what he had done. Odin could never take back Balder's murder. And he would never be free of the terrible knowledge that he had let it happen.

He closed his eyes and felt his form grow smaller, lighter. With a flap of his newly-formed wings, he soared off towards Midgard.

Loki stared out at the stream, his eyes following it as it wound down to the sharp cliff, where the water fell over the side in a continuous rush to the sea below. It was not wide or deep enough to be called a river, but neither was stream the most fitting designation. It moved quickly and submerged him up to his waist in parts. Its span was wider than a strong horse could leap, and as it made its way down the gradual slope it was hindered by rocks that had fallen from higher up on the mountain side.

It would be hard to catch a fish in this stream, he thought, which was why he had chosen this very location.

He knew that the impending confrontation with the Aesir was inevitable. All would learn that it was he who had killed Balder, and this was as he had wanted it. The anguish would be greater if they knew it was he. He wanted them to realize that it was their own actions that had brought this

259

upon them. How much more would they feel the pain of Balder's loss once they learned that their own misdeeds had come back to haunt them?

He wondered what they might do to him if they caught him. Surely there would be no instant death; they would want him to suffer. He was not fool enough to think he could withstand them should they come together. But he did not need to withstand them if he could elude them.

He had built the shack quickly, shifting himself into a giant so that his strength and size were greatly increased. In this form he could easily carry much more and work much faster, and he availed himself of the trees and large rocks nearby to construct a shelter that could almost be called a house, although it was somewhat smaller. Still, it was sturdily constructed, and would serve its purpose till they came.

But was it inevitable that they find him? He had taken precautions—a remote location far from any who might see him, his own power used to dispel traces of his presence so that he appeared to be nowhere, other measures that might serve to blind those who sought him. It was said that Odin could see all when he looked out over the Nine Worlds, but many things were said on Asgard, and many of them were not true or even possible. Odin's vision was far and wide, but perhaps it was not all-seeing. Perhaps he had taken enough precautions to prevent himself from being discovered.

It was useless to ponder things he could not control, and so he instead thought on those he could. The stream, at least, provided an easy escape route should they find him. And if this proved necessary, then he would go somewhere else. In time he would find what he sought, and then running would be unnecessary.

He sat down on the ground and closed his eyes. The

power flowed seamlessly out of him now, coming instantly when bidden. It felt more like an intimate piece of his person than an outside thing, and he had learned to manipulate it for purposes other than shifting.

He felt it flow out in dozens of slim, questing tendrils, each taking a different path. In moments they had scanned hundreds of leagues, each seeking signs of the two he sought. He did not know how long it would take, and the Nine Worlds were vast, but he felt sure that he would find them. He had time enough for now. He would find his sons, and when he did, the need for retreat would be over. Then would be the time for facing the Aesir on their own terms. Together they would raise armies that would make the gods tremble.

Chapter Twenty-One

Loki stood on the edge of a deep pit, so deep that the blackness swallowed the bottom. He knew, however, that it was not bottomless, that there was something down there. He had been brought here, but he did not know how or by whom.

There was a sense of pain and anguish, and he heard low groans of agony rising up out of the pit. At first they came from one source, but as he listened closer, he realized there were hundreds of low voices there, perhaps thousands, just beyond his sight in the blackness below. He could not make out what was being said, but he thought they spoke to him. He got down on his knees and leaned further over the edge to hear the voices more clearly.

Fear crawled across him like a wave of spiders. Something was down there that he did not want to see, and yet he knew that it must be revealed. As he leaned over further, there was the sensation of falling, the desperate wheeling of hands to grab onto something before he spilled forward and fell headlong into the pit.

He stood on some sort of shifting ground, ensconced in the darkness at the bottom of the pit. He did not remember striking ground after he fell, but as he craned his head back, he could see a small circle of light far above him.

He walked slowly forward, the ground shifting and pulsing underneath his feet like a living thing, the moaning of voices louder and yet more indistinct; more like an amorphous group who all spoke at once, but none of whom could do more than moan in despair. As he put one foot precariously in front of the other, he realized that he was being slowly funneled forward, the voices leading him toward something. He was not sure that he wanted to continue, but he knew that he must, that he was being led towards a revelation.

In his periphery he could see movement. It was slow and shambling, and there were snatches of pale white that appeared and then melted back into the surrounding darkness. He could also hear raspy, labored breathing, and the sound of wet flesh rubbing against wet flesh. The smell was fetid and rotten, but there was a strange and pleasant undercurrent, something that redeemed it in some way that was unclear.

The blackness faded, and a solitary figure stood across from him, a large hall just behind. It loomed over the figure and looked as if it might fall. It was patterned after a face, with two rows of windows creating the image of makeshift eyes, and a massive door with jagged top and bottom that looked like a toothed maw ready to devour any who entered.

The figure who stood in front was female and slight of build. As he approached her, he could not tell if she was the destination or if it was the imposing structure that rose up behind her. She wore a black, hooded cloak, but her face was visible underneath the hood; a beautiful, young face, with tufts of raven-black hair that spilled out from the corners. She held out a hand, her pale white skin contrasting with the dark of the cloak, and beckoned him forward.

The familiarity was palpable; this was someone he knew. He was doubly certain that he had never met her, which made the sense of familiarity even stranger. He stepped forward, unable to refuse her summons.

She spoke from within the hood. "Have you found what you sought?" She asked the question with the air of someone who already knew the answer.

"I have found some things, but others are hidden." He paused, trying to peer deeper into the darkness of the hood. "Do you know where my sons are?"

"I am not your son," she replied. She reached up with her hands and pulled the hood back. For an instant, her face was bare of flesh and muscle, a powder-white skull that stared back with eyeless sockets, but the image was gone quickly.

She was young, with pale beauty that rivaled Freyja's. Her skin was white and flawless, and her black hair fell in gentle curves just past her shoulders, which he could see now that the hood was down.

"You do not know what you seek," she said.

He eyed her curiously. For all her youthful appearance, she seemed far older. She reminded him of Idun, an ancient timelessness that exuded the wisdom of the distant past. But with this one, there was a difference. Where Idun radiated life, she absorbed it. He could feel her presence pulling him in, intent on devouring him. It was not evil or monstrous; like Idun, she was a primordial creature, one who existed outside of the normal realms of the Nine Worlds.

"I will find them soon." He felt a sliver of defiance rising up in him, but he knew that it was misplaced. This girl was not his enemy.

"Your army is incomplete. You will fail." Out of the folds of her cloak she produced an infant swaddled in black. She held it out for him, and he stepped forward, taking the small bundle. He let the swaddling cloth fall, and he could see the gaping, bloody hole in its throat, so wide that it nearly encompassed the whole neck. As he held the child at arm's length, shocked by the wound, its head lolled backwards and fell to the ground. In disgust, he dropped the headless infant at his feet.

He looked up to meet the eyes of the girl, and saw her cloak fall to the ground. From her waist up she was flawless perfection. Below that, her body was shriveled and black, with bones visible where the flesh had been eaten away by the maggots still crawling on her, giving rise to the clouds of flies that buzzed around her.

Beneath his revulsion was the hint of a discovery that he could not fully grasp. As he stared at her, her smile wide with satisfaction, the hall began to fall toward them. With no way to avoid its immensity, he reflexively put his arm up to shield himself. The hall crushed them both. He felt his bones snap like dry timber, and his body was reduced to pulp. The pain was a white torrent blinding him to anything else.

And then he was back in his cabin. It was night, and he lay on the floor, the pain fading as quickly as his memories of what had just happened. He felt himself for injuries, but there were none; he was intact and unharmed. He rose slowly, shuddering once more with the remembered pain of being crushed by Hel's massive hall. He shook his head and rose to his feet.

A figure was there with him, cloaked in black.

As before, she was slim and her face was lost deep in the recesses of her hood. She was less substantial, however; he could see through her, and she wavered like the mist forms of the Norns.

"You will come to me," she said. "I will give you the means to take your revenge."

He stepped forward, but she held up a hand. The flesh was rotted, and skeletal fingers poked out from blackened skin.

"Seek me out when you find my brothers. Farewell, father."

The form disappeared, leaving Loki alone.

He did not understand how this could be. Hel had

existed for eons. How could she be his daughter when she had been ancient long before he ever took in his first breath? How could an infant who had been murdered only a dozen seasons ago somehow become ruler of the realm of the dead?

And she had brought him to her realm, he was certain of that.

She had said that his army was incomplete, and so it was. But now he could raise the army he needed to storm Asgard. He would lead a horde of giants, and his three children would be at his side. They would be backed by an army of the dead, of all those who had died and failed to achieve Valhalla. And how they must thirst for revenge on the Aesir they had worshiped, and who had sent them to Niflheim to rot in darkness.

He dismissed the confusion he felt at the realization that his daughter was the mistress of Niflheim. It did not matter how—or even if—it was true. What mattered was that he would lead an unending army against Asgard, and even the might of the Aesir would fall before him.

The faint smile that began to spread across his features was cut short as a thunderclap shook the cabin. He looked out the window. The night was clear, but he saw a rolling line of thunderheads in the distance, a dark bank of clouds that portended something more ominous than any storm. Lightning flashed, a massive strike that arced across the sky.

"No," he muttered, the impending peril quickly setting his nerves on edge. "Not now. Not now."

He turned to the door, ready to dash out before they could reach him. He stopped in mid-stride as another flash of lightning silhouetted the figure at the door. He was lean and muscular with sword drawn. He was also missing a hand.

"You cannot run from us," Tyr said.

266

Loki quickly considered his choices. Even in the peak of health, he would not be able to best Tyr. And Thor was with him somewhere nearby, making any attack futile. He felt for the chaos inside him, barely there after sending it out to find his sons. There was enough for a shift into a small, weak form, a form that he had planned on using when he first found the stream.

He took a step back towards the window. Tyr matched him and took a step into the house, sword held at the ready. Loki glanced at his other hand, noting the metallic sheath that covered it.

"You will never lay hands on me, Tyr." If he could not harm him physically, at least he would do so with words.

Tyr sneered at him. "Your insults do you a disservice. They only give us further reason to cause you pain." He took another step forward.

Before Loki could reply, there was a great rending sound from above as part of the roof was ripped up. Eyes flashing with lightning, red hair and beard ablaze, Thor threw the roof from him with no more effort than a child discarding a blanket. He clutched Mjolnir with one hand, and he stared at Loki, rain dripping from his face.

There was one more here, he was certain of it, probably the most dangerous of the three. While these two could most certainly kill him, he might be able to evade them by quick and decisive action. Frey and his magic, however, would be more difficult to escape. But time had run out; if he did not attempt to escape now, he would never get away.

He turned quickly and called up the chaos within him, the shifting of form effortless despite his weariness. He had done it so many times that it was as simple to change his shape as it was to breathe, an unconscious willing of the chaos to mold the body into a different form.

As his shape changed, he leapt out of the window and

267

landed directly into the stream, his newly emerged tail shooting him amongst the rapidly churning water while his fins and water-sense guided him around obstacles. He let the flow of the water ease his effort, trusting to the rushing water and many obstacles to mask his progress. He did not go as quickly as he could, fearing that it would attract their attention, but kept his speed consistent with other fish.

He had shrunken down to a small size—no more than the span of two hands—finding it easier to shed a larger frame for a smaller than the other way around. It would be difficult enough for them to find him in this form, much less capture him. Once at the end of the stream, he would ride the falling water down to the sea, and then all hope of finding him would be gone.

As he made his way down the stream, he sensed the water flowing differently ahead of him than it did an instant ago. He slowed, wary of something that did not belong. As he drew closer, he swam behind a large rock that slowed the flow of water around it. He used his chaos to probe just ahead. The obstruction went across the width of the stream, allowing water to flow nearly uninterrupted, but halting anything his size or larger from its continued passage. He spun around and went back the way he had come, realizing he could not get by the net they had placed to catch him.

He darted back, fighting the current, and sensed a narrow pass between two large rocks, the only way to continue back up the stream. As he darted toward it, there was a large disturbance as something—he recognized it as a man—jumped into the water, directly in his way and blocking the path between the two rocks.

He built up his speed and approached the pass. With a final thrust of his tail he flew up out of the water and over the rocks. At the bottom of his arc, the stream an instant away, he was roughly snatched from the air. No matter how much he wriggled, the grip would not loosen, and he found himself looking into eyes that flashed with lightning.

He reverted back to his normal form, hoping that he could take some action to release Thor's hold on him. As he completed the change, Thor yanked him up out of the water and spun him around with one hand, tossing him into a tree on the edge of the stream. He hit it with his back, sending intense pain through his body. He crumpled to the ground, unable to do more than get to his knees. He could not force himself upright, and he thought that his back might be broken. He did not have time to contemplate it, however, before the Thunderer was upon him again.

He reached down and grabbed Loki by the throat, lifting him up to eye level. His grip was unnecessarily tight, and Loki could not breathe, but the look on Thor's face was more intimidating than the lack of air. Even through the haze of pain, he knew there was nothing he could do to stop or even harm Thor. If he were rested and strong he could trick him and then flee, but he was completely helpless now. If Thor wanted to crush his neck, he could do so easily.

Thor brought him closer. He could feel the Thunderer's hot breath in his face. "I would kill you for what you have done," he said, "but your torment would be over too soon. You need to suffer more." He pushed Loki up against the tree, his head slamming back into the hard wood. He looked down to see Mjolnir gripped tightly in Thor's other hand. He brought the hammer back and Loki shut his eyes in anticipation of the pain to come. Thor sent Mjolnir hard into Loki's midsection.

There was a white hot moment of pain, and then there was nothing as Thor let him go and he slid down the tree unconsciously.

He woke to agony, immobility, and darkness. As his eyes slowly adjusted to the dim light, he realized he was in a cave. His arms were spread out and tied tightly, causing his back to arch, and his feet were tied down. He could not move even the slightest bit. Above his head, several feet up, was an outcropping of rock, and there was something . . . sinuous attached to it. He concentrated and tried to shift forms, but he was unable to do so.

"Hello, Loki. It has been long since we last met."

He recognized the voice and realized that this was why he could not shift forms. "You have done something to me," he spat out to the air, unable to see Frey.

"It is your fetters. You will not be able to escape them." Frey's voice was quiet but unmistakable. Loki had suspected that he was with Tyr and Thor, and he had feared it. His Vanir magic had cast the net in the stream, and now it prevented him from using his own power to escape.

"Release me. I have no complaint with you."

Frey laughed coldly. "You have complaint with nearly all in Asgard. But you know better than any that there is a price to be paid for your misdeeds."

Given time, he thought that he might be able to escape the bonds, despite Frey's magic. But he needed time to gather his strength. Perhaps he could weaken the spell by distracting Frey. He would appeal to him. They were both outsiders; it was possible that there might be empathy there.

"We are not unlike, Frey."

The Vanir prince walked around a large rock and into his view. He tilted his head. "You will not trick me, Loki. Your ways are too well-known."

"Perhaps they are. But what tricks could I accomplish here? I am completely at your mercy. Have you considered why I am punished so?"

"It does not take much considering. You murdered Balder."

"Yes, I did. But why?"

Frey paused for a moment. "Jealousy? Spite? Revenge on those who were your brethren?"

Loki laughed to himself, just loud enough for Frey to hear. "Despite your wisdom, you are still new to the ways of the Aesir. They deceive you by setting you against me. For his crimes against me and my kin, I had to slay him, by the very code of the Aesir. It is not for his murder that they punish me."

Despite his wariness, Frey looked the slightest bit intrigued. "Why then, if not for Balder's murder?"

"Tell me, Frey, how has it been to be away from your homeland? Has life in Asgard been the same as what it was in Vanaheim?"

Frey curled his lip slightly. "You seek to bait me," he said calmly. "You cannot. I am at peace with my choices."

"Were they your choices, Frey? Did you decide for yourself to leave Vanaheim to be a hostage to erstwhile enemies? You would sacrifice much for peace. Tell me, are you appreciated for this sacrifice? Do the Aesir offer you tribute and accept you fully into the fold?"

A quick flash of something other than contentment crossed Frey's face, and then was gone. He did not, however, respond to the question.

"Do you begin to see, Frey? My children were punished as well. What crimes did they commit?"

Frey narrowed his eyes, but again did not respond.

"You do not answer because you know the truth already. They were punished not for what they had done, but for what they are. They were kidnapped and imprisoned for daring to be my kin. Do you begin to see, Frey? Do you see how ones such as we are treated?"

271

Frey responded, somewhat weakly. "It is not the same. You and I are—"

"It is the same!" Loki willed his voice stronger. "I am here on this rock because I dare to be unlike those I lived with for so long. I am here because my blood is stained with the taint of an enemy. It is no matter that I have saved Asgard and the Aesir countless times; there is always the one sin that can never be forgiven!" He paused and gauged the expression on Frey's face. He was not sure if his words were convincing, but there seemed at least to be some effect.

"If I am here now because I am not one of the Aesir, how long might it be before you find yourself at odds with those you now call your kin? I once thought that I belonged. Do you remember how I was cast out, Frey? You were there. You heard Odin's words. I was ever to be an enemy to Asgard by the word of the High One. When will it be your turn to be cast out? When will you and your sister face the wrath of the Aesir for the brazenness of being unlike them?"

Frey met Loki's silent stare with equal silence. There was a glimmer of hope that he had found a common thought, that the Vanir prince that he had never trusted, never liked, had seen the similarity. He felt some strength returning, but it was not enough, and there was something about the bonds that drained him, prevented him from using his power.

After long moments of silence, Frey spoke. "You twist the truth. We are not as alike as your mind has conceived. It is true that both our ways are different from the Aesir, but you ever seek to subvert the order around you. You claim it is your person and not your actions that condemn you, but the two cannot be so easily separated. I can sense the disorder raging inside of you, as can the High One. It is as clear to me as it is to Odin, I am certain, that you will be the cause of much death and destruction."

"So I am to be cursed for what I might possibly do? How can you be so sure that Odin tells the truth about the future? The Allfather schemes and manipulates to suit his whims. He allowed Balder to be murdered! He knew I was there in Gladsheim! Has he revealed this to his 'children'?"

Frey stared at him, an uncertain look on his face. "You lie."

"Are you so certain? Do you trust all that he tells you? How many Vanir did he slay in the wars?"

"We were at war. There is peace now."

"For now, while it serves his purpose. But do not fool yourself that he will not turn on you and your kind when his whims change. I was once at his right hand; he raised me as his own son. And now I am sacrificed. If he will sacrifice two of his sons, do you truly believe that a former enemy is safe from his schemes?"

Frey did not answer.

"Set me free, Frey. We have had our differences, but together we can convince the others of Odin's manipulations. He cannot be allowed to use those around him as pawns for his arcane purposes. He must be opposed."

There was the slightest hesitation before Frey spoke. "I have long known the enmity you hold for my sister and I. I had not felt the same for you, and had hoped that we could be like kin. But that time is past. Your crimes are too great, and you will not ensnare me with your words."

Loki felt the disappointment stab into his gut. His hope of kinship dashed, he spit out venom. "One Eye will regret sparing me, for I swear to you that I will be free from these bonds."

"Perhaps. I do not understand why the High One has decreed that you yet live, for I sense that no good can come of your continued existence. You will suffer for it, however.

He has said that you will suffer as no other has before."

"When I am free, I will bring carnage to the Nine Worlds. None," he stared pointedly at Frey, "will escape my wrath."

"You will have little time to think on it. Notice the serpent embedded in the rock above you."

Loki looked up to see the sinuous thing that coiled over his head. It barely moved, resembling a carved figurehead more than anything else, but he did see its faint breathing and the regular flicking of its forked tongue, sensing the air around it. He heard Frey chanting the sacred runes and carving out invisible signs in the empty air in front of him. He cried out as something acidic touched his cheek and began boring a hole into his face.

"You will not be left alone in your torment, however."

Out of the corner of Loki's eye he saw a familiar figure stride into view. Her face was red and tear-stained, and she held a small bowl in her hands. Along with the physical pain of the acid burning into his face, he felt the bitter regret of his betrayal of Sigyn. She who had never wronged another, who had stood by his side no matter what, she who had accepted him as one of the Aesir even while the others spurned him. He had left her, had cast her away without a second thought. And now to have her company in these hours of his impending doom added further injury.

He knew why they sent her, and he felt a rage in his chest at their foul play. It was not enough that they hurt him and his descendants; they had to further increase the insult by bringing in this blameless creature—one of their very own!—to suffer alongside him.

"Sigyn, you should not be here," he said, the sorrow and regret overpowering even the pain. "I have not been kind to you."

"She will not answer you, by Odin's decree. But she will

274

ease your pain, allow you time to heal."

Frey nodded to Sigyn and she moved next to Loki, holding the bowl up over his head. The pain lessened to a dull burn. He looked over at her and followed her upheld arms to the snake embedded above him. From its bared fangs issued a thin ribbon of venom. The bowl caught the stream, and he could feel his flesh reknitting itself. But it was shallow and would soon be full.

He looked back down to Frey and noted that it would be long moments waiting for Sigyn to empty the bowl and return. In that time, the venom would flow freely down his face, into his mouth, and through his body. He had felt a mere drop; the agony from the continuous running of this slaver would be inestimable.

He screwed his face up and sent a look of utter hatred at Frey. The momentary respite that Sigyn's bowl offered was no favor. If the venom continued to flow he would die, his immortal flesh only capable of so much regeneration before he simply succumbed and sank into painful oblivion. Instead, he would have time to heal, just enough to mend the scorched and bloody path of the venom so that when it started anew, there would be newly grown flesh to melt through. And if Odin commanded it, faithful Sigyn would stay by his side for eternity, the two locked in a twisted embrace that bound them far more than their wedding bed.

"It is my crime, not hers! You cannot leave her here with me!"

"The will of the High One is not to be questioned." Frey turned and then paused. Looking back over his shoulder, he said, "Perhaps you do not deserve this fate, but that is not for me to decide. I hope that your suffering does not continue forever." He turned and walked out of the cave, leaving Loki staring after him.

Eventually he looked up at the bowl held over his head.

His wife's tears flowed freely, and they struck his face where the venom had burned him only moments ago. His mood changed from rage to bitter sorrow to hopeless despair, and cycled back again and again in the space of mere minutes while he watched the bowl slowly fill with venom.

Sigyn looked down at him with deep sorrow on her face, and then the bowl was filled. She pulled it away and let the venom stream downwards.

Chapter Twenty-Two

Fenrir's agony was constant, the blade of the sword continually slicing into his maw, Gleipnir digging into his skin and muscle, every small movement causing it to tighten further. Worse was his all-consuming anger, the rage at his powerlessness becoming more and more furious. He could not accept the eternal torment he was faced with, and the thought that he would never be free only caused him more anguish, turning his soul blacker.

At first his dark thoughts of revenge centered on Balder and Tyr. He envisioned sinking teeth into them and ripping them apart. He would crack open their bones and swallow the marrow while they watched, helpless while he devoured them slowly, savoring every bite.

As the pain and anguish increased, he included all of the Aesir in his fantasies, imagining rending flesh and spilling innards, always with them still alive as he tore them open. Freyja's neck would be ripped out, he would chew on Thor's severed arm with hammer still in hand, Odin would be choked down his throat still alive, grasping for some handhold to pull himself out of Fenrir's steaming gullet.

When even these thoughts failed to give him satisfaction, he became more bestial and blind to anything resembling thought or reason, and instead envisioned nothing but abstract images of violence, blood-red and intense. He ceased sensing the things around him and became nothing more than what they had thought him to be: a crazed and wild beast intent on pure destruction. But the inability to exact this fury only drove him further and further into an insane rage that fed itself and continually failed to be sated. If he had not been so tightly bound, he would have ripped himself to shreds in his unadulterated fury.

There was a moment, however, when the slightest sliver of consciousness returned to him. He became aware of his own berserker rage, and in that awareness some of the fury faded, if only the slightest bit. The world outside of him returned to his consciousness, and the agony of his predicament became more concrete, less of an overwhelming and unbearable suffering. The pain did not recede, but his ability to grasp his circumstances returned. His bestial nature, while still aroused and furious, waned to give voice to understanding.

What had changed? What had brought him out of the all-consuming, blind rage?

He saw nothing, but there was a presence. It felt oddly familiar. It felt as if some outside force was there with him, but it was a force that he was connected to. He realized that someone or something was trying to contact him.

He closed his eyes, sending the pain from Gleipnir and the sword to a distant place where he could focus on the other presence. He realized that he would not have been able to dampen the pain without the existence of this outside force.

There were no words, but there was a clear communication being attempted. He felt sadness and pain, and above all, anger. This presence echoed his own primal thoughts. Without clearly understanding why or how, he opened himself to it, welcomed it. He felt the presence pervade his body, awakening something within him that he had not been aware existed.

He felt a roiling energy within him, something that had fed his strength without him knowing it, and promised him

278

more power than he had ever known before. Almost unconsciously he willed the energy outward, and for the first time since his binding he was able to loosen Gleipnir's coils. He did not apply physical force so much as will Gleipnir to release tension. The surprise he felt when the bond relaxed was palpable. He seized upon this faint hope of reprieve and focused his attention again on using the force of his will to further stretch his bonds.

Gleipnir strained against him, its coils resisting. He used his emerging power to increase his strength while he simultaneously pulled on Gleipnir. He felt his muscles expanding, pushing further and further against the slowly loosening coils. The bonds cut into him, but still he strained, ignoring the fierce resistance of the fetter. Fenrir tossed his head and shoulders to and fro, each violent jerk loosening the bonds further, ignoring the pain of the sword slicing into his muzzle.

Gleipnir fought him. The dwarfen craftsmanship defied his continued assault. It was not alive, but the dwarfs imbued all their works with their souls and spirits, and these objects did not break or fail easily. Gleipnir was no mere silken strand, but a thing that came as near to a primal force of nature as a creation could be. But it was now facing the determined wrath of a creature carved from pure chaos, one who was now being awakened to a sense of his true nature.

Fenrir arched his back, bringing the full power of his muscular body to bear. Muscles strained, coils dug into flesh. Fenrir's jaw was clenched tight, every iota of his being focused on pushing Gleipnir's boundaries, both physically and with the force of his will.

There was a tearing sound, and Fenrir had so extended his muscles to their breaking point that he was not sure if the tearing was from Gleipnir or his own taut sinew. A toss of his shoulders and neck created a release of tension, and the once-coiled lengths of the fetter snapped.

Standing up fully for the first time in ages, feet firmly planted on the rock that would have been his grave, he let loose with a howl that shook the earth. Far away in Asgard, the gods stirred uneasily in their halls, anxious with the thoughts of what this baleful sound portended.

The cycle had continued for ages; moments of suffering and brief periods of reprieve where he would heal just enough to survive and regenerate for the next onslaught of venom, forever denied the merciful relief of death. But it was nearly over, and every drop had now become tolerable, if only by the smallest margin.

Sigyn could feel it as well. Her face, long the portrait of sorrow and betrayal, had become a mask of trepidation and anticipation. She felt the tremors, heard the howling, but was unsure of the meaning.

Loki's regret at his wife's treatment was always in the back of his mind. But even more than regret, the rage he felt at the Aesir for including her in his torment was insatiable. Her inclusion only proved their desire to destroy all that he had touched. But now he would be able to return the insults and injuries.

The continued rumblings sent dust and small chips of rock falling throughout the cavern. He could see the snake just above Sigyn's bowl, and he thought he felt an uncertainty in the creature. It was not much, but it was enough to indicate that the snake, too, realized that its infinite purpose might be coming to an end.

His energy had been continually drained by Frey's bonds, but their power had faded. It was gradual at first, but Fenrir's release had sent waves of chaos that had disrupted the spell. Slowly he felt the buildup of chaos inside him, desperate for release.

The bowl was nearly full with venom, and soon Sigyn would withdraw and allow the assault to renew. But he would no longer be victim, unable to prevent the pain the serpent delivered. He could not shift his form, but he was able to send a small tendril toward the snake. In the instant before Sigyn released the bowl, he wrapped it around the snake's neck and willed it to constrict.

He could see the indentation from the invisible tendril cutting into the snake's neck, strangling the creature. The venom did not completely stop, but the smaller amount that drizzled onto him was bearable and did not distract him from his purpose. He forced the tendril to squeeze harder, to dig deeper into the snake's neck.

The slow drizzle of venom stopped, and the snake slumped down, hanging lifeless from where it was embedded in the rock. Loki laid his head back and closed his eyes, savoring the respite that had been denied him for ages.

When he opened his eyes, he saw Sigyn standing over him with a worried and anxious expression on her face. She still held the bowl, clinging to it as a symbol of her purpose. She opened her mouth to speak, then closed it, perhaps remembering Odin's command for her silence, but still unsure if such a command held now. Always dutiful, she remained silent and stared at Loki imploringly, desperate and frightened to know what would happen next.

He did not speak, instead focusing on the bonds that held him immobile. With each passing second he could feel his strength returning, and he could feel the magic draining from them. The disruption caused by his son's breaking free had allowed him to finally be released.

He tensed his muscles and pulled on the chains, feeling their taut resistance. Curling his fingers into fists, he closed his eyes and concentrated, forcing all of his energy to the bonds that held him. He slowly pulled, arms and legs becoming like steel as he brought the full force of his rapidly returning strength to bear. The bonds stubbornly held, but he continued pulling, steadily and with unrelenting force, using both his own strength and the energy within him. Sinews ached and his arms and legs were strained to their limits, but the chains could no longer withstand the pressure. They broke on both sides at the same time, the release of his bondage sending waves of satisfaction throughout his entire body.

Sigyn dropped the bowl, sending hollow echoes throughout the chamber, then she put her head in her hands and wept. Loki did not fool himself that he could ease her pain. It was far past the time for begging forgiveness, for him as well as for all others. Atonement could no longer be achieved; the crimes were too severe, the injuries too deep. Now was the time for revenge.

He got down from the rock and stood at her side for a moment, putting one hand on her cheek gently, as if he were still her husband in anything but name. She brought her hands down and stared at him, communicating something with her silence. Forgiveness for her own imagined crime? Mercy for the Aesir? As for the first, there was no crime; the guilt for her role in this was his. As for the second, there was no mercy in his heart for those who had brought evil unto themselves by their own twisted and perverse actions.

He turned and left the cave, leaving her for the final time.

Jormungand had been thrown violently and had hit the surface of the water with great force, the pain of contact stunning him, but the freezing waters had quickly revived him and made him appreciate the full horror of his situation. He had writhed as he sank into the depths, a desperate attempt to reach the surface and fill his lungs with air. His ineffective movements soon slowed and he closed his eyes, consigning himself to his fate.

Eventually his eyes opened, and he was confused. He was not dead. He no longer took in deep drafts of air and felt life swell his chest. Water was everywhere—both outside of him and inside. It conveyed motions and disturbances of all the living things that swam or pulsed or breathed around him. He was changing, slowly becoming part of the tapestry of this underwater world.

As his body adjusted more and more to this environment, he saw that larger creatures were more likely to survive, and so he grew larger, effortlessly extending himself and taking on a sinuous shape that enabled him to navigate the murky depths. He found that this shape also allowed him to burrow into the ocean bed, wriggling down just under the surface and waiting there silently for any prey that might pass by.

He was challenged as his size increased. Larger creatures attempted to consume him. They saw prey that was smaller, when he had been smaller, and considered that he might make a quick and easy meal. Some escaped him before they themselves were eaten. Most did not.

He was not aware of his enormous size compared to those who had cast him into the water. All he knew was that he was larger than anything he encountered, that he often made meals of creatures who themselves dwarfed most others. He was the unspoken lord of this place, and so he ceased growing, no longer finding it necessary.

He vaguely remembered the time before, but it was quickly fading. There were others his size, and some who were larger. He had felt an attachment to them, a bond that he could not describe. And there was a hollowness inside him now that they were gone. He did not have the ability to wonder about it, and so it simply lingered inside him, which made the familiar presence that suddenly contacted him so welcome.

It struck him while he was near sleep, his belly full with the boneless body of a large creature with many arms. Curious, he slowly swam upwards to seek out the source of this strange presence.

Sensing the unstoppable mass, thousands of smaller creatures moved from his path. He swam just under the surface of the water, his wake sending breakers crashing onto shores far distant. When he finally broke the surface, tall waves violently overturned several boats that had been unfortunate enough to be nearby.

As he drew closer, the sense of familiarity grew stronger. He began to see images behind his eyes of things he faintly remembered, and he desired to feel more. He saw one who he immediately identified with the presence, one he had not seen for so long that he had nearly forgotten what it looked like.

He began to realize that this presence was sent to him by the creature in his memory, and even more, that the creature sought him out, called to him.

He increased his pace, sending ever larger waves with each flick of his long tail. He could not know that the waves grew large enough to drown entire seaside villages, but it would not have mattered. The only thing that mattered to him now was reuniting with this one. And as the call became clearer and clearer, he was driven by one repeating idea. He had no language, but his primitive brain understood the concept well enough.

The image of his father loomed in his consciousness, and he would find him no matter what stood in his way.

Hel saw the three approach, and despite the immense size of the snake, the only one she truly considered was the weakest one. She knew him, although their time together had been so brief as to be almost non-existent. And the memory itself was even more faint. It was a lifetime ago that she had seen him, although that lifetime had taken stranger turns than he would understand. Still, there was a bond that could not be denied, and she was eager to see him again.

He did not understand how she could be both his daughter and the Mistress of Niflheim, but it did not matter. It would be enough to offer him what he sought. Even if he did not wish to see the truth, he would accept her words, or at least appear to do so for the sake of expediency. As powerful as his two sons were, he would still need more to conquer Asgard. He would have the support of Jotunheim, and she would grant him the unending armies of Niflheim, as well, but there was a final element that he needed, one that only she could grant.

She crossed to the window and watched them approach. The dead gathered around them to watch their progress to her hall. They had only a bare understanding of what they observed, but the giant serpent carrying the wolf and the fallen god were enough to distract their attention from the dull misery of their deathly states. It was an event, at least, something different in a realm where nothing different ever happened, where each dark day was as miserable and bland as the one that preceded it. And even though they were dead, they still harbored a residual humanity that made them achingly aware of their wretched existence.

She noted the dead hanging back, making themselves only barely visible to the three visitors. It would be enough to unsettle most who came to Niflheim, but it was likely lost on these three. The serpent was too dim to understand that this was a place to fear, the wolf was too filled with rage and raw power to fear anything, and the small one had already visited this place at her own invitation and would not be easily shaken. She smiled to herself, noting that any being wielding the power of the Midgard Serpent and the Fenris Wolf would likely fear little.

The door to the chamber opened, its movement so slow that it seemed to take hours to create a crevice large enough for her servant to walk through. When he finally did, his movements were only barely detectable; it would appear to any but Hel that he was simply standing still. And yet she could see each movement he made, each step, each twitch of muscle. When, after days, he reached her side with his message, she nodded once and then dismissed him. He took slightly longer to turn and leave the room. It suddenly occurred to her that time was passing quite differently for her approaching visitors outside the hall; such was the way of Niflheim, as Loki would soon discover.

She was satisfied with the message that the guest she had summoned had arrived. He would be waiting nearby, and she would see him soon enough. But now it was time to meet with Loki and discuss his request. It had been too long since she had seen her father.

There was a sense of familiarity in her presence. Even before Loki had crossed through the iron gates, he was reminded of the vision she had sent him. He did not think that he had truly been in Niflheim that previous time, but he knew this place nonetheless. And he knew her, as well.

She was as ancient as any of the gods, perhaps even more so. When the first being took breath and thus began its journey to its ultimate fate, she was there, waiting to bring it into the dark regions of Niflheim.

There were some who thought of her as evil, but most accepted her as simply another aspect of the Nine Worlds. There was no life without death. She and her realm completed the balance of the Nine Worlds. Still, although most could accept the eventuality of passing over into her realm, none wished to actually meet her.

She was much as he had expected, but also different. Radiantly and darkly beautiful from the waist up, he could only guess at what lay below since she sat on her throne and was covered with a long, black gown that fell to the floor. Aside from her looks, however, she was suffused with the pure chaos that he held at his own core.

She greeted him, the sound of wind blowing through a forest of dead trees. "Welcome, father."

He narrowed his eyes at the greeting. "You were murdered by Balder as an infant. And yet not only are you alive, but you have been ruler of this place since the time of Ymir. How can you be my daughter and still Hel, the Mistress of Niflheim?"

Hel smiled knowingly, betraying her ancient nature. Her eyes held secrets, he thought, much like Odin's.

"I remember that day. There was a struggle, just out of my sight. She who gave me birth faced down those who would harm us. But she failed."

"What were you aware of? Did you understand even then what happened?"

"It was not understanding as you might call it. There was an awareness that was part of my being. I saw from my own eyes, but also sensed presences and feelings from those around me. There was fear, fear of what we might grow to become."

"Yes, they feared you would be the harbinger of Ragnarok, along with your brothers." He paused, the question still on his tongue. "How is it that you could be my daughter and also ruler of Niflheim since before I existed?"

She stood and walked towards him, passing by closely, the black fabric of her gown brushing up against him. There was a smell, dank and unpleasant, that emanated briefly from her as she passed. She walked to the window and stared out at the dark misty plains beyond. "I am no longer your daughter. You hold no thrall over me. You are here to serve my whims, not the other way around. Do not deceive yourself into thinking otherwise."

He knitted his brow. He sensed her power, and there was no denying that she could destroy him if she wished it. Still, he was here because she had summoned him. "I beg forgiveness, mistress. What do you bid of me?"

He smirked inwardly at how easily he had fallen back into his old role as sycophant. Would this be like it was on Asgard? Would he perform endless duties for her benefit only to be cast out? No, this would not end that way. He was not here to serve her, no matter what she may think. He was here for only one purpose: to raise an army.

There was a soft noise as the door to the chamber opened. Loki turned to see a dark figure walk behind the throne where a curtain hung, separating the room and keeping part of it hidden. Someone was there, waiting.

"I know what you seek, and my goals are not opposite from yours," she said.

He sensed in his daughter a duplicity; there was an air about her that indicated that there was more to what she said. Their goals coincided, but something was held back.

"Is this why you sent me a vision?"

She did not respond, other than to glance at him from over her shoulder. She finally turned her head back and looked once again out over the plain. "There is a place on the edges of the Nine Worlds, one of fire and flame . . ."

"Muspelheim," he said, more to himself.

"In that realm is a being whose power dwarfs all. You have heard of him."

Loki nodded. "Yes. Although it has been said that he is

a myth." All knew of the legendary existence of Black Surt, the giant who embodied that fiery realm. Loki knew none who had been there or even confirmed its existence. From what he had heard, none *could* exist there; it was nothing but fire and flame, and instant death to any but Surt himself. Odin had spoken about both on rare occasions, but always vaguely. For all Loki knew, One Eye had made up the stories of the creature who wielded a fiery sword and was death to all living things.

"He exists, although not in the same way as we of the Nine Worlds." She turned to face him. "We contain a force of the universe within ourselves, and are able to wield it to our whims. Black Surt *is* a force of the universe. With him, the Aesir will not be able to stop you."

"How do we convince one such as he to help us?"

She smiled. "There will be no convincing Black Surt."

"Then what will we do to enlist him?"

She did not answer, but instead walked over to him. "What are you willing to sacrifice to gain vengeance on Asgard, father?"

He did not hesitate. "There is nothing I would not do to see them pay for their crimes."

"That is good, because in order to use Surt, you will need to give up that which is most precious to you."

"What do you mean?"

As if in response, her flesh rippled and turned black. Her skin sunk in upon itself and he could see the contours of her skull. Her eyes liquefied and oozed down her face as her lips withdrew, revealing her white teeth. Her hair stayed on her head, disturbingly, even while the skin fell off in pieces. She raised a clawed, skeletal hand and offered it to him.

"Come, father. I will show you the way to the Land of Muspel."

With only the barest hint of reluctance, Loki took her

boned claw and allowed himself to be led out of the chamber.

Ragnarok

The sun will fade and the world will be enveloped in darkness. Earthquakes will wrack the lands, and monsters will be set loose from their bonds. Worst of all, the wolf Fenrir will be set free, and he will roam the land devouring whatever he sees. He will yearn for the final conflict, when he and the other forces of chaos will face the gods.

His terrible brother, the Midgard Serpent, will rise up from the depths of the ocean and carve a swath of destruction wherever he goes. He will level mountains with a swipe of his tail, and will yearn to take revenge on the gods for throwing him in the ocean all those years ago.

Loki will not be idle at this time. His vile sons, Fenrir and Jormungand, will so shake the earth with their destruction that he will be loosed from his bonds. He will gather an army of the dead from Niflheim and gather them on a ship made of dead men's nails. His daughter, Hel, the ruler of Niflheim, will be at his side, and she will be horrible to behold. Half of her body is beautiful and desirable, while the other is decayed and dying. She will wish nothing but death on the gods for banishing her to Niflheim.

Loki and Hel will converge upon Asgard with Fenrir and Jormungand. Together, they will bring the combined might of all of Jotunheim, marching steadily upward on Bifrost, the rainbow bridge, along with the legion upon legion of the dead, eager to escape their fate in the underworld. Heimdall will sound his horn, Gjall, the signal that Ragnarok has begun.

The gods will meet the forces of chaos, and the sound of their clashing will shake the Nine Worlds. There will be vicious fighting and terrible battles, and age-old enemies will meet, steel against steel, tooth and claw upon axe and shield.

Odin's spear will stab out the eyes and brains of many a giant, and he will leave the battlefield strewn with the massive corpses of his enemies. He will turn and face Fenrir, eager for revenge, and the two will engage. The Allfather will not be able to match the ferocity of the wolf, and will find himself stuck between his two slavering jaws. Fenrir will choke Odin down his gullet, and that will be the end of the Allfather.

Thor will see his father swallowed by the Fenris Wolf and will fly to his aid, but a terrible shadow will fall upon him. He will look up only to find himself bound in the jaws of Jormungand, the Midgard Serpent, and the snake will whisk him up and away from the battle. The two will struggle mightily, and in the end the Thunderer will smash the skull of the snake, who will fall to the ground with a thunderous crash that will knock all Asgard to their knees. Thor will rise, weakened, and will stagger nine steps before he is drowned in the lake of venom spewed out by the dying snake.

One-handed Tyr will search the battlefield long for Fenrir, eager to avenge the loss of his hand to that ravenous beast. His sword will swing in a mighty arc, cutting off the heads and limbs of any giant he meets. When he finally spies Fenrir, bloody and engorged from swallowing the Allfather, he will move swiftly to bring his steel to bear against him. But he will not move swiftly enough. His way will be barred by a cousin to the wolf: the hound, Garm, who will long to close his jaws around the throat of the fierce god. The two will launch themselves at each other and battle long and hard, each inflicting massive wounds on the other. In the end, they will both lie dead from their wounds.

Frey will also bring ruin to the sons of Jotunheim. His path of destruction will lead him to the foot of Black Surt, brandishing his flaming sword overhead. Frey will battle the fire giant valiantly, but in the end will be overcome and crushed under his flaming heel.

Heimdall will meet Loki, and the two age-old enemies will

engage. Though Loki will be outmatched by Heimdall's strength and battle prowess, he will still have his wits and wiles about him, and will prove the match of the Guardian of Bifrost. They will trade blows, meeting steel for steel. In the end, they will slay each other, Heimdall's blade cleaving skull while Loki slides his sword up under Heimdall's ribcage and into his heart. Their corpses will be trampled down into the dirt by further fighting between the Einherjar and the sons of Jotunheim, and their bodies will be lost forever under the soil of Asgard's bloody plain.

Odin's brave son, Vidar, will watch in horror as his father is swallowed by Fenrir. He will stride forward to attack him. Fenrir will gape wide to swallow the son, as well, but Vidar will be ready for him. He will put his hands on Fenrir's upper jaw while his boot trods on the lower. This boot will protect his foot as he stomps down hard and, with his hands, pries apart Fenrir's jaws and rips the beast wide open. Fenrir's bleeding corpse will not even be fit for the carrion birds who flock to feed on the bloody battle grounds. Thus will Odin be avenged.

In a fury, Black Surt will whirl his flaming sword and cast fire throughout the Nine Worlds. All those gathered will burn, both living and dead. Asgard's spires will burn. Midgard will erupt in flames. The whole of creation will be set afire, and all those living and dead will die. Thus will the entirety of creation be sundered to ash and smoking coals. Only Yggdrasil, the tree that always was and always will be, will survive.

Chapter Twenty-Three

Odin dismounted Sleipnir. One hand on his mane, he communicated his wishes to his steed without saying a word. The massive horse stepped backwards and disappeared, leaving Odin alone in Midgard. The Allfather did not look back, but in his mind's eye he could see the horse fade into the space between the Nine Worlds, becoming more and more insubstantial with every passing second. Odin pulled the hood of his gray cloak over his head and walked toward the village in the distance.

Gungnir was with him, but it was only visible as a long and gnarled walking staff. It would not do to walk into a strange village armed with a weapon that could slay the entire populace. The spear had an effect on those who viewed it; sometimes spurring them senselessly towards it, usually to be impaled on its tip. The mortals in the village would still have some fear of him, but Odin wanted to avoid unnecessary slaughter for the moment.

As he reached the outer edge, some of those outside took notice of him. Two men were skinning a sheep that had been slaughtered and strung up on a wooden crossbeam, four young children—three boys and one girl—were wrestling on a trampled patch of thick grass, several older boys were hauling wood in armloads with axes slung over their shoulders. All paused when the gray-cloaked old man wandered towards them, his long gray beard poking out from the shadows of his hood.

They ceased their activities as he walked past them. There was something strangely captivating about this wizened old man who so blithely traipsed into their village as if he belonged there. The old man radiated an aura that inspired awe and fear. They did not know why they were afraid, for all could see that the thin old man was no threat, but a dread existed, nonetheless, one that kept them all fixed where they stood.

He reached the center of the village and sat on the large tree stump that served as the seat of power. That action unfroze most of those watching, and they first looked to each other with perplexed stares before slowly walking towards the stump where Odin sat. A few ducked into longhouses to alert their elders and the others, and it was not long before Olvir, the brawny, blond-haired chief of the village, came out of the largest longhouse, a thick piece of cured meat in his hand and a large chunk of it in his mouth.

Chewing slowly, he approached Odin, flanked by three of the village warriors, none of whom were armed. Having seen many battles and formidable foes, these four were not awed by Odin's presence as the others had been. Some wondered if the chief would be incensed by this old man's presumptive actions, but as Olvir approached, he looked more amused than anything.

"Old goat, what do you think you're doing?" he said to Odin as he reached within axe distance. There was nervous and scattered laughter, but most watched in silence.

The remainder of the village began to drift over to see the scene of the old man confronting Olvir in the middle of the village. Like many chiefs, Olvir was not unduly loved or hated. His prowess and strength were admired, and his ability to make quick decisions was prized, even if many of his decisions were not favored by the rest of the village. Still, they had been safe and mostly prosperous under him, and these two qualities trumped affection for a leader quite easily.

Odin reached up and pulled his hood down, exposing his craggy, weathered face. He stared up at Olvir with his one good eye and said nothing. Gungnir lay innocently across his lap.

The chief's eyes went slightly wide at the sight of the Allfather's gnarled face. He swallowed the chunk of meat he had been chewing and then laughed mockingly. Taking the cue, his warriors did likewise.

"By Woden's beard, you're older than dirt!" Odin was amused to hear Olvir use one of his ancient names.

There was more laughter from his cronies, but nervous glances from the villagers. They sensed trouble, and their initial awe of the old man faded with the implied threat that Olvir radiated. It was clear to all gathered that there might be violence, and they felt a natural sympathy for this ancient creature who faced down three warriors in their prime, spurred on by a chief who had little regard or patience for anyone who challenged him.

"Look, I've been patient till now, but you need to get out of my seat and pray to the gods that I don't cave your old skull in."

Odin looked beyond him, seeing a scene yet to come. "You will not be mollified so easily," he said, shaking his head slightly. He returned to the present and stared up at Olvir. "Would you be so brave without your warriors at your back? Do you need six extra arms to deal with one old man?"

A silence overtook the crowd. Olvir stopped smiling. He was not unnaturally intelligent, but he perceived the dilemma. He was being taunted by this foolish old man in front of the entire village. Normally, that would require a show of strength to keep order, but it was clear that he could not gain much from delivering a beating on this old man.

If anything, he stood to lose stature because of the clear

imbalance; he and his men would look like nothing more than bullies. He was smart enough to grasp that he ruled not just with his fist, but with the agreement of those under it.

"I don't need anything other than my boot to deal with you. This is the last time I will tell you: get out of my seat and leave this village before I split your skull."

"I know you, Olvir. I have seen your birth."

Despite himself, he was curious. "What do you mean? Just who in the Nine Worlds are you, old man?"

"I saw your mother spread her legs wide to birth you, just as I saw her do the same as she laid down with dogs to conceive you."

Olvir felt red-hot rage creep up his spine. He struck out quickly with his open hand, intending to cuff the old man on the side of the head.

The blow did not hit Odin. Instead, Olvir's head jerked back as his hand was in mid-strike, and he fell violently to the ground, blood and three teeth flying out of his mouth after meeting the butt of Odin's spear.

The three warriors, shocked momentarily by the completely unforeseen turn of events, quickly gathered their wits and lunged at Odin. His staff rang out quickly, striking one man in the stomach, sending him doubled over to the ground. The second felt the hard wood crack against the side of his face, and he, too, went tumbling to the ground. The third found his throat in the old man's iron grip, and his breath left him in an instant. His hands going instinctively to his neck, he was brought, like a struggling infant, closer to the old man's face. Forced to look him in the one remaining eye, he saw the Nine Worlds reflected there, and he had an inkling of the magnitude of mistake he and his fellows had made. He ceased struggling, and Odin released him. He sank down to his knees, grateful that his miserable life had been spared.

Odin stood and slowly looked around the stunned village. They were all on their knees, their heads bowed in supplication. They did not truly comprehend who he was, but they realized they were in the presence of the sacred and reacted accordingly. Olvir and his men were likewise prostrated. They would recover from their injuries soon enough; he had used the barest amount of force on them, just enough to teach them humility and wisdom.

"A dark time is coming," he said. "The time of axes, swords, and wolves is at hand, to be followed by Fimbulvetr, the Winter of Winters." He did not add the prophecy he had heard from Mimir time and again, that 'brothers would slay brothers, mothers would sleep with sons, clans and families would be rent asunder . . .' He had seen the visions himself, but saw no purpose in telling mortals the entire truth. It was enough for them to know that they faced dire times. They would need no extra prodding to bring these predictions to light.

As he spoke, their curiosity and fear at what he foretold overcame their awe, and though they remained prostrate, they eventually met his eye. As he looked into each of their eyes he further spurred their fear and base instincts. None of the mortals in this village would survive Ragnarok, and that was as he intended.

After delivering his message, eyes were wide and fearful, but left with purpose. Even Olvir and his three warriors looked as though they had overcome their initial rage and embarrassment. An understanding of a changing time to come permeated their being, and though few knew exactly who he was, all understood that he was at the very least a messenger from the gods themselves.

He pulled his hood back up over his head and left the village, slowly walking out while leaning on the disguised Gungnir. Dozens of eyes followed him in silence, a quiet that

298

lasted till long after he was out of sight. Tales would be told of the gray traveler in the weeks and months to come. It would be said that he was the Spirit of the Gods, the human embodiment of Yggdrasil, a ghost. A scant few named him as Woden, after Olvir's oath about how old he looked, but none were wholly certain of his identity.

Odin spent the next few weeks traveling from village to village to inform the mortals of their impending trials. For most places, it went much the same way as in Olvir's village: a few brash warriors would challenge him and be swiftly silenced, the ensuing mortals would listen with rapt awe, and he would leave them to astonished silence and reverent whispers of the mysterious gray traveler.

Word of this harbinger of doom spread. As he traveled, mortals were already beginning to sow discord and chaos throughout Midgard. From village to village he heard the sounds of fear and anger, and was greeted with the sights of grinding axe and sword blades, of spikes being sharpened and stuck in the ground to skewer incoming enemies, of boats being laden with supplies and prepared for quick launch. The looks of trepidation and terror were on the faces of many, alongside the steel-set jaws of the fighters, eager to shed blood.

Odin smiled grimly. It was all as he had foreseen time and time again. He wondered if the horror to be visited upon Midgard was because of the impending doom of Ragnarok, or because of the word of it that he spread. Either way, the result was unavoidable. And the lives of a few mortals—briefer than the wink of an eye—were not of consequence when measured against what must come soon. Indeed, Odin would sacrifice the gods themselves at Ragnarok; those on Midgard must suffer and die as well. It was the way of things.

*   *   *

He did not bother to disguise his appearance as he walked into Jotunheim, still appearing as the gray traveler who brought words of doom and despair to mortal villages. Cliffs towered on either side of him as he plodded slowly into the homeland of his enemies.

In the outlying places he saw a scattered few giants. They stared incredulously at this foolish lone mortal who wandered into a place that was doom for him. Amused, they simply watched him walk by, clearly unaware of where he was or where he was headed. They thought him likely to be an addle-brained old human, and they knew he would meet his death soon enough when he wandered too far into Jotunheim. In the meanwhile, they enjoyed the humorous and incongruous spectacle.

The villages and citadels of the giants were as massive as he remembered them, dwarfing the structures of the Aesir and making them look as if they were places for children. When he finally reached a large village—and the village was indeed large, with long houses that could house human armies—he had several dozen giants in tow, following him out of pure curiosity, eager to see what would happen to this foolish human.

As in the human villages, Odin went to the center. But the seat of power, so similar to those he had seen before, was taller than he was. He stood next to it instead, and turned to face the crowd of giants that had gathered.

The smallest was at least twice Odin's height, and there were many of this size. Others were far taller and more massive. There was no correlation between age and size— the range from smallest to largest was different than that for humans, and gods, even.

They drew closer, still keeping some distance from him.

300

Fear did not register on a single face. That would soon change.

"Bring me your leader," Odin said, his voice sounding weak amongst the towering figures around him. At this point he was loosely surrounded by a small army of giants, a group that might be able to lay waste to Midgard if they wanted. It was lucky for the humans that the giants rarely took interest in their affairs.

He was first greeted by stunned silence, but that gave way to thunderous laughter, so loud that the ground shook in its wake. Giants doubled over and roared their amusement to the heavens; the thought of this lone scarecrow of a human demanding anything of them was the most ridiculously bold and absurd thing that any of them had ever heard.

Odin silently waited for the laughter to die down. When it did, he said again, even more quietly than the first time, "Bring your leader to me." He let his cloak drop to the ground, and they could see that he wore gray mail underneath, emblazoned with the image of a raven in black. Although the giants had not taken their eyes from this ridiculous creature since he had entered, none saw him don a black helmet with horns curving downward. It sat firmly on his head, and the expression on his face was grim. Gungnir shed its disguise as a gnarled walking stick and stood revealed, a battle spear with a long, menacing, razor-sharp head.

They did not laugh, but instead felt their lips curl up in sudden enmity for this brazen human who arrogantly strode into their land expecting to survive. Still, most were unsure if they should simply rush forward and stomp him into the ground, or wait till their chief had made a decision. A few brash, younger giants made the decision for them, striding forward with fists clenched and prepared to crush the life from this foolish human.

Gungnir flew from Odin's hand and skewered one of the giants through the chest. He fell to the ground forcefully, clutching the shaft of the spear with both hands while blood spouted from the wound and his gaping mouth. The other giants who had moved forward paused, mouths wide in surprise, before looking back at Odin. Gungnir was in his hand once more, clean and poised to inflict more damage, the shaft of it still sticking from the chest of the now-dead giant on the ground.

There was first an interminable silence, followed by a roar of fury and a sudden onrushing mass of giant flesh charging forward to kill the old man, without any thought as to how he had so easily slain one of them or how the spear could be in two places at once.

At the center of the mass, Gungnir flashed out again and again, spearing one giant through the eye and slashing open the throat of another, drawing blood and life from every victim it struck, sending the towering creatures tumbling to the ground in bloody heaps around him. Each time it left his hands and opened the innards of another foe, it was inexplicably back in his hands, being let loose again to skewer another.

As the intensity of the slaughter increased, the houses in the village emptied themselves of their occupants, and a slew of giants witnessed the battle at its center. Brandishing whatever weapons they held or their bare fists, they joined the fray, not even certain who the enemy was, only knowing that someone or something was slaying their kind. The blood haze hung in the air, obscuring all but a fury of movement and violence, blood, and death.

When the carnage was finished, nearly all lay gutted and bloody on the ground around him. The piles of bodies obscured the thin figure in gray mail at the center of the scene. The village was devoid of almost all other life; a few had fled, but nearly all had joined the fray and fallen under Odin's spear.

He had left nine giants alive. They were injured and in agony, but they would survive. They had fallen neatly near each other and were wheezing or moaning in pain. He approached them, navigating the maze of massive corpses.

They stared up at him, the anger pulsating on their faces, punctuated by biting stabs of agony from numerous wounds. Odin had chosen these nine to survive, and had tempered Gungnir's attacks so they would do so. He had swung the spear like a staff on some, breaking legs and sending them to the ground, had pierced shoulders on others, ripping muscle from bone, crippling without killing.

"You want my name," he said, a statement more than a question. They did not respond, but stared at him with undisguised loathing. "You want to know who could do this to you."

He stabbed Gungnir into the ground next to him and took off his helmet. It faded into nothingness as he pulled it off, as did his armor. He was left with his gray cloak, hanging loosely on his thin frame as it had when he first entered the village.

"I was old when the mountains were new. I created the lands you tread on, the clouds in the sky, the oceans surrounding Midgard. I carved them from the giant, Ymir, the first of your foul kind, after my brothers and I slew him.

"I am the Allfather, the High One, the Hanged God. I am the Lord of the Gallows, One Eye, the Master of Poetry. I am the Feeder of Ravens and Wolves, He Who Sits Above, the Gray Traveler. I am Eternal Wisdom and the Bringer of Death, the Lord of the Valkyries and the Einherjar. I am father to your greatest enemy, the World Shaker, the Thunderer, the Giant Slayer."

There was a mixture of hatred and fear on their faces, but he did not relish it. He said what must be said, not for the sake of ego or arrogance, but for pure necessity that could never be explained or understood. None could fathom his burden.

"You have been spared to spread the message of my coming to others of your kind. I will not rest until the giants have been expunged from the Nine Worlds. I will lead an army of the Aesir to destroy you, to burn any trace of your existence. I will slaughter your women, your children, your infirm and elderly. I will create from your bodies a carrion feast for the ravens and wolves to devour.

"Limp from this place and curse yourselves for having survived, for having to deliver this message throughout Jotunheim: Odin comes for the giants."

They blinked and he was gone, left with their white-hot anger and humiliation, their simultaneous loathing and passion to deliver his message hot in their bellies.

Mounted on Sleipnir once again, he urged the steed forward. His preparations were nearly complete; there was only one more task.

Chapter Twenty-Four

The time had come. Perhaps it had been inevitable, but Heimdall could not say for certain. For ages it had hung over all of their heads, a distant yet unavoidable threat that colored all of their actions, all of their words. While he had always been able to fulfill his role as the guardian of Bifrost regardless of what came to pass, Ragnarok lingered somewhere in his head; an ever-present, if hazy, reminder of mortality.

It could not be denied now. As he stared down the multicolored arc of Bifrost to Midgard below, a cloud of dust rose up in the wake of a many-legged mass moving toward the base of the bridge. The mass was wide—wider than any army he had ever seen—and unstoppable. As it moved forward, it lay waste to everything in its path.

He expected such power from the mass of Jotunheim, although it was still striking to see. Despite its distance from Bifrost—it would take several days before it reached the foot of the bridge—its size was daunting, both in numbers and in the sheer size of those who constituted its bulk. At the very least, their ears brushed the tops of the trees they passed by. But there were many among them, at least in the first rank, who dwarfed even these giants. The tallest rivalled the size of the mason, and Heimdall recalled the destruction wrought by that monstrous creature. How much more devastating would dozens or hundreds of them be?

As he brought Gjall to his lips, he ignored all thoughts of the upcoming battle and focused his entire attention on letting his clarion call cry out across the Nine Worlds. This would be the final time alerting all with its warning of impending battle and, perhaps, doom. Its cry was clear and piercing, and he relished the unerring simplicity of the sound. One single note from a horn intended to forewarn all who heard it of the end, and yet it caused inspiration to well up in his breast, inspired confidence and defiance, a denial of the fate the gods were saddled with.

It took little effort to blow the horn. His lungs exhaled only the barest hint of breath, but still Gjall's cry sent a wave that spread across the entirety of Asgard and beyond. It was as if the horn itself originated the sound and he was merely the instrument of its delivery, rather than the other way around. When he finally pulled the horn from his lips, the sound ceased issuing forth, but continued to reverberate throughout the Nine Worlds and returned to his ears in echoes that bespoke of the power of the original blast.

Despite the impending death that Gjall foretold, Heimdall would not have been afraid of the coming conflict, but he might have gone to the final battle with resignation. As Gjall's cries faded, he was suddenly hopeful, emboldened and eager to face the threat, imposing as it might be.

They had dreaded Ragnarok for as long as he could remember, but he wondered if the constant threat that hung over all of their heads made them more pessimistic, more willing to accept the prediction of doom that supposedly awaited them. It was true that the Allfather was wise beyond reckoning, but he was not infallible. Perhaps in this one thing, this event of such overwhelming magnitude, he was wrong. Or maybe he simply chose to let the rest of the gods interpret his prophecies—had the High One ever actually said that Ragnarok would be the doom of them all? He could not remember.

It did not matter. What would happen, would happen, and that fate could not be changed. He would meet it as they all would, with cold steel in his hands and fire in his heart.

He might fall—they all might fall—but they would bring the mass of Jotunheim with them when they did.

Tyr heard the wolf's howls of triumph and felt the dwarfen fetter snap long before he had been alerted by Gjall. The chill sound had woken him from a troubled sleep, jarring him and setting his nerves on edge. In the cold darkness of his keep there was an accompanying presence, a maliciousness that pervaded the chambers of his large hall. He recognized it. Its malingering aura had haunted him ever since Fenrir had sunk his teeth into his forearm and ripped away his hand. He could not do the simplest tasks without the echo of the incident surfacing in his mind.

Tyr's preoccupation with his missing hand was more than simply an aching loss of flesh. Instead, he felt the wolf haunt his every waking—and sleeping—moment, as if there was a venom in his bite that had spread throughout Tyr's body and poisoned him with the remembrance of that single incident.

It angered and frustrated him that he could not remove the wolf from his thoughts. He had suffered injuries before, but never had an enemy so intruded upon his every breath. The harder he pushed the beast from his thoughts, the more persistently he returned, always taunting. Sometimes there were images: jagged teeth and dripping blood, the feral almost-smile, his hand dissolving in an acidic gut.

Tyr rose from his bed and walked to the window. Looking out on the pre-dawn darkness, Gjall's warning call still ringing throughout Asgard, he felt the presence of the wolf even more. He knew that Fenrir would come, along with all the other enemies of the gods.

He had pondered this day, as had all of the Aesir, for countless ages. Although he held scant hope that the High One was wrong, he had wondered if it would come in truth, and what it might look like to see all of their enemies gathered together, storming Asgard. He had always felt sure that Ragnarok would visit its doom on Asgard, and had made sure that he was prepared for the battle.

But Tyr had never considered that his thoughts would be so single-minded, that his entire focus would be on one lone foe. In his mind's eye, he had seen himself at the center of multitudes, his sword cleaving and dismembering. He had seen a mound of victims growing ever higher, his bloodlust growing more intense with each enemy that met his steel. He had even imagined how he might fall. It would be a wave, a mass of enemies that overtook him as he stood firm and dropped dozens before he was finally overcome by sheer weight of numbers and the exhaustion of continual fighting. He did not fear this death, but merely expected that it would occur in some similar way.

When he thought of the final battle now, he was fixated on one thing only: killing the beast. He imagined facing Fenrir across the corpse-strewn field, the two knowing that there was an inevitability to their conflict. They would engage, but he would not seek glory in this battle, would not fight as if skalds would sing of this conflict for ages. He would fight only to slay this creature, to destroy the beast who had taken his hand.

Out beyond the arc of Bifrost the giants moved inexorably towards Asgard. Every step brought Ragnarok closer. It might mean the death of them all, but Tyr could only think of his own personal demon, the beast who haunted him every moment.

He turned and walked to a large chest near his bed, where he had laid his sword belt. It was difficult to buckle with only one hand, yet another reminder of what he had lost, but he was by now accustomed to it. He could have summoned servants to help him, and he would do so to don his armor, but he would have no other touch his steel. It would remain unblemished till it was drawn in anticipation of the bloodletting to come, when the forces of chaos would desecrate the holy ground of Asgard.

Despite the vastness of those forces, despite the crushing weight of giants, monsters, and demons they might face, he would find the wolf. He would find the wolf and would not rest till he had let his blade carve a bloody trail into the beast's flesh.

Odin's journey to Niflheim had been quick. On Sleipnir he had no need to cross the true distance between places; he could instead slip between them, exit the Nine Worlds in one place and reenter them in another, without having actually traveled the distance between those two places. And Sleipnir needed no guidance to take him where he wanted; the horse simply knew his whims and took Odin to his next destination.

Treading on the hard rock of Niflheim, Sleipnir retreating back into the darkness, he stared up at Hel's towering hall. He could feel the cold presence of the dead, even if he could not yet see them. They hovered on the edges of the mist, sensing the power he emanated, fearful of this being who radiated death in such a way that even they feared it.

Among their fetid masses he did not sense the one he had come to see, but he knew that he would not. That spirit was just inside, and he had been deposited at Hel's gate so he could enter directly.

He walked forward slowly, all necessity of disguise gone. He was well-known here, and no veil he could construct would hide his identity. Nor was Gungnir masked; the cruel head of the spear was visible and threatening, a visual reminder of the death that Odin wielded.

The tall, black gates to the narrow bridge opened wide as he approached, although there were none to actually open them. The doors to the hall did likewise, and he passed through. Countless premonitions of this very scene had unfolded before his eye since he had hung on Yggdrasil, and he could have navigated the hallways and stairwells even without his one good eye.

He reached two large doors leading to a throne room beyond. Unbidden, the doors opened wide and he stepped through, knowing who waited for him beyond.

Black shimmering curtains hung, maze-like, throughout the chamber, giving the room the illusion of being broken into smaller rooms. Vague shapes and shadows danced within the folds of the curtains, some human-like, others not. He did not see the shadow he sought, but he knew it was there. His attention was drawn to the throne and its grotesque occupant.

"Welcome to my realm, Allfather," Hel said. Half of her face and body were beautiful: delicate porcelain skin, raven hair, perfect features. The other half was corpse-like and rotten, fetid, and shrunken, with only wisps of leftover hair sprouting out from the raw, green-black scalp, trailing down in uneven strands.

"Expelling you was wise on my part. You are a foul creature."

She looked at him strangely, cocking her head to the side. As she did, the dead side of her expanded in tendrils to the living side, sending meandering tributaries of putrescence across her face. "You did not expel me. I was sent here by your son, the murderer."

"Were you? That is not how I recall it," he said.

The expression on her face made it clear that she did not like his response. "I stared up into his eyes as he stabbed me with his sword. He can verify his crime." She turned her head and said quietly, "Come forth."

The shade flowed through the shimmering black curtain, not parting it, but rather walking through. It was unclear whether the curtain or the man was more insubstantial. Odin had not seen his son since his death, and the shade that faced him now was both like and unlike Balder.

In form he looked the same: The eyes, the face, the lean musculature, the youthful features. At a glance it was Balder, just as he had been in life. And yet there were differences, difficult to name, but still there. There was a sense of dimness about him, a lack of fire or light in his eyes. His skin color was tinged with gray, and his motions were just the slightest bit hesitant, as if his body was reluctant to obey his commands.

"Greetings, father," he said, bowing his head slightly as he had done in life, but with a curious lack of animation. Odin knew it would be so, but still it was difficult to see. He had been used to seeing his son full of life, sometimes to a fault, but always with boundless spirit. He spoke now to a shadow of what his son had been, the form of Balder without the essence. This was what it meant to reside in Niflheim. Those pitiable souls who came here became shades, and all ties to life were extinguished.

"My son, it is good to see you again." And it was. Despite Balder's current state Odin could feel the emotion stir within him. He had not felt this for countless ages, and had not anticipated it here, but found himself full with a mixture of happiness and regret, sadness and anger. And also hopefulness.

"Tell him," Hel said. "Tell him how you drove your blade into my throat as a babe and sent me here, robbing me of my life."

Balder cast his eyes down. It was clear to Odin that she

311

had him in thrall and was relishing her power over him. And over Odin, as well, at least at the moment.

"I came across an infant. I held my sword poised over it for a moment before running it through. It had committed no crime, yet I slew it without hesitation." His voice was somewhat halting, as if he forced the words to come. Yet there was no doubting the truth behind the words, as Odin well knew. He had seen it happen dozens, perhaps hundreds of times, and he knew also that he would not have lifted a finger to stop it. This event, as all others like it, was necessary.

"The words come straight from the mouth of the fiend himself. You cannot shrive this one. His guilt is clear, and his penance as my slave has only just begun."

Odin's eye grew hazy, as if he was seeing things beyond the immediate time and place. He chanted, "The spawn of Angrboda and the Sly One were brought before me. Sensing their threat, I cast the snake Jormungand into the ocean surrounding Midgard. There he grew till he encircled the world and bit his own tail. The wolf Fenrir was spared through the pleas of he who would soon be known as One Handed Tyr—to his regret—and was allowed to roam the fields of Asgard till the time of his binding. The monstrous Hel, half living and half dead, was cast by Odin into the darkness of Niflheim, there to rule over the dead till the time of Ragnarok." His eye cleared, and he looked at Hel directly.

She narrowed her eyes at him. "Stories and legends do not comprise reality, High One. It is obvious that more than your eye was lost when you plucked it from your head and pitched it into the well."

"Perhaps," he said.

She regarded him carefully, the dead flesh of her face healing and becoming white and pure as she did so, a complexion and visage to rival Freyja's. "Why do you come here? You must know that you cannot avoid that which comes for you and your kind. Even now, the armies of Jotunheim march on Asgard, to be followed by those of Niflheim, and one other who will ensure your defeat and death."

"I would speak with my son," he said.

"He is your son no longer; he is now nothing more than my slave. A fitting punishment for his crime, would you agree?"

"You will let me speak with him," Odin said.

Hel's now full lips smiled thinly. "Do you threaten me, High One?" There was a mocking tone in her voice, a subtle hint that she reigned supreme in this place of the dead. Despite his power he could not best her here, where she could draw on the spirit of every soul in Niflheim. It was not necessary, however. There would be no physical confrontation this day.

"It is not a threat. I have foreseen it. Let us not waste time in pointless posturing. Our true confrontation will not take place here, but in Asgard."

Hel looked from Odin to Balder's shade. "Your father wishes to speak with you," she said, and suddenly she was gone, dissolved into mist.

Balder looked up at Odin, a mixture of sadness and resignation on his face. He did not move from his spot, however. Odin stepped forward to meet him.

"The time is short, my son. Ragnarok approaches."

"Yes . . ." Balder said absently, his voice trailing off into nothingness like the ghost he was.

"The armies of the dead will join the fight against Asgard."

"Yes . . ."

"You will not be among them." At this, Balder came out of his stupor. "Your hand will not be raised against the

313

Aesir."

A look of confusion crossed his face. "Hel is my mistress. I must do her bidding. She has told me that I will slay my own kind."

"It will not come to pass. You will not fight at Ragnarok, for either side."

Balder looked even more confused and disconcerted. He looked around anxiously for Hel's reassuring and controlling presence, but she was nowhere to be found. "I cannot refuse her will."

It pained Odin to see his son so conflicted and enthralled. "Sleipnir will come for you. He will take you away from this place. There is a larger role for you than mere combatant." Balder's apprehension was palpable. "You will understand when the time comes."

Odin reached out a hand and placed it on his son's shoulder. Balder's flesh was cold through his loose clothing, and felt vaguely insubstantial. "I bid you good journey once before, when you were sent to the flames, knowing that I would see you only once more. I bid you farewell now, knowing that I shall not see you again, but also knowing that your death served a greater purpose than you can now comprehend."

Odin squeezed the shoulder of his son's ghost once more before letting his arm drop. He turned and left the chamber, summoning Sleipnir. His work was finished and the result unavoidable. He gripped Gungnir tightly. Soon enough the spear would see more blood and death than it had ever seen before.

Chapter Twenty-Five

Freyja's reflecting pool rippled with the sound of Gjall's cry. While it was not entirely unexpected, she still found herself distraught by the summons. All life was destined to end some day, she knew, and even the gods were not immortal, but Ragnarok was different. This was no natural life cycle; this was the senseless death of all things, chaos imposing itself forcefully across the Nine Worlds. This one thing would end the balance of the universe and banish order forever, in favor of a state of endless entropy. The enemies of the gods did not fully contemplate what they did in assaulting Asgard. Or if they did, and they still pursued this destructive course, then they could be considered no less than pure evil.

She stilled the ripples as best she could and gazed into the pool's depth. She could only hope to find a way to avoid the unnecessary destruction and death that would soon threaten all. While she could not hear sounds issuing forth— the pool only allowed her to see images—there were reverberations in the water that hinted at thunderous footsteps crashing upon the earth, countless numbers of them sending waves and tremors across Midgard.

As the cloudiness of the pool dissipated, the water becoming a crystal clear window into the outside world, she saw mass movement. She saw giants—legion upon legion of them—marching towards Bifrost.

She dipped her fingers in the pool and stirred the water, upsetting and dispelling the image. She and all others on Asgard knew that the sons of Jotunheim would one day rise up against the gods, and that it would signal Ragnarok. While it was a fearsomely impressive sight to see the collected mass of Jotunheim striding forward as one, it was not new knowledge.

Nor was it inevitable that the giants would be able to best Asgard. They would face legions of Einherjar, battle-tested warriors whose only purpose was to fight the enemies of the gods during Ragnarok. After endless battling of each other, they would be eager to be let loose and spill blood on true enemies. The Valkyries would also be there, swooping down on their phantom steeds and stealing life after life with their fierce, spectral blades. The giants knew little of the Valkyries who would surely inflict grave casualties on the strong but firmly flesh and blood giants. And then, of course, there were the gods themselves.

The Vanir would weave such sorcery as the giants had never seen, causing some to die in mid-step, others to attack their own ranks, and sending the land itself to rise up against them. Then the giants would face their most terrible foes, the Aesir, who would wade in with steel flashing, each god like an army unto himself. They would lay waste to giants by the thousands. Even then the outcome would be uncertain, for the mass of Jotunheim was vast, the power of the giants fearsome, and the anger and fury of their kind undaunted.

But there were undoubtedly others who would seek the destruction of Asgard. As she swirled the telling waters of her reflecting pool, she intoned the sacred runes that would shift the scene and allow her to see what was as yet hidden.

Once more the mist of the water began to clear and settle, producing images from distant places and times. Even Freyja could not always be certain from where and when the images came. At times she could not be sure that the scene would even occur as it was shown to her. Still, there was usually a truth to be had in the pool, and she could do no worse by attempting to see it.

The waters grew darker as the image formed. Freyja knitted her brow momentarily before realizing that the image was of a darkened place, and that the pool had not grown dark. Within the blackness there were white circles, countless numbers of them. They floated eerily along in a jerking motion, sometimes halting briefly to bob up and down, other times speeding up. All went in roughly the same direction, but they jostled for position within the river of blackness. That was how she thought of it: white circles floating on a black river.

As she continued to stare, she noticed other movements, sometimes accompanied by brief glimpses of white—although not circular—and always below the innumerable floating circles. Gazing deeper into the pool she could make out lines and creases on the circles, and she was unsettled to find that they were faces, gaunt and ghostlike. The wretched, rotting bodies they belonged to were ensconced in the darkness below, darkness that began to unfold so that she could see the shambling forms in its shadows.

The armies of Niflheim stretched out as far as she could see in the pool, even more vast than the mass from Jotunheim that drew steadily closer. She concentrated on the image and brought it closer, drawing in on the individual faces and bodies of the dead who moved forward, slowly and relentlessly. On their faces was a hunger that repulsed her.

Some of the dead were cast in rotting flesh, while others were little more than bones. Some lacked limbs, others were merely a bone house with a thin covering of gray skin stretched tightly over it. Most had been old when they died, claimed quietly in their beds. Most disturbing were the small ones that she had not initially noticed. Thousands upon thousands of them toddled to and fro, their faces hovering far below the general line of ghostly circles. Some crawled, while others could not even manage that, so they merely pulled themselves forward, dragging their empty bellies on the cold ground of Niflheim.

While Freyja had seen countless children die and had accepted it as part of the cycle of things, she felt horror at these little ghouls, plucked from their mothers' teats and cast down into the darkness and gloom of Niflheim, there to contend with all those other poor souls who lingered in the emptiness and despair of that world. She could not deny the unfairness of a universe that took even the barest chance at life from these humans, but she also knew well that there was no arbiter of fairness.

Staring down at this doomed army that slowly plodded towards Asgard with the sole intention of spreading death and destruction, she was stung by the cruelty of fate that would first take the life of a babe, and then send its shade to kill and destroy.

Sickened by the image, she stuck her hand in the pool and disturbed it, causing ghostly circles to change, creating grotesque images and distortions, black mixing with white, faces elongating and eventually breaking apart. And then the image was gone.

She sat back and felt despair creeping over her. The giants would be bolstered by the armies of Niflheim, all the mortal beings in the entire Nine Worlds who had died throughout history. These vast numbers would shortly find themselves on the fields of Asgard, engaged in a bloody onslaught against the gods. The gods were powerful, but she did not know if even they would be able to defeat all the combined forces that were amassing against them. They had all dreaded the coming of Ragnarok, had hoped that it would be averted, but it was apparently not to be.

Heavy with the crushing weight of despair, she stood and turned to leave.

A flicker in the pool caught the edge of her vision, and she turned. The pool swirled crimson and orange, colors alternating and shifting, blending and separating. The entire pool became suffused with the colors, but there was more. It began to radiate heat, which it had never done before. Even more, the heat seemed to contain something else, something sinister that she could not name.

She was drawn back to it, dreadful curiosity overcoming the foreboding. The pool continued to swirl, becoming more and more agitated. Two spots of red appeared next to each other, each roughly the same size and shape, but appearing to be made of flame. They grew in size and intensity, as if they were eyes that had opened. Indeed, she felt as if they were looking at her. Even more so than the gaze, there was a malignant presence from elsewhere, an entity that gazed back at her through the pool.

Fear clawed at her insides. Her pool had never been used by any but her, and only at her bidding. Odin was able to occasionally communicate some gesture or look through the pool, but even then it was clear that he was only aware of being observed; he did not, could not, control the visions themselves. This being on the other side used the pool to observe her, and it exuded a lust for destruction. She had never felt such pure maliciousness before.

Freyja tried to pull away, to will her body to leave, but she felt tied to the pool and the entity's magnetic force. She opened her mouth to speak the sacred runes, but no sound would escape her lips. Panic began to course through her as a third red spot appeared, below and between the two eyes. Her fear intensified as it elongated and took on the dimensions of a mouth, a malevolent smile etching itself on what appeared to be a face of flame.

Her muscles tensing, she attempted to force her voice to whisper the words that would end the vision in the pool. She did not know if the spell would work even if she could say it, but the power of this entity was leaking from the pool and snaking into her chamber, and she felt an urgency to stop it from crossing over onto Asgard. She was not sure if she imagined it or not, but the pool looked as though it was swelling. She became certain when she saw thin tendrils of water, arrayed in shifting oranges, reds, and yellows, creep over the edge and move toward her.

A low moaning coincided with the advancing tendrils of water, a sound that only barely registered, but which was full with menace. It grew, and she felt it reverberate throughout her body, the sounds leaving echoes within her, remnants that rattled her frame and sent pain into her like small worms boring through flesh.

The image in the pool gained more definition, the face becoming clearer. And as it did, its flames faded and became more flesh-like. In the moment when she recognized the face, she was released from the pool's thrall. Quickly, she chanted the runes as she felt the presence attempting to snare her again. The questing tendrils lost their cohesion, and the water, now set loose from the entity's control, spilled across the stone floor.

Freyja rose to her feet and fled from the room as the pool went dark, the presence leaving a residue that would taint any image that followed. It did not matter; she knew she would never use the pool again. There would never be another opportunity. Time was short, and Ragnarok was even now closing in upon them.

As she raced down the empty halls of her keep, all doubts of the end left her. Odin must be told, although perhaps he already knew. Soon enough it would be plain for all in Asgard, and then Vanaheim and Alfheim, followed by Midgard and its surrounding realms. By the time all knew what came for them, it would be too late.

It had been surprising enough to see the face in her pool, and even more so to feel its influence despite the distance between them. More upsetting was the second face, the one that she had always feared would lead to destruction and chaos. And Loki had looked more certain, more filled with power and hatred than she had ever seen him.

Even more threatening than the armies of Jotunheim and Niflheim combined was the utter destruction represented by Black Surt, he whose existence was partly only legend. Somehow Loki had made that legend manifest and had given a force of nature a corporeal form. Worse, Black Surt was little more than an extension of Loki himself, and now, with this power in his grasp, his victory may well be inevitable.

Servants were summoned and quickly dispatched to Odin. She wondered if any of these preparations even mattered. When Loki crossed into Asgard bearing the power of Black Surt, it was unlikely that anything would survive.

Chapter Twenty-Six

Loki overflowed with obscene power.

He stood on the bridge of a massive ship that sailed without need of water or wind, but was powered by the ghastly presences of the armies of Niflheim. It was bound for Asgard.

Fenrir stood next to him. Loki could feel the anger emanating from his son, his eagerness to take revenge on those who had wronged him. Down below, Jormungand's enormous bulk slithered steadily forward, the rumble and destruction of his passing clear for leagues in all directions. His was a basic, instinctual intelligence, filled with longing for the destruction of his enemies, although it could not be articulated in such terms. Loki's third child remained behind with her slave, Balder. She would sense the battle from afar, feel every death as the gods were sent to Niflheim to become her servants.

Black Surt welled up within him in anticipation of the destruction to come. Surt's purpose was solely to destroy, and Loki could feel the dim and vague consciousness of the thing bristle against him, desperate to break the yoke that he held it with. If it could, it would destroy everything it touched. Loki would keep it in check, use it against the gods and, when they were all gone, would let Surt loose back in Muspelheim where it would be contained. He could not hold onto it forever, but he was strong enough to possess it for the time it took to wreak havoc on the Aesir and their allies.

The armies of Niflheim—vaster even than those of Jotunheim—were pressing up against him with their desire to bring others into their fold. He had purposely held back, increasing their lust for the slaughter to come, and also to coincide with the assault by the armies of Jotunheim.

The gods, powerful though they were, would not be able to withstand all the forces aligned against them. Soon he would stroll through the blood-soaked fields of Asgard, noting the dead and dying Aesir around him, and his revenge would be complete.

The lush grassland between Bifrost and the towering spires of Asgard was filled from left to right with the armies of the Aesir, a clear line of warriors marking the spot beyond which they would suffer no enemy. This was where they would cleave skulls, lop off limbs, and rip open entrails till all who sought to destroy them were dead at their feet.

At the forefront, in the exact center of the line, was Odin, clad in gray mail and helmet, Gungnir firmly in his fist and blood-red cape flying out behind him. He was a grim visage of death, made more so by his skeletal frame. His ravens circled overhead, acting as Odin's eyes while they waited for the giants to cross Bifrost. His wolves waited impatiently at his side, eager to feast.

To his right, dwarfing all the other warriors of the Aesir, was Thor, the Thunderer. Mjolnir was gripped in his hand and lightning crackled around the hammer, as if the weapon itself anticipated the battle to come. Thor's eyes were lit and sparked with energy, his red beard and hair looked as though they were made of fire, and his armor seemed that it could only barely contain his mass.

To Odin's left were One-Handed Tyr, sword in his remaining hand and gleaming shield strapped to the other, and Frey, clad in Vanir battle armor but with sword still sheathed and looking—unlike the Aesir around him—less intensely focused, more serene. Next to him was his sister,

Freyja, clad in similar armor, but also with sword unsheathed. Prepared for battle in such a similar way, the twins were difficult to distinguish from each other with their delicate features.

Spread out across the front rank were the other Aesir: Frigg, mother of Balder and wife of Odin; Magni and Modi, sons of Thor and Sif, along with Sif herself; Ull the archer, with expertly crafted yew bow and arrows with shafts of bone; Vali and Vidar, sons of Odin; Forseti, son of Balder; Bragi the poet; Honir, released from his war-bond by the Vanir, further strengthening the ties between the Vanir and the Aesir; along with hundreds of other Asgardians, each skilled and fierce in battle, each longing to draw giant blood.

Behind the front ranks of the gods were the Einherjar. These grotesque warriors were even more eager for blood than their masters. Since the moment each of them arrived at Valhalla, they had done little but fight. Each day was a litany of battle where they bloodied each other in anticipation of Ragnarok. Each night was a feast where those who had survived the day raised cups and bowls to the fallen. And each morning, all would rise—those who had survived and those who had died—to fight again. The cycle repeated each day, with Ragnarok always in the forefront of their minds. This was what they had been brought to Valhalla for, and they savored the thought of finally slaking their thirst for the blood of the enemies of the gods.

The Valkyries were everywhere; ghostly, translucent battle maidens astride similarly ghost-like steeds. They did not stay in one spot for long, but would disappear and reappear among the massed armies. Each was armed with a sword and bow, and they could engage in vicious melee or skewer the enemy from afar with spectral arrows.

The Aesir were joined by the armies of the Vanir, the mystical gods from Vanaheim who had at one point been their bitter adversaries. Now the two groups, long uneasy allies, tossed aside all thought of old injuries and banded together to face the common enemy that threatened them both. They brought with them their spells and sorcery, their mastery of all living things. They had made fearsome enemies; now they would be equally devastating as allies.

And yet all of these armies together only constituted a fraction of the armies of Jotunheim. They could hear the giants even now, stomping on Bifrost, row upon row of massive, towering creatures of chaos, intent on destroying any and all in their path. A quiet unease went through the armies briefly, only to be quelled by the calm and focused ferocity of the Aesir at the forefront. These gods were the anchors upon which all others depended. Their steadfastness lent strength to those around them.

The armies were silent. The time for noise and battle and death would come soon enough. For now, they stood their ground and waited.

The marching of massive feet on Bifrost was all Heimdall could hear as he stood at the edge of Bifrost with his few dozen retainers, awaiting the giants. Swords were out, faces were grim and determined, as they formed a wall separating the end of Bifrost from the plain that led to Asgard. The giants would have to smash that wall to gain access, and Heimdall would not allow that to happen so long as he had breath left in his body.

Heimdall had seen them for leagues before they even set foot on Bifrost, but as the legion upon legion of giants marched inexorably forward, he realized how much bigger they were as they closed the distance. And even more daunting were the numbers. As the first ranks came into view of Heimdall's retainers, he could hear gasps from the brave warriors. The snake-like procession of enemies encompassed the whole of the bridge and the land leading up to it. Heimdall had not known that so many giants existed, and the thought of them marching on Asgard was intimidating, despite his dauntless nature.

As the first wave drew closer, he gripped his sword tighter. Whatever the outcome, this would at least prove to be a battle for the skalds to sing of.

There was space enough on Bifrost for the giants to march about ten abreast. Since Heimdall's small band was spread out as they were, shoulder to shoulder in four ranks, it would be difficult for the giants to flank them unless they actually crashed through the lines. While they would probably be able to do it, it would cost them dearly when his men dug steel into giant flesh.

He wondered if he might be able to halt all of the armies here, at Bifrost, and lay waste to the entirety of Jotunheim in a glorious battle that would earn him the envy of all the Aesir. He smiled at the thought. To stir up Thor's innards with jealousy and deny him a role in this battle would be supremely satisfying, for ever was there competition between the Aesir for the title of strongest, boldest, most fierce warrior. Heimdall had seen Thor's fury at being denied battle, and he and the others had made good sport of it. If that could be done today . . .

He ended the thought, amusing as it was. If he were to maintain this position and keep the giants off the sacred ground of Asgard, it would require his full attention.

The first line of giants was nearing. They were mostly the same size—tree height, at least—but there were several who were more than twice that size and far more bestial looking. Heimdall saw the danger and scanned the faces of his men.

"Stay firm on the line!" he called out. "Keep your ranks tight! Leave the big ones to me!" He noted their grim and determined nods, and turned back to the giants. They had halted, taking full measure of the small force that stood between them and Asgard. They were armed primitively— clubs, hammers, bare fists—trusting their massive size to overwhelm their enemies. Heimdall noted the looks of overconfidence; they smirked, laughed, and even pointed derisively at the small opposing force. It was clear they considered this to be an easy battle and a foregone conclusion.

Without warning they let loose with battle cries that shook the sky and charged forward, weapons and fists brandished high. Heimdall's band stood firm and awaited the onslaught.

The first wave of giants met the steel fury of the Asgardians, and blood sprayed out and above, coming down again like thick, red rain. The line was pushed back as the giants pummeled with fist and club, and several of the men fell, but the ranks behind quickly stepped up and filled the holes, and the line held. The men, though hopelessly outmatched in both strength and number, made up for their deficiencies with fury and skill.

Giant legs were hacked off with broad swings from the front ranks, guts were stabbed through with short, quick thrusts from the back ranks, hands and fingers were lopped off as they sought to grab and crush these annoying insects that defied them. Their initial momentum had carried them forward strongly and had moved the Asgardian line back. But where it held it had become an assemblage of stabbing and biting steel, drawing blood wherever its dozens of stingers struck.

The giants tried to pull back, but the force of the bodies behind pushed them into the line, and swords and axes continued to hack and slash at anything they could touch. As the giants fell, some of them roaring and screaming in agony and bitter frustration, they created a wall to those behind them, and the Asgardians were able to use these giant corpses as barriers from which to strike behind. As giant upon giant fell, the fervor of the Asgardians increased, and their blades bit deeper, hit harder, slashed faster. This furor enraged those giants who could not yet reach them, but who could see these tiny creatures laying waste to their brethren. They doubled their efforts to reach them, thus pushing those in front ever more into the biting teeth of the Asgardians.

While Heimdall felled giant after giant he watched for the larger ones. They would move forward and toss the fallen bodies aside, making holes for the others. He had killed two of the larger ones already, but there were many more behind, and they were able to reach or even step over those on the front line to wade into the Asgardian ranks.

He slashed off the arm of one giant at the elbow and then plunged his sword into its side all the way to the hilt. Blood and gore sprayed as he pulled the sword out and the creature crashed onto the pile of dead giants. Heimdall felt the ground rumble near him and he whirled to face the threat, but he was too late. The giant picked him up in his hand roughly—he felt and heard ribs crack—and then he brought Heimdall to his gaping mouth, intent on either eating him or simply biting him in half.

He struggled to free his sword arm, and when the giant brought him close he stabbed out with his suddenly free sword, directly into the giant's eye. The creature screamed and reflexively let Heimdall go, but he held onto the sword with one hand while he swung around and grabbed it with his other. The giant flailed wildly and stumbled over the bodies of the slain at his feet, Heimdall dangling from the sword still sticking into his eye.

The giant crashed down face first, the impact driving the sword deep into his brain, and he died instantly.

Heimdall, however, had been caught underneath and slammed to the ground, bearing the full weight of the massive giant. After long minutes, he still did not rise.

The Asgardian line held, most unaware that their leader had fallen, oblivious to all but the need to hack, slash, and stab at any giant flesh that pressed near them. Several larger giants moved forth, however, and bodies were cleared away to create an opening. As a massive giant stepped into a hole created in the barrier, several warriors rushed to fill it, their swords flashing. They cut deep into the giant's leg and were rewarded with a roar of pain and anger, which was shortly followed by the other foot stomping down and crushing them into the ground.

Back ranks moved forward and attacked the large giant, but enough of a gap had been created that some of the smaller giants were able to break through and engage the men. As the men fought off the smaller giants—who still nonetheless towered over them—the massive giant reached down and scooped up man after man; crushing some in his hands, blood and guts spilling over his tightened fist, ripping off the legs of others, biting off the heads of still more.

The line was eventually broken and the warriors swarmed upon those giants who tried to go through it. But they were now forced to fight on two fronts since the line of giants continued to press forward. They fought valiantly, desperately, and many, many giants were slaughtered. But slowly, one by one, the men were crushed, beaten, stomped on, pulled apart, or even eaten, and with each death, every warrior had that many more of the enemy to contend with.

As the streaming legions of giants walked through and over the bloody battlegrounds, eager for more death, none even paused to witness the hundreds of dead giants or the few dozen Asgardian warriors who were now nothing more than broken, littered bodies and bloodstains on the once lush field. Not a man survived, and as the giants continued to stream unrelentingly over the field, their numbers interminable, Heimdall never stirred from the spot where he had been crushed under the massive weight of the giant.

Chapter Twenty-Seven

The two armies faced each other across a flat emerald plain, the one vastly outnumbering the other. Tyr could not believe that so many giants existed; they stretched as far as the eye could see, mass upon mass of giant, each at least twice as tall as Thor, and many so large that Thor himself scarcely equaled their thumbs.

The armies of Asgard were silent and brooding. They stared at their enemies across the field with resignation and quiet rage. Once the battle was on they would let fly with battle cries and shouts of fury, but for now, silence reigned. The armies of Jotunheim, by contrast, were eagerly engaged in noisy, mocking behavior, like the savages they were. They did not move forward yet—this was a prelude, an attempt to intimidate—but they would soon, and the field would run scarlet with blood.

Tyr knew it was impossible but he searched the ranks for any sign of Fenrir. He did not see him, but that did not mean he was not there. Still, he did not feel the beast's presence, and he was fairly certain that he would if the wolf was near. He needed to meet this one enemy on the battlefield, and he would slay the entirety of Jotunheim to get to him if need be. He could no longer rest knowing that Fenrir was out there, mocking him, taunting him with the old injury.

The giants grew suddenly quiet for a few brief moments before beginning the charge towards the armies of Asgard. The gods and their allies held their ground firmly, steel at the ready, knowing that these initial few ranks of giants would be the first of many to die at their hands. They may have bested Heimdall's retainers, but now they faced gods of battle, and they would soon enough find out what that meant.

As the giant army came closer Tyr noticed something overhead, just above the tree line in the distance. It drew part of his attention despite the imminent threat of the giants. It was a shimmering of the air, followed by a materializing of the largest ship he had ever seen, floating on the breeze. All those assembled paused for a brief moment, even the giants, as the ship became more fully corporeal, and Tyr felt a mixture of rage and anguish wash over him. Standing at the helm was Loki—although he looked different—and next to him was a large wolf.

He had grown much since Tyr had seen him, but it was undeniably the same beast who had chewed off his hand. Tyr felt his grip grow tighter, his teeth clench. In the final seconds before the clash of these massive armies, his lust for blood increased tenfold.

The brief respite from the appearance of the ship ended quickly as the giants resumed their charge. A ripple of trepidation ran through the armies of the gods, however, as the ship moved over them. All the collected dead of Niflheim streamed downward into their midst, just as the wave of giants crashed into the front ranks.

The downward streaming line of ghost-like dead seemed endless, but they were met by the combined forces of the Einherjar and the Valkyries. The shades swarmed over every opponent they could see, their lack of skill outweighed by the crushing force of their unending numbers. Einherjar were each beset upon by ten or more of these dead souls, clawing, biting, striking with whatever weapons they had— knives, clubs, axes, even bare finger bones. They fought back viciously, each of these hand-picked warriors trained for pain and battle from a relentless routine of fighting, dying, and resurrecting to fight and die again. They cleaved heads with their swords, smashed skulls and bones with heavy two-handed axes, ripped out whatever guts remained with long daggers.

Valkyries danced in and out on their pale steeds, appearing here with flashing blade to lop off arm, leg, or head, and then just as quickly appearing elsewhere to stab an enemy in an empty, gaping eye socket. They were able to keep mostly free of injury due to their speed, but they could not always avoid the constantly questing hands and claws of the dead. Valkyries, once made corporeal to strike, were found to be vulnerable to counterattack, and some were swarmed in mid-strike, their sword arms immobilized by the weight of twenty or more ghouls dragging them down, pulling them from their horses and piling upon them with flailing arms and biting teeth. Those who fell thus did not rise again. Their horses, deprived of the direction of their warrior maidens, were also dragged down and mauled mercilessly.

The gods were pressed hard by the onrushing multitude of giants, and could not even see the havoc that was happening behind them. Each of the gods was already surrounded by scores of giants they had slain, but those remaining were endless. They held their line fiercely, supported by the Einherjar behind them, who stabbed and slashed with viciousness born of an eternity of bloody fighting, and the Valkyries, who appeared suddenly to send their swords screaming into giant flesh and then disappeared just as quickly to attack another.

Tyr's sword hacked mercilessly, slicing through the thick, trunk-like legs of one giant, sending him tumbling to the ground to join dozens of his kin in the blood and muck. With lightning speed and precise movements, his sword danced in and out of the bodies of any giants who came near, while he dodged their clumsy attacks with ease. A larger giant swung a tree trunk at him; he positioned himself to his right and ducked at exactly the right instant. The cudgel struck a smaller giant directly in the chest, breaking ribs and sending him crashing backwards to the ground. Tyr swung high and sliced off the giant's left hand. A scream of pain and anger was followed by a shower of blood and the dropping of the tree trunk. The giant had reflexively stood up straighter, making his vital areas an open target. Tyr stabbed the creature in the groin. He bent double and fell to the ground, bleeding and mortally wounded.

He heard a growling behind him, a sound more bestial than those made by the giants. He whirled just in time to duck the lunging of a feral beast with a mouth full of jagged teeth, while at the same time slashing out with his sword, drawing a shallow wound on the underbelly of the creature. He was rewarded with a howl of pain, and he pivoted once more, facing the beast squarely, eager to continue the fight that he had anticipated for so long.

Ardor was quickly replaced with disappointment. It was a massive wolf-like creature with slavering jaws and tightly-bound muscle under slick, black fur, but it was not Fenrir.

He had heard tales of this creature. It was a foul beast that guarded the entrance—and exit—to Niflheim. It was Hel's servant, and it would attack anything that it thought it could kill, whether that be god or ghoul. As he faced it the beast's jaws opened, hot spittle spilling to the ground. He wondered if there was any intelligence behind those red eyes or nothing but spite and malice.

He did not have long to ponder before it launched itself at him. He stepped to the side easily and scored another shallow hit on the hound. From behind a giant tried to grab him and was rewarded with Tyr's sword in his throat, but his attention had been diverted just long enough for Garm to sink his jaws into the back of his leg, sending white-hot streaks of pain through his body. Using his massive shoulder muscles, Garm wrenched his head to the right and ripped out a bloody chunk of Tyr's leg.

Tyr screamed, more in rage than pain, although it hurt nearly as much as when Fenrir had taken his hand. He swung, his normal precise and calculated movements thrown off by his anger. The blade missed, but the hilt struck the hound's snout and broken teeth fell to the ground. Garm did not react to the pain. Instead, his jaw up against the arm of his attacker, he clamped down on it hard, hearing and feeling the crack of bone as his teeth dug into the meat of Tyr's arm.

Garm did not release his jaws, but instead wrenched his neck and head once more, pulling Tyr off his feet and sending him to the ground. Caught underneath the hound with his forearm still trapped in the beast's iron jaws, Tyr was forced to resort to brute strength and tactics to break free. He smashed the metal end of his lame arm again and again against the hound, bludgeoning it with all the strength he could muster. At first the attacks only enraged the hound, and he whipped Tyr about, each time sending deeper spikes of pain through his body and making it more difficult for him to hit the beast with full force.

Eventually he was able to lodge his foot underneath Garm's body and push upward. The hound, losing his foothold, loosened his jaw muscles involuntarily. Tyr rolled over on top of the beast and smashed the metal end of his lame arm into the side of his face again and again. Still, the beast would not relent, and the scratching of his claws dug through Tyr's armor and into his chest, leaving deep, bloody gouges.

The two rolled on the ground, Garm refusing to let go

of Tyr's arm, which by now was nearly cut in two with the intense and acute pressure of the hound's jaws. Blood oozing from the wound, each shifting and movement causing him intense agony, Tyr reversed strategies. Instead of trying to free his arm from Garm's jaw, he began to force it down into the beast's throat.

Garm, surprised by the sudden change, released the pressure on the forearm somewhat, although the jagged fangs still held fast in Tyr's flesh. Steeling his nerves, Tyr bent over and jammed his free elbow into Garm's throat. Using his weight, as well as every ounce of strength he could muster, he leaned his body onto the beast's windpipe. Garm struggled wildly, raking armor with his claws, but he could not dislodge the god or release the pressure on his throat.

Bleeding from deep wounds in his torso as well as his now-useless forearm, he summoned every iota of strength and pressed down even harder onto Garm's throat. The hound's flailing increased wildly for a few brief moments and then died down, and eventually stilled as the blackness he had been spawned from claimed him back.

Covered with sweat and blood, weaker than he had ever remembered being, Tyr pried the jaws open and withdrew his mangled forearm. His hand dangled limply at the end, and splintered and broken bone were visible amidst the ragged flesh and dripping blood.

He saw his sword lying on the twisted corpse of a giant, and he limped over to reclaim it, not realizing that it was now useless to him. He reached down to grab it without thinking when the shadow fell across him. He turned to see the angry scowl of a bloody giant, the large, stone-headed axe in his hand coming down too rapidly for Tyr's wounded and exhausted body to dodge. The stone head met the flesh and bone of the god and pummeled him to the ground. Still conscious, Tyr turned his head and thought he saw another wolf in the edge of his vision, perched and watching with a smirk on its long snout. Then the axe came down again and blotted his existence from the Nine Worlds.

The Thunderer was a wall unto himself, barely needing any other god to help him maintain a line against the giants. Mjolnir flashed out again and again, carving a swath of destruction as it sailed through the brains of giants, dropping them to the ground, only to return to Thor's hand in time for him to shatter legs or crush ribs. As he fought, thunderclaps deafened those around him, tearing open the eardrums of any nearby and sending hands flying to the sides of heads in agony. Lightning crashed down from the clouds, exploding the bodies of some and sizzling the flesh of dozens more.

Even without Mjolnir, Thor was a force to be reckoned with, as he caught the club of one giant in mid-swing and threw him to the ground, still clutching the weapon. Others were lifted as they attempted to step on him, and then thrown into their comrades. Thor's fists smashed giant bones, his boots broke open wide fissures in the ground, his shouts set his enemies to trembling. It was not long into the onslaught that the giants wondered if it would even be possible to defeat him.

Captivated by his radiant energy, the dead warriors of Niflheim sought him out. As he shattered the knee of a giant, sending him to the ground, and then drove Mjolnir into his head, he was overtaken by a swarm of the dead. Like a wave, they poured over him by the hundreds, each one weak and feeble, but making up for their paltry natures with sheer numbers. Thor was pulled under, and more continued to pile on top of him, each one biting, scratching, striking anything they could reach, including each other. It was a feeding frenzy of the dead, and Thor was buried under it, hundreds of corpses weighing him down.

A violent burst created a tunnel through the bodies, limbs and dead flesh flying up and away as Mjolnir flew free. One entire side of the pile shifted, the dead tumbled to the ground, each scrambling to regain position. From every side bodies and body parts were being forcefully ejected, the entire mountainous pile quaking.

Finally, the pile of the dead was forced forward and crashed to the ground. Thor was now visible, ripping apart dead warriors with his bare hands and shrugging off any attacks mounted on him. Mjolnir returned to his hand and he sent it flying again. It struck dozens of dead warriors, blowing holes through their bodies, and they crumpled to the ground, unable to rise again.

When it returned to him once more he held it aloft, and lightning streamed outward from the hammer in multiple arcs, each one striking dozens of ghouls, frying their rotted flesh and exploding their bodies. When the smoke cleared, Thor stood alone, facing down scores of giants still battling. For the first time, there was fear in their eyes.

The ground roiled, and all those near Thor—scores of giants and hundreds of others—were thrown from their feet with the force of the quake. For a brief instant, the sun was blotted from the sky as a massive shadow loomed overhead. Thor got to his feet quickly, uncertainty spread across his features for the first time as he turned around to see the source of the shadow.

There was barely time for him to register the awesome sight of the giant snake before it crashed down upon him, mouth first. He continued driving into the ground, sending tremors for leagues around and shaking the battlefield so intensely that all assembled wondered if they might truly be experiencing the end right then. Jormungand continued to drive ever downward, Thor caught in the trap of his jaws, until his tail disappeared into the hole he had created.

For long minutes the battlefield continued to quake, tossing the combatants about as if they were children. Thunder roared from underneath the ground, although none above could tell if it was from Thor or from the pounding of the massive snake smashing through rock and whatever else lay under Asgard's soil. Battle continued on, but uneasily, each tremor from underground creating wariness, the thought that at any moment Jormungand might rear up from the ground and kill all in his wake.

There was an eruption near where the snake had driven into the ground, rock spraying out violently, striking and killing those nearest, injuring countless others, followed by a great plume of dirt that obscured the vision of all in the immediate vicinity.

All battle ceased then, each warrior on the field eager to know the outcome of the struggle, to know if the Thunderer had been finally laid low by the Midgard Serpent. The Aesir feared the worst, and considered the consequences of losing the most powerful warrior the Nine Worlds had ever seen. Their fears were realized when the dust and dirt settled, and they could see the head of a massive snake poking out from the hole he had created, with no sign of Thor to be seen.

The cheers of the giants were deafening, and the magnitude of the loss weighed on the souls of the remaining Asgardians like a millstone. They would fight on, and giants and dead warriors would fall by the thousands, but for the first time, defeat was not just some distant possibility.

The cheers died down, however, when the armies of chaos noticed no movement from the snake. Its head merely lay there, its lidless eyes open, but still. There was silence as the head began to move slightly, but it was clear that the movement was not of its own volition. It was being moved by something, and realization fully dawned on all gathered that Jormungand was no longer alive.

Underneath the head was a tiny figure, miniscule in size compared to the enormous serpent. Yet this figure, arms over its head, was lifting the snake up and off of him, and the blue-white flash of lightning could be seen in his eyes.

It was the Asgardians' turn to cheer, and though their numbers were far fewer, the sound that issued forth from their lips fully overshadowed that of the giants.

Thor threw the head of the snake from him, its twisted and broken neck and skull now evident. Mjolnir still gripped in his hand, he staggered forward nine steps then crashed down face first into the dust and lay still.

One Eye was near; Fenrir could sense it through the mass of bodies. He had torn through Einherjar with a fury, shredding limbs and body parts, a trail of blood and dismemberment left behind him, gore coating his slick fur. He knew that One Eye would be near his precious warriors, and if he slaughtered enough of them, perhaps he would seek Fenrir out, to his woe.

As he prowled through the blood-soaked fields, striking out at unsuspecting victims with his iron jaws when he saw an opportunity, a pale maiden clad in armor and wielding a broad sword appeared suddenly in front of him, swinging hard at his head. He ducked, barely in time, and felt the sting of her blade take off the tip of one of his ears.

He sprung then, faster than a beast his size should have been able to do, catching the maiden unprepared for the counter attack. His paws struck her breastplate and knocked her from her horse while his oversized jaws closed on her head and cracked her skull open like a brittle egg. He spat her out and turned on the frightened horse, ripping its throat out with one brutal bite. The corpses of both maiden and horse faded into nothingness as he continued through the maze of dead bodies and embattled warriors.

He cleared a mound of dead giants, each with spears sticking from their throats, and saw a gaunt, thin figure in gray mail, two wolves at his side and wielding a grim battle spear dripping with blood and gore. One Eye looked like death incarnate, and Fenrir wondered how any could worship this evil god who preyed on the weak, who stole babies from the teats of their mothers, who chained and tortured those who threatened his tyranny. He would not survive this day, he thought, and Fenrir relished the idea that his jaws would soon be around One Eye's throat.

He would dispatch the wolves first. One quick snap would break a spine, and he would toss their limp bodies on the heaps of the dead around them. Then he would advance upon One Eye, always wary of the spear. He would not underestimate this god; he would move carefully, striking at the right time, gutting him and swallowing his innards while he slowly died at Fenrir's feet.

The god faced him, the wolves growling and adopting a feral pose, ready to spring at their master's command. Then One Eye did a strange thing. He put a hand on one, soothing it, and spoke softly to the other. The wolves ceased their aggression and abruptly loped away from his side, disappearing amidst the chaos around them.

Suspicious lest they circle back, Fenrir slowly advanced, warily sizing up the god. One Eye simply stood there, his spear pointed upward, its butt end resting on the ground at his feet. He looked completely unprepared for an attack of any kind.

Fenrir growled at him, "You die today."

"Yes," he replied.

Keeping a cautious eye open for a trick, sniffing the wind to see if any of the other Aesir were close and planning an attack, he decided that even if there was a trick, a rapid attack was still the best way to take him down. Even if his initial advance was unsuccessful, he would be in a better position, and perhaps any who might be waiting to attack him would be less aggressive if he were in close with their leader. Bracing his paws on the slick grass, he leaped forward quickly.

One Eye fell under his weight like a crumpled old man. Surprised that there had been no counter attack, he hesitated for the barest instant, suddenly realizing that this might have been his plan, that he might have been lured in close so that One Eye could spear him or grapple with him while his allies attacked from hiding.

But in that brief instant of pause and regret, nothing happened. The god lay underneath him, Fenrir's paws on his chest, his hot breath heavily in his face. Perplexed though he was, he could see no reason why he should not press his attack. His jaws clamped onto One Eye's throat and he wrenched away a bloody chunk with a quick jerk of his powerful neck muscles.

The god groaned in pain, and his eye rolled back in his head, but he offered no resistance, his arms still and outstretched on the ground, almost in an inviting pose. Sparked by blood lust, Fenrir's jaws dipped down again, ripping mail and digging into torso. Skin was torn, ribs were cracked, blood spurted everywhere, but still One Eye made no attempt to resist or even plead for his life.

Emboldened and frenzied, Fenrir doubled his efforts, ripping the god open and swallowing whole chunks of him right there in the middle of the battlefield. When he was done, the life was nearly gone from the god and his innards were now mostly inside the wolf. Still, a small spark of life persisted, although it would not last long.

Fenrir looked down into his eye. He mouthed something, but Fenrir could not hear it. Feeling more confused than sated, the revenge he had craved so long somehow becoming bitter, he turned and left the old fool to die alone.

Mounted on Sleipnir, Freyja found herself at the base of Yggdrasil. She was confused and distraught; she had not wanted to leave the battle, to leave all her kind to their fate against the armies of chaos. If they were to seize victory despite these overwhelming odds, then they would need all to fight on, to give their last dying breath to defend Asgard. If they were to lose, then she wanted to die with them, not slink away like a fleeing coward. She was not one of the Aesir, but that did not mean she would shrink from a battle, and Odin knew that well.

She had been faring as well as could be hoped, probably because she appeared less of a threat than the Aesir. That was to her advantage, for she was able to use her sorcery to strike from afar without her enemies realizing it was she who attacked them. Let Thor and Tyr gather giants to them with their well-brandished weapons; she would help them slay enemies without even realizing they were being helped.

Odin had been insistent. She had found him next to her of a sudden, during a lull in the battle around her. He had appeared from nowhere; she had not even known he was near.

Taking her arm gently, he had said, "Sleipnir will come for you. You must go with him."

She had given him a strange look. "Where? Why do I need to go with your horse?" She assumed it was a battle strategy and she would do as he said, but craved the reason why so she could better prepare her spells and attacks.

"He will take you to Yggdrasil. You will enter the tree and wait there. You will know when it is time to leave."

She was incredulous. "I cannot leave the battle, my lord! I am assisting in ways that our enemies do not even suspect. We need all here to win this battle! The loss of my sorcery could be devastating!"

Odin looked at her solemnly, calmly. "The battle will be lost. It is a foregone conclusion. That is not what is important." He gripped her shoulder gently. "You must survive, and there is one other who must also survive. When Sleipnir comes for you, go with him."

Even there, amidst all the blood and chaos, it was impossible to deny a command from the High One. Freyja nodded her head wordlessly, closing her eyes for a moment. When she opened them, she saw him staring over her shoulder.

"What is it? What do you see?"

"My death," he said. She turned to look, finding nothing, and when she turned back he had disappeared.

Sleipnir came soon after Thor's death. As she had promised, she mounted him quickly and he took off, his eight powerful legs propelling him faster than any living thing could from the battlefield.

She had seen Yggdrasil from afar many times, but had only been close occasionally. The staggering size of it drew an awe-filled gasp, even from one who had existed for eons as Freyja had. Standing at the base of the World Tree, she could scarcely take in anything else, so overwhelmingly immense was the thing. She had a thought of what it must be like to be a flea standing at the base of a mountain, but realized that even that comparison was not enough to appreciate the colossal nature of the tree.

She dismounted Sleipnir, and the horse paused for a moment before turning its flanks and galloping off, a plume of dust arising in its wake. She walked toward the tree.

Yggdrasil seemed to shrink as she approached, the bark

taking on the normal dimensions of a large tree, and yet it also retained its boundless size somehow. She did not question it, but merely reached out a hand to touch the warm bark. There was a living pulse there, something not unlike what she might have expected from a living creature's body. It also radiated a silent wisdom, a primeval intelligence that was unmistakably different from anything she had experienced before.

She was intimidated by this entity—for entity it surely was—this thing that was older than the Nine Worlds themselves. Yggdrasil made even Odin look young and rash. Yet she was also drawn to it, felt as if there was an ancestral quality that bespoke of nurture and . . . love? Was that the feeling the tree radiated? Not lustful, but parental, a feeling of consummate care and safety.

Freyja felt herself drawn into the tree, her hand merging with it, gently pulling her inside. She could have resisted. It was not insistent, but more like a warm tide that tenderly nudged her. She did not resist the pull, but stepped forward, acquiescing to the soft lure. She watched her arm disappear, completely submerged in the wood of the tree, and then stepped forward once more, her entire body swallowed up. Her last thought was vague recognition of another before her consciousness was subsumed by the World Tree.

Chapter Twenty-Eight

Loki stared down at the battlefield with an ever-increasing sense of satisfaction. The ship was now empty save for him. The legions upon legions of dead covered the battlefield. Despite the massive number that had been slaughtered, so many of the dead of Niflheim remained that those who had been lost amounted to a drop in the sea. They were like a plague upon the armies of Asgard, and no Asgardian could so much as spit without hitting a dozen of them.

The giants were faring well, too. Although their legions were not nearly as exhaustive as the dead, they still outnumbered the enemy by at least tenfold, and their size and strength—coupled with their hatred of Asgard—made them formidable foes.

And the gods had lost many, each death causing the remaining warriors to double and redouble their efforts, to fight harder, to kill more. But they were beginning to tire. Though their power was legendary, even these gods were not tireless or invincible. They had lain waste to countless enemy armies, but never had they faced such unending and furious foes as this current onslaught.

When Thor was killed Loki's faint doubts fell away, and he became more certain that Asgard would be stomped from existence. He thought he should feel some regret at the death of Jormungand, but he did not; merely elation at the role his son had played in killing the Thunderer, the most powerful of all the gods. There was a very brief moment when he wondered why he felt nothing when his son's head was lifted and tossed by the mortally wounded Thor, but it was

346

gone almost instantly, replaced by increased savoring of the destruction being wrought before his eyes.

The height of his rapture came when Fenrir devoured Odin, choking down bits of him while his life slowly seeped into the grass. He gave no thought to Odin's lack of resistance, but merely delighted in the destruction. He who had banished him from Asgard, who had spurned all his contributions, now lay digesting in the gullet of his other son, who had also been wronged by One Eye. Only the deaths of Frey and Freyja could begin to compare to the gratification he felt, and as he scanned the fighting below he spied one of them locked in furious battle.

He leaped off the bow of the ship, his body erupting into flames and streaking down to earth like a comet. As he touched down flames exploded outward, incinerating all near him, friend and foe alike. Frey, just outside the perimeter of the flames, looked up as he cut down the last of his undead attackers. Loki smiled at the thought of what was to come.

The Vanir god waited with sword in hand as Loki approached him. All other combatants—mostly the dead of Niflheim—sensed the destruction inherent in their flaming leader, and gave the two a wide berth. They could see that this one god was being claimed by he who had brought them here, and though their consciousnesses were dim and basic, they realized that there would be repercussions should the Asgardian be claimed by other than their leader.

"You are not as you were," Frey said.

Loki smiled. "I am the same—one who was banished and hounded, one who suffered for his love of Asgard. I merely return to repay the debts I owe."

"No," Frey said. "It is plain that you relish this death, that your purpose has transcended revenge only and has become pure chaos and destruction. While we were never friends, there was a part of you that I admired once. And though I could see that your pride and arrogance would take you down a dark path, I could not have foreseen this. There is an evil about you."

"You seek to bait me," Loki said, grinning fiercely. "I am the same, yet different as well. My will and vengeance have brought me here, but I carry one other with me, one who will ultimately spell the death of all in Asgard."

Frey's eyes went wide. "Surt. Black Surt. You have brought him here."

Loki laughed. "I *am* Black Surt! I wield his power, and I will see all of you scourged from this plane!"

Frey's face was grimmer than before. "You are a fool. Your arrogance has doomed you. None can wield the power of Surt. You have become a vessel from which he can leave Muspelheim and spread destruction across the Nine Worlds."

"Perhaps," Loki said calmly. "But that is a destruction you will never see." With a gesture, Frey's sword erupted in roaring flames. His hand and arm burned black, he hissed in agony, dropping the weapon to the ground.

Frey closed his eyes and began to speak the mystic runes, but he was silenced when Loki's flaming hand grabbed his throat. Instinctively, Frey brought his hands up to wrench the grip loose, but was rewarded with seared flesh. His breath would not come, but even worse was the sizzling of his skin around the throat, the flames creeping up his face, now setting his hair alight.

Loki grew larger, lifting Frey off his feet and dangling the agonized god. Slowly his entire body was engulfed in flames and he tried to scream, but Loki's iron grip on his throat would not allow it. After long minutes, his flesh bubbling and blackened, he ceased struggle and lie limp in Loki's hand. He threw Frey's charred, lifeless body down onto the ground, still smoking. He turned to see Odin's own corpse nearby.

He walked over to the dead Allfather, intent on savoring the pain that Fenrir had caused in the final moments of his life. As he bent down to stare into the face, Odin's one eye flew open.

Loki jerked back. How could he still be alive? This husk of a god, half-devoured and lacking most of his insides, unbelievably survived. Recovering from his initial shock, he realized that even if he still lived, it would not be for long. He decided that he would allow One Eye to remain alive while the remainder of Asgard was destroyed so he could see what his decisions had wrought.

He glanced away, only to hear a faint murmuring. He turned back and saw that Odin's mouth moved, and his eye beckoned him forward. He leaned down to come face to face with him. He was caught by something in Odin's eye, a sense of depth. He stared into it and, as when he had stared into the depths of the Well of Urd so long ago, he saw swirling mists that slowly began to take shape. Despite the carnage that still occurred around him, despite the revenge that had been satisfied by the slaughter of the Aesir, he could not banish the curiosity he felt as he stared at the unfolding scene in Odin's eye.

It felt as if he were drawn into the eye itself, that he was witnessing some event unfold in front of him. No longer was he hovering above the near-corpse of his once-father; he now saw three distinct shapes forming before him, two large and one small.

The shapes began to form specific features: arms, legs, and finally faces. He did not recognize them as faces he had ever seen in his life, but there was no doubting the familiarity. One shape had formed into a man of about his own size and appearance. He was handsome and well-formed, but the unmistakable signs of fear were spread across his face. The second shape formed into a woman, beautiful but terrified, and she clutched the third shape—a small child still young enough to suckle.

They were in a dark, enclosed space, and it was clear from the way they huddled together that they were hiding from something on the outside. A door formed and was violently opened. The figure that stood silhouetted in the doorway was absurdly small, about the size of the child, but thin and not of the right proportions to be a child. Loki was confused for only a moment before he realized that the man, woman, and child were giants, and this intruder was not.

The child began to cry, a high-pitched wailing that the woman tried to stifle without success. The small figure in the doorway radiated fear and death, and Loki could feel the waves emanating from him even though he knew this was nothing more than the shade of a scene long past. The figure stepped into the dim light of the room, and his face could be seen.

He did not look the same as he did now. The skin was smoother and without lines. The beard was shorter and less gray. And even though he was thin, Loki would not have described him as wizened and gaunt. Yet the deathly glint in the one eye was unmistakable, as was the bloody spear Gungnir, clutched tightly in his hand.

Odin was clad in blood-drenched armor, and Loki could just barely make out the outlines of what appeared to be bodies piled up behind him before that part of the scene went dark. He lifted his free hand and pointed at the two. He did not speak, but Loki did not need to hear words to know his intent. The woman turned away from him, exposing her back but adopting the posture of a mother protecting her child. The man took a step forward, standing between Odin and the woman and child. Odin gestured toward the child, and Loki could see the defiance on the giant's face.

He hefted Gungnir and threw the spear with full force. It pierced the giant and his woman and pinned them to the wall. The man hung dead on Gungnir's shaft, but the woman, stuck between husband and wall, still clung to life, but only just. Blood flowed from her mouth, and she attempted to keep her grip on the child, but her strength was rapidly fading.

Odin walked up to her and held his hands out for the child, who slipped from his mother's dying arms. The child was nearly as large as Odin himself, but he had no trouble holding it. He set it down on the ground at his feet and opened the swaddling around its head. He knelt down and stared into the child's eyes, and as he did so, he carved glowing symbols into the air with his finger while chanting the sacred runes.

The child's wailing slowed and then eventually ceased. As he continued to chant, the child, still staring up at Odin, grew smaller and smaller, until eventually he was no longer a giant. Odin scooped him up with one hand and gave him a last look before turning to the door and heading out the way he had come, the scene fading as he went.

Back on Asgard, Loki felt a stab in his gut. Deep in the recesses of his memory he remembered that scene. He remembered staring up at a face with only one eye, and he remembered feeling comforted. It was his first memory, and one that he had clung to, one that he had hung his service to Odin upon. His first memory was of looking up at the face of the Allfather and feeling a sense of protection and safety.

And it was a lie.

The one who had adopted him as his own, the one who had raised him and guided him for countless ages, was the one who had murdered his true parents. He had sought them out specifically, had sought *him* out. Odin had slaughtered his parents and the entire village just so he could take Loki to Asgard.

Rage intensifying Surt's flames, Loki reached down and grabbed hold of Odin's hair. Putting one foot on the ragged remains of his chest, he ripped the head loose and held it up to his face at arm's length. He stared with unvented fury at this despoiler and manipulator.

Odin's eye was still open, and his mouth still moved. Loki was certain that the mumblings were incoherent tracts of agony, but he let the head hang there, savoring the anguished look.

"Bastard," he said. "Why did you do it? Why take me from my kind only to throw me back like a dog? Is this the result you wanted? All of your kind are dead or dying, and Asgard will be burned to cinders. Is this what you foresaw would happen? You alone are responsible for this. Your twisted schemes have caused the death of all that you knew. I only wish that at least one of the Aesir lived so that he might see how foul you truly are."

Odin's mumblings looked repetitive, as if he were saying the same word over and over again. Loki could not quite make it out, however. Bringing the head closer to him, he said, "What is it you are trying to say, One Eye? What final words could you possibly have for me now?"

Odin's mouth stopped, and the eye·fixed on some distant point beyond Loki. Amazingly, the head smiled as it refocused its attention back on him. It opened its mouth just once more, saying one definitive word that Loki clearly heard.

Loki narrowed his eyes, wondering why Odin would say that one word. He said it out loud himself, reflexively, feeling it on his tongue: "Heimdall? Why would you—"

Loki felt pushed forward, his breath forced out in one

352

violent burst. Still clutching Odin's head, he looked down to see an arm's length of sword sticking out of his chest. He turned his head, each slight movement sending flares of sharp pain through him, but desperate to see the face of his attacker.

The sword was pushed even deeper, and he caught one fleeting glimpse of Heimdall's blood-streaked face before the sword was wrenched upward with all the strength the Guardian of Bifrost could muster. The blade slid upward, racking bone and rending innards, and continued in its path with increased violence, cleaving Loki's neck and then, finally, his head, brains spilling out as the sword flew out the top of his fractured skull.

There was no time to savor the death of his enemy, however. Before Loki's brains could even strike the ground, Black Surt was released, and there was a massive explosion of fire that flared outward in an instant. Heimdall and Odin's remains were the first to burn, to be followed by all those in the immediate vicinity who were instantly incinerated. The fire swept out in broad, recursive waves, each one stronger than the one before, Surt's power growing with each life claimed, with each act of individual destruction.

In a matter of seconds, all life on the grassy plain was extinguished—the dead of Niflheim turned to ash and cinders, the flesh of all the giants was roasted and charred before disintegrating and falling to the ground, the Asgardians and their allies who remained—few though they were—were hardy, and did not die easily, which only prolonged their suffering, but they were not spared. Fenrir, even then ripping throats and limbs from enemies, was transformed into a ball of furred flame, roasted alive and howling in agony before finally succumbing.

The tall spires of Asgard were first blown apart by the concussive force of the onrushing fire before the timber and

353

stone ignited and burned the realm to ashes. Beyond the city itself, the forests roared with flame, and the denizens of those woods were burned alive where they stood.

The fire continued to spread, offering respite to none. Alfheim burned, Vanaheim burned, Bifrost shattered in flames. Nor were the higher realms the only casualties. Midgard was not spared, and every mountain, every structure, every tree, every mortal thing on that middle world was turned to cinders. The dwarfs in Nidavellir naively thought themselves safe in their mountain strongholds, but their caves acted like ovens, and the entire race perished. The dark elves in Svartalfheim used their considerable magic and sorcery to protect themselves and their land, but the all-consuming might of Surt was not to be denied.

Sitting on her throne in Niflheim, Hel soberly weighed her mistake. She had known Surt would destroy Asgard—indeed, this was why she had sent Loki to him—but she had not realized the extent of his power. The fiery death reigning in the realms above sent no new souls to her; its consumption was complete and total, an utter destruction of body and spirit. Niflheim was empty save for her alone. She had sought out Balder after she felt Loki's death, but he was not to be found.

She pondered only a moment on the impossibility of him breaking free from her, but found that her attention was diverted by the wave of heat and light that began to rip through her realm. Looking out her high window, she saw that Niflheim's mist and darkness were gone. Every crag and black valley, every dark river and lake, were lit up as if the sun itself hung directly overhead. And then she was gone as a wall of flame that dwarfed her hall swept her and all she knew away into oblivion.

Epilogue

The flames died down after a time, when they had consumed all that they could consume and naught was left but ash. The Nine Worlds were no more: Asgard, Vanaheim, Alfheim, the upper realms; Midgard, Nidavellir, Svartalfheim, Jotunheim, the realms in the middle; Niflheim, the underworld; and Muspelheim, the realm of fire and destruction that touched on all the other realms. All had been destroyed; only one remnant of the Nine Worlds had survived.

Yggdrasil was badly blackened and charred, but it still stood. The tree that always was and always will be had not been claimed by the fire. It could not, however, continue on without any life to feed it. Even while the ashes smoldered, it sent out its roots far and wide, gathering all that remained, using whatever life had been destroyed to create anew. Land reformed above its roots, spreading out as far as could be seen.

From high atop its branches, it sent seedlings floating throughout the new world that was being created. Wherever a seed landed it burrowed its way down into the newly-created soil, and a sprout appeared. In time, these sprouts would grow into trees and vines of their own, lending their strength and life to the land around them.

Its highest leaves, dancing amongst the heavens, floated off and formed clouds in the dark sky, clouds which sent gentle rains across the land, dampening the few remaining fires and sending life-giving rivulets into the soil to nurture the new sprouts that had recently arisen.

Yggdrasil then released those who had been nestled inside it, safe from the flames. Their numbers were few, and their confusion and fear were great, but both those things would change in time. The important thing was that life would begin anew, that Yggdrasil would continue to preside over the universe as it always had.

Freyja walked across the fresh, new grass, reveling in the softness of the tender shoots. She reached the edge of the cliff and stared out across the sea. The water was bluer than any water she had seen before, and she could feel the spray of the waves as they crashed against the cliff walls below. Her feelings were mixed, as ever.

There had not been much time yet to adjust to this new world, and she longed for those who were gone forever, but she could not help her feelings of awe and bliss at seeing a new world created right before her eyes, of every day seeing something that had not existed before made anew by Yggdrasil. She would not have thought it before, but she was humbled by the presence of this entity that was greater than the gods themselves. She felt blessed to be a part of this rebirth.

Soft footsteps behind made her turn her head slightly, but she had no need to see to know who approached her.

"Are the seas wider than they were yesterday?" Balder said, warm curiosity and anticipation in his voice.

"Stand next to me and see for yourself, my lord."

He laughed softly as he took his place next to her. "There is little need for titles here. We are gods no more."

"So you remind me each day," she said, not unkindly. "But such habits do not die easily, and I find a . . . comfort in their use, a link to what was lost. I do not want to ever forget what was lost, even if what we have gained is so much greater."

He nodded. "Magni has found something that will never let us forget what we have lost."

She turned to him. "What is it?"

"You must come see it for yourself."

Magni Thorson stood with his back to Freyja in an open glade of burgeoning saplings, his frame partially blocking her view of a large rock he stared at intently. She and Balder—a smile spreading across his face—approached, and she touched Magni lightly on the arm. He did not turn, but grunted a greeting at her. She was reminded of his father in both size and manner, but he lacked the wildness that permeated Thor's being. Or at least it had disappeared after his release from the tree.

Her eyes went wide with surprise when she saw the object on the rock. "Where did this come from?" she asked.

"Good question," Magni replied gruffly.

Balder added, "The rock was here from before, but there was nothing on it till this morning. Magni found it and sent for me, perhaps thinking I knew something of it." Magni gave a look that affirmed what Balder said. "But it is a mystery to me."

Freyja was confused, but not unpleasantly. Indeed, it seemed an omen, a sign that the past was not forgotten, would never be forgotten.

"Does this mean that Thor may have survived?" she asked.

Magni's response was quick and to the point. "No, my father is dead."

"Then what . . .?"

Balder spoke. "Despite all his ferocity, Thor was a god of rebirth, as well. No matter how violent the storm, it always brought life-giving rains to the earth. After destruction, life always returns somehow. Perhaps that is the meaning of this." He looked up at Magni. "Have you tried to lift it?"

"No."

"Will you try?"

Magni tore his gaze from where Mjolnir lay on the large rock. "It is not here for that. It is not here to be wielded as a weapon." He looked back down at his father's legendary hammer, looking still as if it were newly crafted by the dwarfs. "Only my father could lift Mjolnir. I will not try."

Balder nodded. "It will be our symbol then, and the center of a new village, which will one day grow into a great city. Tales will be told around this rock of the bravery and might of the Thunderer, of the sacrifice of the Allfather, of the mischief of the Trickster." And even while he said it, he realized that his enmity against Loki was gone, that he would tell the tales of his mischief, but without venom.

He no longer burned with anger and hatred at Loki's misdeeds. He felt some measure of sorrow for the banished god, and even some sympathy. This new world somehow allowed him to view the past more clearly, to see it without the stain of emotion and fury. He now saw Loki as a necessary part of the cycle of the universe.

His father, he now knew, had seen this clearly from the beginning, had orchestrated the events so that Ragnarok would not be avoided, if indeed it could have been avoided at all. Both Odin and Loki had played their parts, and Balder would not sully this new world with bitter thoughts of the past, would not bring back up what was meant to lie fallow.

He put a hand on Magni's broad shoulder and his other on Freyja's soft cheek. They were gods no longer, but this new world did not have need of gods.

This was now the time of men.

About the Author

Mike Vasich teaches English to gifted and talented students in suburban Michigan. This book was inspired by the teaching of Norse mythology in his class, and is dedicated to all the students who have ever said, "Mr. V, you should write a book!" He lives with his wife and two sons, who were almost named Loki and Thor, and who cause more destruction than any Norse god could ever hope to equal.

7272941R00210

Made in the USA
San Bernardino, CA
30 December 2013